The Silversmith's Daughter

ANNIE MURRAY

The Silversmith's Daughter

MACMILLAN

First published 2019 by Macmillan
an imprint of Pan Macmillan
20 New Wharf Road, London N1 9RR
Associated companies throughout the world
www.panmacmillan.com

ISBN 978-1-5098-4154-7

1 3 5 7 9 8 6 4 2

A CIP catalogue record for this book is available from the British Library.

Typeset in 12.42/14.9 pt Stempel Garamond by Jouve (UK), Milton Keynes
Printed and bound by CPI Group (UK) Ltd, Croydon, CR0 4YY

Visit www.panmacmillan.com to read more about all our books
and to buy them. You will also find features, author interviews and
news of any author events, and you can sign up for e-newsletters
so that you're always first to hear about our new releases.

'The art and craft of the silversmith calls for appreciation and understanding of something more than the technical and materialistic elements. A true craftsman, one whose work is his [sic] own conception and for the execution of which he is directly responsible, puts all his being, body, mind and spirit into his work.

    . . . The value of all the things men and women make must be measured by the degree they succeed or fail in satisfying their whole being.'

Bernard Cuzner, silversmith, 1935

Glossary

annealing Heat treatment of metal to alter its composition and make it more workable.

burnishing Rubbing metal with another hard metal surface to remove marks – work, like **polishing**, often undertaken by women in the jewellery trade.

chasing and *repousée* Ways of moving the surface of metal with hammers and punches – **chasing** is done from the front side, pushing metal inwards, while *repousée* is done from the inside, pushing a design shape outwards.

damascening Decoration made by cutting incisions into metal and introducing a thread of gold or silver wire, which is beaten into the cut for embellishment.

die-sinking The process of carving a shaped cavity into a steel block to make the pattern into which a thin sheet of metal can be stamped. The **dies** are in two halves and the metal is stamped between them.

doming-block Wood or metal block with concave cavity in it, used for shaping a sheet of silver into a curve.

drop-stamping The same process for larger objects where the shaping of the metal is deep, for example a salt cellar or sugar sifter. The weight, worked by ropes, drops from a greater height to hammer down on to the metal.

enamelling Laying colourful powdered glass substances on to metal and fusing with heat.

champlevé A design is cut down into the metal's surface and the powders laid within the indented shapes.

cloisonné Compartments are created on the metal surface by soldering shaped wire on to it, and the spaces are filled with the vitreous powder, then heated.

engraving Cutting of an image or writing on to a metal plate.

flux A white fluid made from mixing solid borax with water, used to assist in the soldering process.

gem A precious or semi-precious stone, especially when cut and polished or engraved.

lemel Metal filings.

mandril Curved wooden or metal block round which metal can be hammered into shape, for example a bangle.

metal stamping The shaping of sheets of metal using, in those days, a heavy iron stamping press to make the basic metal shape, for example for a brooch. The metal is pressed between the two halves of a steel die into which the pattern has been carved.

muffle Receptacle into which items are put to go into a furnace to protect them from the direct flame.

niello A black decoration made by use of a compound of sulphur with silver, lead or copper, used for filling in engraved designs in silver or other metals.

peg A specially curved workbench with a leather pouch attached to catch metal waste and a wooden 'peg' fixed on the bench for the worker to rest objects on as they sawed, hammered, etc.

pickle A liquid compound used to remove oxidation and flux from newly soldered jewellery.

raising Creating a vessel from a flat sheet of metal by hammering it.

setting and mounting (gems) A prong setting has three or more metal tines, or prongs, that stick up and hold the gemstone in place. Gem settings that contain prongs are called heads. A head can be soldered or welded on to a piece of jewellery, such as a ring or pendant, to allow the mounting of a gemstone.

shopping Local name for a workshop, often in the back yard of a business.

smithing The treatment of metals by heating, hammering and forging.

snips Hand pliers for cutting wire.

Twenty-Four Chain Street, Hockley

Birmingham, 1898

'Take the child out of the house. For pity's sake – get her away from here!'

Pa was on the landing, not with a candle but in strained, dawn light, his eyes red. He must have been weeping, but in her mind those eyes were shocking as glowing coals and that was how she remembered it afterwards. Pa with hot coals in his eyes as he stood outside his own bedroom door.

Mrs Flett was there and he said in a rasping voice, 'Get her dressed, will you? Take her away 'til it's over.'

Daisy had woken suddenly, knowing that something wrong and terrible was happening. She could hear footsteps hurrying up and down the stairs and along the passage and the muffled, urgent sound of voices.

And there was another faint noise, not like anything human or that she recognized, yet even then she knew instinctively it was her mother. She climbed out of bed and crossed the floorboards barefoot, in the freezing dawn, taking her comforting scrap of cream wool shawl, an old one of Mom's which had been torn into strips a few inches wide. She hugged it to her with one hand, reaching the other up to turn the door handle.

Dear Mrs Flett, who helped in the house, had mouse-brown hair in those days. She dressed Daisy and hauled her out and along the iron-cold streets until they saw the light of a little coffee house just opening its doors in the winter gloom. There was a dog inside, with a white hairy face, but that was all Daisy ever recalled of it.

The next thing, she was standing outside Mom and Pa's bedroom door again, later in the morning because it was properly light. Pa was there and Mrs Flett and this time it was his hand turning the handle. They went into this room which until now had been a place of morning love, where she went to snuggle between them for a few minutes while they drank a cup of tea before the day of work began. They would laugh and tell rhymes. Before the three of them got up, Mom, her coppery hair falling loose and thick and smelling of soap and lavender, would kiss her on one cheek and Pa on the other. His whiskers tickled and made her giggle and often his beard gave off the metallic smells of the workshop because that was Pa's smell.

But this morning, Mom was in bed by herself. All items connected with the bloody struggle to produce that second little baby had been cleared away by then. Mom was just Mom to Daisy, but her outside name was Florence Tallis and this morning she did not look much like Mom; she looked public and formal, like Florence Tallis.

She lay with her auburn hair brushed straight, her eyes closed. Everything except her hair was white: the sheet, her nightgown, her face. It was so cold: the room, the silence. Daisy could hear her father's broken breathing as he tried to stifle his weeping behind her.

'Mom?' she said, her voice very small. She didn't understand. With a finger she tapped her mother's leg, wanting her to wake up and smile, sit up and draw her on to her lap as she would have done before, to smooth her finger over the little silver bracelet on Daisy's arm which she had made for her, with her name engraved in tiny letters: 'Daisy Louise Tallis'. But the leg was cold and lifeless.

'Your mother's resting now,' Mrs Flett said kindly, but firmly, drawing her away.

Daisy was four years old then.

The gravestone, in the new cemetery in Warstone Lane, read:

FLORENCE MARY TALLIS b. 1870 d. 1898
Beloved wife of Philip Tallis

'But Pa,' Daisy asked, when she was a little older and people had talked to her about her talented mother. 'Why didn't you put on it that she was a silversmith?'

He considered for a moment, burly like a bear beside her in his coat as they made their Sunday visit to the grave.

'Well . . . people don't do that really, do they? Not on stones like these – they don't tell much of us in the end.' He turned and looked down at her, smiling gently. 'Maybe it's for the best.'

'Can she see us?' Daisy asked. It was something she often wondered and it troubled her.

Her father looked away for a moment, breathing deeply.

'I don't know, is the truth,' he said and his voice was so sad, a sadness that every day she longed to make better. 'I'd like to think so, but I just don't know the answer to that. But –' he looked down at her, eyes smiling – 'just in case, we'll have to do her proud, won't we?'

I

1915

One

January 1915

The front door of number twenty-four Chain Street closed with a bang, followed by the sound of feet hurrying past the front office and along the passage.

Margaret looked up at Philip across the front office and saw him roll his eyes.

'*Now* what's the matter?' he said wearily.

Margaret got to her feet with a careful smile. Her gentle, bearded husband was the most loving man she had ever met, but he was baffled by the moods of his daughter, Daisy. Over their ten years together, Margaret had become used to the girl's mercurial temperament.

Now aged twenty, Daisy had grown into a beauty. She stood five and a half feet tall, thick hair of a soft gold swept stylishly back from a strong, lovely face, the blue-grey eyes looking out at the world with passionate solemnity or, at times, with challenging amusement. She was also a talented artist and silversmith, having grown up in the trade. In addition, her father had sent her, at fourteen, to train at the School of Jewellery and Silversmithing in Vittoria Street, where she was now skilled enough to be a teacher.

The classes at Vittoria Street were done on a part-time basis, for young people already employed in the trades. It was what Daisy was born to – they all knew that – and she had loved her years at the school. Even so, when she came charging into the house, they were never sure whether it was going to be a furious crashing in through the front door or an ecstatic deliverance of good news.

'It's all right.' Philip smiled at his wife. 'You're going out. And it didn't sound too much like trouble. I'll pop in and see in a few minutes. Give her time to calm down, whatever it is.'

Daisy sat waiting excitedly for her father in the back room, with a cup of tea all ready for him. She had told Mrs Flett she would do it herself and set out a tray: a nicely swaddled pot and cups and, as ever, the silver milk jug with the beaded edge, made by her mother, Florence Tallis. As she had grown older, she and Pa had had their disagreements. Daisy knew that a lot of this was due to her own stormy nature. But Pa expected a lot of her as well. Whenever she could she tried to find something to tell him that would please him. She liked to be able to give Pa good news and see his face crinkle and his eyes glow with pleasure.

Only a few months ago, just after the war began, she had waited for him here just like this, jumping up when she heard him coming.

'Guess what, Pa?'

She had only just got home herself from Vittoria Street and was bubbling with excitement. Pa was going to be so proud of her!

'What, Daisy-Loo?' he said. He had never called her this when she was a little girl, but for some reason – perhaps to reassure her when her two half-siblings came along – over the past few years, he had adopted it as his pet name for her. As he said it, she could hear all the fondness in his deep, rumbling voice.

'They've made me a full teacher!' She bounced on her toes in her black boots. 'Mr Carter from the smithing department has gone to join up, and they're short-handed. Mr Gaskin came and told me himself!'

She saw her father take in this news and his face broke into a smile. Though she had finished her five years of study at Vittoria Street in the summer of 1914, she had only expected to work as a student teacher because there had been no vacancies. But the war was quickly changing a lot of things.

'Well, well,' Philip Tallis said.

He came closer to her and looked into her face. In his own features, fleshy cheeks half concealed by a bushy brown beard, she saw something: a twitch, a hint of inner emotion. It passed in a second but she knew he was thinking of her mother, beautiful, talented Florence and the baby sister for Daisy who had died with her. The small cloud passed and she saw a smile light her father's grey eyes. Even though Pa was happily remarried to Margaret, those last moments of her mother's life haunted them both.

'It's what you wanted, isn't it? You've just got there a bit quicker than you expected.' He put his hand on her shoulder. The smells of acid and metal came from his clothes. 'You've done well, wench.'

Daisy smiled, glowing at this. Her father was never one to gush compliments, but she could hear all the pride in his voice. She felt as if she was flying, riding the wave of her life to where she was meant to be. Daisy Tallis, prizewinning student and designer, talented silversmith. A Tallis – worthy of her mother.

And now she had more news that she thought would please him.

This time she heard him coming from the front office

of 'Philip Tallis, Silversmithing and Engraving' and she jumped up to pour him some tea.

'All right?' she said, smiling as he came through the door. The room was cosy, the fire crackling. 'Where's Ma and the others?'

'Oh, she's in the front – but she'll join them round at Kitty's house in a minute, I think.'

Daisy's stepmother, Margaret, had given her father two more children, John and Lily, now nine and seven. Daisy was pleased they were out visiting friends. It was nice to have Pa to herself for a while.

'And guess what else?' she said, beaming as she put his tea on the table beside him.

Nodding his thanks, he looked up at her.

'You know I'm teaching in the elementary smithing room? Well, Mr Snell from the advanced room has joined up – and guess who's coming back to teach advanced?' Pa was going to be so pleased. 'Mr Carson!'

'Carson?' Philip Tallis said, offhand. 'Oh – that old fop.' It was spoken with a smile, but Daisy could hear an edge of something in his voice.

She frowned, feeling crushed. She had been hoping he would find this news exciting.

'He does wear some funny clothes,' she said. She had always found Mr Carson very dashing. 'He's an *artist*.'

A muffled 'huh' came from her father as he reached down to shovel some more coal on to the fire.

'But Pa,' she reproached, 'I thought he was your friend?'

'Well . . .' He shifted the poker about in the embers with an expression of distaste. 'I've known Carson a long while, that's true.'

Which, Daisy realized, for the first time, might not be quite the same as being friends.

*

She had started her classes at the Vittoria Street School in 1908. Vittoria Street was a short walk along the blue brick pavements away from Chain Street in the heart of the Jewellery Quarter, a district that, among many other power-houses of Birmingham, provided the world with a vast number of items of beauty and utility. The school was founded in 1890, especially to develop the skills of young smiths and jewellers coming up in the trades. There were classes in the afternoons and evenings and Pa had said that Daisy could go in the afternoons, while working for him in the workshop in the mornings. He did not want her going there in the evenings, he said. She would get too tired.

How excited she had been the first day she started there aged fourteen, almost running to the imposing brick building in Vittoria Street! She knew this was what she was born for. Her memories of her mother, Florence Tallis, were of a woman who knew this trade, someone skilled, an artist. In Daisy's mind she was a pale beauty with glossy auburn hair and a tall, slender figure like her own. She had stood at her workbench, hands busy with a hammer and mandrel, snips and rounding dome, shaping some lovely object, be it a ring or a jug, a bowl or a neck-lace. Florence had learned her skills from her father and married another silversmith. Daisy wanted to be just the same. If anything, she had to be better, to show Pa she could live up to her mother. And Daisy had been design-ing and making things already since she was very small, as soon as her little hands could grasp the tools.

Though it was perfectly normal to Daisy that a silver-smith should be a woman, in the school she found herself to be one of only a handful of girls amid a great crowd of lads all apprenticed in the jewellery trade and coming to classes on release from their employers. But it meant that the girls stuck together and soon she was good friends with Gertrude and Ida and especially with May Gordon, who became her best friend of that time, though now, sadly, life was so busy that they rarely saw each other. She had loved every day of her training – or almost every day.

The school offered what seemed to her a feast of classes: lectures on the work of the silversmith and the goldsmith; classes on smithing, on *niello* and damascening, raising and chasing, *repoussé*, enamelling . . . Precious gems, which had rather passed out of fashion when the old Queen settled into mourning her husband and gave up all personal adornment, were now back in vogue and there were classes on gem mounting and setting.

But there were the other classes she had to do, which had resulted in some of those stormy arrivals home, in door slamming and sulks.

'Why do I have to learn to *draw animals*?' she had demanded furiously. 'I want to make bowls and teapots and . . . *silver* things, but not animals, or people! And the goat did its business on the floor!'

Philip and Margaret had laughed helplessly at this outburst.

'You just make the most of it, Daisy,' Pa said. He had never had the benefit of such a training. 'The more things you can learn the better.'

'But why do I have to do *all* these things?' Daisy groaned.

'It'll be to improve your eye,' he said. 'The way your hand and eye work together. Just take my word for it.'

Thanks to the former head of the school, Robert Catterson-Smith, who had introduced all sorts of initiatives to fuse together the technical and artistic, life drawing was indeed from life. As well as human portraits, which Daisy taken against from a young age – *I can't draw stupid fingers and noses, why do I have to?* – now there was also an Animal Room.

Daisy found herself having to draw all manner of things she had never suspected would be part of her training: dogs, cats, rabbits, a fish, the goat. All, as Mrs Flett said, 'Large as Life and Twice as Natural.' Whatever that was supposed to mean.

For similar reasons (fingers, noses and so on) she had set her face against clay modelling until she discovered that she was really good at it. Her hands seemed in harmony with the material and, to her delight, objects appeared at her touch. Drawing stuffed birds and flowers was more successful too: 'At least they keep still – and they don't have . . .'

'You must have learned to draw fingers by now?' Margaret had said absent-mindedly, running her eyes down the accounts in the office as Daisy chattered to her. After a moment she looked up. 'You really do complain a lot, miss. I should have loved to have your training.'

For a moment, Ma punctured Daisy's self-absorption. Her stepmother had fallen in love with the crafts and skills she saw when she came to live in the Jewellery Quarter, and Pa taught her things when there was time, but it was not often. Daisy knew, guiltily for a moment, how lucky she was.

Before too long, she won one of the local prizes, the Messenger Prize – five whole pounds! – for, of all things, a life drawing, accompanied by a study of a head in profile, and at this point her complaints almost ceased.

As she worked her way round the different rooms and classes of the school and concentrated more and more on her real love, working with silver, she was in heaven. She worked and studied and did well in the examinations. She loved attention from her teachers and won more awards.

Each year, those who had won local prizes could be entered for a national one. All the work was sent down to South Kensington and Daisy began to appear as a runner-up. Finally, by the summer of 1913, she was rising high at the end of her studies. And to cap it all, she was First Prizewinner of a major national award for a silver teapot she had made, wrought in simple, elegant lines.

She knew she was good – and that she had made her pa prouder than he could ever say.

And now she was a fully fledged teacher at the school alongside the people who had taught her – and Mr Carson, who she had known all her life. Mr Carson even remembered her mother! She really was feeling very pleased with herself.

Two

Two households sat side by side: twenty-four and twenty-six Chain Street, in the busy and prosperous Jewellery Quarter, barely a mile to the north-west of the heart of Birmingham. The area, roughly shaped like a triangle, was a teeming warren of activity extending away from the spire and graceful Georgian architecture of St Paul's church. All around it were streets of terraces crammed full of living quarters and workshops. In some, six or eight different businesses shared one building, each with just one room: jewellers, gem setters, smiths and enamellers, die makers and engravers. And in addition one could find a whole range of specialities, from the making of glass eyes to that of sports trophies; from spectacles to the ornate silver chalices, pyxes and candlesticks gracing the dark interiors of churches.

This had been Daisy's home all her life and she knew the place and its people almost the way she did her own body. She and the other children of the quarter all played out together and she knew almost everyone by sight. Her only insight into any other life was hearing from her step-mother about her upbringing in the village outside Bristol from where she and her sister Annie had moved in 1904.

The black front doors of each of the ornate brick houses, twenty-four and twenty-six, were close together, their halls divided from each other simply by a sturdy wall. Each of the houses now had wide bay windows, their frames painted black to disguise the soot which came to rest in every crevice of the city's brickwork, their panes the widest they could be to let in all possible light on to the jewellery maker's trade. Number twenty-six had an entry running along its far side; each house had a yard at the back with an extra workshop, or 'shopping', where many of the firms' employees sat bent over unusually shaped workbenches, cut in wave-like curves along their sides, each workstation called a 'peg'.

Most of these employees had always been lads but now, in these early months of the war, there were fewer of them than there had been before. Autumn last year had seen the recruiting offices mobbed by crowds of young men eager to take the King's Shilling and go to war for their country against the invading Germans. The local Territorials had all been recalled to their drill halls and other lads had come from the counties around and all across Birmingham to join up. Familiar faces had disappeared and it was hard to replace them. Some businesses in the quarter were already struggling.

Inside number twenty-six, behind the sign 'Ebenezer Watts & Son, Goldsmiths', ran the thriving business of Margaret's Uncle Eb, his wife Harriet and son Georgie. Daisy was not related to Georgie by blood, but he was Margaret's cousin and over the years, quiet, kindly Georgie had become to her like an older brother, teasing her or taking her portrait with his beloved camera. Georgie's wife, Clara, who had once worked as a burnisher, came in to lend a hand at times, even though they had three children.

When Margaret and Annie first came to Birmingham, their uncle and aunt were still living over the shop. Now they lived in their new, spacious house in Handsworth, a mile further out of the city from Chain Street, and number twenty-six was filled to the brim with commercial creativity – from the shopping in the yard outside, to the rooms occupied by other craftsmen all contributing to the gold items pouring out of Watts's business – gem setters, Caleb Turner the die sinker who had moved next door from number twenty-four, and Jack Sidwell's enamelling business. Even the office could now be referred to in the plural since it had spread into two rooms.

And Margaret's beloved Uncle Eb, a prosperously paunchy man with a walrus moustache, cheerful and kind in his ways, arrived daily from Handsworth in a horse-drawn gig, usually beaming around him as he did so like a man who couldn't believe his luck. Aunt Hatt also could not seem to keep away for long and came breezing into both numbers twenty-four and twenty-six for chats and cups of tea and at times, general interference.

In number twenty-four, the premises of 'Philip Tallis, Silversmith & Engraver', this was now the sole business, because the house also needed to accommodate the growing Tallis family. Mrs Flett, who was getting on for sixty and was a widow of many years, had cooked for the family even since Florence Tallis was still alive. Though she no longer lived in the house, Joan Flett still insisted on coming in every day to cook and help look after the children, and Margaret, who also now worked in the business, found her a godsend. Daisy could not imagine life without Mrs Flett. She was a funny old thing, gaunt and rather severe looking but kind with it. She had long been almost a part of the family.

And this, all her life, had been Daisy's whole world.

Three

'Coo-ee!'

Margaret was sitting in the office working away when there was a tap on the door and a smiling face appeared.

'Hello, Auntie!' She got to her feet, smiling. 'Oh – don't you look nice!'

Aunt Harriet, or Hatt as they had always known her, never failed to look nice. She set great store by her clothes and today she was dressed in a very becoming outfit: a silver-grey skirt almost to her ankles, a knee-length dress over the top in a warm cream colour, with a lacy neck and sleeves to the elbow. Her thick black coat, against the January weather, was draped over her arm.

Though she was in her sixtieth year, and very definitely more ample in size than she had once been, Harriet Watts's hair was only a little streaked with grey and while she was growing broader in the beam, she was a fine-looking woman, still with a beautiful, dark-eyed face. A gold band shimmered at her neck and as ever, she gave the impression of being an exotic bird which had escaped from a less workaday place.

'All right, Margaret, dear? Heavens, we haven't set eyes on you all since Christmas! How are the children? They'll be back any minute, I suppose? Philip out the back, is he? Can you spare a moment to come next door for your tea? Thought I'd pop in. Georgie's here and it'd be nice to see you all together.'

'Of course,' Margaret said, giving up the attempt to

18

answer any of the torrent of questions. She tidied her paperwork a little.

'Won't be long, Muriel,' she said to Muriel Allen, a middle-aged woman who worked in the office. Miss Allen gave a stiff nod, implying that it was none of her business what her employer did.

Aunt Hatt launched herself like royalty into what had once been her own house, number twenty-six. The office staff had all changed since Margaret's time working there, except for sweet-faced Bridget. Five years ago, Bridget had married Jack Sidwell, who still had his prosperous little enamelling business upstairs.

Margaret remembered Jack as an awkward young man who had once harboured a fancy for her sister Annie (a true exercise in futility since Annie had always declared that she would Never Marry). But Bridget, a plump-faced, bespectacled young woman, with flyaway brown hair and a kindly way with her, seemed to be doing wonders for Jack.

'He seems almost human these days,' Annie had remarked recently, seeing him in passing.

Jack and Bridget had two little boys, who Bridget's mother looked after in the daytime, and Jack's business was flourishing. It was all a happy arrangement.

'Hello, Mrs Tallis,' Bridget said, a smile spreading over her pink cheeks.

Margaret smiled, pleased to see her. Despite living next door, she was so busy that she seldom went into number twenty-six these days.

'Would you like a cup of tea, Mrs Watts?' asked Sarah, the other girl in the office.

'Oh, that would be nice – I'm dropping!' Aunt Hatt said, flinging her coat over the arm of a chair and then collapsing into it, as if to illustrate the point. 'Running about after three grandchildren will be the death of me! And I've got to sort out all these women and their knitting tomorrow – socks and gloves for the troops, they say, but how many people know how to turn a sock? It was all Clara's idea, but there it is, I'm left with it and there's the fundraiser for the poor Belgians . . .' She held out a hand as the girl went to go to the kitchen. 'Pop and tell Eb and Georgie I'm here, will you?'

A few moments later, Margaret heard her uncle 'pom-pomming' along the passage and his large, endearingly plump figure appeared in the doorway.

'Good heavens!' he cried, holding out his arms in mock dismay. 'An office full of wenches!'

'We're not wenches, Eb,' Aunt Hatt said crossly. 'I'm sure Margaret doesn't take to being called any such thing.'

But Margaret was laughing. 'Hello, Uncle,' she said, going to kiss him.

Georgie appeared close behind him, a slender, handsome man who looked very like his mother and was a good deal quieter than both his parents.

'Hello, Margaret,' he said. 'Long time no see.' It was in fact only a couple of weeks since their lovely Christmas Day spent together at the Wattses' spacious house in Handsworth, but it did feel a long time ago now. 'Kids all right?'

'Everyone's doing well,' she said, pleased to see him. Even though they worked next door to each other, sometimes weeks could pass with them exchanging hardly more than a brief greeting. 'I'll have to bring them out to Handsworth one Sunday soon. What with everything slumping, we'll have more time on our hands.'

'It's terrible – terrible, all of it.' Uncle Eb's face fell into despondent lines. 'Bad for business, this war, bad for

20

everything – what do they want to go and fight over flaming Belgium for? I've got lads leaving left and right . . .'

'Those lucky stars of yours are starting to take off though, Eb,' Hatt said. 'In fact, they might be your best line yet!'

Eb grinned. 'Yes, we're not doing so bad with those. You want to get Philip to come up with something like that,' he said. 'It was our Georgie's idea in the first place.'

'Like the lucky horseshoes?' Margaret said, pressing herself back against a shelf full of ledgers to let Sarah through the door with the tea tray.

Georgie smiled, moving a little sheaf of spiked orders out of the way so that he could lean up against the work table at the front of the office. The lapel pin of a lucky golden horseshoe, made by W. Stuart Turners', had taken off like mad once the war started: 'Send a lucky horseshoe to your boy in the trenches!' Uncle Eb, who was always one to leap on any truly commercial idea, had gone about muttering, 'That's what we need – summat like that,' for days, until Georgie said, 'Well, what about "Thank your lucky stars"?'

'We reckoned one star would have to do,' Eb said. Caleb Turner the die sinker, who now worked upstairs, had designed a beautiful star about three-quarters of an inch across, with a thin line cut just inside all the way round and echoing the shape – and the star lapel badge was born. 'And then there's this other model with one star and a little one attached to it – see?' He picked up a blank that was lying on the table.

'It's not doing as well as the horseshoe,' Georgie admitted. 'They got the papers advertising it and everything – but badges and buttons are the way forward. Jack's doing a roaring trade for the army.' He nodded towards the ceiling, to the room where Jack Sidwell had his enamelling business.

'He can barely keep up,' Bridget said. 'They're just pouring them out. He's hardly got time to breathe.'

Margaret stood amid the chatter, wondering whether she and Philip should not have thought of producing something similar when the war started, as trade had shrunk back so much. Daisy had been talking about the MIZPAH jewellery, even designing things, though not having been brought up in a religious household, she had to ask Margaret what the word meant.

'It's from a story in the Old Testament,' Margaret explained. 'There was a man called Jacob who wanted to get away from his father-in-law, Laban. He took all his family and animals and ran off in the night. But when the two men met to discuss the situation, they made a pile of stones – a sort of sign of agreement, a Mizpah, or the bond between them – to say that the families would now not live together. So that's why it's about a bond between people who are separated.'

Philip, who was of a rather purist mind when it came to commercial jewellery, had not shown any enthusiasm about this so far.

They were all drinking their tea and chatting when footsteps approached along the passage and there was a tap on the office door.

'Who's that then?' Eb peered round it, then stood in the doorway. 'Oh ar, lad – what're you after?'

'Sorry, Mr Watts.' Margaret recognized the deep, shy voice. It was Den Poole, Mary Poole's only son. She had known Den since he was a lad of nine, when she first came to the city and he was a poor little thing, man of the house on the tragic death of his father, when they were going through terrible times. He had become very attached to

Margaret and he and Daisy had been playmates for a time.
Uncle Eb had promised that once Den left school, he
would give him a chance in the business. Den had grown
into a sturdier looking lad than they had ever expected, for
such a poor little scrap as he had been. He was hard-
working and had got on well, learning the trade of a metal
stamper.

Margaret was about to call hello to him when, still outside the office door, he burst into speech.

'I've got to talk to yer, Mr Watts. I've gotta do it now
and I'm sorry I dain't come around the outside . . .' The
workers did not usually come through the house, but
passed along the entry at the side to reach the workshop.

'Not to worry,' Eb said. Margaret wondered if Den
realized how many people there were in the office, listening to this conversation. 'What's on yer mind, lad?'

'I've got to go and join up!' The words burst out of
Den like an explosion waiting to happen. 'I've got to go,
tomorrow, like. I've just got to!'

She saw Uncle Eb stand straighter, pulling his shoulders back.

'Not you an' all, Den? You don't have to, you know.
No one'll think the worse of you if you stay here – there's
work to be done. We need you here!'

'But the other lads are going. It's the thing to do, Mr
Watts – fight for your country – ain't it? I've held off and
held off, but now I've gotta do it!'

Margaret and Aunt Hatt exchanged dismayed glances.
Aunt Hatt mouthed, 'What about Mary?' across the
room. Mary Poole, Den's mother, had never been much
of a coper and life had in any case dished out to her far
too much to cope with.

Aunt Hatt looked across at Georgie as if to say, *You
talk some sense into him.* But Georgie stayed where he

was, a solemn expression on his face. Surely to goodness, Margaret thought, a chill going through her, Georgie wasn't thinking of joining up himself? She had become very fond of her kindly, clever cousin with his wry sense of humour. And she knew what it would do to her aunt if Georgie went.

'My mind's made up, Mr Watts,' Den was saying. 'I'm going to join up tomorrow – only I wanted to let yer know first, like.'

Eb shook his head. 'It sounds as if I can't change your mind, lad,' he said sorrowfully. 'You're a good worker – I hate to lose you. But there'll be a job waiting when you get back.'

There were mutterings of 'very grateful' and 'sorry' from Den and an awkward silence. Then they heard him say, 'Will yer tell Daisy I'm going, Mr Watts?' Those in the office looked at each other and shrugged.

'All right, yes. Off you go then, lad, if you have to,' Eb said. 'Good luck to yer.'

'Thanks, Mr Watts. I 'ope I'll make you all proud.' They heard his footsteps receding towards the back door.

Four

It was only a couple of days before Daisy ran into Mr Carson.

The Vittoria Street School of Jewellery and Silver-smithing had been founded as a branch of the Birmingham School of Art in Margaret Street, which was about a mile away in the middle of Birmingham. It was set up for the specialist training of smiths and jewellers and some of the teaching staff, working artists like Mr Carson, gave classes both at Margaret Street and Vittoria Street. Daisy loved being in the school with its long, echoing corridors and rooms full of people bent over benches or tables creating things, many of them very beautiful.

She had just come out of the class she was teaching that afternoon, showing her students the tricky process of shaping a bowl from a flat circle of metal using a raising hammer, and was feeling weary. As she set off along the corridor, amid the milling crowd of students, the relentless sound of hammers banging (something which even now she would still sometimes hear in her sleep) was replaced by their excited chatter. Mr Carson emerged from the Advanced Silversmithing room.

He was no stranger to her: she had known him all her life. But James Carson had not been present in the Vittoria Street School, or indeed in Birmingham, for several years. During this period, Mr Carson had taken up a post at the Sheffield School of Art and he and his wife, Victoria Carson, also an artist, had moved there. Now, Daisy assumed, he had come back to fill some of the gaps left by the war.

Catching sight of her along the corridor, Mr Carson set up a roar from a distance, so that most of the students turned and stared.

'Is that who I think it is? Miss Daisy Tallis? Daughter of that old genius and curmudgeon Philip Tallis? Ahoy, Daisy Tallis!'

Daisy felt herself lift out of her fatigue as he came sweeping along the corridor like a huge bird, clad in a black cape which billowed out behind. He was a tall, lean man, his hair such a dark brown as to be almost black, parted in the middle and falling in waves down to his collar, his face punctuated by a neat goatee beard and a moustache. He was bareheaded today, though Daisy could remember him appearing in an array of colourful hats and berets of the artistic, rather than conformist, kind. And he always gave off a rushing, exhilarating energy.

Daisy turned hot with blushes at being addressed like this in front of everyone else and her heart was hammering. But she couldn't help an amused smile spreading across her face. Mr Carson was always so larger-than-life and extreme. Throughout her childhood he had turned up in Chain Street from time to time, booming through the house, demanding to see her father and bellowing at him about why he was such an old hermit and why did he for heaven's sakes not join the Guild, the meeting place for artists and craftsmen in the area? And Pa always rolled his eyes and grumbled. Come to think of it, she thought, as Mr Carson halted in front of her like a racehorse stalled at a fence, she was not sure even now what the answer was to that question herself. Her Pa could be a mystery sometimes.

26

Mr Carson's brown eyes smiled down at her in apparent glee. He seemed so tall, such an awesome figure to her. She tried not to notice the other students gaping as they jostled past along the corridor.

'Well, well – little Miss Daisy Tallis. I must say you really have grown up in the last – what is it? – five, six years? As lovely and as winning as ever! In fact, my dear, you do look very like your remarkable mother. Except a beautiful golden-haired version of her, of course.'

Daisy blushed even more, but this remark warmed her to the core. It was lovely to meet anyone who had known Mom, who could talk about their memories of her. At home, now that Margaret was there, her mother hardly got a mention out of tact for Pa's second wife.

Mr Carson reached forward as if to tickle her under her chin as he used to do when she was a little girl, but he seemed to think the better of it. Instead, he straightened up and hooked his thumb between the buttons of his startling, emerald-green waistcoat. In fact, Mr Carson's bearing and outfit – the bright weskit, his trousers of a mole-coloured velvet, that cape and his whole vivid presence, made Daisy feel dull in comparison, like a pigeon set beside a peacock. And though she had not long passed her twentieth birthday, in this man's presence she suddenly felt like a child again.

'Goodness me,' he said teasingly. 'I go away for a few years and what do I find? I leave a delightful little girl sitting on the steps of number twenty-four Chain Street, and I come back to find her not only at Vittoria Street and on the teaching roll, but to cap it all, quite grown into a ravishing beauty! Whatever has happened?'

Daisy giggled, flattered but unsure what to make of these remarks. Mr Carson had always been rather overwhelming. But then his face sobered.

'I hear you've been doing exceptionally well, my dear,' he said. 'Winning prizes – a veritable little Hester Bateman, or Florence Tallis for that matter, had the poor lady been spared! I always knew you were going to be something rather special. And you are teaching the beginner silversmiths, I gather?'

Daisy felt even more overcome, being likened to such a famous craftswoman as well as gratified that he seemed to have heard about her and what she was doing at the school.

He dropped the teasing tone then and began to speak to her seriously, as to a fellow colleague.

'Well, I'll be teaching the more advanced groups. We shan't be far away from each other. So, my dear, if you need any help of any sort, don't ever doubt that you can come and ask, will you?'

'That's very kind,' she said, though resolving at the same time that she would never need such help. She was not sure what to say next, and still blushing under his penetrating gaze, she said awkwardly, 'Well, I'd better go.'

'Of course.' He stood back, gave a courtly little bow and let her pass. Daisy hurried away, but glancing back a moment later, she was startled to see that Mr Carson was still standing in the same spot, watching her.

A few days later, Daisy walked out of the main door of the school in Vittoria Street. She had been teaching an afternoon class and her head was still full of the sound of hammering and of the pupils' questions which she hurried about the class to answer, bending over the not always sweet-smelling lads at their workbenches, instructing them about this and that. There was only a handful of girls. She drew in a deep breath, unwinding after all the demands of the afternoon.

28

It was already almost dark. The air was damp but the wind had died for the moment, so that smoke hung in the evening air and all the sounds, the clopping hooves of the horse pulling a cart with a few remaining blocks of salt, a mixture of voices and the crash as something was loaded on to another wagon, came to her pure and clear. The streets of the quarter were always busy and now they were full of people bustling along, some on errands, boys with basket carriages and messengers scurrying back and forth. However, despite appearances, in many firms, instead of long hours into the evening during a rush period, some workshops were shutting up earlier these days – even at dinner time. The war meant a decrease in orders and there was just not enough work coming in.

Daisy was in her own little world, her mind full of the class, of thinking she must go and see her friend May Gordon, who had been at Vittoria Street with her for their five student years and had been taken on in Mr Cuzner's business in Bournville . . . But another thought intruded as it had begun to do over these days. Mr Carson. She had seen him frequently during his first few days back in the school, careering about the building, people turning to stare.

And today, as they passed each other in the corridor, there was the way he had looked at her. He had met her eye, giving his little bow from the waist. 'Afternoon, Miss Tallis!' spoken with a mischievous smile. The man was so full of life and intensity that she could not help being fascinated by him. She was so caught up in all this, walking along now, that she did not notice the young man, among many others in the street, who was standing propped against a lamp post just along from the main doors.

*

He was nineteen years old, not a great deal taller than Daisy, who was rather tall at five foot six. He had a strong, masculine frame, with broad shoulders and a pale face, the eyes seeming dark in his face by contrast. His cheekbones were prominent, almost as if he had been chipped from a block of stone. Under his cap, a lock of brown hair fell across his forehead. He stood slightly hunched, hands pushed into the pockets of his heavy jacket, and his face wore a serious, watchful expression. When he saw the girl emerge, still absent-mindedly in the process of pushing her hat on to her lovely, pale hair, he felt his heart speed up and with one foot, he pushed himself off from the lamp post.

Daisy was walking along, head down as she pulled her coat round her and fastened the buttons. She appeared to be in a hurry, but then Daisy always did seem in a rush.

'Dais?'

'Oh!' She started, staring at him without recognition for a few seconds. 'Oh, Den – it's you! Goodness, you didn't half make me jump! You off home?'

'Yeah. No.' He cursed himself for being flustered, for feeling like a servant compared to her. It was the way he had always felt, coming from the slums of the Jewellery Quarter and her related to the boss – well, sort of. He felt that she was above him, Daisy Tallis, daughter of prosperous Philip Tallis the silversmith. She was like a goddess, so beautiful with that hair, that lovely face of hers, so lovely that he became suddenly aware that his jacket was a couple of sizes too big and he felt rough and awkward in his cap and big boots. But they had known each other so long, him and Daisy, and all he wanted was . . . Well, in fact, what he wanted – her, just *her* – was too much, and he knew it. 'Can I talk to you a minute, Dais?'

She stopped, puzzled. She and Den were close in age,

though in little else so far as she was concerned. They had played together sometimes as children – Daisy usually in charge – when Margaret and Annie had brought Den and sometimes his little sister Ivy to the house during the Poole family's hardest times. Since Den had been apprenticed at Watts's next door, they had seen each other now and then in passing. Daisy had always known that her life was very different from Den's. His family lived on a broken-down yard off Pope Street. She had been born into a more fortunate situation, and even though she too had lost a parent at a young age, she had not lived in poverty like the Poole family. She was fond of Den like a sort of distant brother, but the truth was she felt rather superior to him. She, Daisy Tallis, was a star of the art school at Vittoria Street, a prizewinner, now a teacher! She scarcely ever gave Den a thought.

Looking at him, amused, she said, 'Fire away then!'

Den seemed overcome by confusion for a moment and looked down at his boots. But as they stood there, Daisy became suddenly aware of him in a different way. She saw how strong he had become, the muscular thickening of his face and neck, the fact that now, slightly, she had to look up at him. Only then did she suddenly see Den as a man. A light blush rose in her cheeks as his eyes dared to look back up into hers.

'Come over 'ere,' he said.

Daisy, unused to being spoken to in this commanding way by Den, followed, bewildered, as he led her into a narrow, mucky entry along the street. She felt her boot land on something squashy and there was a stink of refuse. They were out of the way of passers-by, but were forced to stand uncomfortably close together in the gloom.

'What is it, Den?' she said, beginning to feel irritated by being dragged into this stinking alley. She was unsure what to do with her hands, so she clasped them behind her.

He squared himself up and stood tall. 'I'm joining up.'

Daisy stared at him. When war was declared on 4 August last year, it had seemed a distant thing. Germany, the Schlieffen Plan, Belgium – what did any of these have to do with her? She barely knew where Sarajevo was, this place where it all seemed to have started when someone shot the Archduke Franz Ferdinand – someone she had never even heard of. It had made more impact on her when Joseph Chamberlain, the city's most famous man, had died at the beginning of July. One thing that had brought the war a fraction closer was that they now had a couple of Belgian lads being trained at the Vittoria Street School.

'What does it really mean, being at war?' she asked at breakfast, soon after war broke out. She had no memory of any other war.

Her stepmother looked across at her. 'We don't really know yet,' she said. 'But I do know that that butter and bacon on your plate cost a lot more this week – and that started even before they declared the war. Prices are going up like anything. Sugar's gone up from tuppence ha'penny a pound to fivepence ha'penny!'

'I'm going to have to put the whole works on short time,' her father said. Daisy saw suddenly how pale and worried looking the war had made her father. 'People are cancelling their orders or sending in wires saying hold them for the time being. We've hardly anything coming in. And with so many men rushing to join up there won't be anyone to do the work soon in any case!'

There had been a great rush into the forces in the autumn, all those lads hurrying into Kitchener's army, the man's pointing finger and moustache looking down from walls all over the district. But although a few of the staff had gone from the school and Arthur, the fiancé of Edith who worked in the office, was now in the merchant navy, Daisy knew of no one really close to her who had joined up. And though the war had not ended before Christmas as they had all predicted, surely it couldn't be long? What was the point in Den going now?

'What – you mean the army?' she said.

'Yeah. Course.'

'Doesn't Mr Watts need you at the works?'

'Nah. Not really. There's not so much work since it started – we're on short time.' Den drew his shoulders back, standing tall. 'I just feel I gotta go, Dais. Be a man, like.'

Daisy found herself suddenly moved by this. She smiled gently at him, though uncertain whether he could really see her face in the gloom. She released her hands, clasped them in front of her instead.

'That's brave, Den. It is. But – what about your mother?'

Den made a slight squirming movement, as if Daisy had touched some nerve in him. Poor Den had been the man of that household since the age of nine.

''Er's working now Florrie's old enough to go to school, like – and Lizzie and Ivy've both got a wage coming in.'

'Oh, well then . . .' She was not sure what to say. She was impressed that Den was taking this step – but why was he telling her? Lightly, almost teasing, she said, 'I suppose you'll be over in the park, training then? They're saying it won't be for long in any case, so I expect you'll be back soon.'

Den nodded, solemnly. 'Ar, that's why I want to go now – before it's all over . . .'

There was a long silence and Daisy thought she might as well be moving on.

'I'm impressed, Den,' she said, starting to turn away. 'So, are you going tomorrow – to the recruiting office?'

'Yeah – I've just told Mr Watts. 'E weren't very happy. Listen, Dais, don't go!'

He grasped her arm and she turned back, startled by him touching her. Up close, she suddenly caught the smell of him, sweat and the residue of chemicals that clung to everyone's garments in the workshops. A man – strong and urgent. For a second she felt almost afraid.

'What is it?' she said, trying to keep her voice steady.

'If I . . . when I go – will yer write to me?' She could see it cost him courage to say it and she managed to stop the laugh of surprise which tried to escape from her.

'*Write* to you? What, me?'

'Yes,' he said awkwardly.

She did laugh then, something she often felt sorry for later. 'Are you going to write back, Den? *Can* you write?'

'Course I can,' he said and she was instantly ashamed that she had injured his pride. But he had not spent much of his time at school. 'I'm not very good though. But, Dais – will yer promise? There's no one else'll write and I'd . . . Well, you'd . . .' He was stumbling over his words. 'I know you'd write a good letter. You do everything better'n anyone else. You're just . . .'

He ran out of words, but even the silence in which he gazed at her was full of intensity and she didn't know where to look. What was going on? Was he saying that he . . . ? No, surely not – not little Den Poole? Even seeing him suddenly as a man, she could not believe he would be saying something like that. But in the almost darkness, she could sense the intense feeling coming from him, making her feel almost as if her very flesh was being caressed. It was unexpected and unsettling. She did not want to hurt his feelings, but she now felt desperate to get away from him.

'All right, I'll write to you if you like,' she said casually, hoping to goodness she would remember. 'But I must go home now, Den. Ma'll wonder where I've got to.'

'Yeah,' he said quickly. 'Course.' If there was one person in this world Den had everlasting respect for, it was Margaret.

They walked out into the street and she hurried away, giving an awkward little wave. 'Bye then, Den – and best of luck!'

She heard his goodbye drift along the street behind her.

'That's another one Eb's got leaving,' Margaret said that evening as they sat round the table.

'Who is it this time?' Pa said, helping himself to a mouthful of cabbage.

'Den Poole,' Daisy said.

'How do you know?' He looked up at her, chewing.

'He came and met me out of work and told me,' Daisy said.

'What – just now?' Her father frowned.

'He wants me to write to him.' She cut up her kidneys in the thick, tasty gravy, only then glancing up to see that both her parents were looking closely at her.

'That poor lad's been sweet on you for years,' Pa said.

'No, he *hasn't*,' Daisy said, laughing in astonishment. 'What're you talking about?'

'Want to bet?' her father teased, his face crinkling with amusement.

'Philip,' Margaret cautioned him. She did not approve of any sort of gambling, even in a joking sense. 'And poor

35

Mary – just another thing for her to worry about. Perhaps I'll go and call on her.'

'You're just being silly,' Daisy said. 'But I can write to him if he wants. And Pa – I want to do a bit more on my jug tonight.' She was making a straight-sided silver jug, playing with shape and dimension, always wanting to create something new and different. She had a little workroom of her own in the attic now, where she could try out more novel things than they made in the works.

'It's too dark,' he said.

'I can see for a while with the lamp, you know I can!' She was jiggling with impatience, wanting to get up there, to get started. 'My sight's perfect.'

Pa rolled his eyes, forking up potato and cabbage. But he seemed in a good mood. 'All right then, Miss Argumentative – just an hour. But no longer, all right?'

Carrying the oil lamp, she climbed up to the front attic room and the half workbench which used to be downstairs and was now set under the window. Three curved shapes had been cut out of the side of the bench, each for a person to sit at and work on the wooden block or peg which was set over it on a support at eye level, for hammering and shaping metal. In Pa's shopping and Eb Watts's, the men sat round whole tables like these, with six pegs, all working away with their gas jets and blowpipes to steer the flame more accurately on to the exact spot where they were working, with their tools for shaping and cutting and the skin pouches hanging from the edge of the table to catch the lemel and dust left over from the work.

Daisy stood the lamp on the bench, put her overall on and sat down, drawing in a deep, happy breath. Even after her work down in Pa's shopping, or teaching at the school, this was something she had to do, a habit she had

had since childhood when she came home from school: 'Pa – I want to *make* something!' From her youngest days she could remember her mother bent over this very peg, working on her own creations in silver.

Daisy knew she was talented. She could feel the materials work and shape under her hands and she needed to be able to do her own work like this, preferably every day. It was almost like breathing to her, or like food. Her one real ambition was to be a professional, respected, artist silversmith – even if she was a woman! – to be someone in the trade and to have her own thriving business.

As well as the workbench under the dormer window, the room contained a spare single bed along one wall, which looked spartan as at present it had no bedding on it except one pillow and a pale pink candlewick counterpane covering the thin mattress. On the other side of the little square room were a small cupboard and some waist-high shelves. On the lower shelves she kept tools and work materials. Along the top were a few of her treasures – items she had made and two made by her mother. One was a shallow, hand-beaten silver dish, the other a little silver jewellery box, the lid set with semi-precious stones, agate and opal. Inside was a tiny silver christening bracelet which Mom had made for her and which had been on her wrist from a time before she could remember. It was a slender ring with overlapping ends, neatly fixed so that the bracelet could extend its size as she grew. Engraved along the side, 'Daisy Louise Tallis' had taught her to spell her name. She had worn and worn it until it made a weal on her arm from pressing so tightly and she had wept when Philip had to cut it off when she was eight years old. She always kept it close to her as one of her most precious possessions.

Seated on the stool in front of the bench, she looked

with satisfaction at all her tools neatly laid out: her pliers and snips, her files and saws, the rawhide hammer and Archimedes drill, her doming block and mandrel ...

She placed the half-made jug before her and inclined her head to look at it, her eyes feeling along its shape, assessing every line. It was of an austere design, straight sided with a pointed, triangular spout which she was in the process of fashioning. But it was not right. She frowned, offended by the thing and by her own lack of judgement. Too big? Yes, just a little bit – out of proportion to the rest of it. Wrong.

Picking it up, she was full of a sense of dissatisfaction. She was never going to be good enough!

She took hold of the unattached spout to work on it. Usually her mind would be completely absorbed, the precision and choices involved in the work occupying all the space that might contain other thoughts. But tonight they kept intruding.

The talk she had had with Den came back to her; his dark, imploring eyes, his begging her to write. And that feeling she had had as he stood close to her. Was Pa right about Den, that he was sweet on her? As she had stood with him, she had felt something, a sort of power over him that she had never known before – or not in that way. She was an innocent as regards men. Most of the males she met were either older men, local workers or teachers in the school, or younger lads who she was teaching.

She pushed some strands of hair back from her face and picked up her piercing saw, preparing herself to cut with all possible care. Bother Den – she couldn't help what he felt, could she? Why should she feel disturbed by it? She would write him an occasional friendly letter when she got around to it – what more could she do?

But as she worked at the edge of the spout, her heart

started racing when another thought would not be shut out. Mr Carson. He had only been back in the school for a few days, but she could not help noticing the number of times she had caught him looking at her – the way he seemed to watch her with a slight smile on his face, his eyes still following her if she glanced back. She was becoming more and more aware of having grown up into a young woman – a woman who men found attractive.

'For goodness' sake, don't be such a silly goose,' she said out loud, leaning her head back to ease her neck. 'He's . . .' She stopped talking out loud. *He's nearly twice your age and he's married. He's not looking at you like that.*

But however many sensible talks she gave herself, she could not chase away the reality that this flamboyant and powerful man was paying her a very particular kind of attention – one that each time she met him and his eyes fastened on her, sent the blood pumping madly round her body.

Five

Margaret, who was serving out a dinner of chops, heard the knocking. She saw Daisy, who had been sitting with a dreamy expression on her face, jump as if she had been brought back from somewhere far away.

'I'll go.' Philip got up from the table and in a moment Margaret heard sounds of greeting and laughter.

'Annie!' she called, her voice rising with happiness. 'What're you doing here? I thought you had no time to breathe, let alone come to see us.'

Her younger sister's pink-cheeked face arrived around the door, smiling and looking energetic as usual.

'Surprise evening off,' she said. 'We do have to get out now and then, you know. I thought I'd pop over and see you all!'

Annie was dressed not in her nurse's uniform but in her own clothes – a dark blue skirt and blouse and a long green cardigan. Clothes usually looked long on Annie because she was so petite – not that she could care less either way most of the time. Her hair was dragged hastily back into some sort of bun and her big-eyed, elfin face was full of life.

'Hello, Auntie Annie!' Daisy said, beaming at the sight of her. She loved Annie and had a joking relationship with her which included trying to improve Annie's dress sense, without much success. Annie was always far too busy saving the world to think of such fripperies.

'Hello, Daisy dear ...' She stopped to kiss Daisy's

cheek. 'Hello, Mags. I suppose I've missed the little ones – are they in bed already?'

'No!' John said indignantly from the other end of the room where he and Lily were playing on the floor. 'We're not babies, you know!'

Lily ran up and hugged Annie in her intense way. 'Are you looking after lots of wounded soldiers, Auntie?'

'Yes, I am, Lily,' Annie said, kissing her. 'But they are getting better, or most of them, anyway!'

'Trust you to arrive just when the grub's up,' Philip teased, settling in his chair at the head of the table, his jacket hung over the back.

'I know,' Annie said, inhaling gleefully. 'Like a dog, I can smell a good meal from miles away – and that gravy smells *delicious*! It's got to be better than what we get over there.'

'There's plenty – sit down,' Margaret said. 'John, Lily – you can stay over there and play for a while.' They had had their tea earlier with Mrs Flett. Standing at the other end of the table from Philip, serving out the meal, Margaret eyed her sister. 'Everything all right?'

Annie, who had done all her training at the Dudley Road Infirmary, had applied straight away to work in the new war hospital at the university in Edgbaston as soon as it got started. Already, when Archduke Franz Ferdinand was shot in Sarajevo on 28 June, as tensions rose throughout the summer of 1914 and war was declared once the Germans moved into Belgium, plans had been well advanced. The university had been transformed in not much more than a week into the First Southern General Hospital.

'Oh – yes,' Annie said. 'Very busy.' She looked down for a moment, her face sobering.

At the beginning of the war, everyone had been talking

about what was happening to the poor Belgians, with the Germans overrunning their country and committing unspeakable atrocities. Then when the fighting began, after all the rush to volunteer at the start of it all, had come news of the British Expeditionary Force having to retreat from Mons.

When Annie started at the First Southern General, she had been full of details of all the efforts to get it ready, the way that now the university's grand main hall, with its stained-glass windows, was lined with rows of iron bed frames all made up and ready, as were a number of its academic departments. With five hundred beds in place they had filled a number with lads injured in training. But by the beginning of September they were waiting for the first convoy of casualties to arrive from France, through Selly Oak station. Nowadays, Annie said less about it, as if it was a relief to get away, or perhaps she had just become used to it.

Margaret sat down, pulling her chair in. 'Do start.' She said a silent prayer of thanks. Despite her and Annie's strict Christian upbringing a few miles from Bristol, where their father was a Congregationalist minister, she had never managed to instil any observable religious feeling in either her husband or Daisy.

'Guess who I've just been to see on the way here?' Annie said, after they'd all started eating.

'Who?' Margaret said.

'Mary Poole.'

The sisters had known the Poole family, in which Den was the only boy, for some years. It was Annie who first got to know them as she had worked for a while with her daughter Lizzie, at a time when things for the family had been especially bad. The Pooles still lived on a yard in Pope Street on the edge of the Jewellery Quarter.

'Oh,' Margaret said. 'How is she?' Despite her show of interest, she had a sense of misgiving, and knew she had not been wrong to feel this when Annie looked round the table and announced, 'She's expecting.'

Margaret almost choked on her mouthful of cabbage. 'What – *again*?' This all the more remarkable, being Mrs Poole's second occasion of bringing forth a child after she no longer had a husband – nor had she had one for a long time.

Frowning, she glanced at John and Lily, her own cheeks flamed with blushes. It was bad enough even Daisy hearing all this – Annie was the end, really she was, always coming along with some terrible story! Daisy, however, was listening with avid interest. John and Lily kept their heads down, wise enough not to show that they had their ears thoroughly pricked.

'I'm afraid so,' Annie said. 'She's only just showing, but she told me straight out.' Annie knew the Poole family well and had been a great support to them at one time. She knew Mary would not hide much from her.

All of them had grown used to the fact that Annie was prone to airing subjects usually considered too indelicate for discussion – the state of people's anatomy, unexpected pregnancy and such – over the tea table. It was one of the reasons the children all looked forward to her visits. There was a kind of devilment in Annie, as if she liked to rub your nose in the earthiness of things. When she had first gone to train at the hospital on Dudley Road, she had been full of mischievous remarks about how every other building along the road seemed to be a public house, as if to provoke Margaret. And now here she was at it again. However, all of them baulked at asking any of the more obvious 'how?' and 'who?' questions about this particular development.

Annie, being less reserved, went on, 'I said to her, "Oh, Mary – not again!"'

'You *didn't*?' Margaret gasped. How could Annie say something so personal – to anyone?

Annie looked at her in surprise.

'Well, what would you have said? I mean now, of all times, when there're already so many out of work – and she won't get a separation allowance, will she, not without a husband? I felt really exasperated with her. And Den's gone, of course – I don't think he knew or he might have thought twice about it. But then she said such a sad thing to me. She said, "I know it's foolish of me, but I can't seem to feel right – not since Nellie went." I really didn't know what to say to that.'

To all their surprise, Annie's eyes filled – she was not one to shed tears easily. But they had all known Mary back then. It had been at one of the worst times in her life when she had just lost her little twin girl Ada through sickness and her husband had died. Because she had Nellie, the baby, she was hardly able to bring any money into the family herself, leaving it all to poor little Lizzie, who was only fourteen.

In desperation, Mary had taken Nellie to the orphanage. She always swore it was only for a while, that she would go and get her as soon as she was back on her feet. But she had never seen Nellie again. When she did go back to the home, even though it was only a short time later, they told her that Nellie had been adopted by a nice family, that she would have a good life and that Mary mustn't bother herself about her again. They would never tell her where she was.

'Of course someone'd want my Nellie,' Mary sobbed afterwards. 'She were lovely – the most beautiful baby I ever had.'

And Nellie had been lovely – blonde and blue-eyed and plump.

Annie wiped her eyes. 'She said that she still feels as if a piece of her is missing – it's her way of trying to feel better, I suppose.'

'But she's got little Ethel,' Margaret said. 'I mean, she must be, what – five? – by now.' She was astonished by the sheer immorality of Mary Poole's life, of how she ever managed to get herself into quite the messes she did in the first place. But by now they had all realized that not much was likely to change.

'And goodness knows what poor Lizzie thinks of it all,' Annie said. 'She didn't say much, but she'll be the one who ends up doing all the work as usual.' Lizzie Poole, Mary's oldest daughter, had long been the one to carry the can for the family's problems. 'She had to birth Ethel by herself, the midwife was so long in coming.'

'Have you seen Aunt Hatt?' Margaret said, feeling compelled to change the subject.

'No – I popped in and saw Uncle Eb though,' Annie said.

They exchanged news about family – had Margaret heard from Father and how were Aunt Hatt and Georgie and Clara and the children?

'Oh, Aunt's happy as anything,' Margaret said, 'running round after those grandchildren. It suits her down to the ground. And thank goodness she and Clara get along so well.'

'Aunt always wanted more children herself, didn't she?' Annie said, laying down her knife and fork.

'I imagine so, yes,' Margaret said, hoping to head Annie off again before she steered the conversation back along paths which might involve unnecessarily physical details. 'Rice pudding?'

They sat chatting for a time after John and Lily had gone to bed. When Annie got up to go she first hugged Daisy. Then embracing Margaret, she looked up at her, her face sombre, and Margaret suddenly saw that there was a world of things Annie was not talking about. She felt vaguely ashamed. Seeing Annie in her own clothes and not the grey dress, white apron and red cloak of her uniform, it was easy to forget what her work involved day after day.

'See you as soon as I can,' Annie said. 'Time permitting.'

Oh, I expect it'll all be over soon, they would have said not so long ago. But now everyone seemed less sure. 'I'll walk to the tram with you,' Philip said. 'It's even harder with the lamps painted over – it's not as if they gave off that much light in the first place.'

The city streets had been blacked out for fear of what the Germans might be intending to do with those Zeppelin airships that they had in their possession. Street lamps had been painted black halfway down the shade and vehicles were expected to muffle their lights. And Annie was going to have to change trams in town and walk from Colmore Row to the terminus in Navigation Street to get another tram down the Bristol Road.

'You'd better get one of those buttons,' Margaret joked. You could buy little white buttons that shone violet in the dark if you warmed them by the fire.

'I don't think I've ever seen one of those,' Annie chuckled. She did not seem at all worried by being out in the dark. 'I should've thought looking where you're going would be a better idea.'

Margaret watched Philip and Annie set off along the dark street. They were soon out of sight and she closed the door and stood for a moment, alone, in the pale gaslight of the hall, a smile on her face. How blessed I am, she thought, having all this, my family, and Annie close by as well – even Father only a train ride away. And when all these boys are going off to war – those mothers never sleeping well again. She sent up a prayer for them, and felt guiltily relieved that she did not have a son old enough to fight.

Six

'Daisy?'

She looked up from the desk, realizing that her father had already said her name more than once by the expression on his face.

'For goodness' sake,' he grumbled, 'are you with us, or not? I said, have you found order ninety-one yet?'

'Oh – yes, sorry,' she said, jarred back into reality. It was so hard to keep her mind on anything. Pa was not a difficult man, but he was exacting where the business was concerned. 'It's here.'

'Good,' Philip said testily, taking the sheet of paper from her. He loomed beside her in his overall. 'It's hard enough getting any orders these days, without you losing them.'

'I haven't lost it,' she pointed out carefully, seeing this was not a moment to argue. Things were tense and she saw Edith, the younger of the two women who worked in the office, give her a sympathetic smile.

The order, from a grand house in Cheshire, was for fifty silver napkin rings. Daisy had worked on some of the rings herself on her days out in the workshop. And it was true that while sitting in the office for one day a week drove her to a fever of boredom, it was she who had suggested that she should do it. She knew her mother had known about running the business, as well as seeing Margaret and Aunt Hatt involved in the office side of their gold and silversmithing businesses for most of her life. She realized it was something she needed to know.

She had been allocated a seat at the large table in the middle. The lamp suspended over it was lit most days, except at the height of summer, its burning mantle a background hiss as it cast a pale ring of light on their papers and blotters.

Mr Henshaw, who had worked at Tallis's for years and, being close on sixty, was far too old to go off to war, was very much the boss in the office. He sat, enthroned on a Windsor chair, at a side desk facing into the room. All too often, Daisy would look up from her daydreams to see him observing her over his half-moon glasses, beady eyes peering from under those shaggy grey brows as if to say, *I hope you're getting on with your work, young miss?* It always surprised her how hairy his eyebrows were when his head was nearly bald. Though he was not an unkind man, she always felt a great distance between him and herself. There had never been any chin tickling or teasing from Mr Henshaw as she was growing up.

And there were two ladies. Miss Taylor, on packing, a sweet, blonde, softly spoken woman in her twenties, whom Daisy could call Edith, was walking out with a man called Arthur, now away at sea. And there was Miss Allen, who wrote many letters and was goodness knows how old, at *least* forty, who she definitely could not call Muriel because she was always Miss Allen and tart as a lemon with it. They all sat round the table, as did Margaret when she was there. Daisy did whatever she was asked to do by the others, and very tedious she found it most of the time.

Her attention was even harder to discipline these days, when her mind drifted constantly towards the extraordinary, dangerously delicious things that were happening to her that she could not mention to anyone, that she just could not stop thinking about . . .

'Pa?' Desperate for distraction, she straightened up from her slump over the desk. 'Why *don't* we start making MIZPAH brooches – or rings? They're nice.'

'Huh,' he said, meaning, *Not that again.* 'Sentimental tat,' he said scornfully, on his way out of the room. Pa was a bit of a purist – an artist at heart. He ran a commercial business because he had to, but he would have preferred to be working on his own creations in silver, instead of snatching only the occasional hour here and there when he could.

'But Pa,' she said in a low voice, having followed him out into the passage. He stood before her in his overall, clearly impatient. 'Why not do it? You're worried about not getting enough orders, aren't you? Blenkinsop's have all but closed down – we don't want to end up like that.'

Her father rolled his eyes as if to say, *You don't need to tell me.*

'Other firms are doing well with them,' she pleaded. 'I'm sure I could design something lovely! They're such a popular thing – they sell ever so well. Imagine if you were having to join up and leaving Ma – you'd wear a MIZPAH brooch, wouldn't you?'

'No,' he said drily, 'I don't s'pose I would.'

'Even if I'd made it?' She appealed to him, looking up with her most winning smile.

Her father softened in a resigned way, giving a sigh. 'Well, all right – if you'd made it I'd have to, wouldn't I?'

' "The Lord watch between me and thee when we are absent from one another." ' Daisy felt her heart swell with feeling as she said it. MIZPAH – the emotional bond between any two people who loved each other and were parted. She thought of him, of James Carson, his eyes looking down at her. 'It's beautiful! Oh, Pa, let me design something! Mr Watts is doing very well with his lucky stars. And I could make something better than everyone else's, I know I could!'

'What can you do better than anyone else?' Margaret's voice was tinged with reproach as she came out from the kitchen. She wasn't given to boastfulness and did not like to hear it in Daisy.

'She's on about us making some of that MIZPAH stuff,' Philip said, trying to sound dismissive, but Daisy could already see that she had him hooked – a little bit at least.

Margaret put her hands on her hips. 'Good idea. We could do with rather more income from somewhere, the way things are going.'

'And it is from the Bible,' Daisy said, feeling this would win her religious stepmother over even more. '*Can* I, Pa? I could go up and design something now instead of being in the office today?'

Outnumbered and outflanked, Philip Tallis held out his hands in defeat. 'Well – all right then. I suppose so. You see what you can come up with.'

Seven

Daisy dashed up to her workroom. The lower staircase was covered with well-worn brown linoleum, but the treads up to the attic stairs were bare wood and her boots clattered eagerly to the top, taking the stairs two at a time. She felt as if she had been let out of school early to play. Now she could draw and make her own designs all afternoon if she wanted!

This floor was now her realm in the house. She slept in the back attic overlooking the yard, but had chosen to have her workroom at the front where there was more light. She tried to stop her half-brother and -sister, John and Lily, coming up here and messing about with her things. They knew from hard experience not to touch the box her mother had made, however much Lily begged to be allowed to play with it.

Lily was all right most of the time, Daisy had to concede. She was only seven and a sweet little thing with a pudding basin of thick brown hair and big blue eyes. She looked up to Daisy and loved it when Daisy deigned to spend time playing with her. It was quite gratifying being adored like that. All the same, she was glad to have her own bedroom and workroom up in the attic and let the rest of the family get on with it a floor further down.

John, on the other hand, was downright annoying. Daisy found it hard to admit even now how jealous she had been when Margaret had two more children – especially when John, the eldest, had arrived. It had come as a shock to Daisy, who had been on her own for the first twelve years of her life. When John was born, she had been afraid she would be pushed aside because their mother was not her real mother, even though she loved Margaret now almost as if she was.

And of course he was a boy and she had felt sure he would now become the important one, the one who would inherit the business from Pa. That was how things went in the world, wasn't it? – it was always the boys who got everything. And he looked so like Pa, solid and strong, with Pa's big eyes and frizzy hair.

Though angry, she was ashamed of her feelings and had never said anything about it to Pa, but she knew she had often been mean in her behaviour to John, and Pa had ticked her off for it. Sometimes she refused to play with him, or ignored him as if he was not there. Her half-brother needed keeping in his place, she felt.

Daisy went to the table and took her design notebook from the drawer. It was nothing special, just a little brown covered notebook with lines. Instead of sitting at the desk, she took her pencil and lay on the bed leaning forward on her elbows. She flipped through the book of drawings: experimental sketches for her jug, various handles and spouts. There were the teapot and sugar salver she had designed, the bracelets and pendants, the engraved silver tray . . .

'MIZPAH,' she whispered, opening up a clean page. '"The Lord watch between me and thee . . ." What would I want to wear if *he* went away?' A pang went through her. This was a desolate thought. Would she want a ring? A necklace? Or a brooch? What would *he* wear?

A delicious, excited feeling came over her. At last she was alone and she could give herself up to her fantasies. She knew, really, that they were just dreams. Mr Carson was a safely married man, but she enjoyed his attention, the way he looked at her with those dark, intense eyes. It might not be real but it was intoxicating being able to pretend he was hers, this romantic, artistic figure, sweeping round the corridors at Vittoria Street.

She rolled over on to her back, inserting a finger under the edge of her corset to ease it, and breathed in as deeply as she could. Resting the notebook on her stomach she stared up at the sloping white ceiling. But she did not see the chipped paint, the bare room with its blue-and-white checked curtains at the window. She was seeing his face, wondering, Would he wear a brooch for me?

Over the past couple of months, as she taught her two weekly afternoon classes at Vittoria Street, between two and four o'clock, he had gradually started to pay her more and more attention. Mr Carson's afternoon classes were in advanced silversmithing and in raising, chasing and *repousée*. He also taught one of the evening classes which ran between seven and nine o'clock, but she was not in the school then.

All afternoon and evening, Vittoria Street School was abuzz, the various teaching rooms throughout the building full of activity. All the day-release classes related to trades in the district: as well as the numerous skills associated with smithing metals, classes were given in clay modelling and drawing from life, as well as enamelling and die sinking, and mounting and setting jewels.

Daisy noticed nowadays that when she emerged from the Elementary Silversmithing room, she hardly ever failed to find Mr Carson's tall, striking figure positioned somewhere in the corridor, often walking slowly along as if he was on the way to or from somewhere and they had just happened to coincide. At first she thought that was all it was. But after a while, he just always seemed to be there. Increasingly, as well as the intense look and smile, the raising of his hat should he be wearing one – for he was the sort of person who often wore hats indoors – he would find a reason to stop her for a brief conversation.

'Is everything going along all right, Miss Tallis?' he might ask, with a smile which slightly mocked the formal way in which he was speaking.

'Yes, thank you, Mr Carson,' she would say, because in general, although a few of the students could be a bit trying, she had no real problem and she loved her work.

'And how's your pa getting along?'

'He's very well, thank you.' If you want to know how Pa is, she couldn't help thinking, why don't you call and see him? But she had noticed that, since coming back from Sheffield, Mr Carson had still not been to their house. When she was young she had always found it exciting when he arrived, and in those days, he had seemed to keep popping up like a jolly rabbit rather often. Only now she was coming to realize that back then, Mr Carson had assumed he could influence her father, take him under his wing as some sort of protégé for his own glory. But Pa, proud, stubborn, mostly self-taught, would have none of it. He had dug his heels in and rejected Carson's patronage. And in the end, there was an almost magnetic repulsion of personality between the two men.

'Well, it's still astonishing to me to see you here,' Mr Carson would sometimes say, in a bemused way. 'And of course a great pleasure.'

Yesterday, he had come into her teaching room. The last of the lads were clearing up their pegs and hurrying from the room and Daisy was still supervising a slow, painstaking boy called David as he finished soldering together the two ends of a bracelet.

'No, Jack,' she called to another boy as she stood over David. 'You can't leave it like that. What about the person who's going to use that peg after you?'

She was busy concentrating on David, a serious boy for whom she had rather a soft spot, when she became aware that Mr Carson had come into the room and was ambling up and down picking up objects in what seemed an arbitrary way and putting them down again. She felt immediately self-conscious and torn between wanting him to go away and curiosity about why he was there.

'All right, David, I think that will do,' she said. 'You can leave it in the pickle – I'll see to it before I go. You get cleared up now.'

She turned, as if she had only just noticed their visitor.

'Ah, hello, Mr Carson?' She spoke very formally, though her heart had speeded up and she scarcely knew why.

'Good afternoon, Miss Tallis.' He glanced at David, now the last one in the room, who was stolidly tidying the tools. 'I just wanted a quick word.'

They stood awkwardly for a moment as David finally took himself off.

'Everything all right?' Mr Carson said, as if to fill the time.

'Yes, thank you,' Daisy said demurely. She realized then that she was still wearing her overall and took it off. Beneath she had on a wool frock in cornflower blue with a darker blue cardigan over it. After hanging up the overall, she patted her hair and turned to see Mr Carson's eyes fixed on her and a look in his eyes which made her feel strangely prickly all over, and as if she was aware of every line of her body.

'I'm full of admiration for your work,' he said, as if he

must say something. 'I have seldom seen such excellence in one so young.'

'But you haven't seen any of my work for a long time,' she laughed, gratified, but knowing he was just flattering her. 'It's all at home. You'll have to come and visit us if you want to see. I'm sure Pa would be happy if you called round.'

To her surprise he looked uncertain and glanced away from her a moment, along the room, with its windows down one side.

'I'm not so sure about that.' He laughed suddenly and looked back at her, his dark eyes filled with such merriment that it warmed her and made her like him even more. It felt almost as if they were in some conspiracy together. 'I'm not sure your pa really approves of me. But I tell you what – how about I walk you home and say hello to the old so-and-so?'

They walked the streets side by side in the chilly wind. Mr Carson, in his dashing black hat with a wide brim and sweeping cloak, talked about his students and made jokes, turning to look down at her when he laughed. He had a loud, full-hearted blare of a laugh which made her join in with him. And Daisy, in her sea-green coat and brown hat with a brim and a strip of peacock-green silk she had twisted round as a band, felt rather something, walking along with this dramatic, artistic-looking figure who somehow also always made her feel special and cheerful.

When they reached Chain Street, Eb Watts was outside his front door at number twenty-six. He looked Mr Carson's eccentric attire up and down and disappeared inside. Eb Watts didn't hold with these Arts and Crafts types – he was a businessman and that was that.

'So, are you coming in to say hello?' Daisy asked.

'Not today. I must get myself home.' Mr Carson

removed his hat, gave a sweeping bow and made a face of mock dread. 'Or I shall be in trouble.'

Daisy laughed and said goodbye, still smiling as she went indoors. She wondered exactly what Mrs Carson was like because he always painted her as an ogre. But she seemed a rather free lady and an artist, especially as the two of them had no children. Daisy liked this idea, of being free and not having children. She very much hoped that one day she might meet the artistic Mrs Victoria Carson.

Since that day, Mr Carson had appeared more and more often, to exchange a word and offer to walk her home. She had been flattered, especially when he kept saying how good her work was, how talented she was – the exceptional child of gifted parents.

She couldn't help being fascinated by this man. He was so noticeable to look at, handsome and dashing, with a male power that seemed to have fastened on her. Yet in her innocence she thought of it in the way of two kindred spirits meeting. He understood her, her work, her artistic soul.

But yesterday . . . She lay on her bed, feeling her heart's forceful rhythm as she remembered. Yesterday something had changed. She had been in the room with the last few students. The slow boy, David, had not been there, the last handful of students hurried away and the workroom stilled. And there he was, standing in the shadow of the doorway as she had somehow known he would be.

Her blood speeded up. She grew aware of a vein pulsing in her neck. But she carried on with what she was doing – tidying, making sure nothing had been left in the bath of pickle, washing her hands, removing her overall.

As she did so, he came into the room, gently pushing the door closed.

'Afternoon,' she said lightly, looking across at him.

'Good afternoon, my dear.'

She finished bustling and went to fetch her coat. 'Shall we go?' His walking her home had quickly become a habit.

'Of course.' He stood at the door, holding his hat, the cloak over one arm. As she went to pull the door open, he said, 'Wait, my dear. Just one moment.'

She looked up at him, half expectant, half nervous. He was standing so close to her that she could not fail to be affected by him.

'I face a dilemma,' he said, looking down at the wooden floor. She waited, wondering what on earth this might be and why he would be talking to her about it.

'I'm a man,' he said, looking at her with solemn eyes. 'I am no jingoist, but I feel I should do my duty to my country. That perhaps I should follow the call . . .'

She almost cried out, *No – oh, no, don't do that!* But she stopped herself. She saw Den's face in front of her for a moment and felt a shock of guilt. Despite his asking her to write, she had heard nothing from him since he left and she had completely forgotten to write to him.

'But,' she protested, 'surely there is no need? It can't go on much longer?'

'I fear that view may be mistaken,' he said solemnly. 'After all, the war is spreading already, in the east, and they're digging in – a stalemate.' He held out a hand in an expansive way. 'Look what they did to the Belgian people – such cruel barbarity! They have to be stopped.'

'But aren't you . . . ?' She had been about to say *too old*. She corrected herself quickly. 'Surely you must be of more use here? And your wife won't want you to go.'

His glance flickered at her. 'Perhaps not. But there is another thing.' He stepped even closer to her. Eyes full of emotion, he reached a hand to her face and very gently shifted a little lock of hair hanging at her temple. 'My dear Daisy ... Oh!' He removed his hand as if afraid of himself. 'Every day when I see you ... You are simply the loveliest thing I have ever seen! So gifted, so beautiful! Everywhere I go, I see you before my eyes. I can think of little else – it's as if you have bewitched me!'

She stood very still, washed in his words. She could scarcely believe what she was hearing. It affected her like a spell, though she had no idea what exactly this meant or what to say in reply. She had known a few lads pursue her before, but she had brushed them away like flies, not interested in return. They were like children! But this man – this *married* man, she reminded herself. What did this mean?

'I'm sorry.' Seeing how at a loss she was he retreated, lowering his hand. 'I should not have said anything. But you do something to me, Miss Daisy Tallis ...' He was smiling now, those eyes lighting up. 'I am filled with adoration, like an acolyte at the throne!'

Fortunately, before she could even begin to think of anything to say in reply to this, he opened the door again and swept out through it. 'Come along, my dear – I must return you safely to your home!'

Daisy lay in the slanting light of the attic, reliving these moments over and again in her mind. Mr Carson, worshipping her, thinking her work was something exceptional. He thought far more of her than Pa had ever done – it was utterly extraordinary and exciting. And her feelings of unease at this, she told herself, were unnecessary. Mr Carson had a wife who was a successful artist. Everything was right and proper and what she had seen in his eyes was the burning admiration of one artist for another. And this, she admitted to herself, was all she had ever wanted! It was intensely exciting and gratifying. She could have lain there dreaming about it and let the hours drift past.

'Come along, you silly thing,' she said, dragging herself off the bed. 'MIZPAH. That's what you need to be getting on with.'

Eight

There was a day that changed everything. Despite his intense manner and his interest in her, Mr Carson had never been anything but courteous. Wherever she went in the school, he would appear. After a time she could sometimes sense him even before she saw him, would feel a tingling at the back of her neck, almost as if he was breathing on her. She might turn and look about her and there he would be. He asked after her classes, he gave advice and praise, told her about some of his smithing students, about his own painting. And often he walked her home. Only once, though, had he finally come into the house to greet her father. Pa had been in the workshop and Daisy did not follow Mr Carson out there to see what sort of greeting he received, though afterwards Pa did not seem exactly excited by this event.

And then, that afternoon as they stepped out into the raw, smoky air of the street, Mr Carson turned to her from under the wide brim of his hat. To her bewilderment she saw that he seemed shy, tense, almost as if he was afraid of her.

'Perhaps, if you're not in a hurry, you'd like to come in for some tea?' he said.

Although his lodging place was nearby, Daisy had never been there. She was excited. Did this mean that she might at last meet the mysterious Mrs Carson and see some of her paintings? Though she had never yet had a glimpse of Victoria Carson, Daisy already held up

Georgie Gaskin, the wife of the head of the school, Arthur Gaskin, high in her mind as if she were a god. She was hoping Victoria Carson might be another woman and artist she could worship. Perhaps Mrs Carson might even take an interest in her?

'Well,' she said. 'If it's convenient for . . . for you both.'

She knew he lived in rooms, rather than the grand house she might have imagined, but she had never really given much thought to why Mr and Mrs Carson did not live in bigger, more impressive accommodation. At the far end of the street, he said lightly, 'Here we are,' and steered her in through a doorway. 'Just up the stairs there.' He stood back politely as if to let her pass, then changed his mind. 'I'd better lead the way.'

Daisy climbed the stairs, wishing she had known in advance she was to make this visit. She was in her old working dress, the cornflower-blue one, and the old blue cardigan. Even in overalls there was a risk of soiling her clothing with flux or any number of other substances in the classroom, so this was the dress she almost always wore to teach. But the soft, comfortable stuff of the dress now made her feel drab. She imagined that Mrs Carson would be draped over a chaise longue wearing silks and velvet slippers, with pearls and blossoms in her hair like a pre-Raphaelite heroine. Though she was taken aback by the dingy darkness of the staircase.

On the first floor, Mr Carson stooped to insert his key in the lock. She looked at his long slender back, the thin, very slightly bowed legs in his black trousers, so close to her. Taking in his physical presence in this new place gave her a peculiar feeling. How strange it was to be this close to a man! She realized that while some girls her age were married with several babies round their legs, she had no idea really about men. Her heart started to thump harder

63

and she found it hard to understand her sudden sense of misgiving, as if her instincts were running before what her mind could understand. But at least Mrs Carson would be there. She did not need to worry about anything.

'Here we are!' Mr Carson flung the door open. 'Come along, my dear. And let me see about making us some tea. It will take me a little while to get the fire going, I'm afraid.'

'But,' Daisy said, astonished, 'don't you have a maid?'

'Not at present,' Mr Carson said, immediately laying kindling on the fire and filling the kettle from a pail of water beside the fireplace.

Daisy watched, amazed. Was this how Mr and Mrs Carson lived? The room – one of two from what she could see, since there was a door leading off this one – had what she decided to think of as a simple, artistic charm. She looked about her. So this was how real artists lived! The floor was simply rough boards, the walls white and the only furniture a table and chairs, a cupboard and two other very old French-style chairs, the back and seat upholstered, with slender wooden legs. There was no range, simply a fireplace with a pair of fire dogs, a hook on which to hang the kettle or a pot over the flames and, lying tucked behind the brass fender, a long-handled iron skillet.

There were sagging brown curtains at the windows. In the corner behind her stood an easel with a board tilted on it and there was a muddle of paints and spirit bottles and a rough pile of sketchbooks on the floor beside it. Other than Mr Carson's cloak and hat now lying on the chair, there was very little else in the room. As she looked about her, she found an enchantment to this bare, careless room. None of the domesticity of children and wet nap-kins hanging and all the stifling, tedious work that went along with that – all of which had arrived in twenty-four Chain Street with the birth of her half-brother and -sister. This, here, was a life given over to art. Oh, this was what she wanted – to be with these people, to learn from them!

'Is that a painting of Mrs Carson's?' she asked, as the fire began to crackle into life. She did not presume to walk round and look at the picture, as it was turned to face the wall.

Mr Carson shovelled coal on to the flames before coming over to her, gently, almost like someone about to impart bad news.

'The room will soon be warm,' he said. 'Why don't you take your coat off – put it with mine, umm?'

Daisy did as he suggested, laying her coat and hat on top of his, which somehow made her tingle with a sense of intimacy. Mr Carson indicated one of the chairs for her to sit. The upholstery was threadbare and of a very faded old gold.

He drew the other one closer and perched on the edge of it, legs bent, leaning solemnly towards her.

'I need to explain the situation to you, Daisy,' he said. 'The reason I am living in this rather straitened way. I have only been back here a matter of a few weeks, so I do hope to make better arrangements eventually. But I am having to lend support . . .'

Daisy was wondering even more where Mrs Carson was at this moment, but she soon found out.

'What I have not explained is that my wife . . . that Victoria did not come back here with me. She has stayed in Sheffield, where she has teaching work and a small studio and where she wishes to continue her life – without me. However, I must of course continue to support her financially, which stretches me rather . . .'

He looked down for a moment as if in distaste at having to discuss matters of money.

Daisy stared at him, feeling that her expression must look foolish. She was finding it hard to take in what he was saying. And the idea of having to be 'paid for' like Mrs Carson – even an artist like Victoria Carson! – repelled her. Why was Mrs Carson not here? What a strange thing. And why, if you were a woman, did you always have to be dependent on a man's money? It seemed humiliating. She cleared her throat and tried to appear more intelligent.

Looking deeply into her eyes, he said, 'Mrs Carson and I are now married purely in name. What I mean, Daisy, is that while I am a married man, it is in law only – not in matters of the heart.'

Daisy's first feeling was of disappointment. She would never meet Mrs Carson now. Could you just stop being married like this? Didn't that mean . . . ? She had never met anyone who had done that terrible thing – *divorce*. Mr Carson leaned even further towards her.

'My heart is changed now from what it was,' he said softly. 'I realize that I have known you since you were very young, my dear. But when I came back here and saw you – little Daisy Tallis – grown into such a fine woman . . . And not just fine but so brilliant, so talented like her mother before her, I . . .'

Again he removed his gaze from her for a second as if afraid, but he seemed compelled to go on and he got to his feet and took her hand, drawing her towards him.

'It has been a terrible time – such a lonely time, my dear. I had never imagined that Victoria could be so cruel . . . I look at you and you are so young, so utterly lovely, Daisy, I can hardly believe you are in this poor little chamber with me. I've tried to behave in the right way because I have such a deep respect for your father – and for you. But ever since I saw you for the first time in the school, my heart has been yours. That's all I can say, foolish man that I am.' He spread his hands, palms up. 'I just can't seem to help it.'

He reached out and took one of her hands, holding it between both of his cool ones as if it were a precious bird. She dared to look up at him, into his handsome face, which appeared afraid and joyful and desirous all at once. His eyes held her gaze, his face attempting a smile, but her fingertips could feel the pulse of a vein at his wrist, his blood beating like a bird's heart.

She was moved beyond words, by the poverty of the room, by him living in the way of a suffering artist after the desertion by his wife, by his adoration of her. Her heart swelled, filling with tender, protective feelings.

'Oh,' she said emotionally. 'Oh, Mr Carson . . .'

'James.' He squeezed her hand for a second. 'Please, my dear – call me James.'

'James.' She tried it on her lips the way she had often tried it in her daydreams. And she smiled up at him. It was delicious to be adored, to feel the force of this astonishing man.

'Is there any hope,' he asked humbly, 'of your having any feeling for me? I know I am old in your eyes – I am what? Thirteen, fourteen years your senior?'

'It doesn't matter,' she said, thinking of her father and Margaret, whose ages were also far apart. She already saw the years ahead, Daisy Tallis and James Carson – a pair of artists who would be known and admired.

Mr Carson laughed joyfully. 'Oh, Daisy – you're a miracle, you truly are!'

Moments later they heard the kettle getting up steam and he released her gently.

67

'Come – sit and we shall make merry!' he said quaintly. He poured water into the teapot, steam billowing about him, and Daisy watched, entranced. This man was in love with her and she – oh, yes – she was in love with him. Oh, now life was really beginning!

Nine

She knew she must say nothing at home.

Almost every time now, she went to his rooms after classes were finished. She invented other reasons for being later home than before: demands of the school, or May Gordon had asked her to visit.

Margaret kept saying, 'It's nice that you and May are seeing such a lot of each other again, Daisy – why don't you invite her here for a change? She's very welcome.' May used to visit often while they were together at Vittoria Street. Daisy, who had no real intention of seeing May, gave vague responses. She did not want to give up any of her secret times with Mr Carson in his rooms.

They were very careful. The second time she had been there, he said, 'I'll go on ahead and get that kettle on the fire!' And Daisy followed. This became a habit which they did not discuss. They never went out together. Daisy would glance about her before stepping into the doorway to his staircase to ensure that no over-familiar face – one of Pa's office workers like Mr Henshaw or stiff old Miss Allen – were about to swim out of the crowd. And then she would hurry inside, full of excitement at this intrigue and at being alone with someone who adored her. She did not examine closely why they needed to act so secretly.

Sitting by the fire, they drank tea. Mr Carson usually bought something nice like crumpets or pikelets which they toasted on the flames, eating them hot and dripping with butter. He joked that they were living 'bohemian style'. It was obvious that he enjoyed treating her, sometimes bringing special little cakes as well, and Daisy lapped up the attention, something in short supply at home these days.

He asked her about herself, her mother, her new family. He quizzed her about what she was working on and she described her tea service and the designs she was thinking of. And he told her about his boyhood in a place near London called Middlesex, and that he had always painted and drawn since he could hold a pencil.

'My parents were quite humble souls,' he said. 'Father worked in a market garden. But they did not prevent me. My elder brother followed my father so I was given freedom to find my own way. I went as apprentice to a smith in Clerkenwell – that's where I started learning my trade. Silver was always my first love – although I've always drawn and painted as well.'

And he told her that he had once been to the great William Morris's house at Kelmscott and been introduced to John Ruskin himself. To Daisy these were the names of giants: they seemed more than real people.

Another time he popped a lump of sugar into Daisy's teacup with a pair of delicate tongs which he then held up to regard fondly.

'Imagine if we had not had tea introduced to this country in the seventeenth century – why would we ever have needed all those tongs and sugar sifters and toast racks?'

Daisy laughed and told him that she was now making a toast rack for her tea service.

'And I'm sure it will be extraordinary – you must let me see,' he said, licking the butter delicately from his fingers. He always sat with his legs splayed, leaning forward in the chair as if about to leap to his feet and do something urgent, even when eating toast. And she loved the way his thin face and dark eyes were always so full of life and humour.

One dark, windy March afternoon, when they had sat awhile with tea by the fire, James Carson got to his feet, as if on a sudden impulse.

'Daisy?' He came close and held out his hand, drawing her to her feet. 'Oh, my dear, dear girl.'

She could hear a change in his voice from the light entertainer of other days. There was an urgency which sent a feeling through her, of excitement, of danger, she was not sure which. Because whenever she was with him it was as if her skin was sensitive, as if the hairs had all been stroked back the wrong way and were waiting to be rearranged.

'Might I . . .' He faced her, laying his hands on her shoulders. She saw a little twitch of the flesh under his right eye. 'May I take the liberty of holding you, my sweetest dear?'

Her heart thudded. She answered with her eyes, while hardly knowing what she was supposed to do, but wanting to find out. A moment later she was in Mr Carson's arms and by instinct she wrapped hers timidly about his long, wiry body, amazed at what was happening. She could feel the beat of his blood, smell on him the odours of the teaching rooms. He drew in a breath and released it, his lips touching her hair.

'Oh, Daisy, Daisy.' Releasing her slightly he looked into her face, his own full of longing. When he kissed her, his lips were warm, buttery, extraordinary. She was not sure if this was exactly enjoyable. The desire, the idea of being wanted by this man, felt somehow separate from these lips, this tongue probing at her. She was full of confusion, but her arms pulled him tighter to her because she felt that was the right response. She loved him, didn't she?

James Carson took this as encouragement and kissed her all the more.

When he released her that night, after they had stood for some time in each other's embrace, he running his hands over her body, she walked home to Chain Street in a daze. Had that really happened ... she and James Carson? But her bruised lips told her it had. Reaching the front door, she straightened her shoulders and smiled secretly to herself.

I am a woman now, she thought. I know now – and no one else knows that I know.

Days later, she realized her mistake – she had not, in fact, known anything at all. After that first afternoon it was as if a bridge had been crossed. There seemed no way to go back to how things had been before, sitting drinking tea by the fire, talking and joking.

As soon as she went into his room the next time, James Carson pulled her into his arms.

'My dear girl – I can't think of anything but you.' His body pressed hard against hers and she could feel a kind of tremor in it.

'Your heart,' she said, pressing her hand over his chest. 'It's beating so fast!'

'I'm crazed with wanting you.' He spoke quietly, into her hair. 'I can't help myself.'

But you've got me, she thought, bewildered. What more did he want? She embraced him more tightly, trying to show that she too was in love, she too felt desire. She felt things, in her body, a longing, a burning – such a mix of her body and soul that she could hardly decide which. But she had no real idea what was to be done with this desire.

'Do you feel the same?' he asked, looking urgently down at her.

She looked into his eyes and solemnly, hoping for the best, like a leap into the unknown, she whispered, 'Yes.'

'Oh, my dearest.' He looked emotional. She almost thought for a second that he was going to weep and she was deeply moved by the effect she had on him. 'Would you . . . does this mean that you would really give yourself to me – lovely young thing that you are?'

Give yourself to me? Was this what she was supposed to do? And how could she answer no now, anyway?

'Yes, James,' she said, overcome by him, by her own emotions and the pull between them, her heart, her body and the force of his wanting.

He took her face between his hands gently and kissed her. 'You are astonishing,' he said. 'I shall worship at the throne.' Seeing her uncertainty, he said humbly, 'You are a sweet young innocent, aren't you, my love? Come, we must be gentle. May I?'

He helped her unfasten her dress. At first, she felt panic. What were they doing? What was happening? Seconds later as he pulled the garment from her shoulders, added to this came a burning embarrassment. She never showed herself to anyone else naked, ever. She wanted to ask him to stop but she felt she could not now. She had said yes, hadn't she? How could she suddenly change her mind after that? He peeled the blue material down slowly, unveiling her so that she could step out of it, and she stood in her corset, her white camisole and petticoat, her wool stockings, feeling foolish and passive, her cheeks hot with blushes. Goose pimples rose on her flesh and she shivered.

'It's all right,' he said soothingly. 'This is how it's done. This is how I worship your body. I know it's strange at first – it takes a little getting used to. But it is of the soul, Daisy my beauty. And I love you, dearest. I shan't hurt you. Come ...'

She felt a little encouraged by this. He took her hand and led her, still in her undergarments, into the second room that until now she had never seen, and to his bed, the bedclothes untidily peeled back and open, as if waiting.

Lying in her own attic bed that night, she felt confused and very alone. What had happened had not taken long. Mr Carson fondled her breasts for a few moments – the best moment of the whole encounter, which had been a revelation of sensation, though still so very mortifying to be suddenly naked in front of a man. After that he had seemed to go into a sort of trance, quickly undressing himself so that now she was subject to the shock of a naked male, with all those dark, shadowy places, and smells and that astonishing thing ... She had only ever seen male private parts in the form of little John when he was a baby and they had looked nothing like that.

And then he had done *that* to her, forcing into her even though it hurt when he had said it wouldn't and she had writhed under him, trying not to cry out, thinking, This can't be normal, can't be ... He kept saying, 'It's all right, it's all right,' until he gasped and made odd sounds, lost in his own world. After his seizure of pleasure, he had been utterly sweet to her, holding and stroking her, whispering adoring words which had, in the end, made it all feel a bit better.

But now she felt dirty and shamed, even though she had managed a quick wash. She had come home feeling soiled, with a terrible, whelk-stall smell about her that she felt everyone must notice. All she had wanted was to run a bath and climb into it. But though Pa and Ma had put in a bathroom on the floor below, they had certain days for baths and today was not hers so she had done the best she could with a basin of water.

She lay curled up small, longing for comfort, for someone to talk to. It was not true that it had not hurt and she wondered, was this love? This thing which left her sore and slimy and desperately embarrassed? Surely this was not what Pa and Margaret . . . ? No, it could not be. If only she could ask someone whether this was really how it was.

Years ago, when Margaret had first had John, Daisy had asked her where babies came from. She had not meant the birthing of them – her own dim memories of her mother and other overheard snippets of conversation had given her some clue that babies came from a woman's body; that giving them life entailed pain and mortal danger. What she really wanted to know was how they got there in the first place. But she had scarcely known what words to use. Margaret had given her a guarded look which said, *I'm going to give you an answer and don't you dare ask any more.*

'Well, dear,' she said. 'A baby is made from the love of a man and a woman. It's all a rather private thing and you'll know more about it when you're older.'

So was that what had happened? Or was there something else, completely different, that you had to do?

She pulled her knees up even tighter, close to tears, feeling the dull burn between her legs. Mr Carson had been so sweet and kind afterwards. He had helped her dress again with all the care in the world. He *was* kind – he was a marvellous man. She loved him – didn't she? But she was still shocked at the thought of his body. Was this something he would expect her to do again? And why did

75

they have to go on keeping everything a secret? Surely soon they should declare themselves and get married if this was love? But even that didn't feel right. It filled her with panic. At last the tears came and she lay quietly sobbing out her confusion, before sleep arrived to relieve her.

Ten

At the end of her class the next Tuesday, Daisy hustled the students out, put her coat on and looked cautiously into the corridor. There was no sign of James Carson and she hurried out along the corridor and into Vittoria Street, still buttoning her coat. She tugged her collar up, hunching her shoulders, and strode along in the late afternoon gloom.

She had not seen him since they had parted at the door of his rooms last Thursday and the thought of meeting him gave her a sick, nervous feeling. Her mind was in a total state of confusion.

'Whatever is the matter with you, wench?' her father had snapped eventually the day before when she seemed to be constantly in another world. No Daisy-Loo these days. She was driving them all mad.

But her mind felt shattered. What she had done with Mr Carson – or rather what he had done *to* her, that animal thing, crude yet with pleasure coiled somewhere in it, most especially the pleasure of being wanted, adored . . . But a terrible chill reality had come to her. Was she now a fallen woman? Was that what it meant? Was this supposed to be love? And now what should she do? These terrifying questions boiled in her mind.

The thought of seeing Mr Carson again filled her with horror. If they could have gone back to how it was before, those times when she had sat with him, his eyes alight with humour and adoration as they drank tea – that was one thing. She had thought of them as innocent but in some instinctive way she had known she was being courted, that there was a flare of attraction in the air between them at all times. But the shock of that man who had stripped naked in front of her, who had laid his forcing body on her, his eyes rolling back as if she were not really there . . .

She knew she could not avoid him for ever. Her next class was only two days away.

'Today we're going to begin something new,' she said.

The class were all seated at their pegs, light from the windows falling on their expectant Thursday faces. She walked up and down as she addressed them, trying to wrench her mind into concentrating on the class. Was he in the next room now, teaching?

'We are going to start on a small cup – for a child, let's say. The main body of the mug will be made of a seamed tube – a neck, we call it. Now with any piece, when we start thinking of the design, what do we first have to bear in mind?'

Several hands went up and she pointed at one. 'The capacity,' the boy said.

'Yes. And what else? Simple, but vital?'

David, the rather slow boy, raised his hand, his face flushing pink.

Today, she knew it would not be possible to avoid him. He was bound to be waiting for her – what would she say?

'Sorry.' She felt a mortifying blush rise in her own cheeks. 'Could you repeat that please, David?'

Now he looked worried. She had not heard a word but he thought it was his fault.

'It's all right,' she reassured him, feeling foolish. 'I'm sure you're right. What did you say?'

'The shape,' he said timidly. 'I mean – it needs to look like what it is, don't it?'

'Yes,' she said. 'That's right – simple, but true. Good.' For goodness' *sake*, she chastised herself, dragging her mind to the task ahead. 'So – we need to cut our blanks and prepare them for soldering – very much as you did for the boxes you made. Make your template out of card first . . .'

Somehow, she made it through the afternoon of drawing and sawing and hammering. The lads packed up, thanking her. As four o'clock drew closer, her nerves took over. The moment she stepped out of the room – as she had somehow known she would – she saw him hurrying towards her.

'Miss Tallis!' he greeted her from a distance. It felt false, as if they were acquaintances and *that* had never happened.

'Mr Carson,' she said coolly, turning to face him. There were lads swarming all around them.

He seemed taken aback. 'All well?' he said lightly.

'Yes, thank you,' she said with a formal nod.

She turned to walk from the building, her skin prickling all over. She knew he would follow, that she would be affronted if he did not, while dreading it at the same time.

'Daisy,' he murmured, the moment they were out in the chilly air. 'Don't be cold with me, my sweet. I can't bear it.'

She looked round to find his eyes fastened on her, full of affection and longing. He smiled and she could not help smiling back.

'That's better – I don't like to see you looking glum,' he said. 'By the way – did you notice that that poor lad, David, has the most enormous crush on you?'

'No!' Daisy said with a little laugh. 'I hadn't. He's a

79

clumsy lad – well-meaning, though. He'll be a good work-man in the end.'

Mr Carson gently took her elbow and steered her to-wards his house. They talked of day-to-day things while underneath there was *that, that* waiting because she knew what he wanted, why he was leading her ... And she, who was so forceful about what she wanted normally, could not seem to refuse him. She felt changed – a Daisy Tallis who she did not recognize, who had lost her will. Soon, they were climbing the stairs into his room.

This time he went through the motions of making tea once again, but as soon as the fire was burning well, he came to her, where she was sitting tensely by the hearth, took her hands and gently pulled her to her feet.

'My, what cold hands! Come to bed, my little angel.' He gazed down at her. 'Let me release your lovely hair again.' His fingers were already working at the pins in her hair. 'Oh, you are so beautiful, I can hardly believe it.' He stroked her cheek. 'All I can think of is kissing you – having you. You make me new again, Daisy – I feel years younger when I'm with you, d'you know that? Come, my dear – give me one of those dazzling smiles of yours.'

His face was so impish that she could not help but smile back at him, while shrinking inside.

'I don't ...' She tried to protest. 'I don't think we should – that I should have ...'

'Shh, my dearest. Come to me – that's right!' Laughing with joy, he pressed himself close against her. 'What is all this shivering? Come, let me warm you. My dearest, sweet one, don't you worry. There's nothing to be concerned about. It's all the most natural thing in the world. You'll see – it takes a little practice. But it is where the body and the realm of the soul clasp hands together, my little love – it is nature, the two of us dancing naked together. It is the

Garden of Eden for we artistic souls. Let us lie together – come.'

How could she refuse? Was it right – that he was introducing her to a realm of art, of the soul? Here was a man who had met William Morris, who was a painter, an artist . . . And was that not what she wanted more than anything, a life of art, of creating?

Once more, some moments later, she was almost naked, and he, already overwrought with desire, fumbling out of his clothes and bearing down on her. And she told herself, even with the smell of him, this alien, forcing body, this was right – she was an adventurer of the soul, an artist. And she held him tight.

Afterwards, she stepped out into the dusk, her collar once more pulled high up round her ears, the feel of him still on her body. It felt as if there must be a sign above her head shouting to everyone what she had been doing. And when, after a few paces along Vittoria Street, a familiar face came towards her among the afternoon crowd, she was so startled that she almost screamed.

'Oh!' Her hand went to her racing heart. 'What are you doing here?'

Den planted himself in front of her. He was dressed in uniform, his hair cut very short. Looking him up and down, at the strong boots and gaiters, the army cap, she felt suddenly awed. Though there were many more men about in uniform these days, it seemed so strange to see Den wearing khaki like that and he seemed older, appeared to stand taller.

'All right, Dais?' he said. 'I was waiting for yer. Where've yer bin?'

'Oh – just . . .' She waved a hand vaguely. 'Had a few things to do. Are you on leave, or what?'

'Yeah. Done basic training, like. I've been to see our mom and the others,' he said.

'How are they?' Daisy had met most members of the Poole family. She suddenly remembered what Annie had said about Mrs Poole expecting a baby, but she didn't think she had better mention that.

'Ar – they're going along all right,' he said gruffly. He seemed stiff, on his dignity and somehow like a much older man, she thought. She remembered he had sometimes been like that as a boy, as if the weight of the world was already pressing down on him. She waited, not sure what to say.

'Will yer write then? They're sending us away – tomorrer.'

'I couldn't write,' she said guiltily. 'I didn't know where to send it.'

'You just send it to the army.' He kept his eyes on her face, reaching into a pocket, then handed her a scrap of paper. 'That's my service number – for the post. I think you need it – with my name, of course, but that should find me.'

'I'll try,' she said guiltily. Den's face lit up as she said it and she was touched. If it meant so much to him she really must remember to do it. Suddenly she realized she was pleased to see him. It was a relief being with someone closer to her own age. And all he wanted from her was a letter or two. As she folded the piece of paper and slipped it into her pocket, she smiled and said, 'Where are you going to?

'Oh – up the cut in a coal boat.' He shrugged, with a wry expression. 'Dunno. More training, I think. You just do as yer ruddy told. Any road – wherever it is, I'll be able to think of you, here, like normal. Making all yer fine things. It'll be nice to think of that.'

82

To her surprise, tears filled her eyes at the sweet sim-
plicity of the way he said it. She was so caught up in
herself all the time that even the lists of dead and wounded
in the papers did not get through to her very often. But
now someone so close was in uniform.

'Oh, Den – good luck,' she said, moved.

'Ta.' If he saw her tears he did not say anything. He
kept his eyes steadily on her, beginning slowly to back
away. 'You keep on being our Daisy Tallis,' he said. As he
turned away he added, 'T'ra for now, Dais.'

'Bye, Den.' She stood in the street as his khaki-clad
back moved away. Little Den Poole from Pope Street.
They'd known each other since Den was nine years old
and she ten. Suddenly she found herself convulsing, and
the tears ran down her cheeks.

Eleven

Margaret looked at Philip across the office table as they heard the front door of twenty-four Chain Street open and close with a bang followed by hurried footsteps along the passage to the staircase.

Margaret frowned. It was a while since Daisy had come thundering into the house like that. In fact, she had been remarkably quiet lately. Miss Allen kept her eyes on her work as if there had been no sound, Edith smiled at Margaret and Philip raised his eyebrows.

'Sounds as if someone's had a bit of a difficult day,' Edith said fondly.

They had all grown used to Daisy slamming into the house either furious or elated while she was a student at the Vittoria Street School.

'They made me draw *portraits*!' Daisy had never seen the point of drawing people – she wanted to design beautiful *things*, not draw people. Why must they make her do all these *pointless* exercises?

Or on other days, 'They sent my bowl to Kensington – and I won first prize!' or, 'Mr Gaskin came into the class today and he spent ages looking at my designs – he said they were *excellent* . . . !'

Mr Gaskin had picked Daisy out as a star pupil from the beginning.

These days, however, she seemed to be even more up and down than usual. It was true things in general were so uncertain with the war on. But Margaret had noticed that Daisy had started coming back late, often did not want her dinner, saying she was not hungry. And precisely because of the war and all the wider concerns on everyone's mind, this kind of moodiness and lack of consideration was especially exasperating to Margaret. She had been brought up to be much more self-controlled. Really, she thought, trying to quell her irritation, Daisy shouldn't be storming about like that – our Lily doesn't behave as badly and she's only seven!

Philip, still in his Holland overall from the workshop, was frowning over something at the desk with Mr Henshaw. Seeing that he was in no position to do anything, Margaret reached inside herself for an extra supply of patience. She loved Daisy like her own, but she really was the limit sometimes.

'I'll go up and see her.' She touched her husband's shoulder lightly as she passed him, and he gave her a distracted smile.

In the passage she could hear sounds from the back room of Mrs Flett, who was giving John and Lily their tea. Margaret paused, brushing bits from the lap of her calf-length skirt. It was of a deep rust colour and the soft sateen material felt somehow comforting against her palm. She could hear Lily chattering to dear old Mrs Flett. Things sounded cheerful enough. She drew in a deep breath and went to face her less than harmonious step-daughter.

Two flights up, she peeped into Daisy's workroom. No one was there, but the bedroom door was shut. She listened, expecting perhaps to hear a storm of tears from inside. But instead, there was an ominous silence. Margaret tapped on the door. There was no reply.

'Daisy, dear?' She found her heart was fluttering nervously. Daisy's was a personality to be reckoned with. 'May I come in?'

She turned the handle and gently pushed the door open, thinking she might find Daisy sprawled dramatically across the eiderdown. Instead, the girl was sitting bolt upright on the edge of the bed, one leg crossed tensely over the other. In the afternoon light through the attic window, she looked arrestingly beautiful. Her head was in profile from where Margaret was standing, a strong, well-proportioned outline, her thick blonde hair fastened softly back from a middle parting and twisted low in her neck into a thick knot. She wore her blue work dress and brown shoes with stylish Cuban heels. But she had her knees primly together, hands clenched in her lap and her pretty, usually animated face wore a tense look of misery. Margaret could see from her red eyes that there had already been tears.

One brief look was enough to send her hurrying to sit on the bed beside Daisy. This was obviously not just a little tantrum about something trivial. Margaret was only ten years older than Daisy and when things were easy and friendly between them, as they often were, it could feel almost as if they were sisters. As Daisy had grown older though, there had been more flare-ups.

Of course, Daisy missed her mother. But she had very much wanted Margaret to marry her father, Philip, when they met after Margaret moved to Birmingham in 1904. In fact, she had almost campaigned for it with the emotional force of a nine-year-old. And Daisy could be a handful, there was no doubt, but today, seeing the girl looking young and so upset, Margaret felt very much in the role of mother, and tender towards her.

'My dear,' she said, resting her arm round her step-daughter's slim shoulders, 'whatever is the matter? Your father and I hate to see you so unhappy.' She imagined friend troubles, or someone outdoing Daisy, who was fiercely competitive in her work.

She half expected Daisy to be angry and throw her off. It was not the first time Margaret had asked if there was something wrong over the past few weeks but she had never seen the girl looking as desperate as she looked this afternoon.

'A trouble shared?' She tried to sound light-hearted, not wanting to make too much of things. And after all, it really couldn't be so bad, could it? 'Why don't you tell me about it, dear? I'm sure it would make you feel much better.'

Daisy hesitated, rubbing her fingers together restlessly. Margaret noticed that all her nails were bitten down to the quicks. For a moment Daisy turned with a direct, hungry gaze, her big eyes searching Margaret's face as if for an answer, but then, with a twist of misery coming over her features again, she looked down into her lap.

'I can't.' It was only a whisper. Then louder, 'Pa will . . .' She stopped, shaking her head, before looking up at Margaret again. Her expression was not hostile, just desperate, and a second later her features crumpled and she burst into tears. 'I can't,' she gasped, bent over, her hands covering her face. Margaret was disturbed to feel the sobs convulsing her body. 'I just *can't*, Ma.'

Margaret softly stroked the girl's back, trying to offer what comfort she could. She could see that for the moment she was not going to find out what was wrong. At the same time, though, something was nudging at her; a worm of misgiving, which had been turning under the surface of her mind, began to push itself fully into view. Surely not . . . ? No. She told herself she was being ridiculous. How could that be possible?

'Look' she said, getting to her feet, 'let me bring you up a cup of tea. Perhaps we could have a talk about it later, umm?' The ache in her heart at the girl's suffering was now accompanied by a stab of dread. What was going on? This was definitely something more than one of Daisy's little moods about being forced to do things in classes that she did not want to do, or some other passing thing.

She went down to fetch her a cup of tea before going back into the office. Philip was still in there with Mr Henshaw and he looked up as she came in.

'I tried.' She shrugged, giving him a smile which said, *We'll talk about it later.*

But as she went back to her office work, checking the payment of the business's invoices, the thought which had begun nagging at her when she saw Daisy's pale, sickly face, took hold. She felt a surge of panic so strong that it felt almost like rage. But she forced the feeling down. It was so unlikely, so unthinkable, that she told herself not to consider such a terrible thing. Daisy would never be so immoral, so stupid . . .

But the thought would not leave her.

As the two women of the house, she and Daisy could not help but share a certain intimate knowledge of each other. Soon after she and Philip married, instead of making do with the tin bath and the lavatory in the yard, they had a proper bathroom installed upstairs at the back of the house. The pads that she and Daisy made for their monthly periods, folding them from strips of muslin, were soaked in a pail, tucked discreetly in the cupboard in the corner of the bathroom. Only now was she beginning to look full in the face the fact that for the past couple of months, she had been the only one to put any cloths in there.

*

Daisy sat holding the teacup while Ma's steps receded down the stairs. Cries of playing children came from the street outside, with the clop of horses' hooves and the rumble of cartwheels, but she was oblivious to all this, locked as she was into the world of her own aching heart.

Putting down the untouched cup of tea on the chair next to her bed, she slipped her shoes off, desperate and sick, to lie curled on her side. She screwed her eyes closed, trying to shut everything out, but she could not get away from the aching dread inside her. Muffling her mouth with the eiderdown, she gave way once more to her tears.

Twelve

Annie Hanson hurried along Pope Street. It was one of the poorer rows of houses fringing the Jewellery Quarter, where the more ornate buildings and variegated brick of the bigger, prosperous factories gave way to rows of shabby, tightly packed brick terraces, many of the front houses backing on to others behind, crammed in around narrow yards.

Annie was a nimble figure in a simple dress the colour of milky coffee, a baggy brown cardigan flung over it. She had coiled her straight brown hair carelessly into a bun and plonked her brown felt hat on the top. Familiar with the street, she did not look about her. She hurried along and turned into an entry leading to the yard of houses behind. Though she did not come here often now, its chill darkness was familiar and by habit she knew to step round the holes in the path, picking her way until she reached the gloomy light at the other end.

The entry opened on to a yard paved with broken blue-bricks, four dingy houses strung along one side with a gas lamp bracketed to one of the middle ones. At the end of the yard, against a blackened wall, were two dry-pan lavatories and a brick wash house.

Annie's heart sank as it always did when she came into the Pope Street yard. Not every yard was as drab and gloomy as this one – why ever didn't Mary Poole move? She tutted to herself. There were surely enough of them earning in the family now for them to go somewhere better? But Mary stubbornly clung to what she knew. Her neighbour, Mrs Blount, was one of the few people she had ever been able to rely on.

And with Mary about to become a mother herself, yet again, this was all the more important. Annie had made a special point of coming, knowing she must be nearing her time.

The door was not fastened but Annie knuckled the rough planks and waited, wiping her fingers against the dark wool of her cardi to shift the sooty grime of the door. A moment later the pale, worried face of a young woman appeared.

'Annie!' Her expression lit up. 'Hello, stranger – come in! Mom, guess who's here? Oh, thank heavens, Annie. Mrs B's gone for Mrs Geech – I dunno know what's keeping 'er. You've come just at the right time.'

Oh, Lord, Annie thought, have I? She could imagine just what Lizzie meant, and even before she crossed the threshold she heard the groan of a labouring woman.

Lizzie Poole stood back, her sweet features lifted by a smile, though Annie could see she was anxious. Though now in her mid-twenties, skinny little Lizzie looked hardly older or bigger than the young girl Annie had worked with at Marshall & Hogg's pen factory, when she first moved to Birmingham and got to know the Poole family and their troubles.

The one living room of this dwelling, half a house which shared, back-to-back, the roof of another house facing into the next-door yard, had not changed much over the years. There had been more than one attempt to shore up the damp, bowed ceiling, the purchase of a new table and chairs and a few extra knick-knacks. A new peg rug covered the bricks next to the range at the side of the one living room. But it was a poor, sagging place like those around it, damp and bug ridden. Annie, brought up to have a social conscience, thought of it like a warren or hive, to keep the workers as close to the factories as possible with the minimum investment and consideration of their health. It always made her angry, seeing what rotten little places they were. Yet yards like these were tucked in out of sight behind streets all around the city.

Mary Poole was standing braced by the table, her head bowed and clearly well on in birthing a child. As the pain swelled, then receded, she let out another low keen of pain.

'I've only just got in myself,' Lizzie said, frantically shovelling coal and slack into the range. Though now in her mid-twenties, she was still living at home, still propping up her mother. 'Found 'er well gone. I've put the water on.' She gestured at the two pots she was heating.

There was no sign of Ivy, who must still have been at work. But six-year-old Ethel, or Etty as she was known, a blonde scrap of a girl, was sitting on a stool right in the corner, quiet and wide-eyed at the sight of her mother.

Annie, who had rather been hoping for a cup of tea and a friendly chat after many days on duty in the hospital, gave a brief sigh and took her cardigan off, trying to find the energy she would need to get to work once again.

'Mary?' She went over to her.

The woman had been in the midst of such intense pain that only now did she notice someone had arrived.

'Oh!' She looked round, mortified that anyone had seen the state she was in. 'Oh, thank the Lord it's you, Annie! I wondered who was here for a moment!' She even raised a welcoming smile. 'I dunno where Mrs Geech's got to.'

'Never mind, we'll manage,' Annie said, though rather

hoping Mrs Geech would come and rescue her. Lizzie always thought Annie could do everything, being a nurse, but she had little experience with birthing mothers.

Annie had seen the Pooles through many times of sadness, but she had never seen Mary birthing a child before. Mary was a scrawny woman with straggly, faded blonde hair that had almost turned to grey now that she was in her forties. As she straightened up, her belly looked like a vast growth against her thin body.

'How are you coming along, Mary?' Annie asked carefully.

'Oh . . .' Mary groaned, sinking on to a chair, leaning back to give room to her swollen body. 'When it started off, I thought, oh, Lor' no, not this. I can't do it all again. But 'ere I am . . . Oh!' Her face tightened and she struggled to her feet. ''Ere we go again.'

Once she had panted her way through another pain, Annie said, 'Don't you think it's about time we got you upstairs, Mary, away from Etty? And Ivy'll be back in soon, too.'

'Mrs B give me some papers for the bed,' Lizzie said, holding out copies of the *Birmingham Gazette*. 'And the water's coming on.'

'You've done well,' Annie said. She smiled wearily, taking Mary's arm to help her to the stairs. 'Make sure there's some string handy – have you got scissors, Lizzie? It was rather quick last time, I seem to remember? Best get her up and comfortable, I think.'

Annie watched Mary Poole's face as she laboured on the bed in the dingy upstairs room. With every seizure of pain her lips contorted in a wide grimace. She had turned over on to her hands and knees, the newspaper rustling under her and getting all in a mess, and Annie kept trying to tidy the bed.

'Here . . . I bet you need this.' Lizzie carried another cup of tea into the room and a slice of bread with a scraping of lard. 'There's a bit of broth . . . ?'

'This'll do me for now, thanks, Lizzie,' Annie said. She smiled gratefully, thinking what an astonishing person Lizzie was, the way she had somehow coped with so many things life had thrown at the family. She sank her teeth into the stale bread. Her head was swimmy with exhaustion. A couple of hours had passed and the light was beginning to die outside. 'Have you got a candle you can bring up?'

Mary Poole gave another low cry of pain and sank forward on to her arms to rest her head, her backside high in the air.

'I can't,' she moaned indistinctly. 'I've no strength.'

'Can you drink a sip or two of tea?' Annie said. 'It's sweet, dear – it'll help.'

Mary pushed herself up with what seemed like a super-human effort and took a couple of mouthfuls of the tea.

'I'll get you another cup, Annie,' Lizzie said, disappearing.

Soon Mary was lost in her world of pain again. Annie was starting to feel uneasy. She had thought this birth would carry through more quickly and that she could say goodbye and hurry round to see Margaret and the family. Should she call someone? she thought. A doctor? But that would mean payment. She could offer to pay, but she knew Mary would be embarrassed and not want it. If only there was a decent midwife. Lizzie had said they would far rather have her here than smelly old Mrs Geech, but at least the woman had more experience than she did.

In the moment's quiet, she heard Ivy and Lizzie

exchanging a few words downstairs and then Lizzie coming back with another cup of tea.

Mary gave a pitiful whimper which turned into a cry of agony. She twisted back up on to her knees again, panting. 'It's coming! Oh . . . Oh, my . . .'

Her waters broke with a gush over the bed and almost instantly the pains overtook Mary with terrible intensity.

'I caa-a-n't . . . !'

Annie jumped into action, trying to wipe her down with one of the squares of rag Lizzie had brought up. It was too late to change the newspapers on the bed. 'All right, Mary – don't fret now.' She tried to keep her voice steady. 'You'll be all right. You know what you're doing.'

Which is more than I do, Annie thought, suddenly panic-stricken. The room was so dark, the air thick with the cloying smells of sweat and discharges from her patient. She wished powerfully for a moment that she had not come, and was sitting in Margaret and Philip's room in Chain Street catching up on news and being spoilt with cake and chatter . . .

'Lizzie . . .' The girl appeared with another cup of tea, but seeing the situation she put it down and rushed to her mother.

'Can you lie on your back now, Mary?' Annie said, close in to the woman's ear. Her body was saturated, her hair hanging down over her face.

'No-o-o,' she moaned, head down.

Annie felt her innards clench even tighter. Surely she wasn't going to deliver in this position? It was like a dog! A blush spread over her.

'It's coming!' Mary cried. 'Get my drawers off . . .'

The two young women fumbled about in the half-darkness, lifting Mary's frock, pulling at her loose bloomers.

95

'Oh!' Lizzie gasped. 'Look!'

Annie could see, too, the dome of a head already bulbing from Mary's body. Relief coursed through her. Very gently she guided the child as Mary's body ejected it, twisting the little one out into the world and down on to the bed as Mary dropped forward again, panting, spent.

'Mary?' she said, as the streaked little child roared into life. 'You've got another little girl.'

'Oh ...' Mary said faintly. 'Another ... I seem to make girls ...'

Annie cut the snake of cord and tied it off, squinting to see what she was doing, and Lizzie held a candle high over her.

'Lizzie?' Ivy's voice floated up the stairs. 'It's 'ere then? What'd she 'ave?'

'Girl,' Lizzie called back.

There was a pause, then Ivy called, 'Mrs Blount come round – said 'er couldn't find Mrs Geech anywhere.'

'Well, no need for 'er now – we've got Annie.' Lizzie was laughing with relief.

'I'll call 'er Ann – after you,' Mary murmured.

Annie smiled. 'How nice.' She looked down at the little one who seemed remarkably vigorous, all things considered. 'Now, little Ann, you go to your sister for a minute, while I see to your mother.'

She massaged Mary's belly while she gave out low sounds of discomfort. It took some time for the afterbirth to come away. The room was so dark, Annie could hardly see a thing. She scooped whatever had emerged into the sodden layers of newspaper and screwed it all into a bundle which she left by the door.

'We'll put that on the fire,' she said softly to Lizzie.

She opened the window wider to let some air into the

fuggy room and covered Mary with the one blanket. The woman lay back, spent.

''Er's sucking my finger, Mom!' Lizzie giggled. ''Er wants you.'

Annie helped prop Mary up a bit and the two girls watched as she introduced the little girl to her breast and she began to suck.

'Well . . .' Mary looked up between damp strands of hair, softer now, almost like a girl. 'I thought I'd like another boy – but now 'er's 'ere – lovely, ain't 'er?'

'I'll go and make more tea,' Lizzie said. She seemed full of energy now, so relieved that it was all over and that someone had come to share the responsibility. 'And bring some water up.'

'You just give her a little feed and then we'll get you properly cleaned up,' Annie said, sitting down beside Mary.

'All right,' she heard Mary say faintly.

Annie realized she must have dozed herself, in the quiet, because later – was it just a few moments, or longer? – she opened her eyes and saw that Mary, with the child still tucked beside her, had fallen deeply asleep. She looked peaceful enough, her haggard face smoother now, free from pain. But there was something about her that caught Annie. And there was a smell in the room, unpleasant, like pennies, metallic and bitter. She felt a sudden eerie prickling at the back of her neck, a feeling of foreboding she could not make sense of.

'Mary?' she said sharply. Her heart began to pound and she leapt to her feet and leaned over the exhausted mother. Mary was breathing. Of course she was. It was all right – she was being ridiculous. And now she could hear Lizzie's feet on the stairs again, bringing tea.

But the feeling would not leave, like an icy premonition spreading through her. As Lizzie came into the room, saying, ''Ere yer go, Annie,' she gently peeled back the blanket. In the flickering light the two of them took in the black stain which was spreading like a tide across the bed. 'Ivy!' Lizzie ran screaming down the stairs. 'Get the doctor – quick!'

In seconds she was back and joined Annie in trying to rouse Mary Poole.

'Mom – wake up!' Lizzie shook her shoulder and Mary gave out a slight, drowsy sound. 'The doctor's coming!'

'Lizzie – get me anything you can to staunch it,' Annie cried. Seldom had she felt such panic. She had fallen asleep and let this happen! How could she? She was full of fear and rage at herself.

Lizzie ran to the room next door and came back with what looked like an old sheet which Annie rolled and pressed between Mary's legs, desperate to stem the life blood which was pulsing from her. She had seen horrific things, the deaths of men far too young in her care, the terrible inheritance of war, their amputations and wounds, the poisoning of their bodies. But that was war and this was giving life and this was Mary who she had known for a decade. Unreality mixed in her with desperation. This could not be! Mary had had so many children. Why now, this sudden draining of life from a mother with five children and no husband . . . ? She felt like weeping, even as they waited and waited for the doctor.

Dear Lord, she prayed desperately, *grant us thy help, breathe the force of thy loving life into her and save her . . . And please, for heaven's sake, let him get a move on – get him here now, please . . .*

Lizzie looked at her across the bed, ghost-faced in the candlelight. 'What can we do?' she said desperately. 'Annie – help her. I don't know what to do.'

*

It was an hour and a half before the doctor came, a small, harried-looking man clumping up the rough stairs. He took one look at the woman on the bed beside her sleeping infant and flicked back the blanket. The sight of the mattress told him all he needed to know. Delicately he pressed his fingertips to her pulse. With a sorrowful tilt of his head, he replaced her hand on the bed.

Thirteen

Daisy could not eat her dinner. The smells of meat and gravy which she usually found delicious were making her sick. She had already got to her feet to slide open the window which gave on to the backyard and the workshop. She was desperate for some fresh air to thin the atmosphere inside.

Normally she loved it when Auntie Annie came to visit. She adored having these older women around after so many years of living just with her father. She enjoyed hearing Annie's stories and the way she made Ma blush at times, the things she came out with. And she would have been chattering away to Annie as well, about the school and her own latest projects. But the queasy feeling which had been plaguing her now for a couple of weeks rose up in her and she could hardly take in what any of them were saying.

Annie had managed to arrive early enough to play with John and Lily, who adored their auntie, and she read them a bedtime story. They kept saying, *Why can't you come more often, Auntie?* They knew Annie's work at the hospital was so busy that it consumed most of her life; and Daisy knew that Margaret, who was a more measured, domestic person, worried about her passionate little sister. But Annie seemed in her element. Usually, over tea she regaled them with sad stories of lads who had come home and died of infections or told her about their girl-friends who had not waited for them – but also the jokes and pranks that went on in the wards. Philip, Margaret and Daisy would sit rapt, listening to her.

But tonight, all Annie could talk about, tearfully, was Mary Poole, what had happened last week when she had meant to come to see them and never made it and how Mary had bled so much that she had sunk into unconsciousness and never come round again. The doctor had said it was not her fault, but she felt terrible, as if she should have been able to do something to stop it. She needed to talk and talk. And they all worried about Lizzie and what the family were going to do.

'Even in these times, this seems worse somehow,' Annie said miserably. 'Nothing to do with the war. Just . . .' She stopped, shaking her head. 'I wish . . . Oh, dear, if only the doctor had got there sooner, or perhaps I should have . . . I don't know.' She shrugged helplessly.

'I'm sure you did all you could.' Margaret tried to reassure her, but they all felt shaken up by what had happened and so sorry for Lizzie and the rest of the children.

'They just all expect me to know everything about anything like that,' Annie said.

'But Lizzie's not blaming you, surely?' Philip asked.

'No. Dear Lizzie – no, she isn't . . .' She frowned, suddenly catching sight of Daisy. 'Are you all right, Daisy dear?'

Daisy, who had been trying desperately to get any of her food down her without bringing it straight back up again, felt even sicker and more desperate on hearing what had happened to Mary Poole.

'Yes, thanks,' was all she managed to mutter. If she said anything else she thought she might either cry or be sick. How horrible this was – it was not like her! She kept her head down, a surge of heat going through her body, the blood singing in her ears. Her stomach began to clench

101

and she knew for sure that she was going to have to run for it.

'I don't feel too good,' she managed to say, before getting out of the room as fast as she could. She pulled the door closed and dashed on tiptoe into the scullery, just reaching a pail to lean over in the nick of time.

Kneeling on the cold tiles, she retched until nothing else would come, then sat up straight, breathing heavily, listening. She had managed to close the kitchen door and no one had followed her, thank heavens. Getting to her feet, she hurriedly rinsed out the pail and took a drink of water, with the unpleasant feeling of sweat turning cold on her forehead and down her back.

Creeping upstairs she readied herself for bed. She did not want Margaret coming up later, asking her more questions. She must pretend to be asleep, to be ill . . . When now the suspicion that she was not ill, that it was that other thing she still hardly dared think about, was taking over her mind.

And tomorrow she would have to get up and struggle through another terrible day, feeling ill, and now, increasingly frightened to death, alone with her terrifying secret. And what happened to Mary Poole might easily happen to her . . .

'Please God!' Up in the attic, safe from listening ears, she let out a desperate moan. 'Help me – please don't let this be true! I know I don't usually pray or anything, but please,' she whispered tearfully, 'if you're there, please help me.'

Lying in the dark, dozing queasily, she heard doors opening and closing below and knew that Annie must be setting off for home. Soon she heard someone coming up the attic stairs. The door opened and light appeared.

Through half-closed eyes she saw Margaret with a candle, coming over to the bed.

'Well, my girl, what's going on?'

There was a steely solemnity to her voice which Daisy knew meant that she was not going to get away with pretending to be asleep. Groggily, she sat up. Margaret stood over her, which was ominous.

'There've been no rags in the bucket.'

The words were brutally direct, like a slap. Daisy looked up at her. The terrible truth crashed over her like a wave. All this time she had felt this dirty secret locked inside her, but even so it had not felt real, not until she heard those words which exposed all her shame. She hugged her knees up close, curled up to press her face against them and burst into convulsions of tears.

'Oh, Lord in heaven.'

She felt Margaret sit on the bed beside her. Raising her head, she saw her stepmother lower the candlestick to the floor and sit staring at her, appalled, in the flickering light.

'So it's true?' Margaret's voice was still controlled, but it was like a trap about to spring.

'I don't know,' Daisy sobbed. 'I just know I feel bad – sick – and I haven't come on, not for . . . I don't know . . .'

There was a silence. Daisy stared at her knees. She sensed that Margaret, virtuous Margaret, was trying to take this in. But she knew there was something in Margaret's voice that she had never heard before from her firm but gentle, godly stepmother. Daisy heard it as anger, as condemnation of her – what else would it be? Only now, the weight of her disgrace reached her with full force.

'You've –' she could hear that it pained Margaret to ask – 'been with someone?'

Still not looking at her, Daisy nodded miserably.

'Did he force you?'

Her tone made Daisy look up again, truly startled. 'Well . . . No. Yes. It was . . .' Forced? Persuaded? She had not felt as if she had a choice. She was so confused. She had allowed something when she scarcely knew what it was . . . But could she say he forced her?

'I couldn't seem to stop him,' she said, feeling small and foolish. 'He was . . . Oh, Ma – you don't know what men can be like!' she cried dramatically.

'Don't I indeed – what makes you think that?' The bitter force with which this came back at her startled Daisy to the core. The memory came to her of those days, years ago, before Margaret and Pa were married. Margaret had disappeared and her father had been deranged with worry. No one had ever explained to her then exactly what had happened but she did know it involved a man called Charles Barber.

'Did he attack you?' Her voice was steely, like someone determined to face the worst.

'No,' she said more quietly. 'Not exactly.'

Margaret looked away for a moment across the room, lost in thought. Her hands were clasped tightly in her lap as if it was the only way she could keep control of her emotions.

'Who is it?'

'I can't tell you.' Daisy's tears flowed again. 'I just can't. Pa would . . .'

'I didn't say tell your pa. I said tell *me*. Is it still happening?'

Miserably, she nodded, feeling awash with shame. It was as if he had taken her over; she was trapped by him and could not get away. At first, even though she did not like what he did, she had loved the way he held her afterwards and talked about art and famous people and made her feel chosen and exalted. And once she had crossed the

104

bridge into letting him do as he pleased, out of her own romantic longings, her adventurous curiosity – there had been no going back.

Margaret seized hold of her upper arm, hard, as if wanting to shake her.

'*Listen*, Daisy. In – what? – seven or so months' time, you are going to have a baby. A *baby*, born out of shame.' She kept her voice low but the force of feeling behind it pierced into Daisy. 'For the love of God, don't you understand what that means? You are going to be mother to a bastard child. And you bring all of that down on *all of us*.'

Margaret got to her feet, pacing back and forth in extreme agitation. For a moment she veered close and Daisy shied away, thinking Margaret was about to slap her. Instead she kept her hands gripped together.

'Your life is going to change for ever and you will be changed for ever in everyone's eyes! You *stupid, stupid* girl – how could you let this happen?'

She sat again suddenly, bent over with her hands covering her face. Daisy was appalled to see Margaret's shoulders shake with emotion. But in her disciplined way, she dragged herself back to self-control and sat up, hands in her lap, though Daisy saw the tears in her eyes.

'I do not believe you are to blame – or not entirely. But your father . . .'

Pa. *What would Pa say?* The thought of her father's face froze her inside. And if he knew who it was?

'And *he* –' Margaret went on – 'whoever he is, will go on with his life carelessly, just the same as he has carelessly used you.' There was a silence and then, with such emphatic rage that Daisy jumped, Margaret burst out with, 'And I am *damned* if I'm going to let that happen without whoever it is knowing and taking some responsibility for himself. I won't tell your father, not yet. There is no need for him to know at this stage.' In a quiet, gritty voice she said, 'Tell me – and I shall help you.'

Daisy gazed back at her with astonishment. She had never seen Margaret so hard or so alight with fury before. But she still could hardly bear to own up to it. He had known the family for so long, even known her own mother, and having to admit it felt dirtier still. For a few moments their eyes burned at each other in the dim light. Until at last, in a whisper, she gave his name.

Fourteen

All night, Margaret lay awake. By seven the next morning she was dressed, her hair coiled hurriedly into a bun, a shawl flung over her blouse and skirt. Going out, she slammed the front door harder than she had intended and, in the pale spring morning, went storming along Chain Street.

It was not many minutes' walk. Even though she had not broken the night's fast, her body was so full of pulsing energy that she could hardly contain it. She realized, as her feet pounded along the cobbles, that she was more explosively angry than she had ever been in her life before. So much so, she felt as if rage had taken over her entire being.

That ridiculous, strutting, puffed-up idiocy of a man! . . . Thinking he can just take and lay hands on her with not a care . . . The thoughts boiled in her mind. It was made even worse by the dim memory that when she herself first set eyes on James Carson, she had for a time found him charismatically attractive.

But this also brought back her memories of Charles Barber, the man who had assaulted her when she was a young woman. The feelings had rushed up like a water spout under pressure. All the more so because Barber had completely disappeared. There had been no consequences for him, no punishment. They realized he must have gone abroad.

Let the Lord punish *that one*, she thought. But upon my soul, I'm going to have a word with this article here . . .

Coming upon the door Daisy had described under her close questioning last night – where does he live? Upstairs? Does he live alone? – she hurried up the scruffy wooden stairs and without pause, slammed and slammed the flat of her hand on the wood of the door.

'All right, all right,' she heard grumpily from within as she kept pounding it. 'I'm not deaf – coming, coming.'

When the door opened she saw that he was only just dressed – still buttoning his shirt, a dark red silk cravat dangling loose about his neck. In the second it took him to register who it was, his expression flickered from irritated to startled and then, in bafflement, resorted to an ingratiating smile.

'Mrs Tallis – how very ni—'

'You viper!' Margaret strode, uninvited, past him into the room. 'You vile, selfish, *disgrace* of a man!'

James Carson reached out and swiped his hand feebly at the door. It failed to close but was no longer wide open for all to hear this altercation. 'Mrs Tallis – whatever is the—?'

'Have you *no thought* for anyone but yourself?' Hands on hips she leaned towards him, blazing her anger at him, and even as she did so, was rather amazed at herself. 'What in heaven's name made you think that you could just toy with, just take and *take* whatever you wanted with no thought, no *conscience*? Well now, Mr Carson, she's carrying *your child* – your *bastard* child. So what do you have to say about that?'

He stood utterly still, hands paused in the act of tying the cravat, face stunned into shock.

'Daisy?' he said huskily. 'Not Daisy?'

'Yes – Daisy! Or is there a whole collection of young

108

women of whom you've taken advantage, who I might have come to discuss?'

James Carson sank down on to a chair.

'It's not like that.' He looked up at her, face fraught with appeal. 'You mustn't think that of me. I am not that sort of man. I love her – I *adore* her.' Agitated, he got to his feet again. I would never do anything to harm her – she's . . . She's brought me to new life. She's an angel – she's utterly astonishing.' He stepped towards her. 'I would never dishonour her. I want to marry her!'

Margaret gaped at him in incredulity.

'You're already a *married man*. You *have a wife* – or had that inconvenient fact slipped your attention?'

'But I didn't . . . I mean, Victoria never . . . What I mean is, I thought it took longer – for a child . . .'

'Oh, for goodness' *sake*!' She almost screamed the words, clenching her fists at this towering stupidity. 'Don't you know *anything*? Daisy is a healthy young woman – and now you've had your way with her she's carrying a child for which you bear responsibility . . .'

She was so caught up in her anger that she hardly heard the footsteps on the stairs. The door swung open and both of them looked round. Margaret was aghast to see her husband standing in the doorway, hatless and in his shirtsleeves. He looked huge, imposing. Margaret, bewildered at seeing him here at all, was also relieved. She had wanted to keep this from Philip, but in reality, how was this to be done? And Daisy was his child, the silly, ridiculous girl!

All three of them stood, paralysed for a moment. James Carson's face took on the look of a trapped animal. Margaret saw in her husband's eyes a granite-hard expression which she had only glimpsed before on the rarest of occasions.

'Did I hear right?' His voice was quiet, but she could hear the terrible force behind it. She hesitated, then gave a faint nod.

She watched as Philip stepped over towards James Carson.

'My Daisy's not been right these last weeks. Is that because of you?'

James Carson clasped his hands together imploringly at his chest. 'I love her, Tallis. She's the pattern of all—'

Philip Tallis drew his arm back and punched James Carson with full force so that he lurched backwards clutching his jaw and fell to the floor, hard up against one of the chairs. Philip stood over him.

'Don't you ever, *ever* come anywhere near my girl again, you filthy, jumped-up little bastard!'

'But . . .' James Carson tried to protest, scrambling to his feet, with blood running down his chin. 'I mean – I want to—'

'Don't get up or I'll hit you again!' Philip roared, readying his fist. 'That's a girl who could knock the spots off you and your arty bloody poncing about a hundred times over – and now you've ruined her!'

He lowered his fist again and strode out of the room.

'Philip—'

Margaret managed to catch up and grab his arm as he tore along the street. He was breathing heavily, his chest heaving. She could see how much rage and distress was locked up in her husband's large frame. She found herself full of astonishing, disturbing feelings. Even amid her concern for Daisy, her anger, seeing Philip so stirred up, so violent, gave her a strange sense of excitement. If only they were alone now, in the privacy of their room, and she could take him in her arms, make love to him, comfort him. She was full of desire for him, and deeply shocked at this turn of events in her own emotions, she found a blush of embarrassment rising in her cheeks.

'How did you know where I'd gone?' she said breathlessly, as they made their way home. She had thought he had been asleep.

'You made enough noise getting out of the house.' A wagon passed laden with milk churns, wheels rumbling along the cobbles, so that she was not sure of the tone of his voice when he added, 'Weren't you going to tell me?'

'Of course, dear. I was just so angry.'

He allowed her to slip her arm through his and they walked back to the house. In the hall, from where they could hear Mrs Flett rattling about in the kitchen, they embraced, silently, pressing each other close.

'I could kill him,' Philip murmured into her ear. She could hear his ragged breathing.

'I know.' She had, in those moments, felt the same. It had been a terrible shock to her. She drew back and looked up at his kindly face, which was now darkened with anger and sadness. 'The main thing is – we've got to think what to do about Daisy.'

He drew in a deep, anguished breath. Then, to her horror, he said grimly, 'And as for her . . .' And before she could stop him he had raced up the stairs.

'Daisy! Wake up!' she heard him raging. 'Sit up and look at me . . .'

As Margaret reached the bedroom, she saw him standing over the bed where Daisy was hauling herself upright.

'You stupid, *wretched* girl!' he roared at her.

Margaret tried to shush him – did he want the whole neighbourhood to hear?

'You've thrown your life away on that fool . . .' Words poured out of him. 'After all you've done – you're

111

brilliant, wench, more than ever your mother was – and look at you now, nothing but a cheap tart . . .'

Daisy, with her hair tousled, face white, looked like a terrified little girl. She pulled her legs up under the covers, hugging them as if trying to protect herself. She looked very unwell and she rested her head on her knees in a despairing way.

'Philip . . .' Margaret tried to stop him, feeling distraught now. This was not her Philip, this angry, blaming man. She could hear the pain he was in, and he did not know what to do except attack Daisy with it. She wondered, with a shudder, whether John and Lily could hear all this on the floor below.

'What've you got to say?' Philip raged, flailing his arms. 'Are you pleased with yourself? Selling yourself like a cheap whore to that . . . that . . . that ridiculous popinjay.'

'I'm sorry, Pa,' Daisy pleaded. Her shoulders shook and the tears ran down her cheeks. She buried her face against her knees. 'I'm so, so sorry . . .'

'You're sorry?' he yelled incredulously. 'It's a bit late to be sorry, isn't it? All that training, all your . . . All those days, thrown away. What d'you think your mother would have said? Eh?'

Daisy's head jerked up and Margaret saw the look on her face, like someone having a spear thrust into their side.

Philip caved in then, suddenly, as if the sight of her was too much for him. He sank down on the bed, leaning forward, and rested his elbows on his thighs, head down.

Margaret stood beside both of them, a hand on each of their shoulders, feeling as if her family was turning to wreckage in front of her and she could do nothing about it.

'Ma . . .' Daisy lifted her head suddenly. 'I'm going to be sick.'

Margaret grabbed the enamel bowl from the side of the bed and Daisy heaved over it, lying back afterwards with a little moan, limp and defeated looking.

Philip sat up, wiping his face, looking stunned. He got up and made a dismissive gesture with his hand. As he strode out of the room, they heard him say, 'For God's sake . . . I can't . . .'

'My life's ruined,' Daisy sobbed, curling up in her bed. 'Now I'll have a baby and no one will ever want to marry me and Pa hates me. I shan't be able to do anything else ever again. And everyone'll be gossiping about me!'

Margaret stood beside her, unable to contradict. What the girl was saying was all too true. The extent of what had happened, the thought of Daisy's disgrace, all the wagging tongues, the looks and condemnation that they would face. And now Philip – how was she to deal with her husband? She ached with sorrow and worry. She hated them falling out in any way.

'He wouldn't leave me alone, Ma,' Daisy sobbed. Though reluctant to hear any more about this, Margaret sat down on the bed. 'He said he loved me – and I thought . . . Well, I didn't know anything. He flattered me, I suppose – and I . . . I didn't know about . . . you know, babies, and . . .' More tears ran down her cheeks. 'I don't want to have a baby – not like this. Not ever!'

'Look.' Margaret suddenly felt incredibly weary, as if all the fight had gone out of her. She laid a hand on Daisy's shoulder for a moment. 'I'll deal with your father. But we're going to have to face up to it now. This is how it is and we've got to think what to do.'

*

Later, once she had got John and Lily out of the house to school and Philip had gone into the workshop, she carried a cup of tea up to Daisy, telling Mrs Flett that the girl was feeling unwell.

'Our Daisy's been looking a bit under the weather this last while,' Mrs Flett said. 'I hope there's nothing wrong.'

'Oh, I don't think so,' Margaret said lightly, while thinking with dread, My goodness, if Mrs Flett has already noticed! And what of the other women, in the office?

Daisy, who had been dozing, sat up groggily. She drank down some of the tea quickly, gestured for the bowl, which Margaret had restored to its place by the bed, and was sick again, wiping her mouth miserably with a hanky as she lay back down. Margaret handed her the glass of water by the bed and moved the bowl with its tan contents outside the door.

'Is it always like this?' Daisy asked despairingly. She had hardly ever had a day's illness apart from this. 'I never knew it was so horrible.'

'I don't know,' Margaret said gently. She had been quite sick herself with her babies. 'Mostly, I think, yes.' She waited, perched on the edge of the bed. 'Daisy, what Pa – what we – didn't tell you earlier, was that I went out, first thing this morning, to see that wretched Mr Carson.'

'Did you?' Daisy's eyes widened. She seemed to be feeling slightly better and sat up hugging her knees again. She appeared comforted that someone had done something to intervene. 'Whatever did he *say*?'

'He didn't get the chance to say much, as it turned out. I was angry and I said a few things – and then your father arrived. I hadn't told him anything, but he heard me leave the house and . . . he must have heard what I was saying.'

'Oh!' Daisy breathed fearfully. 'Whatever did *he* say?'

'Well, he . . .' She tried to recall exactly, and looking

back on the scene, she felt a strange, incongruous feeling growing inside her. 'He called him a few choice things and then he knocked him to the ground.'

Daisy gasped. 'Pa did?'

'Yes – he absolutely thumped him one!'

Their eyes met and the explosive feeling overtook her. She found herself breaking out into hysterical giggles and laughing so uncontrollably that Daisy started laughing as well.

'He fell across the room and into a chair, and . . . he looked so ridiculous . . . and then . . . well, he tried to get up and your pa said . . .' She was overcome by another gale of laughter, releasing some of the dreadful tension of the day. Daisy wiped her eyes, looking both appalled and overcome by mirth at the same time. 'He said, "If you get up I'll just knock you down again" – or something like that. And he called him a – oh, I can't remember, but it was ever so rude . . .'

She couldn't believe herself, reacting like this, and it took both her and Daisy a while to calm down.

'He did say he loved you,' Margaret said, wanting to soften things. 'But he's married – and that's that.' The germ of a thought stirred in her mind. It was possible, on some occasions, for a couple to divorce . . . But she dismissed the idea. Carson was nearly old enough to be her father. It was all wrong, in every way. She looked hard at Daisy. 'Did you think you loved him?'

A bleak look came over Daisy's face. 'I thought I did. But I don't know.' She shrugged. 'Not really.' She was working herself up again. 'Everything he did was for him, not me – I can see that now.' With a despairing look she said, 'And now it's too late!'

'Look, dear,' Margaret said gently. A plan was beginning to form itself in her mind and a sense of conviction.

She knew it was going to cost her dear in strength and determination, the way Philip was today. But she had to hold true.

'Things are not going to be easy for you. When you have a child, your life is never the same again. But . . .' She looked into Daisy's face. 'All those lives being lost over there – all those poor boys. It seems terrible to mourn a new life coming into the world. We'll help you. We will find a way. It's not going to be easy, but somehow we must do what we can for this child in love and truth – not shame.'

Daisy's beautiful eyes fixed hungrily on her.

'How?' she said.

Fifteen

Margaret went by herself to tell Aunt Hatt and Uncle Eb and Georgie and Clara what had happened, just a couple of weeks after they found out about Daisy's condition. She was determined to deal with the situation truthfully, so far as close family were concerned. She chose a Sunday afternoon when most of them would be there, because Georgie and Clara usually took their children round for Sunday dinner.

By the time she got to Handsworth on the tram and was shown into Aunt Hatt's lavish parlour by the maid, Margaret was shaky with nerves. Even though her uncle and aunt – and Georgie and Clara – counted among the kindest people she had ever met, and were fiercely loyal to their own . . . Well, when it came to this sort of thing, people could be so cruel. They judged harshly – and above all they judged the woman. It was an awful feeling, going to their contented household where she had always been so warmly received with news like this.

The house still smelt deliciously of roasted meat and the south-facing parlour was full of the promising light of early summer. When Margaret arrived, Uncle Eb was sitting back in his armchair, resting his eyelids, replete and content after Sunday lunch, his pipe on the table beside him. Aunt Hatt and Clara had been sitting chatting, Clara's auburn head close to Aunt Hatt's fading chestnut, on a small couch, and through the long windows Margaret could see Georgie out on the lawn with the three

117

children and hear their shrieks and laughter as they played. She saw Georgie fling himself down sideways saving a goal as Jimmy groaned.

'Oh, Dad! You always get it!'

'Ooh, Margaret!' Aunt Hatt cried as she was shown in. She struggled to her feet and came to kiss their niece. 'What a lovely surprise! Whatever are you doing here? Didn't you bring the family?'

'I need to talk to you, Aunt,' she said.

''Ello, wench – you all right?' Eb said, waking muzzily and wiping a hand over his mouth.

'She needs to talk to us, Eb,' Aunt Hatt said, as if this was something anyone should know by now.

'Oh ar, right.' Obediently he pushed himself more upright in the chair and seized hold of his pipe as if for reassurance against anything the female sex might be about to launch at him.

'You all right, Margaret?' Clara said, coming and kissing her. 'You look a bit pale.'

'Look – I'd better say this quickly, while the children are outside,' Margaret warned them as everyone found a chair again. Her heart was pounding. If she didn't say it now, she thought she might never begin. It would be so much more restful to pretend none of this was happening and just sink into a comfortable afternoon with the Wattses.

'We've . . .' Her face was ablaze with blushes suddenly and she looked down at the fluffy Chinese rug, clasping her trembling hands. She felt close to tears.

'Oh, love – what is it?' Aunt Hatt said. They were all looking at her in consternation.

'A trouble shared,' Clara said, in her rather important way. Since having her own three children, Clara, an ener-

118

getic, freckled redhead, had become rather fond of pronouncing on things.

Forcing herself to look them all in the face, one by one, Margaret said, 'I've got to tell you. I don't want to keep it from you all because no good will come of it in the end . . . It's Daisy. She's . . .' It was a physical effort to get the words to leave her tongue. 'She's expecting a child.'

There was a second's bemused silence.

'A child?' Uncle Eb said. 'You mean . . . ?'

'You mean, she's . . . ?' Clara held her hands in a curve close to her belly, then looked at Aunt Hatt in an ominous sort of way.

Cheeks aflame, Margaret nodded. The tears were so close to the surface that her throat was tight and aching. It felt as if Daisy's shame was her own, as if she had not mothered her or protected her properly.

'Not *Daisy*, surely?' Aunt Hatt said, as if Margaret might somehow have mistaken her own stepdaughter for someone else's.

But seeing the sad confirmation in Margaret's eyes, Aunt Hatt said, 'Oh, my dear . . .' She was hurrying to Margaret's side to comfort her when Clara's voice cut in and Aunt Hatt hesitated.

'Well, how did that happen?'

Margaret was chilled by the hard accusation in Clara's voice.

'Who's the . . .' Uncle Eb bit back more extreme words. 'Who's got her into that mess then?'

Margaret explained, briefly, not shielding James Carson. Why should she, she thought? And she explained that she was planning to take Daisy back to the village near the end of the confinement, that until anything was showing she could continue to work at Vittoria Street and then they would have to see.

'Oh, poor Daisy!' Aunt Hatt cried passionately. Then she added, 'But how *could* she – with *him*?'

'Oh, he spun her a yarn about how he loved her and her artistic soul ...' Margaret could hear her own bitter sarcasm. 'I think she thought he might even marry her.' Even though Aunt Hatt seemed sympathetic, she was uneasily aware of Clara sitting bolt upright, a tight, disapproving look on her face.

'Well, I'd say she's only got herself to blame,' Clara said. 'Silly little girl – she should have had more sense – and more dignity.'

'But Clara—' Uncle Eb protested from his chair.

'No—' Clara held up a hand. 'There's no defending that sort of loose behaviour. I'll say this quickly before my children come back in because I don't want anyone breathing a word about it in front of them. I don't hold with this sort of thing. She may be one of those artistic types – we all know Daisy's very clever, since we've heard so much about it ...'

Margaret was deeply shocked. She knew Clara was a bit of a bossy boots, but she had not seen her as spiteful or envious before.

'All I can say is, I don't want any of this sort of thing going on around my children.'

'Clara!' Aunt Hatt was clearly shocked, but there was doubt in her voice as well. Margaret could see she desperately did not want to fall out with her only son's wife. Margaret felt anguished that she had come and caused all this, though she was repelled by Clara's hard-faced attitude. But now it looked as if she was turning Aunt Hatt against them all as well.

'You can do what you like,' Clara said with a prim tilt to her head. 'Obviously this is your house. But I just don't want this sort of thing coming near to my family.'

'Well, I don't know,' Uncle Eb said, looking bewildered by the whole situation. 'That doesn't seem very Christian to me.'

'Christian!' Clara snorted. 'What's Christian about bringing a bastard baby into the world? That's what I'd like to know. I'm surprised you haven't turned her from your door, Margaret, that I am.'

'Now you look here,' Aunt Hatt said, standing upright again, hands on her hips. And this was the moment Margaret knew she should never have doubted her. 'If the same ever happened to your Ella or Gina—'

'Don't be ridiculous!' Clara snapped. 'My daughters will never behave in such a way.'

'Well, if they ever was to get into trouble – any trouble,' Aunt Hatt said. 'You turn them out on the street if that's your way of being Christian, Clara – though I've not noticed you darkening the doors of a church any more often than the rest of us. You do as you feel right – but you tell them they can always come to their grandma. I'll never turn our girls away no matter what they've done. They're our little jewels.'

Margaret put her hands over her face, unable to hold back her tears as Aunt Hatt went on.

'That silly little wench is going to have enough judgement and tittle-tattle going on about her for a lifetime. We're family and we'll stick together. I don't want us to fall out, Clara, but Margaret's my niece and like a daughter to me. She's come to us with her troubles more than once and we won't be turning her away any more than we did the first time. So, Clara – if you don't like it, you can make your own judgements, but so far as I'm concerned, I'm afraid that's just going to be how it is.'

'Well said, wench.' Uncle Eb stood up and placed himself beside his wife. 'I'm sorry, Clara.' He eyed his daughter-in-law, who sat tight-lipped, but was beginning to look a bit uncertain in the face of this family unity. 'But Daisy's one of the family now. We don't want to see our family broken up so you'll have to decide about that for yourself.' He turned to Margaret.

'It's all right, wench. This is a terrible thing that's happened, but you tell our Daisy we're with her, thick or thin – and bring her over to see us next week, eh? The sooner we all get together on this the better.'

'Thank you, Uncle. Thank you both.' She did not look at Clara.

There was a burst of noise as the children came running in from the garden.

'Is it tea time yet, Nanna?' Jimmy the ever-hungry asked.

Georgie followed them in, closing the garden doors. He turned and smiled round the room, before noticing the state of everyone.

'What's going on?' he said, in bewilderment.

'Do I have to go?' Daisy raged next Sunday.

Margaret had returned from the morning service at Carrs Lane church and Daisy came resentfully down for dinner. Her whole being was in rebellion. All she wanted was to turn the clock back – but since she couldn't do that, she'd rather pretend none of it was happening. It was impossible to forget, though, because she felt so rotten and she could scarcely stand the sight of her own sickly face in the mirror. Not to mention the way Pa was ignoring her.

Her life was not her own and never would be again and she might as well be dead!

However kind the Watts family might be, the worst of it was her horrifying embarrassment and shame that everyone knew exactly what had happened – that she had done *that* with Mr Carson.

'I wish you'd stop ordering me around!' she shrieked. 'I don't *want* to see anybody. They'll all be staring at me and telling what to do and I just want to *stay here* and never see anyone!'

And then Pa lost his temper. He looked up from carving the Sunday joint, wielding the carving fork in her direction.

'Don't you talk to Margaret like that!' he boomed across the table. 'You, girl, are in no position to complain about anything, bringing all this down on us – and wasting all your chances! You're damn lucky we're not putting you out on the pavement to fend for yourself!'

'Well, if that's what you want to do,' Daisy yelled back across a rib of roasted beef, 'why don't you just get it over with and do it? I'll go, if you want – and take my disgrace with me, so it doesn't mess up your perfect little household and your perfect little family. It's not as if you need me, is it?'

John and Lily were sitting, eyes popping, listening to this. Margaret stood up.

'Not a word more,' she said, with such forbidding force in the direction of her husband and Daisy that the two subsided. 'Don't either of you dare say *another word.*'

'Mom?' Lily said, close to tears. 'Why's Pa shouting? What's Daisy done?'

'I will tell you,' Margaret said. 'But not just now, Lily. For the moment, what we are going to do is eat our Sunday dinner, which the good Lord has provided for us, and then we are going to see Uncle Eb and Aunt Hatt.'

'And Jimmy!' John said happily.

'And Ellie and Gina!' Lily also recovered instantly, as

her father carved the meat with his head down and Daisy remained silent, trying to stem her own tears at having made her Pa so hurt and angry. But oh, Lord, she really didn't want to go and face the Watts household.

'Here you are, young lady,' Uncle Eb greeted her sorrow-fully but sweetly, when she arrived. He seemed almost bashful and it dawned on her that suddenly, in their eyes, she had become someone different. Though she had been humiliated, was in this grossly shameful state, she had also, in a strange, sweet way, truly become a grown woman. It was a strange feeling.

Eb was such a portly, rotund figure now with his giant, grizzled moustache and whiskers that he always made her think of a rather sage walrus – like the pictures that went with the 'Walrus and the Carpenter' poem. He had always been warm and welcoming and that afternoon he was bashfully tender towards her, treating her with such great delicacy – 'Come and sit here, my dear, it's the softest chair' – and repeatedly offering her cake – 'Come on, wench, you need to eat' – when she was in fact feeling sick, that she was quite overwhelmed.

And Aunt Hatt embraced her and was concerned and motherly. Georgie, though not referring to anything, just said, 'Hello, Dais – you all right?' and gave his shy smile. All she could see in his brown eyes was kindness. He mentioned that Clara had stayed at home and was not feeling quite well.

'You poor, poor girl,' Aunt Hatt said passionately, pulling Daisy into her arms. 'What a terrible man ... *Wicked*, that's what I call it. He should be hanged!'

Georgie made a mild protest about how this might be taking things a bit far.

'Well, it's all very well!' Aunt Hatt rounded on him. 'You say that. *You men* – I ask you!'

'We're not all the same, if you don't mind,' Georgie said.

'He'll just go blithely on,' Aunt Hatt continued heatedly, releasing Daisy. 'None of it makes the slightest difference to him. *His* life won't be affected! Now Daisy, if there's ever anything you need or you want to know, you can always come to me – and I won't breathe a word to anyone . . .' Her dark-eyed, kindly face looked closely into Daisy's. 'You just remember, that child is every bit as much yours as it's his. I know it's going to be hard, Daisy dear – but don't bring a loveless child into this world.'

Daisy was so overcome by all this that she burst into tears. She had no idea at this point what she might want to know – all she knew was that she felt horrible and wished she could wake up one morning and find out that this whole mortifying experience had just been a nightmare.

Even then she could see she was lucky beyond words to have loving support when she had brought such trouble to their door. But it didn't stop her loathing herself and everything about the way her life was turning out.

For the first week, once everyone knew, all had been in turmoil. Daisy did not go back to Vittoria Street. She could not face running into James Carson and in any case, she felt too ill. She lay down a lot of the time, being sick and weeping in frustration and grief for her own lost life.

Above all, her father's words kept ringing in her head. Out of all that had been said this had cut the most deeply into her. *What would your mother have said?*

Daisy did not know for sure what the mother who she could just about remember, that stately, loving, auburn-haired woman, would have said. But she knew she had let her down. She wanted so much to be like her mother – to be *more* than her: successful, a brilliant silversmith and artist. And now she was never going to be anything. She had thrown her life away.

Soon after all the upset, Margaret told her that James Carson had called at the house once, begging to see her, and that she had sent him packing.

But within two days he was back.

Sixteen

'There's a man asking for you, Daisy.'

It was Miss Allen who had gone to answer and she sounded disapproving. But then Miss Allen, thin faced, in her stiff, dark clothing, usually did. Daisy could hardly refuse to go to the door.

She kept her head down, trying to hide the dreadful blushes coursing through her. She had known she would have to talk to him some time. They lived so close together – and there was her work at the school. She felt she might as well face it now, at least on her own territory. She was not obliged to invite him in.

But it was hard even to look at him. He was standing outside, holding his hat with both hands. At first sight she thought he looked diminished, not quite the man she remembered. Was it just that she had fallen out of love with him? But no, it was more than that. His hair was hanging lank, his beard straggly and unkempt. He looked as if he had not slept for a long time.

'Daisy,' he said quietly, but with a desperate lilt to his voice. 'Oh, Daisy, my dear, *please* let me talk to you.'

She hadn't meant this to happen, to have anything to do with him, but she felt a pang of longing, of the need to talk to him as well. She glanced back into the house. 'We can't go in there. Let me get my coat.'

They walked stiffly side by side. She could tell that James Carson was working himself up to speak, but it was difficult out in the street. They remained more or less

127

silent until they reached St Paul's churchyard. She waited as they passed back and forth along the paths round the front of the church. She did not feel obliged to begin the conversation but her emotions swelled, tears rising to the surface. She wanted to hold back her tender feelings and curse him: at the same time, she longed to let go and weep, to have him hold her in his arms and tell her he would look after her, that everything would be all right.

'Daisy,' he said at last. 'I'm so sorry – my dear girl, are you . . . I mean, are you going along well?'

'No!' she burst out, then tried to lower her voice. 'Of course not! How can I be? I spend every morning being sick and I can't go to the school because you are there. What do you think? You've ruined my life.' Her voice broke and the tears flooded out. 'I'm so unhappy . . .'

Mr Carson made helpless gestures with his hands, as if wanting to reach and hold her, but sensing that she would fight him off.

'I am in *anguish*,' he said.

Hope lit in her. It was not nothing to him – he was upset, he was involved in what had happened to her!

'You've no idea – I've hardly slept. It's all so unbearable.' He gestured wildly with his right hand, working himself up. 'I – I was so carried away with you. With your beauty – with *you*, Daisy. I *do* love you – I wasn't lying, my dear, I promise you. But I was deluding myself, I can see. Your, er, Mrs Tallis put me right about that. I have a wife – loveless a situation as that might be. I never dreamt – never intended all this to happen.' He made a gesture seemingly to sum up their whole situation.

'Well, it has,' she said brutally.

Mr Carson looked at her like a dog caught in the middle of a whipping.

'I have been in *agony*,' he said. 'And I wanted you to know that I have come to a decision.' He pulled his shoulders back with a heroic air.

Daisy waited, her heart starting to hammer. He was going to stand by her. He could separate legally from his wife – was that not possible? And then he could marry her and save her from this agonizing shame and loneliness. It was not too late . . .

He took a deep breath, as if to address a room full of avid listeners.

'I am in your way here – at the school, in this place. And it is a torment to me to be near you, and yet – forbidden. I am going to leave. I have decided to join His Majesty's army and do my bit for the country. Others are going and as a man, I must do my part – I must sacrifice myself, d'you see?' He was in deadly earnest. 'So – I shall no longer be in your way at the school, my dear. I shall be gone.'

Daisy stopped dead and stared at him in a turmoil of feeling. It had never crossed her mind that he might just disappear, not like this. He could just walk away, as if none of this had happened, just as Margaret had said! It was enraging – and yet, there would be such relief in having him gone. Even, just a little, she was moved by his declaration. 'You're really going to do that?

He gave a little bow, pressing his hat to his chest. 'I am.'

'But –' she swallowed – 'what about me? What about the baby?'

His face twitched, then he gave her a sweet, pitying look.

'Oh, Daisy,' he said. 'I do wonder if you are being strictly truthful with me. Is there really a baby? Or even if there is, can I be sure it's mine? Or is it just a way of entrapping me, trying to force my hand?' He gave a little laugh. 'In any case, even if there really was, you know perfectly well you don't need to be saddled with it, my dear. There's plenty of people who desperately want a child. You shouldn't waste that talent of yours in all that ...' He made a gesture with his wrist, a gesture so dismissive of all to do with womanliness, with children. To her amazement, she had to stop herself leaping towards him and scratching his face. All of it – all the experience of women, the pain, the mothering – it was a trifle to him. It was as nothing.

But the shock of this was like a blow. She was so full of hurt and rage that for a few seconds she could not move. There she had been, thinking him capable of being considerate, perhaps even close to heroic. And here she was, unable to do any of the things she most loved, with her pa hardly able to look at her, here in her shame and with this child to bring forth. And he – once again he was caught up in a drama of his own making, of which he was always the central hero. No one else counted.

Standing facing St Paul's church, her heart freezing over, she backed away from him.

'You are not a man,' she said. 'You're a ... a disgusting, selfish fool. You're a clown!'

And as he stood with an ingratiating look on his face, she turned and walked away. As she strode along, Aunt Hatt's words came back to her, giving her a glimmer of determination: *You just remember, that child is every bit as much yours as it's his ... Don't bring a loveless child into this world.*

The street suddenly came into her view – the carts and horses and crowds of passers-by – and for the first time a startling instinct caused her to lay her hand over her still flat belly as she made her way home, to shield whatever was inside from all harm.

She did not think he would keep his word about leaving – about anything. But within two days he was gone.

Seventeen

December 1915

Margaret stood on the platform at Snow Hill station, glad to be in the shelter of the waiting crowds, several lines deep all along. It was a bitter day, the sky hanging low over the chimney tops outside and a wind that cut right to the skin.

On one side of her were an excited John and Lily in their best hats and coats, Lily holding her favourite doll clasped to her as if worried she might get swept away in the rush. On the other side was Daisy, bundled up in layers of clothes. Her pale, swollen face was half hidden in the shadow of a wide-brimmed brown hat which matched her chocolate-brown coat, cut wide and flowing to hide her condition. Over it were draped a shawl and scarfs. The platform was so crowded that there was no room to get much of a look at anyone anyway.

Servicemen with canvas bags slung over their shoulders jostled among all the civilians; trains came and went, their whistles shrieking, trailing banners of smoke and steam; voices called to each other and the air was full of acrid cigarette smoke mixed with the smuts from the trains. A poster on the wall nearby showed a uniformed man holding a rifle: 'Join the Volunteers and Be Ready'. Here, never for a moment could you forget the war.

But for Margaret, that war had been a distant thing

compared with the one going on in her own house for the past months. She felt exhausted, wrung out with emotion and glad finally to be on her way, away from here.

Their train pulled in with a trail of steam and smoke, brakes squealing.

'Can we get on?' John was alight with a ten-year-old boy's passion for locomotives.

'Wait, dear.' Margaret barred him with her arm. 'We have to let the other passengers out first.'

They emerged lumpily, children and bags lifted down the steps, only adding to the chaos on the platform. Margaret noticed, tenderly, that Daisy laid a hand protectively round her belly in the crush. There had scarcely been a moment of the last months when she had not worried about Philip's daughter, despite all the pain and shame brought to their door by the situation.

'Come on now, dears. John – you've got your and Lily's cases, haven't you?' She picked up the bag she was sharing with Daisy in one hand and with the other, steered the girl by the elbow. 'John, Lily – keep behind me. That's it, hold tight to Lucy-Jane, Lily. Let's get into this one.'

Daisy quietly obeyed. They managed to get seats by the window, and John sat beside his mother, Lily next to Daisy.

'I hope there won't be too much smoking in here,' Daisy whispered, leaning across as Margaret sat down. 'It makes me feel sick.' She had not had an easy time with sickness and only now, towards the end of the pregnancy, had she stopped looking gaunt and strained.

Though quite neatly pregnant, in this last month she had swelled uncomfortably, her face and ankles thickening, making her feel heavy and exhausted. Margaret, though often enraged by the situation, felt terrible seeing the effect it had all had on a talented girl who had once been so confident. Now, apart from some flare-ups of anger over the weeks in the face of Philip's stubborn anger, she was like a poorly little shadow. All of this was breaking Philip's heart. Margaret could feel the weight of it on him in the set of his shoulders, as if a great burden rested there.

'I wish I'd flaming killed him,' he said to her once, early on. It was Daisy he could not come to terms with; he could barely look at her, as if the very sight of her was an agony for him. And the agony had also become Margaret's.

The carriage filled with civilians, people fussing with their belongings until they settled down.

Margaret looked across at Daisy. She had removed her scarf and rested her head back, her hat tilted further over her face. Lily looked round hopefully at her big sister, but seeing that Daisy was already falling into a doze, she turned her attention back to her squiffy-faced rag doll. Margaret smiled approvingly at her. John settled with the *Funny Wonder* comic she had bought him, grinning to himself.

Margaret felt herself relax just a fraction. With all the emotion and carry-on in the house over the last few months, it was a relief to leave – even though it now meant facing her own father.

Philip had been sealed like a stone tomb. He would not discuss the matter with Margaret, however hard she tried. He worked long hours and tried to avoid Daisy at all costs. Margaret, caught between them, trying to keep things as normal as she could for her younger children and hide Daisy's secret for as long as possible, had felt overwrought, pulled in all directions. It was taking a toll on how things were between herself and Philip. The easy talking had become strained. They made love far less often, a relief only in that she did not wish to bring forth more children, but in every other way, a loss of their closeness. He was angry, locked into his rage with James Carson and with Daisy.

We can't stay here, Margaret thought. She felt distraught all the time, was bowed down under the strain of it all. She'll manage to hide it for a good while, but at the end, I must get her away from here. And I'll find someone who'll take the baby – there are good people in the village, people who will be kind . . . And when we return, all can be as normal . . .

'Dear Father,' she had written, back in June, when they were all trying to adjust to the situation, 'I am writing to you about a delicate matter. I hope I can appeal to both your sense of charity and your human kindness, when I relate the events that have led me to turn to you . . .'

She had not minced her words. Her father, William Hanson, was still in his post as a Congregationalist minister in the village several miles north-east of Bristol where Margaret and Annie had spent their childhood. In a few, direct words she told him of Daisy's situation, that it was causing great tension and explaining that for the last month or so of her confinement and for the birth, they would all benefit from some privacy and for her to be away from home.

Margaret knew that her father owed her a debt of compassion and apology after doubting her, taking the side of his protégé in the church, Charles Barber, against that of his own wronged daughter. It was this rift that had sent Margaret and Annie to Birmingham in the first place, escaping from home to twenty-six Chain Street to stay with Uncle Eb and Aunt Hatt, who had been kindness itself in taking them in. Only much later, faced by more of Charles Barber's depravity, had her father apologized.

As she wrote the letter, she was filled with swirling cross-currents of feeling. In part she was sorry for the shame she was asking to bring to her father's door. Yet mixed with that was anger: 'This is real life, Father,' she thought, 'for women in this world, a life of men and pain and blood and milk and . . . It's how it is! This is the test of the pure, religious fortification in which you would prefer to hide yourself. And faced by this calamity, this slice of what Annie calls "the lot of women" – are you going to refuse us?' What she actually wrote was more measured and polite, but she did not leave him much room for refusal.

His reply was stiff, formal – but he had agreed. He had even promised to make discreet enquiries in the village. They were to let him know when they were planning to arrive. He would see to it that they were made comfortable. She could imagine his own discomfort at this. He had a new housekeeper, Miss Berry, a spinster in her late thirties. Whatever was she going to make of it all?

Margaret sat back in her seat, letting out a long emotional breath. The past months had been very hard. One moment Daisy would be full of rage and helplessness in the face of what had happened to her, making the household a far more fraught place than her moods had ever made it before. The next she was sick and upset, or sweet and confiding. And though she tested Margaret's tolerance to the very limits, they had had some very tender times together and she felt desperately sorry for the girl and for what had happened. After all – it could so easily have happened to her, had things gone just a little differently.

Her husband was the only one who had truly angered her. It was with Philip where the true healing was needed. Last night, he had sat on the side of the bed for a long time, facing away from her as she lay there. As ever she was caught between rage and tenderness. *It's your daughter – find it in yourself to climb down and look after her* . . . And yet she was aware of all his pain, and longing to reach out and touch him, to hold him and be held. To make love, to be how they had always been . . . At last she could bear it no longer.

'Philip,' she said softly.

He must have heard her tone, the way she was appealing to him to turn to her, to come back to her, hold her, before they were parted for most of the next month. But he sat on, in silence. Margaret felt herself recoil inside, deeply hurt.

Eventually Philip had stood up and got into bed with a long sigh.

'You'll be wanting to get going early tomorrow, I suppose,' he said. He gave her a stiff kiss and turned away on to his side. And this morning, there had been another peck on the cheek, when they all said goodbye, though he had at least shown Daisy more emotion.

As she sat now in the railway carriage, Margaret's eyes filled with tears. She looked across at Daisy, who already seemed to be asleep. How peaceful it would be to have a nap herself. In these quiet moments, while her younger children were occupied and amid the murmured conversation of the other passengers, Margaret leaned back and let her lids slide over her eyes.

Daisy sat with her eyes closed. She felt exhausted but wound tight with emotion. She could still feel her father's arms holding her close when they had said goodbye. It was the first time he had shown her true affection in all these months and her throat ached, thinking of it. It must

137

have come home to him that they were really leaving, that they were all to be parted.

'I'll be down to see you all very soon,' he said. She felt his beard against her hair as he held her, then he drew back to look at her. 'There's my girl.' His face had been full of emotion. He squeezed her shoulders. Suddenly, looking into her eyes, he said, 'Never mind – you'll be back soon, and . . .' He couldn't finish the sentence. She would return. Everything could be put back to how it had always been? Was that what he meant? And then, forcing himself, he said, 'Everything I've done has been for you, Daisy-Loo.'

When she started to cry, held by him as if by a big bear, he made soothing noises. 'It's all right . . .' His own eyes wet, he looked into hers and said, 'It'll be all right, wench.'

But he had looked frightened and it was only then that she really realized how afraid he was. He was angry and ashamed – but most of all he was afraid. He had lost her mother in childbirth and now he was afraid he would lose her too.

Tears stole out of her closed eyes now as she thought about it and she quickly wiped her face. How much trouble and strain her stupidity over James Carson had brought to them all. She had got carried away with his adoration, had let herself be sullied, used . . . These thoughts turned in her mind. But she felt so small and helpless with it all and deeply ashamed, as if she had lost sight of the person she had been before with all her ambitions. She was always so tired that it was months since she had sat happily at her peg in the attic, dreaming and working beautiful things into being.

These months had been full of emotion. As well as her grief and anger, she had been humbled by an even deeper respect for her stepmother. Many another would have seen her put out on the street. But no.

Margaret was adamant about one thing.

'No lies,' she said, right from the beginning. They were all sitting round the table only a day or two after she had been to see Aunt Hatt and Uncle Eb. Margaret actually banged her fist on the table, so hard that Daisy jumped. 'There are things people don't need to know unnecessarily – but I won't live with endless lies. And I *won't* have it that a man has his carnal way and everyone else pays with shame!'

This was such an outburst and so candid in character that they all sat stunned. Daisy saw her father look away for a moment with a pained expression. She at least understood that this was as much to do with events in her stepmother's past as it was with her.

'This is a *child*, not a dirty secret.' Margaret was leaning into the table to make her point. 'And how will it be in the end if we all lie? There'll be nothing but trouble.'

'I suppose we could . . .' her father began hesitantly. He never looked at her, not through all the conversation, as if she wasn't there. 'I mean, someone else might . . . She doesn't have to bring it up . . .' He trailed off into silence.

'We'll have to decide that when the time comes.' Margaret sat up tall, magnificent, as if to say, *There will be a decision, but you needn't think you are the one to make it.*

Daisy grew more bewildered. It was as if they were talking in riddles she could barely understand. This was something she had no experience of at all. It was not as if people talked about it.

'No one in the business needs to know, not yet,' Margaret went on. 'Although I don't think we can keep Mrs

139

Flett in the dark. And as for the family – well, they'll have to know. But I'm sure they'll keep it to themselves.'

'But,' Pa protested. 'They'll talk – you know what people can be like . . .'

'Well, *damn* them!'

Daisy had never seen Margaret like this before – so flushed and worked up, so profane! In fact, she had never seen or heard anything like it anywhere.

In the early days she had soldiered on at the Jewellery School, once Mr Carson had gone. Until Vittoria Street broke up for the summer, things were much as usual. The sickness abated and she continued work, though she felt constantly exhausted. Over the summer she worked in the Tallis business and designed a new MIZPAH brooch, which went into production in the firm.

By the time the Jewellery School went back to work in September, she was six months pregnant.

'You're so slim that you seem to hide it well,' Margaret told her. 'You really are not showing much.' She had still not let anyone on the staff in on the secret, not even Mrs Flett – yet. Sufficient unto the day is the evil thereof was Margaret's way of looking at it. They would deal with all that when it became necessary.

Daisy had gone on with her work at Vittoria Street. Even after the summer break, she was not so big that she could not easily disguise her condition. It was only in this, the final month, that she had suddenly grown obviously large. She had led the school to believe that she was suffering an illness that would take her away for the remainder of the term.

It was a relief to stop teaching. She had found standing all that time utterly fatiguing. But at least it had been her normal routine. Now she was heading off to this strange place in the country which she had only visited a couple of times before. And at the end of the road there was just one terrifying certainty – of having to give birth to this child.

Eighteen

23 December 1915

Once again, the sky was a cauldron of boiling grey, the rain pouring down. The black branches whipped in the wind and the river rose and rose. There would be a few days of calm mugginess before the winds returned and the rain came bucketing down once again. It gave all of them an increased sense of calamity.

By the time Philip was due to arrive for Christmas, Margaret was so pent up with nerves at living with her father, William Hanson, and Daisy, and with John and Lily cooped up inside because of the wet weather, she felt ready to explode. It felt as though they were all living in a bubble, the walls of which were growing tighter and tighter. It was a struggle to remain calm and self-controlled.

As well as all the other emotional tensions, being in the village had brought her awareness of the war much closer. Her father followed the news very closely, his tall, hawk-like figure bent over the newspaper each afternoon, peering through his spectacles. The evacuation of Gallipoli, which had just been accomplished, felt to him like a personal defeat.

And in the village, two brothers from one family, the Pearsons, who Margaret and Annie had known as children, had both been killed at the Battle of Loos. Their

142

sorrow, their crêpe-draped windows, hung like a pall over the whole village. It made life seem so brief and frail. Even though, before she left home, there had been some degree of making up with Philip after all the tensions and sorrow of that year, all she could feel now was a longing for him to be there, for them not to waste another moment of precious life apart and at loggerheads.

They had been separated now for nearly three weeks and she was waiting, following him in her mind every second of the time from when the bus was due to leave Bristol on its way to the village. As the hour of its arrival approached, she could no longer contain herself. She put on her hat and coat and hurried up to the road, regardless of the weather.

When she saw him step down from the bus, a small bag in his hand, it felt like the sun coming out, even though the rain was still falling relentlessly. She saw his eyes light into a smile under the already dripping hat brim as they walked to greet each other.

'Oh, my love!' She almost threw herself into his arms, not caring who saw. 'Thank heavens you're here!' She found herself in tears.

Philip looked startled, then concerned, as she drew back and they linked arms, setting off along the streaming road.

'Eh, love.' He squeezed her arm. 'This isn't like you. Is it that bad?'

'*Yes*,' she said, pouring out all her pent-up frustrations. She had written home, of course, every few days, but she had tried to keep all her letters light-hearted and cheerful. But now she could no longer contain the strain of it all.

'Honestly, the number of times I've nearly packed us all up and come home again! But John and Lily have enjoyed the village school and I'm glad that they're having a chance to live a little differently, as I used to. But oh, dear – Father! I know he felt he had to accept us coming here – and he never says much. But it's there in every line of him, that ramrod back of his, making us all say grace at table and doing a lot of that gazing into the far distance that he does. The children are rather afraid of him. And poor Daisy! She's so sad and angry – and so big now that she's gone into a sort of trance, like a dozy great cow. She just sleeps and doesn't say much, as if she's shutting everyone out. And then there's Miss Berry, his housekeeper – she's such a strait-laced soul that I . . .' She stumbled over her words, upset by what she was having to admit.

'We did tell some untruths in the end – about Daisy. I even put my mother's wedding ring on her finger and so far as the village is concerned she has a young husband in France. But it's all so *awful* – and I keep asking myself whether I'm wrong coming here and whether this is just a way of rubbing things in Father's face after the way he treated me, like a sort of retribution, and I feel terrible . . .'

The gush of words finally ran out into tears. Philip stopped her, gazing urgently into her face. He looked very upset at the state in which he found his wife.

'Margaret, you mustn't think that. You're just trying to do the best you can for everyone – and none of any of it has ever been your fault! You've . . .' Here he sounded emotional. 'Well, you've put the rest of us to shame.'

'Maybe I was wrong to bring her here,' she wept as they drew close to the house. 'She's so unhappy, and it's not really Father – he's been kind enough to her, all things considered.' She pulled out a hanky and blew her nose. 'I just thought it would be a good thing to get away from home – until it's all over. For everyone. But now I'm not sure . . .'

'And I think it is. She would have felt worse at home – cooped up, feeling she was hiding.' He held her gently for a moment and looked, as if with difficulty, into her eyes.

'Have you . . . found someone?'

'Yes.' She glanced away, then back at him. 'I think so. For a sum.' She saw him nod, taking this in. Their shoulders were already dark with rain. 'Come on, love – let's get in out of the wet.'

As they pushed open the door of the little white house, John and Lily gave their father an uproarious greeting.

'Pa, Pa!' Lily danced on her toes. 'Come and see the tree!'

'I rode a horse!' John announced.

'Just let me get my coat off,' Philip laughed, as they flung themselves at him. 'You'll get all wet.' He looked like a giant in the low-ceilinged little house, Margaret thought, just as her father did, forever stooping to pass through doorways. At least Father was out, for the moment. It gave them some time just to reunite as a family.

Philip looked across his younger children's heads to see Daisy standing in the doorway. Her hair was loose in a sheet down her back. She hardly looked like the same girl, her face moonlike and puffy and now so big at the front in a way that made him blush a little on seeing her.

'Hello, Pa,' she said softly.

'Daisy-Loo.' Tenderly, her took her in his arms and kissed her cheek. 'How're you keeping, love?'

'I'm all right,' she said impassively. The tone hurt Margaret. She could hear all the girl's helplessness and regret, knew the fits of sobbing terror that Daisy had shared with her at the thought of the birth – an event she did not even really want to happen. But now it was so close, she was quiet, as if resigned to it, as if nature gave that as a blessing.

'It'll be dinner time soon,' Margaret said. 'Let me take your pa up to unpack his things. John, Lily, you clear up the toys and we'll all come and be together, all right?'

She was sleeping in the old childhood bedroom which she had shared with Annie, looking out over the garden and towards the river. She had been struck by how low the ceiling was and by how much the trees had grown since she left.

'I'm afraid it's separate beds,' she said lightly to Philip. 'But at least we shall be in the same room.'

He had splayed out his coat to dry near the fire downstairs. Now they were alone, he flung his little bag on the bed and faced her.

'Come here, wench,' he said softly.

After these weeks of parting, she went to him, longing to be held and reassured. As her husband drew her close, she heard his intake of breath, felt his hunger for her in the way his hands moved over her, and in seconds they were both weak with desire.

'Oh, my love,' he whispered. 'My dearest love . . . I'm sorry . . .'

As one they moved to the narrow bed, lifting her skirt, tugging at clothes and buttons, everything so that they could be reunited and she was sobbing in his arms, clinging to his back, the big, generous body she knew so well. Moments later, their desire quickly satisfied, they were both laughing, his bearded cheek close to hers, and she could feel the ripples of it through his body.

'I really don't know what's come over me!' she whispered. 'I feel like a terrible, wanton woman.'

'You're an astonishing woman!' he said, raising his head to look at her, and they both laughed again.

'But I used to be so . . .' She searched for words to describe her younger self. 'Proper. And . . . I don't know. Grey and . . .' She shrugged, amazed by the way life had broken her open.

'You were marvellous,' he said, still rocking inside her gently, his face full of joy and pleasure. 'And you're even more so now.'

She raised her head to reach her lips to his. 'I love you so much, Philip.' Her face sobered and she lay back with a sigh. 'Poor Daisy. Oh, heavens – we really do need to go back downstairs.'

William Hanson had returned by the time she and Philip joined the others downstairs and she hoped her father could not see her blushes, still feeling her and Philip's hurried lovemaking in her body. Her father stood, hands clasped behind his back, a rugged, granite-like figure at the end of the table, where the three children were already sitting. Miss Berry, a pleasant but rather stiff-jointed woman with wispy brown hair, was bringing in boiled carrots and leeks to go with a shepherd's pie. As the two men shook hands, Margaret thought with a moment of panic, Oh, my goodness, I hope I haven't caught for another child! Usually they tried to be more careful . . . And her blushes increased.

'Hello, Philip.' Her father inclined his craggy head as the two men shook hands.

'Thank you for welcoming us, Mr Hanson,' Philip said humbly.

How awkward it all was, how embarrassing, Margaret thought, her cheeks burning as they sat down. But it was at the same time comforting to be in her old home for a while, away from the business. As her father intoned a prayer, she glanced at Daisy, who kept her eyes on her plate.

Dear Lord, protect her and be with her through what is to come, Margaret prayed, suddenly full of tenderness for her. And bring us peace this Christmas-tide.

Nineteen

Christmas Day 1915

'Annie – wait for me!'

Annie turned as she let herself out of the nurses' quarters, smiling at Susannah, one of her fellow nurses, whose face she could just make out against the shape of her white veil. They both slipped out into the darkness of early morning, closing the door quietly so as not to wake the others who were not rostered on until later.

'My goodness, it was hard getting up today,' Susannah yawned. 'Oh, my, it's windy out here again – I suppose it's going to pour.' She shivered. 'It's the only time of year I like having a veil to wear!' Wrapping her cloak closely round her, she added, 'I'm glad you're on with me – you move faster than I do and otherwise it's that blasted VAD.'

'Oh, she's not that bad,' Annie said. The regular nurses sometimes made a point of resenting the volunteer VADs and she thought it unkind, especially as the VADs often got thrown in at the deep end. 'Anyway, come on – let's move a bit quicker now!' She tugged on Susannah's arm. The two of them trotted across towards the imposing university buildings which were now their hospital. The lights were burning inside and it looked warm and welcoming compared with the icy air of dawn, where their breath was snatched in white sworls. They could just make out the face of the clock on the university's tower, which showed seven-twenty. Soon they were inside, going to greet the night staff and be debriefed about events through the hours of darkness.

Annie walked into the ward, in the splendid surroundings of the university's Great Hall, with a feeling of excitement rising in her. Though she had not admitted it to Susannah, she had not found it at all hard to get up. After what happened yesterday, during all the Christmas Eve excitement on the wards, getting up that morning had far been easier than usual – though she still could hardly admit to herself why this was.

But Susannah never missed a thing.

'You're very chirpy this morning,' she said, eyeing Annie with a teasing expression. 'That wouldn't be anything to do with the rugged Scots specialist of yesterday, would it? Ooh, Annie Hanson – you can deny it as much as you like but I can see you blushing!'

'Christians awake, salute this happy morn!' they sang in the little Congregationalist church, as stormy light slanted in through the windows, flickering as clouds passed the sun.

This place, which had at first felt so strange to Daisy, seemed almost comforting this morning, as she stood with her father on one side of her – at church as a rare concession to his father-in-law – and Margaret on the other. Around them were the devout villagers and farmers who assumed, rather than being directly told, that the ring on her finger meant that her man was away at the Front. In the weeks they had been staying out here, everyone had treated her with a respect that bordered on reverence. This made her feel both touched and deeply ashamed, like the imposter she was.

Daisy knew she had been impossible at times over the past months, testing everyone to their limits, but she just could not help it. Pa's anger and silence had made it all worse. She had been terribly moody, flown into rages; at other times dissolving into tears in front of her step-mother at the thought of what must happen to her. These facts Margaret had gently explained, one evening in the summer. They had been up in Daisy's bedroom, sticky in their summer frocks after the working day. There were children playing outside which made Daisy feel even worse – all her childhood now seemed like a lost country to which she ached to return.

'I can't do it,' she had wept, leaning despairingly against Margaret as they sat on the bed. 'I don't want to – it's all so horrible. Doesn't it hurt?'

'Yes – I must admit, there is some pain,' Margaret said carefully, hands folded in her lap. Daisy peered at her, feeling that something was being hidden from her.

'A lot? Does it hurt a lot?' Her eyes filled with tears. 'My mother . . . she died,' she sobbed stormily. 'It'll be the same for me – I'm going to die, I know I am!'

'Look, dear.' Margaret's grey eyes turned on her and even as she was getting carried away with her panic, Daisy knew she would be given truth. 'Your mother was very unfortunate. The baby she was carrying was breech – coming out feet first, in other words, which is very difficult. But it's not like that usually. Just think how many women give birth to children every day of the year! So you see, it's a very normal thing. And by the time the baby is ready to come, you will be ready too, I promise.'

Margaret made a point of not saying anything about what would happen then, after the birth. So far as Daisy was concerned, it was still unreal, even now. She just wanted rid of it, to have back the life she had known. The life in which she had shone, had not let everybody down – most especially not her mother, Florence Tallis.

The fierce protective feelings she had felt after James Carson's callousness had come and gone. But when she started to be aware of the child quickening in her and, as time passed, the movements became more vigorous, despite everything she began to be a little curious. But she had pushed such feelings away. She did not want a baby – least of all James Carson's. It was a horrible mistake and the sooner it was over the better. She would be able to go back home and forget about all of it.

By the time they left Birmingham, she was relieved to go, although at first she had been horrified by the idea and fought with Margaret over it. She had been very nervous of Margaret's father. She had met him a few times already over the years and she knew him to be deeply religious; he could be very stern and she wondered why Margaret had thought this would be a good plan. But when she arrived, the Revd Hanson had taken her hand – his head, magnificent as a granite statue, bowing stiffly over it – and said, 'You are welcome, my dear. I hope we shall be able to give you a comfortable stay.'

Apart from day-to-day pleasantries, he had said not another word about why she was there and for that she was grateful. She had been able to go about the village sometimes as Margaret reacquainted herself with her neighbours, and to rest. To hide from the busy life of Chain Street. It was as if she was in a secret, safe cocoon, just waiting to burst out of it.

As she grew heavier, the movements inside her more insistent, she found herself becoming slow and dull, not thinking of anything at all with any sharpness. Nature had brought her to the point, after these long months, when she was ready to deliver up a child. It had to be – it was something larger and more powerful than herself and she bowed to it, having no choice.

As they were rounding off the hymn, William Hanson moved stiffly, magnificently, towards the pulpit as if bearing the burden of heavy responsibility. And Daisy felt an odd warmth begin to spread through the lower portion of her body. It was so strange and striking a feeling, as if something within her was actually melting, that she was seized with panic. Was this it – was she about to start having a baby in the middle of the service?

She sat down hastily, amid the rustling of the congregation as everyone settled to hear the preacher's words. The feeling remained, like a low hum in her. Something had changed, but for the moment, nothing else happened. She let out a long breath and closed her eyes. It will be soon. Help me, she prayed to whatever God might be available. Please help me.

Christmas on the wards felt even more special than last year. The staff were determined to make an enormous effort to put on a cheery show for the lads, all of them away from home – some further than others. And some were so ill or in such a wounded state that they could not enjoy it. But the others who were recuperating had revelled in all the fuss that was made of them.

The beds already had cheerful coloured counterpanes and they had hung streamers and greenery along the walls as high as they could manage and brought in a Christmas tree. The festivities had started off on Christmas Eve with a carol party in the Great Hall. Everyone who was able had gathered to sing and volunteer in taking turns to play the piano – staff and patients alike.

Annie, like the other nurses, had been trained to keep her emotions strictly at bay on the wards. And she had

153

never seen herself as sentimental. But as they all sang, she had looked at the faces of the lads round her, some in bed, some in wheelchairs and a few gathered round the piano. Many of them she had seen at their very worst – feverish, helpless, in terrible pain. Now they were more comfortable and enjoying all of it. But then came thoughts of those who had not recovered, of all the other wounded boys – and the other nurses – in France and across the world, all perhaps stopping to sing a hymn, to pray for peace in the world. She was so moved that by the end of 'Once in Royal David's City' and 'Silent Night', she and some of the others could not prevent the tears running down their cheeks, though they did their best to hide it.

She recovered herself to perform her tasks on the ward and was in the middle of a round of observations when Susannah, a well-rounded girl with an eye for the boys, sidled up and nudged her.

'Look!' she whispered. 'Who's this then? Ooh, he's nice-looking, he is.'

Annie could only agree. The doctor, in his RAMC uniform with the red cross sewn on his left arm, was tall and lean with a neatly clipped moustache and brown hair, and seemed to exude competence and cheerfulness.

'Go on, Annie – Matron's not here.' Susannah looked around. 'You'd better go and speak to him.'

'Me? Why don't you go?' Annie hissed. But it seemed so silly to be seen there squabbling over who should do what, that Annie squared her shoulders and went to speak to him, amid the excited chatter of the ward.

'Good evening, doctor,' she said, very formally.

The man turned with a smile, seemed on the point of saluting her and thought the better of it.

'Yes! Afternoon, and merry Christmas – well, almost!' he said. 'The war is no respecter of the season, I'm afraid.

154

I'm here to take a look at a couple of your patients. But apparently I'm also to be given the onerous responsibility of carving the fowl tomorrow – on this ward.'

The man's crisp Scots accent felt like a fresh breeze and Annie, seeing his twinkling expression, couldn't help smiling. Out of the corner of her eye she saw Matron entering the far end of the ward, a fact she indicated to him with her eyes. She was half sure she had seen him give her a wink as she did so. Matron soon made her way along to speak to the new doctor and Annie slid away.

Twenty

Annie and Susannah took over from the night staff and the day began, everyone wishing each other 'Merry Christmas' and some of the cheekier patients daring to ask for a kiss: 'Oh, go *on*, nurse – it is Christmas!' Annie wagged fingers playfully at them and did not give in.

The ward was given presents funded by the Birmingham *Daily Mail*, all handed out by a well-padded Father Christmas. Everyone enjoyed him so much that the whole day soon began to run late and they had to dash along to hear the Administrator's address in the chapel and then rush back to make sure that everything would be ready for Christmas dinner. Later there would be more presents and mince pies and more singing ...

When the orderlies wheeled the trolley on to the ward bearing the turkey and trimmings, a cheer went up from the hungry lads in the beds and echoed round the hall. Annie, while irritated at herself, could not help turning to see which of the medical staff was to carve the turkey and have dinner with them. Would it be that rather interesting new Scottish doctor as he had said it would? When they saw his tall figure following along behind the trolley, Susannah whispered, 'Aha – look who's here!' Annie was even more annoyed to find a blush rising in her cheeks.

There was a moment when he stood staring at the trolley, slightly at a loss, and when he looked up, he met Annie's gaze, so that she felt bound to go over and help him out, feeling the eyes of everyone on the ward beginning to fasten on the two of them.

'Good afternoon, doctor,' she said. 'Have you come to do the honours for us?'

'Yes – they've certainly thrown me in at the deep end. I'm here to do my best with this –' he waved a hand at the upturned and well-roasted turkey – 'or worst, perhaps, from the fowl's point of view!'

'Well, you're very popular, I can tell you,' Annie said, indicating some of the eager-looking patients.

'Ah, Dr Reid,' said Matron, looming beside them. She was a woman in her late forties and kindly, but my goodness, she made sure you did as you were told. 'You have come to assist. Come along, Nurse Hanson – to work. This dinner will not serve itself!'

There was a pause while the doctor said grace over the turkey, which Annie could not help finding slightly hilarious. Religious as she was herself, there was something about praying over a naked turkey with its legs sticking up . . . The new doctor carved and Annie and Susannah and the other staff filled plates almost to overflowing and distributed them round the ward.

'Is that mine, nurse?' one of Annie's young patients cried eagerly. 'I think I'm going to pass out if I don't eat in a minute!'

'I don't suppose you will,' she retorted. 'But yes – this one's for you.'

'Oh!' He feigned a faint for a moment. 'Stuffing! Roast spuds! Bread sauce! Have I died and gone to heaven?'

'Not last time I looked, no,' she said, smiling as she placed the food on his table. 'Go on – tuck in.'

Once they had taken plates to all the patients, Annie and the other staff came for their helpings. As she was spooning potatoes on to her plate, Dr Reid approached and quietly said hello.

'Fergus Reid.' He bowed slightly from the waist. 'This is all very jolly. May I enquire of your name, nurse?'

'Nurse Hanson,' she said. She was really doing her best to remain formal, but in the face of Dr Reid's infectious smile, she could feel a pinkness suffusing her cheeks and her lips turning merrily upwards. She was comforted by the thought that everyone was far too busy tucking into their Christmas dinner to take much notice of her.

'May I be party to your first name, or is it a strictly kept secret?' he said solemnly.

'I suppose I might stretch a point,' she said. 'It's Annie.'

'It's a pleasure to meet you, Nurse Annie,' he said teasingly. 'And merry Christmas.'

So began an afternoon of jollity. Fergus Reid lingered around long after they had eaten, chatting to some of the lads and helping clear up. Annie was surprised. Most doctors thought they were well above such things and second only to God. She couldn't help looking curiously at him. He was a friendly man, even Matron softened in his presence and Annie saw her smiling. He talked to all the staff, though she was kept so busy she did not see a great deal of him – until he was about to leave.

She was talking to a young man in a bed up towards the high wooden pulpit and suddenly realized that Dr Reid was coming towards her along the ward. He had put his hat on again and seeing his face now looking out from under his cap brim, Annie thought his features seemed sharpened, more distinguished even than before. She felt her entire body prickle, almost as if there was some sort of danger close by. It was odd, disturbing, that he had this effect on her. She tried to put a cool, professional expression on her face.

'Nurse Hanson,' he said, very politely. 'I shall be off now. But might I trouble you for a word before I go?'

'One moment,' she said to the lad she had been talking to. Walking beside Dr Reid, she said, 'You have stayed a long time. I'm surprised no one has called you away – though of course we've been glad of the help.'

'Well, I'm a new boy,' he said. 'Not everyone has caught on that I'm here. But I've had a quick look at the two patients they especially want me to examine. Nerve cases, you see. And it's a good chance to get to know the place a bit. Um, nurse?'

They had just reached the nurses' station, a table at the side of the room, where no one happened to be sitting at that moment. He touched her arm for a second to stop her and they stood face to face. Annie fingered the edge of the blotter on the table.

'I, er . . .' He spoke very quietly. 'I'm new around here, as you know. In Birmingham, I mean. I don't know the city at all – I've come down from Edinburgh, you see. I don't even know that I'll be here all that long. Might I impose on your time for an hour or two, to show me around a bit – when you come off duty, or another day?'

Annie was so surprised that she was speechless for a second.

'I . . .' She took a breath. 'Today, I'm afraid I have promised to go and visit a friend – and family.'

'Well, of course,' he laughed. 'It is Christmas Day.'

'But another day – yes.' A genuine sense of pleasure rose in her and she beamed at him. 'I'd be glad to.'

It was already dark again before she reached the yard in Pope Street.

'Miss Hanson!' Ivy opened the door and grinned with delight. 'You never said you was coming!'

159

'Oh, yes, 'er did,' Lizzie said, coming over with the baby, Ann, in her arms. 'Only I never said – thought it'd make a bit of a surprise.'

As they closed the door, Annie took in the poor little room and tried to assess how things were going. Even though everyone – the doctor, Lizzie and Ivy – had assured her they laid no blame at her door for what had happened, she still felt a terrible sense of responsibility over Mary Poole.

Poor Lizzie, alone now with the family to look after, looked very thin and tired, but she was smiling cheerfully. Ivy, whose childhood blonde hair had darkened to a mousy brown, was a practical girl who had found work learning enamelling at the Trafalgar Works – Thomas Fattorini's factory in Regent Street. She was of a stockier build than her willowy elder sister, and seemed very sensible and older than her years. Annie remembered with a terrible pang the day she and Margaret had found Ivy's sister, Ada, dead beside Ivy in the bed upstairs. This family had had such a lot to contend with and with Den gone as well now, Ivy and Lizzie had to be parents to the two young ones, Ethel and baby Ann.

'It looks nice in here!' Annie said, trying only to see the best of it. The cold and the smell of damp, the mouldy ceiling and the beetle scuttling across the floor, she edited from her thoughts. Because as well, today there were streamers across the ceiling, holly along each end of the mantle and a decorated candle in the middle. Lizzie, who was feeding Ann with a bottle, smiled with pleasure.

'We wanted it nice for Christmas,' she said. Her eyes filled. Their mother had only been dead seven months. What a sad, gruelling struggle it all was, but Annie was full of admiration for these sisters and the way they were pulling together.

'Did you make the streamers, Etty?' she asked the little girl, who was sitting at the table, looking very much as Ivy and Ada had at six years old, when Annie first met them.

Etty, who was playing with some buttons, nodded shyly, pleased to be noticed.

'We did 'em together,' Ivy said. 'Now, d'yer want a cuppa tea, Miss Hanson?'

'I thought you'd never ask,' Annie smiled.

Ivy looked stricken. 'Sorry – only . . .'

'I was joking,' Annie said. 'But yes, Ivy – I'd love one. And do please stop calling me Miss Hanson. Annie's perfectly fine.'

'All right,' Ivy said, busying herself with the kettle. 'Water's boiled, Lizzie . . .'

'Make us a good pot,' Lizzie said. 'And don't hang about. Annie'll be wanting to get off to her family.'

'Oh, there's no hurry,' Annie said. 'It's a treat to see you all.' She reached into her bag. 'Look, I've brought some nice biscuits, shortbread! And a fruitcake – and a few little gifts.'

The girls exclaimed with pleasure and Etty slid down from the table and came to stand shyly by Annie's chair, staring at her in wonder.

'You're pretty,' she said, wide-eyed.

Annie laughed. 'Well, that's nice, Etty – and so are you. Come here and help me hand out these little presents, will you?'

'We've got one for you too,' Ivy said over her shoulder. 'Ain't we, Lizzie?'

'In a minute,' Lizzie said, winding Ann over her shoulder. 'Ooh, that cake's making my mouth water. You are kind, Annie. You shouldn't be spending your wages on us.'

'Well, I don't have much time to spend them on anyone most of the time,' Annie said.

She handed out the little gifts, each wrapped in tissue. She had bought a pretty silk square for Lizzie, flowers and leaves all in blue, red and green on a cream background.

'Oh, Annie, that is pretty!' Lizzie's eyes lit up and she stroked it in wonder. For Ivy she had a bar of perfumed soap and a tortoiseshell comb and for Etty, a wooden jigsaw puzzle of a group of children playing with a skipping rope. Etty gasped at the sight of it and took it immediately to the table, gazing solemnly as she opened the box.

'And there's something tiny for the little one,' Annie said, handing Lizzie a small rattle. 'For when she's a bit bigger.'

'Thanks ever so much,' Lizzie said. 'You're ever so kind.'Ere, 'ave a hold of 'er a minute, Annie, so I can cut some of that cake!'

Annie took the contented baby on to her lap and enjoyed the warm feel of her. She was wide awake, staring round at them all.

'Have you heard any more from Den?' Annie asked. She had been full of questions about how they were coping, but those could wait. So far as she could see they were doing very well – all these girls had had a lot to manage from a young age.

'There was a card when he got to France, saying he was all right,' Lizzie said, bringing a little plate over with slices of the cake. 'Ooh, look at that – I love marzipan!'

As they sat in the warm, Annie said softly to Lizzie, 'You all right?'

Lizzie's eyes filled and she gave a sad smile. 'I'm getting by. Mrs B has this one –' she nodded down at little Ann – 'a day or two and then I pay Mrs Felton up the road to have 'er some of the time.' But her eyes clouded and she seemed troubled.

'What's the matter? Aren't you sure she's doing a good job?'

'I don't know.' Lizzie hesitated. 'I'm not sure. I just don't like handing her over, some'ow.'

'She seems contented enough.'

'Yeah.' Lizzie eyed her sister in Annie's lap. 'I s'pose. Yes, you're right.'

Annie looked at her old friend, her heart full of sadness for her and admiration.

'Never mind, Lizzie – your prince'll come one day.'

'Huh – what, for me? Yer joking. Who's going to want an old maid like me, with all this round me?' She took a mouthful and a sudden look of bliss came over her face. 'This cake is one of the nicest things I've ever tasted.'

Revd Hanson had had rather a shock at their insistence on celebrating Christmas in a less austere way than he was used to – for the sake of John and Lily as much as anything.

'We never had a tree or decorations when Annie and I were growing up,' Margaret told them.

But they had all decked out the house for when Philip arrived, making paper streamers and going out to raid the hedgerows for shining red hips and haws, holly and clusters of mistletoe. William Hanson drew the line at having alcohol in his house, but Miss Berry had made blackberry cordial in the summer and they celebrated happily enough. By the evening, everyone sat round the fire, reflecting on their luck at being together when so many were separated from loved ones. The year had brought increasingly terrible news from the Western Front – huge losses at Ypres and at Loos – and the Hun using gas on the enemy. Margaret had been horrified by stories Annie had reported from the hospital.

'We must be grateful,' William Hanson said. 'These are grave times – grave times indeed.'

And Daisy realized that despite his gloomy words, he seemed happy to have them all there. It was the first time they had all spent Christmas together in his home. As she sat, that evening, the melting sensation began again, as if something within her was cleaving open.

She was sleeping in the smallest room, which Margaret told her had once belonged to their baby brother John, before he was taken from them as an infant by a terrible fever. Margaret and Annie's heartbroken mother had kept the room intact afterwards, unable to bear to change it. Even now, it still looked much as it ever had and Daisy liked the simple little room with its pale green walls and cosy green eiderdown.

But sleep would not come to her that night. The hot, almost tearing feeling in her body continued and she felt suddenly wide awake and bursting with energy, as if her body was on full alert. She had not said anything to anyone all day about these feelings. She heard William Hanson's tread on the wooden stairs as he retired to his room, then Ma and Pa, who had settled an excited John and Lily to sleep downstairs. The two of them had been turfed out of Annie's old bed now that Pa was here. She heard something give an unearthly shriek outside. It began to rain, a swish of sound and a rattle on the window. Let me sleep, please, she thought, wanting to escape what she knew had begun. The force of it was building in her.

It was a while before it became pain. When it came it was shocking in its sharpness – like a crushing band of iron about her body. She leapt up in the bed and knelt, pressing her head sideways into the pillow, gasping until it began to die away.

Oh, my heavens, she thought, what am I supposed to do?

It was pitch dark. With shaking fingers she re-lit the candle, comforted by the light. Every so often, the iron hand grasped hold of her again, its force increasing so that she could not help a moan escaping her lips. She dozed a little, then woke again. On it went, growing more frequent. I must get someone, she thought, but she could not seem to find the impetus, to take in that this was really happening.

'I must get up . . .' she whispered.

She had lost track of all time. The house felt deadly quiet around her. After a bout of pain, she swung her legs over the side of the bed and stood up. As she did so, liquid gushed from her, soaking her legs and into the rug beside the bed. She looked down in horror, but then the pain ambushed her with such force that she bent over the bed again, groaning and sobbing.

'Daisy?' Margaret was beside her. 'Oh, my dear – why didn't you come for me?'

Daisy had no idea what happened next, except that she was in a stormy sea of pain, hurling her forward then receding so that all other reality was lost to her. People were in the room; another candle's wavering light, voices – Margaret, her father, another woman . . . Oh, thank heaven someone was here to help . . .

'Right – we'll get you on the bed, lovey,' the woman's voice said. She had the impression of a plump person, hair in some sort of wrapper and a round face.

Everything was going so fast. 'I can't,' she panted. 'I can't do this . . .'

No one else could do it. She was the only one able to birth this child. When the final pains felt as if they were cracking her apart, she still felt incapable of it, even when the village midwife was saying things like, 'Good, good, lovey, that's right, you keep that comin',' and there was something vast trying to force its way agonizingly out of her and then a slither and a sudden feeling of being released. Everyone was exclaiming and she heard, to her utter astonishment, the loud, outraged cry of a baby.

'My dear . . .' Margaret had tears running down her cheeks. 'She's a little girl – a beautiful little girl.'

Daisy, her body cleft open, lay in blood and sweat, her hair lank about her, limp as an old cloth and full of bewilderment. She felt like someone else, not herself at all. The woman who had helped, whose name turned out to be Mrs White, came to her with a little wrapped bundle, her fleshy face beaming.

'Well, she's a lively one,' she said. ''Ere you are, my dear. You 'ave a look at her, the little princess . . .'

'No!' Daisy protested weakly. All she could feel was fear. Don't let me – don't ever let me see . . . 'No, I don't want to . . .'

The woman either did not hear or did not understand. The bundle was laid in her arms. Daisy felt a surprisingly solid little body find its space against hers, life clamouring through it. She turned her face away, pushing at it, seized with panic. This was not meant to be happening.

'Get it away from me – just take it away!' she cried frantically to Margaret. She was the one who knew what they were to do. She had arranged it all. 'Get it away from me.'

'Oh, Daisy, are you sure?' Margaret rushed over and took the warm weight off her. 'But you should give her a drink . . .'

'No!' Daisy shouted. 'Take it – get it out of here, now!'

She lay back and closed her eyes as Margaret carried the bundle away, whispering something to the midwife.

166

Daisy was suddenly sharply conscious now, attuned to every movement in the room, every sound, the minute snuffle she could hear coming from that warm thing that had lain on her, and just for a few seconds the place it had occupied felt empty, bereft.

The whispering continued. Daisy heard the door open as if Margaret was about to leave and it became impossible, like a tearing apart in her, this now or never, never again.

'Wait!' She shot up on to her elbows. 'All right, wait just a minute – let me see before you go.'

She saw Margaret and the midwife exchange looks, their eyes full of some doom felt between them. Margaret seemed to find permission in that look somewhere.

'All right, Daisy.' She came close again, but did not push the child into Daisy's arms. Instead she leaned down, opening the little cream blanket. Daisy saw dark hair, tiny features, the mouth moving slightly pursed, as if looking for something, but for the moment there was no sound except tiny, squeaky breaths. It was utterly extraordinary.

'So,' she whispered, 'it's a girl?'

'Yes,' Margaret said. Her voice was tight, held in. 'Do you want to . . . ?'

'No.' Daisy recoiled and lay down again, closed her eyes. 'Take her – now, Ma.'

She heard the footsteps leave the room again. After a few moments the other woman spoke. Her voice was calm, but neutral, with little warmth.

'All right, my dear. Now I need to see to you – all right?'

'Yes,' Daisy said faintly.

She lay back, limp and empty. It was over.

Twenty-One

Pain woke her. Her breasts were tight, with that terrible, bursting tingle. When she slept she dreamt that something was sucking on her, both easing and hurting her, and when she woke, again and again she had to discover that there was nothing there. She hurt down below, feeling as if she had been bludgeoned in the privates. Her body sweated at odd times and in odd places.

She had been prepared with all her being for something and was now abandoned, unable to fulfil it. The ache inside her exhausted her, bewildered her. She had not known, had no idea – about any of it. And that weight she had felt lying on her arm, that face, that tiny face . . .

'I'm going to have to go back.' She heard her father's voice, very low outside the bedroom. He sounded distraught. 'I can't leave the business any longer. Bring her back when you think she's ready.'

'All right.' Margaret sounded distressed. 'I suppose that's how it is. I can't . . .' She trailed off, perhaps finishing the sentence with a gesture. 'It feels . . . It's wrong. That's how it all feels now. And it does to her, I think, only she won't say so.'

There was a silence. Daisy felt that sensation again, the feeling that kept haunting her dreams, of something warm and heavy lying on her arm, of something gnawing at her nipples.

'It was what she wanted,' she heard Pa say. 'It's done

now. What can we do? She's young. She'll get over it soon enough.'

'Spoken like a man.' Margaret's voice was harsh.

Even in her odd state, Daisy was shocked. A little face appeared in her mind, the mouth pursed, searching. The face she had glimpsed just for a few seconds.

'I didn't mean . . .' Her father sounded distraught.

'Look – you go. I'll deal with her,' Margaret said. Her voice was weary.

When Pa came in to say goodbye, Daisy pretended to be soundly asleep. He stood by the bed for what seemed a long time, then came close, leaned over and kissed her. She could feel that he was about to creep away and she made herself open her eyes.

'Hello, Pa.' She pretended to wake.

She saw the look of panic on his face for a moment, but he stood, attempting a gentle smile. For a moment he looked like a boy, lost and unsure.

'Are you going back?' she said.

'Reckon I'll have to, yes.' He rubbed one hand down the opposite arm, as if it was aching, though perhaps it was just something to do. 'You'll be home soon?'

She nodded, her eyes filling as they seemed to do endlessly, as if her whole body was weeping. And she saw that he could see and that he could not bear it.

'It'll be good to have you all back,' he said. He patted her shoulder. 'Best get going.'

And he was gone. She lay, weak and bereft, weeping.

'Daisy?'

It was Margaret's voice, soon after. Daisy opened her eyes.

'How are you, dear?'

She hauled herself up, everything hurting, her breasts hard. She could not speak, but her face must have said something so clear that Margaret looked away as if she could not stand to see it.

'What did you tell John and Lily?' Daisy said.

'That you had the baby and that this baby was going to be looked after by someone else. I told them that sometimes it's like that.'

'Did they ... accept that?' For some reason this seemed burningly important, as if her half-siblings' judgement might be purer and more instinctive than that of the adults.

'John did.' Margaret looked down at her hand, which was resting on the blanket.

'What about Lily?' Earnest, sweet Lily.

'She's finding it harder to understand.' Margaret looked up at her then, her face full of sadness and uncertainty.

Their eyes met and they sat like that for a few moments, neither wanting to speak, but as if searching each other's gaze for something. Daisy saw her stepmother's expression change, her eyes take on a fearful questioning look. And in the silence, her heart beating with need, her eyes blurring with tears, Daisy nodded.

Margaret went by herself. She knew the family. The eldest daughter, who had one child of a few months old, had agreed to take another, for a sum of money.

'You don't need to give the money back,' Margaret told her. 'But she just can't do it.'

It was unbearable, the way Daisy had just been lying there, as if half dead.

'I never knew 'ow she could do it in the first place,' the young woman said, in her cottage kitchen. She insisted she was not a money-grabbing person, that she would

170

give most of it back, but Margaret insisted she keep it for her kindness and trouble.

Within an hour, Daisy heard the door and she leapt up in the bed, her blood coursing so hard that she could hear it in her ears. It was as if her whole body was coming back to life and turning towards its purpose. Nothing was the same as before. Since that night when she had been torn open by that little body, she had not been the old Daisy Tallis. She had become someone new. Someone who was bound, body and soul, to another being.

Feet came up the stairs and the door opened. Margaret stood with the swathed child in her arms, her own face open and tender and smiling as if released.

'Here she is,' she said.

And Daisy held out her arms, knowing that now everything was truly changed for ever.

II

1916

Twenty-Two

January 1916

'Let's go and see some of the town,' the note from Fergus said. 'I've scarcely ever had time to see the place at all. Bull Ring? I think this is something you should show me!'

It had been difficult enough trying to find a time when both he and Annie could be sure of a few hours off, and everything had to be organized by a series of notes. At first, even though she was pleased he had asked, she felt so nervous and inexperienced that she almost wanted to back out of seeing him. But he had said he might not be at this hospital for long and – well, it might be enjoyable, she told herself. And she knew, really, that she was not going to refuse.

It was nearly the middle of January by the time Annie found herself scrambling on to the tram to get into Birmingham. By that time she had hardly seen Fergus Reid again, except once in the far distance, a distinctive, tall figure, hurrying across the grounds to the hospital.

'Why on earth did I say I'd go?' she complained to Susannah in the nurses' quarters, searching her scant possessions for something even halfway respectable to wear. Annie had never done fripperies and most of her life was in any case spent in uniform.

'Because you were asked – by one of the most handsome men in the whole hospital?'

'Handsome is as handsome does,' Annie said. She sat brushing her hair, looking at Susannah in the glass.

Susannah rolled her eyes. 'I'll go for you if you've got cold feet?'

'Perhaps you should,' Annie said desperately. But it came to her then, with a shock, how disappointing it would be not to meet Fergus Reid tonight. 'All this sort of vainglory is not me in the least. I look such a mess and it's even worse when I make an effort. I wish I was like my sister Margaret – she always looks beautiful without even trying!'

'Annie,' Susannah said, serious now, sympathetic. She took Annie by the shoulders and turned her towards the mirror again. 'Just give me that brush.' Brushing and twisting and pinning, she arranged Annie's hair into a soft coil at the back of her neck, lecturing all the while. 'You have no idea just how astonishing your looks are, you silly. I mean, it's as if you've never once even seen a mirror. Look at you!'

She put her head next to Annie's. Annie, looking reluctantly, saw a figure with rather romantically arranged hair, a heart-shaped face with impishly prominent cheekbones, and large hazel-green eyes.

'You're so busy trying to save the whole world that you never pay yourself an ounce of attention,' Susannah scolded. 'Why do you think the most astonishingly interesting man in the whole hospital headed straight for you, when he could have –' she made a comical scything movement – 'he could have mowed down most of the female population in one stroke!'

'Including Matron – did you see her face when he turned up on Christmas Eve?' Annie was laughing now, trying to push away her feelings of panic. Men – she just

176

did not tangle with men! They were all out to control and manipulate you in the end.

'Oh, definitely including Matron!' Susannah giggled. 'Now go on – enjoy yourself for once. And tell me *all about it* when you get back.'

And now that she was on her way, wearing Susannah's black hat with a wider brim than Annie had ever worn in her life before, she felt like a complete imposter. Annie, normally bullishly brave, was full of foreboding. She sat on the tram, perspiring in her wool coat – for the weather, after days of being wet and very blowy, was now unseasonably mild. Her hands and feet were clammy with nerves. She pulled off her worn leather gloves and sat clutching them.

When had she ever been interested in men? she ranted inwardly, peering out at the dark streets. Never – most of them were dolts, or worse! And she was never going to get married. So what was she doing here? She allowed the image of Dr Fergus Reid RAMC into her mind and was hit again, inwardly, by that magnetic, baffling feeling that she had to see him.

Once, she thought. Just this once – and never again.

She had scarcely stepped down from the tram in Navigation Street than she saw his unmistakably tall, uniformed figure waiting in the light of a lamp. As soon as he spotted her he strode over and halted smartly, giving a little bow with a slight raise of his cap.

'Good evening, Nurse Hanson.'

'Oh!' She felt startled and unready. She had forgotten the impact of him, his height, the crisp accent. 'Good evening! My goodness, you're very . . . punctual.' Annie realized she had made this sound like a criticism, when in fact she would have been most unimpressed had he *not* been on time, but it was too late now so she hurried on, 'And yes – it is quite a good evening. Not raining for once.'

'Quite. Those gales brought down rather a lot of trees, I believe.'

They stood facing each other in the gloomy street, Annie still clutching her gloves, feeling foolish and nervous as a kitten. If Fergus Reid was nervous too, he was showing it a good deal less than she felt she was. Oh, heaven, she groaned inwardly, what am I doing here? A cup of cocoa and her bed suddenly felt incredibly attractive.

'Now,' he said, looking round. 'I think it might be a little dark for a tour, even of something as intriguing as a Bull Ring.'

'It's really just a market,' Annie said. 'And it's lively in the daytime, but nothing much will be going on at this time of night, I don't think.'

'Well, in that case, let's go and find a cosy spot somewhere, shall we? Would you prefer the Midland – or the Queen's Hotel, perhaps? I'm sure I can secure a good drop of malt in one or the other.'

'Oh – no!' Annie said, realizing this meeting had been a terrible mistake. This was a whole realm of things she had not even thought about! 'I'm afraid I'm only prepared to go into a Temperance establishment. I don't hold with drinking.'

'Ah,' Fergus Reid said, nonplussed for a moment in the face of this adamant resistance. He clasped his hands behind his back and she was not sure, in the dark street, whether she imagined the twitch of amusement in his expression. He seemed to be examining her as if she were one of his more perplexing medical cases. 'Well, I'm afraid you'll have to help me out there. New to the city and so on – and not my area of expertise.'

Annie realized, with burning cheeks and a sinking heart, that it was not hers either. In all the years she had lived in Birmingham, she had never once been out on the town like this.

'Well, in fact,' she admitted stiffly, 'I'm afraid I don't know where we might go.' She felt very foolish and apologetic. And she realized suddenly how much she did not want Fergus Reid to despise her, or call the evening off.

'Look,' she said, fighting all the prejudice of her upbringing. After all, did even stepping into one of those places necessarily make you the most flagrant sinner ever? It was not as if she was unable to resist the blandishments of temptation. 'I daresay if we went into one of the hotels you mention, they might find me something other than alcohol?'

'Yes,' he agreed solemnly. 'I imagine they might.'

As she followed Fergus Reid into the warm, fuggy atmosphere of the bar at the Queen's Hotel, the ruinous stenches of sin seemed to burn their way into her nostrils: the air was thick with smoke from pipes and cigarettes and, snarled into it, the filthy whiffs of beer and spirits from all those bottles of evil, intoxicating liquors . . . Most of the tables were crowded with a mix of khaki uniforms and civilian greys and most were men, though there were a very few women among the throng. She looked at Fergus's long, khaki-clad back walking ahead of her and compared herself to Daniel walking into the den of lions.

And then she felt rather silly. Nothing much was going on. It was true that alcohol had been the ruination of many a family, but here everyone seemed to be sitting having amiable conversations. There were bursts of laughter which teetered on the edge of losing control and this made her uneasy, but it was not as if the place was full of brawls and people lying barely conscious on the floor with bloodied faces. She raised her chin as if bracing herself.

'Shall we sit here?' Fergus turned, having found a small table tucked away from the noisiest drinkers.

He brought over a tumbler of whisky and for her, a blackcurrant cordial. They settled at the table, chat and laughter all around them, Fergus sitting opposite her, their coats hung on the stand close by, his hat on the spare chair beside him. The lighting was soft and Fergus's face was slightly in shadow, his well-clipped hair a dark line round his brow.

'Cheers!' he said, twinkling at her as he raised his glass.

Annie smiled, doing the same, though feeling that he was mocking her. 'Cheers,' she said, gamely clinking glasses. The drink was horribly sour when she took a sip and she tried not to grimace.

'So – a Temperance upbringing,' he said, sitting back. 'There's quite a bit of that in Scotland – on the east side especially, where I come from. Very strict.' Again, he was smiling.

'My father is a Congregationalist minister,' Annie said. 'He became more rigid after our mother died. Sadder, too.' She realized, uncomfortably, how sadness and self-denial had joined hands in their family. She had never seen it quite that way before.

'And how old were you?' he said gently.

'Eleven.'

'How very sad,' he said with genuine sympathy, which for some reason put her more at ease.

'Well,' Annie said, 'we managed. My sister Margaret and I.'

He acknowledged this with a small tilt of his head.

'Look,' he said mischievously, 'you might as well know the worst – I smoke as well. Can you bear it?'

It was her turn to tilt her head. She held his gaze. 'Well, let's see, shall we? Try me.'

He drew a silver cigarette case from his pocket and lit up, blowing the smoke away from her. 'I find it helps me concentrate.'

'And the drink?'

'Oh – well, that's just . . .' He looked at her with a serious air. 'I suppose I don't believe there are many things which are inherently bad. Bombs, perhaps – those have destruction as their very purpose. Guns, even. But most things – it's the purpose to which we put them. This –' he held up his glass with its finger of golden liquor – 'comes from a long and honourable tradition. Did you know it was originally called "water of life"?'

'No. That sounds blasphemous to me.' But she managed a smile.

Fergus Reid sat back, crossing one leg over the other in a way which made Annie, just for a second, imagine his skeleton, the long tibias and femurs. 'Well,' he said, twinkling at her, 'you are at least in agreement with my dog, who turns his nose up mightily if I offer him a sniff of my glass.'

'You have a dog?'

'Yes – old Seamus. An Irish wolfhound – had him for years now. He's a good old chap.'

This was somehow endearing. Annie liked animals.

'Anyway,' Fergus went on, 'I solemnly promise not to turn into a drunken wastrel in the next hour or so. All right? Now, Miss Hanson – do tell me about yourself. Is that a slight touch of the West Country I hear in your voice?'

She told him, briefly, about her family, about the loss

of their infant brother John, about their coming to Birmingham – though she slid over the details of why.

'Margaret and I came to stay with our uncle and aunt and never left,' she explained. She found herself telling him about the Pooles, about how she gradually realized she wanted to be a nurse.

'So – I trained at Muddley Road, as we call it. Dudley Road Hospital to most people. And I volunteered to change over to the First Southern General as soon as the war began. That's about it. Please – tell me about yourself.'

She listened in amazement as Fergus Reid told her, quickly, quietly, with no bombast, about his life. He seemed fond of his parents and sister Isobel, had grown up in Fife, in Auchtermuchty. He had trained in Edinburgh, and was employed at the Edinburgh Asylum before working his way to Australia as a ship's surgeon. After that he studied in Frankfurt and was then taken on by the National Hospital for Nervous Diseases in London. As he talked, modestly but with a keen interest in the subject he loved, Annie, herself now nearly twenty-nine, saw that he must be close on ten years older than herself. He had a long, serious face, but which flared into animated life while he was talking. By the time he had finished she was deeply impressed. More than impressed.

'Another?' he asked, getting up. The thought of more of the blackcurrant was not especially inviting, but she nodded.

'I was well settled in London,' he said, once seated back at the table again. 'Thought I'd be there for life, more or less. And then the war came along.' He leaned an elbow on the table and gave a smile which somehow reached into her. There was a vividness to the man, an intensity. 'I

182

wonder how many conversations over the years will contain that statement. "And then the war came along . . ."'

'It's certainly changing a lot of things – there are women police now and there was a woman selling the tickets on the tram I came into town on,' Annie said. In spite of everything she still felt vaguely shocked by this. She seldom travelled by tram. 'So, they sent you here?'

'Yes – for now. I suspect it won't be my last billet. I spent a couple of months in Manchester. Of course, most of our work now is being directed into trauma – head and spinal injuries, paralysis and so on.'

'There've been the most terrible injuries,' she said. To her astonishment, for a second she felt she might weep, there and then. The tears swelled in her, memories of some of the lads she had nursed, what had been done to them. She knew that he would understand, would not see this as out of place, and yet she desperately did not want to give in to it. She looked down, finding herself unable to speak.

'You nurses spend more time with them,' he said gently. 'Some patients I see repeatedly, of course, try to patch them up the best we can and get to the bottom of their symptoms. But nurses – day after day. I suppose they talk to you?'

'Yes.' She took another sip of the punishing blackcurrant, trying to gather her emotions. 'Especially on nights.'

'Is that not very nice?' He pointed at her glass.

Annie hesitated. 'In fact,' she admitted, wrinkling her nose, 'it's really quite unpleasant.'

'Look –' He leaned over, holding out his glass. Closer to her, she found his physical presence fascinating, enlivening. If he had got up and left, in that moment, the room would have felt dead to her. 'I'm not a tool of the Devil – why don't you have a taste?'

183

It seemed such a little thing but it cut against everything she had been brought up to believe, as if he really was the very serpent, plotting to lure her out of Eden. He was so seductive, so . . . But oh, my goodness, what was the harm? People were going out getting their limbs shot off and worse and here was she being prissy about taking a sip from a glass! Hadn't she always believed you must face things, not retreat?

'All right.' She sat up, very formal, and took the glass, steeling herself.

Fergus sat back and burst out laughing so merrily that she could only join in. 'It's not hemlock, you know! It's the great drink of my nation – a taste of heaven. But it is *strong*. Don't do more than touch your lips to it. Taste and see!'

Annie leaned her head over the golden ring of liquid. The fumes were bad enough! She tilted the glass and let the whisky burn against her lips and into her mouth.

'Oh!' She spluttered once she had swallowed. 'That is *horrible*! It is the most . . . Ugh!' She took a quick sip of the blackcurrant which seemed quite benign in comparison. 'Lord above – how can you *drink* that?'

Fergus was laughing wholeheartedly now and their eyes met. How she liked the sound it. It was like something new opening out, filling her with a sense of joy and excitement. And she was gratified that she had made him laugh.

'If that's heaven,' she continued emphatically, 'I'll happily go to the other place!'

They travelled back to the hospital together after talking easily all evening, in the bar and then side by side on the tram. Fergus walked with her towards the nurse's quarters and as they parted, he said, with a bashfulness that moved her, 'I hope we can do this again, Annie. It's been a wonderful evening.'

She looked up at him, unable to remember an evening she had ever enjoyed as much. 'I'd like that,' she said.

Fergus hesitated and then, with a quick look round to check there was no one about, stepped closer.

'May I?' He laid his hand lightly on her shoulder and stooped to kiss her cheek, almost knocking her hat off so that they ended laughing.

'Goodbye,' Annie said, going off towards the entrance to her quarters.

'See you soon.' He stood watching and as she reached the door, she turned and he waved.

Twenty-Three

Spring 1916

Daisy sat in her attic room, propped against the pillow. At her breast, the little one sucked and sucked and Daisy could feel the power of it coursing through her. For a moment she bent her head back and breathed deeply in before letting out a long sigh.

The baby girl seemed to be the one with all the force for life that she once had herself. Even at birth she had weighed nearly eight pounds and she was hungry for every mouthful.

But now, at three months, she had picked up a cold and had been up and down all night, sniffling and wanting to suck for comfort, finding it a struggle because her nose was blocked and crying all over again. Daisy lay in a haze of exhaustion. At last, now morning had come, the child seemed to be able to suck more easily. The room stank of eucalyptus oil which Daisy had dripped on to a hanky.

'You,' she said, fond, yet close to tears as she looked down at the guzzling infant, 'will be the death of me. That you will.'

Pa had greeted her gently when she and Margaret returned to Birmingham. They had chosen to come home on a Sunday afternoon, when there would be fewer prying eyes about. Not even Mrs Flett was around at that time.

John and Lily ran into the house, delighted to be home. Daisy walked in carrying the baby, feeling utterly raw and strange. First of all she carried the child upstairs to give her a feed. She looked round at her bedroom as if at that of a child. Everything was familiar – the bed, the chest of drawers, the rug and chair unchanged, yet everything felt different, as if she had been away for a hundred years.

She perched on the edge of the bed suckling, holding her baby close and thinking how it would have been if she had come home without her. Tears spilled down her cheeks until she was sobbing, thinking of how she had almost let her go. Now it seemed utterly impossible.

Eventually she calmed herself and went shyly down to the back room, where they all drank tea. Daisy knew that Ma had sent a wire to her father to say what had happened so Philip showed no surprise. Lily had hardly been able to take her eyes off the baby and sat beside Daisy, gazing and talking to her. John, however, had soon declared that she was boring and paid her little attention.

So that now, as they sat together in these hours of privacy, there was a new tenderness in the air. There might be all sorts of trouble to face, but for the time being, Daisy was back home with her baby and both of them were alive and well.

'Well,' Pa said, also with an air of shyness. Once again Daisy realized she had become something new and more mysterious since having a child. 'You must have a name for her by now?'

'Yes,' Daisy said. 'She's called Hester.'

She saw a smile reach her father's eyes. 'Ah, Hester Bateman. Well, she was a fine English craftswoman. It's a good name.'

'Then after Mom – Florence.' She saw him wince

slightly and she felt that stab again. Florence, her mother. The loss she never managed to make up for no matter how hard she tried. 'And then Margaret.'

'Hester Florence Margaret Tallis.' He smiled. She could see how hard he was trying. 'I like that.'

Margaret quietly poured more tea, looking back and forth between them as if she could hardly believe that things sounded harmonious at last.

That night, he had actually come up to her room. She heard his tread, his hesitant tap on the door. She had just climbed into bed with Hester, who was already fast asleep after this exhausting day.

'Mind if I come in?' He stood looking round the door.

Then he saw her faint smile and came up close.

'Just thought I'd come and say goodnight.' He was shifting on his feet, bashful, and she could see that he was working up to something, trying to get used to everything. She was moved, still tearful herself.

Margaret had told Daisy that the night she had given birth, her father had suddenly seemed to fall apart. He wept and wept. Only then did Margaret realize just how frightened he had been all the time Daisy was carrying the baby. He was afraid he would lose her the way he had lost her mother. Seeing her alive, knowing the child was alive, had undone him.

And Pa had seen her at her lowest, seen what it had done to her, giving her baby away, no matter that that was what she had thought she wanted. But what trouble she had brought to their door!

'It's not going to be easy for you, Dais,' he said. Your moth— Margaret's got her ideas about how we're all going to play it. But there's some'll guess, I'm sure.'

'I'll have to take what comes.' Angrily, she added, 'It wasn't all my fault.'

'There's many'll say it was.'

There was a silence. Her father looked distraught, as if he had got off on the wrong foot.

'I'm sorry, Pa,' she whispered, looking up at him. She couldn't explain how lost she felt.

'Oh, Daisy.' He softened and sank down on to her bed. 'Other than your mother dying the way she did, there's nothing in my life I've ever wished away like I have this. But . . .' He eyed the dark-haired little creature lying in the crook of her arm. Dark hair very like that of her father, of whom no one now ever spoke a word. 'Now she's here . . .' He lowered his head and she was moved to see that he was close to weeping again. 'It brings back when you were a little one.'

And his kindness after all this time made her cry herself. She seemed to be one long blart during those days.

She had had to take up her work at Vittoria Street again, feeling she could not stay away any longer when they were so short-staffed. She knew she could just about manage a couple of hours away from Hester, in the afternoon. Her first day back, walking nervously into the school, still sore, still bleeding and so self-conscious it felt as if all the world was accusing her, almost the first person she met that afternoon was the head of the school, Arthur Gaskin.

'Ah, Miss Tallis!' His tone was fatherly and held genuine pleasure at seeing her. 'How delighted we are to have you back!' He came closer and Daisy flinched inwardly. Was it all over her – could he smell her? Her own physical experiences of Hester were so intense that it felt to her as if everyone could see into her, what she had done, the state of her body. As Mr Gaskin looked into her eyes, she felt the aching tingle as milk let down into her breasts and she blushed painfully, praying that she had padded her clothes enough to soak it up. 'Are you well recovered now, my dear?'

'Yes, thank you, Mr Gaskin,' she muttered, all confusion. She stared at the buttons on her boots. They all thought she had been suffering from a bad chest.

'I can tell you it's a godsend you're taking back these two classes. Of course, with the war going the way it is, we can see change coming – we may have to take on war work very soon – but classes are battling on more or less as usual at the moment, even though we have lost more staff . . . Mr Carson on the silversmithing side, of course . . .'

Even the mention of his name made Daisy feel that he must have guessed. But he could not know, could he? Things could not go on like this: she had to take hold of the situation. She looked up and into Arthur Gaskin's kindly eyes.

'Is there any news of Mr Carson?' she said coolly.

'I believe he was sent to one of the local battalions,' he said rather vaguely. It suddenly dawned on Daisy that Mr Gaskin did not have much time for Mr Carson either. For some reason this made her feel slightly better. 'I imagine he might have been posted to France by now, but I am not, as they say, in the know.' He smiled faintly and she managed to smile back.

Once she was in the classroom, she got on reasonably well. In one way she was more relaxed now than before, when she had been in a constant state of anxiety about someone noticing her condition, even though they were all young lads and girls who would not have had much idea of these things. But by the end of the class all she could hear in her head was Hester's hungry screams.

By the time she got home, her breasts were aching and she felt one sticky, horrible mess of milk and blood. She was close to tears. I can't do this! she thought. How can I go on like this? But go on she had to – unless she wanted to give up everything, lose everything she had had in her life before. Because she knew she had to hold on to the threads of that life, of the old Daisy Tallis, whoever she had been, who wanted to make her pa proud – and her mother. Somehow, she still had to live up to Florence Tallis and not disappoint everyone.

When she was alone, going to Vittoria Street or about the place, things were, outwardly, much as before. When she, or she and Margaret, took Hester out in the perambulator, everyone gave the appearance of assuming that the baby belonged to her stepmother and if they were whispering behind their hands, at least no one said anything to their faces.

Within the house it was a different matter. It was entirely obvious to most of the staff in the business and Muriel Allen had given her some hard looks, the dry old stick. Edith Taylor, however, although she didn't make any comment, had been extra kind to her.

'Oh!' she cried when she first saw Daisy holding Hester – for Daisy had said she would not spend her time hiding upstairs. 'Isn't she a little love?'

Edith came and bent over Hester, her already sweet face softening even more. She looked up at Daisy and all her confusion showed for an instant. All those questions and comments – *Where did this baby come from? Who is the father? This is shameful, awful* – showed in her face in those seconds. But she swallowed them down and smiled again.

'Oh, Daisy, she's lovely. I'm longing for the time I can rock my own baby in my arms. May I have a hold?'

191

Warmed by this, Daisy handed Hester over and, placid child that she was, she looked up wonderingly at Edith. They had always got on well, but from then on Daisy felt that Edith was her firm ally, however shocked she might secretly be about the sudden appearance of this baby.

Of course she knew the staff must be whispering behind her back, and might be talking outside as well, but Daisy found she did not much care. She knew her father's staff had liked her before and now there was nothing she – or they – could do about any of it. Any trouble from them and they all knew they could be out of a job. The same applied next door at number twenty-six.

The only person who spoke to her directly about it was Mrs Flett. Daisy had carried Hester down to the kitchen after her feed the first morning, much in need of a cup of tea herself. Her heart pounded hard when she saw Mrs Flett – a stooped, bespectacled figure now, in her apron, stirring something on the range – and she could feel herself blushing.

She came over without a word and looked at Hester. There was that same softening in her old face on seeing the infant and she looked up at Daisy with a smile – though a sad and complicated one.

'I'll say this now, Daisy and get it off my chest. I'd never've expected you to come home shamed in this fashion with no ring on yer finger, for all you've always been headstrong. But I do know I'm not party to the full story and it's always the woman takes the blame. Your stepmother's a fine person and 'er's stood by yer as many wouldn't. And I know I'm only a servant, but I've grown to be as fond of you as my own. So – I may not like it, but you won't 'ave no trouble from me. I'd've done anything for your mother and I'd do the same for you bab.'

'Oh, Mrs Flett,' Daisy said emotionally.

'If you need help, I'm here.' Mrs Flett's eyes filled as well and they both had a little weep. 'She's a bonny babe though, I'll say that,' Mrs Flett added. ''Ere – you sit down and I'll brew some tea.'

Sitting in bed now, after this very broken night, she thought wearily of the day ahead. Apart from her teaching at the Jewellery School on three afternoons, when Margaret looked after Hester, she was helping out where she could in the Tallis business. But life had become so difficult! Even though she knew she was lucky beyond words to be protected, not to be thrown out in complete disgrace, oh, how frustrating life was! How could she ever do anything of her own work again?

Even though she had seen John and Lily as babies, she had not fully taken in what any of it meant. She had still somehow thought that you could just put infants down and carry on with your life as before. But even when Hester was asleep in her cradle she found it hard to separate her mind from her. And so often these days she did not have her hands free! Except for later in the day when John and Lily came home from school and Lily could not get enough of holding Hester.

Daisy loved Hester with a tiger-like devotion. Of course she did! But inside, she felt she would never be the same again. Never could she find that sailing confidence she had had before. She had been brought low, in disgrace, and broken open by another young life coming in to compete with her own. Daisy Tallis felt lost these days, and as though she was nobody very much.

She climbed stiffly out of bed, changed Hester's napkin and quickly dressed before carrying her downstairs.

Margaret was in the kitchen with Mrs Flett, who was peeling parsnips.

'You look a bit weary, dear,' Mrs Flett said.

'Bad night again?' Margaret asked, rather distractedly. John and Lily already seemed to have gone to school but she had plenty of other things to do. She came over and looked at Hester, laying two fingers along her forehead.

'She's a bit warm, isn't she? She'll settle. Just give her lots to drink.'

'Oh, she's getting plenty of that,' Daisy said, pouring a cup of tea. The lonely despair she had felt pacing up and down with Hester in the small hours of the night melted away now, hearing Margaret talking of all this as if it was quite normal. To her it had felt like the end of the world.

She was carrying the tea into their living room when there was a rumpus at the front door.

Margaret hurried to answer, calling, 'I'll go!' into the office. Opening up, she cried, 'Oh – Aunt Hatt! What's the matter?'

'I'll tell you what the matter is.' Aunt Hatt came stumping along the passage and into the back room, still wearing her coat and a fancy hat with a long, pointed feather. 'Oh –' she softened for a moment, coming to lean over Hester – 'what a love she is. She's a bit snuffly, Daisy. Is she all right? Now what you need to do, is . . .' Long instructions followed. 'And you're not to worry about Clara. I know she can be—'

'Aunt Hatt?' Margaret interrupted.

'The Derby Scheme!' Aunt Hatt launched in. 'Oh, yes, Mrs Flett, tea, please, strong as you like! You've heard, of course? Conscription!'

'Well, yes, of course I've . . .' Margaret began. 'It's been on the cards for ages . . .' But Aunt Hatt was in full flow.

'Clara's in a terrible state – thinks Georgie's going to join up any minute and leave us all, even though they're saying—'

'Ma!' None of them had heard the second knock and Georgie appeared from next door as well, looking really worked up. 'Will you *please* stop keeping on like this! I'm not joining up now – not this minute. They say it's only for men with no family – but all I said was, it's coming, I can feel it, and—'

'But yours is a *reserved occupation!*' Aunt Hatt cried, so wildly that she almost knocked the cup and saucer Mrs Flett was delivering to her across the room. 'Surely it is?'

Daisy was amazed by the change in Harriet Watts. She looked older suddenly, and vulnerable, holding her tea and sinking on to a chair.

Georgie seemed caught between anxiety at the thought of the call-up and shame that he was still here, as if someone might hand him a white feather at any moment.

'I can't say it is necessarily reserved,' he argued. 'Not with Pa here running the place and all the other staff – and the women are taking over now . . .' He too came over and smiled down at Hester, though with a certain embarrassment. 'Looking fine, isn't she?' he said in a shy way which warmed Daisy's heart.

'But that's no good at all!' Aunt Hatt erupted. 'Good God, the whole of Birmingham is tooling up for war and it's no good thinking they can leave it to a scrappy lot of women to run! It's bad enough them putting them out on the streets – in the police, I ask you! Whatever next?'

'All I said was—' Georgie tried to interrupt.

'You've got a weak chest, Georgie!' Aunt Hatt pronounced. 'You always did have a weak chest!'

Georgie put his hands on his hips, a helpless expression on his face. 'I *haven't*, Mom. You know I haven't had any problems with my chest since I was about nine years old. I don't want to go, but all I'm saying is, in the end I might have to.'

'Oh, heaven forbid!' Aunt Hatt said. 'I've got the most terrible feeling of dread. It's crouching on my chest like a . . . a . . . Don't let them take my only boy – oh, this wicked, terrible war.'

For a moment Daisy thought Aunt Hatt was going to burst into tears, but then she said, 'Well, I've had my say,' and subsided, helplessly, into sipping her tea.

But Georgie was right. Within two more months the government, desperate to fill their armies, extended the Military Service Act to married men.

The same scenes were enacted all over again the Sunday before he left, when the whole family was at the Wattses' house in Handsworth.

'I don't know whether to be proud or upset,' Clara said tearfully to Margaret.

Clara had been very cold to Daisy on the few times she had seen her through the pregnancy and Daisy knew that if had not been for Aunt Hatt, bossy Clara would have been the sort to turn against her. But today she had other things on her mind.

They all sat in the lavish sitting room, the glass doors open on to the spring garden. Clara looked out at her children, gambolling about with Georgie on the grass, and her face crumpled. 'He's got to go, I know. But he's my man and I don't know what I'm going to do without him.'

Twenty-Four

July 1916

Annie pulled on a cardigan over her summer frock, seized hold of her raincoat and hat, and tore out of the nurses' quarters towards the university's Great Hall. She pushed her straw hat on her head as she went, holding it on in the wind.

'Running again, Nurse Hanson?' one of the VADs who worked with her on the ward teased as Annie went dashing past. Running on the wards was forbidden but Annie always found it difficult to slow down and move in a measured way when under pressure.

Amid the line of ambulances and orderlies moving about them outside the main entrance, it took her a moment to identify Fergus, standing out of the way to one side of the door. He caught sight of her scurrying figure and came towards her smiling.

'Where's the fire?' he grinned.

'Oh, don't you start!' Annie said. She had been on duty non-stop for the last ten days. 'I'm so glad to get out of here for a bit.' She eyed the ambulances. 'It might be the last time for a while – let's make the most of it.'

'Ah, yes,' Fergus teased. 'Wine, women and song?'

'Oh, *stop* it!' But she was so delighted to see him. More than she could ever have imagined feeling about any man.

*

Their times together had been few over the past six months. But ever since that first evening in the Queen's Hotel – a man, a hotel bar and a sip of whisky all in one night, good heavens! – her barriers had been falling one by one until Annie had had to admit to herself that she was falling helplessly in love with this interesting, attractive, maddening man. A man who made her do all sorts of things she had vowed she never would, who would sit and talk to her for hours, whose face she had come to look out for in any crowd as the face she loved.

After their first evening together, it had felt an age until they managed to get time off at the same time again. In six months, there had been few occasions when they had been able to meet away from the hospital in the evening. Otherwise they managed a few snatched conversations in passing or out in the grounds. But this pressure, this scarcity, had lit their emotions all the faster.

On their outings they had been into Birmingham, wanting a change from Selly Oak, where they otherwise spent all their time. She had shown him the city – the Bull Ring and Town Hall, the streets of factories where the air rang with sounds of metal crashing on metal and filled the nostrils with grit. Fergus was interested in everything. And he was gentlemanly, kissing her on the cheek as they parted. But following their third time out together, after they had got back to the hospital and she was in her room, half undressed, there was a tap on her bedroom door. Startled, she picked up her dress and held it against her.

'It's all right – it's only me.' Hilda, one of the other nurses, put her head round the door. She was rather a prim girl and her expression seemed caught between solemnity and disapproval. 'Dr Reid is outside. He seemed rather concerned and says he needs your assistance with something.'

For a second Annie felt horribly guilty and self-conscious. During her training one nurse had been expelled for going out with a man, thanks to another starchy and righteous nurse who had reported her. It even crossed Annie's mind that, until she met Fergus, she might have been the sort of person who would have reported someone in that way herself . . .

But what had she done wrong? Nothing. And perhaps it was indeed a medical emergency.

'Gracious,' she said, frowning. 'I wonder what's happened? I'll go straight away. Thank you, Hilda.'

Hilda backed out of the room still looking suspicious, and Annie, about to put the dress on, thought again and pulled her uniform on instead. It had sounded as if it might be serious, whatever it was. She took her cloak and crept outside.

In the darkness, she saw his tall figure, outlined by the light of the spring moon.

'Dr Reid?' she said cautiously.

'Ah, Nurse Hanson.' His voice was low, but formal, urgent. 'I must apologize for disturbing you – could you come with me a moment, please?'

'Of course.'

He didn't take her arm or explain and hurried along, she trotting beside him to keep up.

'Has a new convoy arrived?' she asked, wondering if they were short-handed.

'Come this way.' Now he did steer her by the arm, but away from the main hospital.

'Where on earth . . . ?'

'Shh,' he said abruptly, adding in a whisper, 'We don't know who's listening.'

Soon they were crossing the green space of the grounds

behind the university, heading for the trees fringing the edge.

'Just stop!' Annie halted abruptly, getting annoyed now. 'What are we doing? I don't like being pushed about like this.'

'Annie.' Fergus turned to her, glancing about him. All seemed quiet. 'Don't you trust me?'

'Well, I did,' she said crossly. 'But I thought you needed help on the wards, and now you're dragging me off into the bushes – what am I supposed to think?'

'God, woman,' he said. His voice was quiet, she heard the change in it. 'Can't you see? This is what I have to do to be alone with you for five minutes. I see you in the hospital – or these snatched meetings in town – and there's never . . .' He looked away for a second, as if steeling himself, then back at her face in the darkness. His face was completely in shadow, but even so, she could sense how intensely he was looking at her. 'All I can think about is holding you in my arms.'

Annie gasped. 'Oh, my goodness!' She gave a shaky laugh. 'So is that—?'

She never had a chance to finish because Fergus pulled her close. It was nothing like all the things she had dreaded. She was moved by him, loved him, even the strangeness of feeling a man's lips on hers, the prickle of his moustache, the way he stroked the back of her neck, so softly, and held her. She was amazed at her own passion, her kissing him back as if she was born to it. They stood for she didn't know how long, holding and kissing. By the time they walked back together, hand in hand and both in something like a dreamlike state, they had exchanged pledges of love, of the future.

'Thank you for luring me out,' she whispered, as they

neared the nurses' rooms. She gave a quiet giggle. 'You're so *naughty*.'

Fergus looked down at her. 'Oh, Annie,' was all he said, but his voice was full of tenderness. 'My lovely Annie.'

It was such a relief to be away from the hospital, from the prying eyes and regulations. Another evening had become possible and they stood on the crowded tram, pressed close together, smiling at each other, quiet while there were so many other people to listen in.

As they stepped down in town, the heard, 'Get yer *Gazette*!'

'Oh, let's get a paper,' Annie said. 'I haven't seen one for days.'

Fergus handed over a halfpenny and they stood back out of the moving crowds and pored over the front page there in the street.

'"An impenetrable wall of steel,"' Fergus read. '"What was done at Loos in the way of breaking through almost on the first onslaught is not likely to be accomplished again during this year when the Germans have been taking most diligent advantage of months of immobility to strengthen their defences . . ."'

He stopped and looked at Annie. His eyes were troubled. For a moment, neither of them said anything. Then he smiled and took her arm.

'Let's enjoy the evening, while we've got the chance. Now – can I tempt you to a dram of our very best malt whisky this evening, Miss Hanson?'

'No, you blasted well can't,' she said, grimacing at him. 'What I really, *desperately* need, is a nice hot cup of tea!'

Fergus laughed wholeheartedly and Annie loved the

sound of it. 'You really know how to let your hair down, don't you? Well, we'll see what we can do.'

That evening in the Queen's Hotel, talking, laughing, discreetly touching hands as often as possible, Fergus's loving eyes looking into hers, was the most precious memory, something Annie had to cling to for the rest of that terrible month. Because following that night, the day's pace of exhausting busyness in the hospital accelerated rapidly.

Gradually, everyone became aware of the calamity that had been the first day of the offensive on the Somme. The newspaper columns of the dead multiplied so shockingly that people stared at them in disbelief. Mourning bands and memorials and black crêpe appeared more and more across the city.

At the First Southern General, the casualties poured in through Selly Oak station, telephones ringing, station parties waiting with stretchers, blankets and pillows, the St John's Ambulance Brigade and extra volunteers sorting the walking wounded into transports and carrying the stretchers to the waiting wagons bound for the hospital. Then came the process of settling them into beds on the wards, praying there would be enough space; the shock at some of the wounds, the poor lads so grateful to be out of it, to be looked after.

'We'll need even more beds,' Annie said to Susannah as the trickle seemed to be growing into a flood.

Susannah whispered to her, eyes full of horror, 'If these are the ones who came through – how many dead must there be?'

A great many – they were already beginning to know. On and on the battles went.

There was not much time for emotion. Annie sank into

dreamless, exhausted sleep whenever she got the chance. They worked and worked. Sometimes she saw Fergus in passing in the corridors and the smiles they gave each other, the occasional snatched squeeze of a hand, gave energy to her exhausted limbs and often heavy heart.

There were young men from all over the place: Australians, Canadians, lads from Belgium and Serbia. And some local. On arrival, the first question they asked, in whatever language they could, was, 'Where am I?' And a lucky few were alight with happiness when they were from the area and found they had been brought to Birmingham.

One evening, once things had calmed down, Annie was doing a round of observations, taking temperatures and pulses, having a word or two with each patient. The beds were crammed so close together that she had bruises all down her shins from clambering about making beds and seeing to her patients.

In a row right in the middle of the Great Hall, she saw that another patient had arrived and was recovering from surgery. As she approached she glanced at him, then focused on him more closely. He seemed somehow familiar.

She looked down the list they were compiling of the new patients and a name jumped out at her. She looked back at him. Yes – it was!

His eyes were closed. His face looked sunken and the top half of his body was swathed in bandages, but he was breathing evenly. The cropped hair made his handsome, strong-boned face look thinner than she remembered.

'Hello?'

She glanced down at the list again. She wasn't mistaken? No, it definitely said Dennis Poole.

'Den?'

His eyes opened then. For a moment utter terror flickered across his features, before he took in where he was. His licked his lips.

'Who're . . . ?' He looked intently. 'Are you . . . Miss Hanson?'

She smiled, suddenly overjoyed to see him.

'Yes! And Den, you're in Birmingham – did you know?'

'Ar,' he said vaguely. 'Think so.'

'What happened?' she said.

'Can't remember, really.' He frowned. 'They said I've got a chest full of metal.'

'Well – not any more, perhaps,' Annie smiled. 'You've been operated on. Are you comfortable?'

'Could do with some water.'

She helped him raise his head and sip a little.

'Will yer tell our Lizzie I'm 'ere?'

'I'll try,' she said, thinking she would have to write – there seemed no time ever to go anywhere at the moment. 'You carry on resting – that's the best thing you can do.'

'Nurse?' He reached out a hand as she was about to walk away.

'Yes, what is it?'

'Will yer . . . I mean, I'd like Daisy to know I'm . . . to see her?'

'Daisy?' She stared down at him, trying to work out this surprising request. Even though Den and Daisy had known each other since they were thrown together as children, she had never thought of them as being close in any way. Of course, Den would have no idea what had happened to Daisy over the last months. Perhaps he just wanted to see another familiar face.

'What about Lizzie and Ivy?' she said.

'Ar – them an' all. But Daisy,' he insisted. 'Ask 'er, will yer?'

Twenty-Five

Daisy stepped down from the tram into the sunshine of the Bristol Road.

Setting out from home on this mysterious mission to the hospital, she had had to leave Hester with Margaret again. As she walked along towards the turning, she felt her spirits lift. Oh, it was nice to be out on her own, to be free again and go somewhere different! Her youthful days of being able to take off wherever she liked in her spare time – wandering through the Rag Market or the shops in New Street – had come abruptly to an end. Her only other reason for leaving Hester now was to teach her classes. They sometimes went out to the Wattses' house with all the children at weekends, but otherwise she felt she had been chained to the same four walls for an eternity.

Walking up the road to the university, as trucks, motor cycles and ambulances came and went, she felt a surge of well-being. Her young body had healed from Hester's birth and though she was still feeding her, those urgent, unpredictable rushes of milk had slowed to something steadier. Striding along in her blue-and-white frock, feeling the breeze through the straw of her hat, she began to feel almost young again.

But as she reached the entrance to the hospital, with its huge, imposing buildings, nerves began to take over. The note from Annie which had arrived yesterday was in her pocket. When it arrived she had been doing some work

205

in the office for Pa, while Hester was asleep after a morning feed.

Aunt Hatt had drifted into the office, as she seemed to do more and more often these days. Georgie being called up had made her restless with worry all the time and she always wanted someone to talk with to take her mind off it.

'I never know whether to dread the post arriving these days,' she exclaimed, perched on a chair as Miss Allen brought in the day's letters. 'At least I know Georgie's safe while he's still here training. I hope they keep training him right 'til the end of the war!'

'I don't think any bad news comes in letters anyway, does it?' Margaret said, eyeing the clutch of post. 'I thought they sent a telegram.'

'Yes.' Aunt Hatt's plump face sank into woe. 'Mrs Illingworth, along the road from us . . . A son and a nephew . . .' She fanned her face with a sheet of card from the desk. 'I just didn't know what to say to her.'

'This is for you, Daisy.' Margaret held out the envelope, then looked at it more closely again, frowning. 'That looks like Annie's writing. How odd.'

Daisy opened it immediately.

'Den Poole in hospital here,' Annie had scrawled, evidently in a great hurry. 'Wants you to visit. Come as soon as possible, Daisy – he's on the ward in the Great Hall at present. Love to all, Annie.'

'Den Poole?' Aunt Hatt's brow wrinkled. 'Oh, yes – of course! Mary Poole – how could I forget? Oh, he must be injured. But he's got plenty of family of his own – why would he want to see you, Daisy?'

'I don't really know,' Daisy said. She felt uneasy. She remembered the last time she saw Den, almost outside James Carson's house, but could hardly recall anything about it. He had said he was leaving, but she had been so wrapped up in James Carson, she had barely given it a thought. And, she realized with a pang of guilt, she never had written to him as he asked her to.

'You'd better go,' Margaret said. 'If Annie's found the time to write to you it must be important. It's Saturday tomorrow, you can go then.'

She was humbled by the place. The buildings were enormous and grand, the corridors echoing with activity, orderlies and nurses hurrying about, telephones ringing. Suddenly she felt small and rather useless.

'Are you lost, miss?' A middle-aged man in a St John's Ambulance uniform asked her. When she explained, he pointed: 'Just keep going along here. It's the biggest room – can't miss it.'

She paused in the doorway. It was like walking into a church, something she scarcely ever did in any case. A long room with a beautiful, arching ceiling and alcoves all along the sides, culminating in the bright, curved glory of a stained-glass window. Had the room been empty, she might have stood for a while and taken in the beauty of it.

However, before her was a packed array of beds, four deep across the floor, a corridor up the middle, with a little table on which stood a fern in a pot, and a nurse's desk to one side. She could feel the eyes of some of the men beginning to take her in and she started to feel self-conscious. Nurses bustled about, a small number of men were also on their feet and more and more heads began to turn. She heard a low, appreciative whistle which seemed to be coming in her direction across the room.

'Daisy!' Annie appeared, walking towards her at high speed. 'I'm glad you came.'

'Oh, hello.' She smiled, relieved to see Annie. She was

struck by the sight of her. Annie had always looked unusual – a vivacious, impish face and those big, dancing eyes. But Annie had always been so occupied with rushing about helping the poor and generally trying to be virtuous that there had also been a drabness about her. Now though, she looked changed. Her face, under the white veil, was glowing with life and she beamed at Daisy. She did not kiss her as usual, though – she was on duty.

Daisy was about to ask why Den wanted to see her, but Annie was already talking.

'Lizzie's here at the moment – his sister. Remember her?' Daisy did, though they did not really know each other. 'I know she's got to rush back and look after little Ann – the baby. As you have, of course.'

Daisy wondered if she heard disapproval in Annie's tone. She must think very badly of me, she thought, being so religious. Annie had always been like a missionary. But she had spoken matter-of-factly, her face giving nothing away. 'Come along – you'd best come and say hello.'

As they walked down one side of the ward, Daisy now began to take in the smells of the place on this warm day: whiffs of private, bodily things, something sickly, iodine and sweat and disinfectant. She began to feel queasy, not at anything she actually saw or smelt but at the thought of what might be underneath the bedclothes of that man, lying so still, his face wrapped in bandages, or another with a cage over his legs holding the sheet and blankets away from his legs. And Den – what state was Den in? She felt sweat prickle under her arms.

'Annie,' she said desperately. 'Before I see Den – what's happened to . . . ?'

But it was too late. They stopped by a bed in the middle section of the ward and she saw Lizzie Poole's slender figure perched on a chair beside it, leaning to rest

208

her hands on the mattress as she talked. And in the bed, Den, catching sight of her so that Lizzie turned to look as well. Lizzie, Annie's old workmate from the pen factory, was a pale, sweet-natured girl who now only looked a little older than the way Daisy remembered her.

'Oh, Annie – it's time I was going.' She stood up and smiled, though Daisy could see the tension in her face. 'Hello, Miss Daisy,' she said shyly. 'It's very nice of yer to come and see our Den.'

Daisy murmured that it was no trouble, but Lizzie was already saying to Annie, ''E don't look too bad, Annie, though I hope he'll be better soon. Least I know where 'e is, though, as 'e's in 'ere.'

'He's going to be all right, Lizzie,' Annie told her.

Daisy felt Den's eyes fixed on her, but it was not until Lizzie had said her goodbyes and she and Annie had walked away together, that Daisy dared look him in the face. She stood by the bed, not knowing what to say. His hair was army short, face unblemished except for one small dressing on his left cheek. But his chest and arms, all lying outside the bedclothes, were bandaged and he lay very still as if moving caused him pain.

''Ello, Dais,' he said. His voice was quiet. Perhaps it hurt him to breathe. 'Sit down, will yer?'

She obeyed, trying to pull herself together. Heat rose in her body. The place was beginning to make her feel faint. She lowered her head for a moment.

'You all right?' Den asked.

'Yes.' She took a deep breath and looked up, feeling truly foolish. Here was Annie working all the time, and Den injured and she could barely cope with a visit. 'How are you, Den? What . . . what happened?'

'I, er . . .' He looked vague for a moment. 'I 'ave a job remembering exactly. Last thing was . . .' He had to keep pausing to draw in a breath. 'I was by the gun – I'm in the Machine Gun Corps, see . . .'

'Where?' Daisy said. She knew so little of France, of where anything was.

'Some place called Serre. The Somme. Attached to the Terriers . . .'

'Have you had an operation? Perhaps you shouldn't talk if it hurts.'

Den shook his head, then nodded faintly. His eyes seemed about to close, but he forced them open and gazed at her.

'It's all right. But there's a bit they can't get. Shrapnel. I was full of it. I got knocked for six.'

'Oh,' Daisy said. She did not know what to do or say. 'Are you comfortable here?' she asked.

'Yeah.' He swallowed, looked away a moment. 'Mom died. After I left. Nurse Annie were there – it's a comfort having her 'ere.'

Oh, heaven, Daisy thought. I'd clean forgotten. She felt very badly. How could she have been so wrapped up in herself, so selfish? Only now she remembered fully why Lizzie was so burdened, what had happened. Lizzie's own problems made hers look very pale in comparison. Not just losing her mother but having the baby to look after and her other sisters, and the house to take care of – all while trying to keep a wage coming in.

'I'm ever so sorry, Den. Poor you – and your sisters.'

He grimaced. 'Yeah. I feel bad. I just went – never even knew 'er was having the babby . . .'

Tears ran down the sides of his cheeks suddenly and his face crumpled. But the sobs that wanted to rise in him hurt so much that she could see him struggling not to give rein to them.

'Oh, Den!' Moved, she gently took the hand nearest to

her that was lying on the counterpane. It felt large and strong, and he grasped her hand with surprising force. She saw him fight to compose himself. He was brave, she thought. A brave man.

'I wanted to see yer,' he said. 'Wanted to see your face looking at me.'

Tears rose in her eyes. He seemed so young, a child that had lost its mother, while so old and battle-hardened already. The pages and pages of deaths from the Somme belied the cheerful headlines which had made it sound as if the battle was going well. More and more households had lost someone, felled on the Somme.

'There's a lad over there . . .' Den nodded faintly. 'Trained with us . . . Horace, his name is.'

'Oh?' she said. 'How is he?'

'Not so good,' Den said. 'Poorly, he is. But I can't get out to see him – not yet. Would you go, after? Say hello from me?'

Though appalled by the thought, she nodded. 'Course, Den. Of course I will.'

'How you been, Daisy?'

He still had hold of her hand, and now it felt too intimate and she would have liked to pull away. He had tilted his head to look into her eyes. She wanted badly to lie, to say all was good, that she was working, making lovely things, winning prizes for her smithing – that she was the old Daisy Tallis who was going somewhere. Not the humbled, shamed person she felt. She lowered her eyes. The truth trembled behind her lips, but she could not tell him.

'Dais – what's up?'

'Nothing!' She raised her head, forcing a smile. 'I'm all right. Everything's perfectly all right – except for the war, of course, I mean.'

Den was watching her. She saw his eyes begin to close

211

once more, as if he was losing the battle to stay awake, but he forced them open again.

'That's good.' He spoke faintly and she had to lean closer to hear him. She smelt the disinfectant from his bandages. 'It's nice. Things being good ... being the same.' He was fading into sleep. 'You just stay the same, Daisy ...'

It wounded her, the sad way he said it. And even more, his belief that she was somehow pure and unchangeable. Her face burned, but he did not see it. She desperately did not want him to know of her shame and embarrassment. She felt terribly stirred up, as if she needed to weep and weep.

'I'd better go,' she said stiffly, feeling she might break down if he said anything else and pour out everything that had happened.

'Come again?' Den pleaded.

Standing up, not meeting his eyes, she nodded. 'I'll try.'

'And say hello to Horace from me, will yer?'

'All right.' Going and speaking to another wounded boy was the last thing she felt like, but she knew she must agree.

Den seemed to be sinking into sleep again. But as she gathered herself to leave, getting to her feet, she heard him murmur something.

'I can't hear you, Den?'

She leaned down. He did not open his eyes but must have sensed her shadow close to him.

'I've always loved yer, Dais – you know that, don't yer?'

She straightened, quickly, in shock. She was not sure exactly what he meant – in love with her, or what exactly?

His eyes opened then and met hers, with a look of such devotion that suddenly she felt the prickling of tears, because it was sweet, hearing someone say they loved you – and it was something she thought no one would ever say to her now.

'Well – thanks, Den . . .' She forced her lips to smile. 'See you soon, eh?'

But he reached out and seized her hand with startling force.

'Love me back, Daisy? Say yer love me?'

'I . . .' She floundered. What could she say? Annie had said Den would be all right, but how could she be sure? How could she deny him?

'Course, Den,' she said lightly. 'Of course I love you.'

His face settled into a relaxed joy. 'Come and see me again soon, won't yer?'

She wandered along the rows of beds in the direction he had indicated. Some of the lads lay prostrate, asleep. Others watched her curiously and one or two, daring to be cheeky, called out to her.

'Eh!' The voice had a foreign accent she could not recognize. 'Come and sit with me, pretty lady!'

She smiled faintly, but she was beginning to realize she had no idea how to identify this Horace person when Annie came back to rescue her.

'Where're you off to, Daisy?'

'Oh . . .' She turned gratefully. 'Den sent me to send his good wishes to a Horace Sanders. Can you show me where he is?'

Annie's face became grave and she gave a tiny shake of her head. She drew on Daisy's arm. 'Come with me a minute, dear.'

They stood to the side of the echoing corridor as orderlies and nurses passed back and forth.

'I'm afraid Horace died last night,' Annie told her. 'His wounds were worse than they had thought.'

'Oh,' Daisy said. 'Oh, God.' She dissolved into tears, then tried to control herself. The war came up close, battering her with its realities. 'Is Den going to die?'

'It's been touch and go,' Annie told her. 'When they operated they found he has a piece of metal lodged an inch from his heart. It's too close to go in there and get it out. So we're hoping . . .' She shrugged.

This was her every day, Daisy saw, with awe. Until now, everything going on across all those battlefields felt to her mysterious, far away. And suddenly here were these boys, these broken bodies. And when she walked away from Den, was that the last time she was to see him? Thank heaven she had said something kind to him, even if it was a lie.

She forced down the urge to sob and sob, and wiped her eyes.

'It was nice that you came, Daisy. 'Annie smiled and touched her shoulder. 'Pop in and see him again, eh?'

Twenty-Six

August 1916

Sitting in the office in Chain Street on a hot, muggy after-noon, Margaret bent her head over the books, perspiring and struggling to concentrate.

Edith Taylor came and laid a sheaf of orders in front of her.

'Thank you, dear.' Margaret glanced up at her.

Edith was an attractive young woman with honey-blonde hair, and of a cheerful disposition. But Margaret could not help noticing how pale and strained she looked. Her fiancé, Arthur, was an artificer in the merchant navy and Margaret knew she had barely a moment when she was not worried to death about him. As if the wind and sea were not enough to fret about, now there were the German U-boats prowling the waters. Even Margaret found it almost too terrible to think about.

She dragged her mind to the orders Edith had put before her, eyeing the top one. MIZPAH again. It really was proving popular, one of their bestselling lines now. Clara was wearing a brooch version, two interlocking silver hearts with the word MIZPAH across them in ornate writing and delicately entwined round with flowers. Georgie had given it to her when he went to begin his training and Margaret could see how much it meant to her.

It was a good job the MIZPAH line of brooches and bracelets and lockets had been such a success, because the jewellery trade had shrunk back and so many of the staff had gone off into the forces. They had taken on a number of women to replace them where they could, three of them girls quite newly trained at Vittoria Street and wanting new positions. Thank heaven old Tom was still here to do drop stamping. The whole atmosphere of the place was shifting and they all had to adjust.

As the months passed, factory after factory in Birmingham was going over to the war effort. 'Total war,' they were calling it. The city was like one great, throbbing machine of war production. There were the big munitions firms like the BSA in Small Heath, making Lewis guns by the thousand, Kynoch's in Witton who made explosives, where Lizzie Poole had now found work, and the Mills grenade factory at Aston. As well as these there were countless other smaller ones. And the jewellery trade was trying to do its share. This great concentration of precision skills was adapting to turning out small parts to help bigger firms meet the targets demanded by the hungry government war machine. Uncle Eb's workshop next door, as well as still making jewellery, had taken on war work, producing huge numbers of brass tapes to go into bomb fuses.

And now 'Philip Tallis, Silversmiths' was about to embark on war work of its own. A couple of weeks ago, Philip and the others had rearranged the workshop, moving the workbenches with their pegs closer together and further towards the back of the workshop to make room for a lathe at the front end. A select few of the workforce – all female – had been trained up to make small components for a factory in Oldbury, tooled up now to make the new armoured vehicle called a tank.

216

They were told it was a thing with caterpillar tracks instead of wheels which enabled it to travel across the mud and other rough ground. Margaret knew that Philip loathed this new development. He scowled every time the thing was mentioned, but they all felt they must do something to support the war effort.

She started to sort the orders, but her mind was on other things. Daisy was so quiet these days, so closed in on herself, that she did not know what was going through her mind. The girl looked exhausted. Of course, Daisy was having to face up to real life with a baby and no one was going to give her any prizes for *that*, Margaret thought drily. And naturally, a lot of attention was now focused on little Hester . . . Sure enough, even though she had been trying to think about whether Daisy was in fact all right and whether she should be worried about her, her musings were interrupted by the squeaking sounds of a small child waking up in the back room.

'Oh – shall I go and get her?' Edith's face cleared and she looked quite happy for a moment. But already they were treated to a back view of Muriel Allen's grey hair in a tightly pinned bun, disappearing through the door. Edith shrugged and made a half-comical face at Margaret, as if to say, *Who would have thought?*

They heard Miss Allen making fussety noises and then she appeared with Hester on her bony hip, wide-eyed and fresh from her nap. Miss Allen, who before Hester's arrival had always seemed a dour character, was all smiles. She had not had much to do with Margaret's own children. But it seemed as if, whatever they thought about Hester's origins, the little girl was so endearing that she now belonged to everyone.

'Here we are,' Miss Allen cooed.

'Now, now, ladies, back to work,' Mr Henshaw said,

looking up over his specs. But though he tried to look superior and disapproving at all this female baby talk, his eyes softened at the sight of the little girl.

Hester was a captivating child, now more than seven months old. Looking at her you would scarcely have known Daisy was her mother. She had hair of a rich, liquorice brown, sallow skin and large brown eyes. She was a sturdy, forceful little character but cheerful, with a gurgling laugh that made all the staff melt and which John and Lily both tried to make her produce as often as possible.

It was such a relief that this little girl seemed to have added to the family in a happy way – or that was how Margaret felt, anyway. Even Philip would chuckle hearing her.

For weeks now the lists – such lists – of casualties from the Somme had come rolling inexorably in. They were pored over by all those who had sons and husbands, lovers and brothers at the Front. All they could be sure of was that their name was not in the paper – not today. It left a refuge of relief and hope for a few hours, then a building anxiety as the time approached to see the next day's list.

The lads who had come home on leave didn't speak much. Once they had been out in France, it was as if they didn't know what to say, or wanted to put it out of their minds. Not like when they were still here and training. Clara had said Georgie told her all about it, then, about the hard bits and the pranks. Aunt Hatt and the family had celebrated his leave days as if it were Christmas. Georgie looked different already, his hair cropped, his face thinner. He made jokes about it all, had his children scrambling over him, played football with Jimmy. And then he was gone, to France – after only three months.

And all they knew at home were fragments they were given by the newspapers – battles and the names of foreign places in France, Turkey, the east . . . And trenches, shells, gas. Terrible words whose reality they could not take in.

Yet here, in the midst of it, was this new life: this beautiful, lovable little girl, Hester Tallis. Despite the disgrace of Daisy's situation, and Daisy being so quiet and subdued, Hester was a sweet flame of young life and loveliness amid such dark days.

'All right, I'll give her her drink – thank you, Miss Allen,' Margaret said, getting up. She took the little girl and kissed her warm cheek as they walked along the hall. 'There you are, you little poppet,' she whispered, gooey as all the rest of them. Mrs Flett, who was sitting having a few minutes' peace in the back room, looked up at her and smiled.

'Ah, look at that little lamb,' she said. 'Shall I give her a drink, Mrs Tallis?'

'Thanks, Mrs Flett – that would be a help today,' Margaret said. 'I'm running a little behind.'

There was a commotion at the front of the house. Margaret heard the door burst open with no knock and then there were voices in the front office. She handed Hester over hastily and hurried back to find Bridget Sidwell from the office next door, looking as if her eyes were going to pop out of her head. Margaret didn't need to ask whether it was bad news.

'Oh, Miss Margaret –' Bridget's voice was barely more than a whisper now – 'you'd better come, quick.'

The front office at twenty-six Chain Street seemed full of people. Margaret stood in the doorway taking in the fact that as well as the normal office workers, most of her family were there. Uncle Eb was sitting sideways on to her at one of the desks while the others stood round: Aunt Hatt, Clara, all her children were there.

There was a quietness which was almost unearthly. It was this which made Margaret stop as she was about to greet them, the words refusing to pass her lips. In those seconds they all seemed to have been frozen into a terrible tableau – even the children. A feeling went through her, as if she had swallowed something leaden and it was sinking deep into her innards.

They took in that she was there. And she knew. She could see. But no, surely it couldn't be. He only left at the end of May. It was not possible . . .

'Georgie?' she whispered.

It was Clara who moved first. She snatched up the telegram lying on the desk in front of Uncle Eb. The expression in her eyes was so terrible that Margaret could hardly bear to look at her.

'I was just boiling the kettle and I was about to give them all their breakfast and he was at the door and I . . .' She was babbling strangely, then stopped like the last tick of a clock.

Aunt Hatt's hands went to her face and Margaret heard a sound of distress come from her which she would never have thought to hear from her aunt. For a second her eyes met her uncle's and his were full of silent pain. He lumbered to his feet and went to his wife, clumsily wrapping his arms about her.

'Oh, Clara,' Margaret said. She was about to embrace her cousin's wife, when she saw the faces of Jimmy, Ella and Georgina all looking mutely up at her.

'My dears, come next door with me – we'll see what Mrs Flett can find for you, shall we? And you can say hello to little Hester.'

'Pa's dead, isn't he?' Jimmy said as they went along the hall.

Even then Margaret could hardly take it in herself.

'I'm afraid that seems to be . . .' She trailed off. 'Look, dears – just give your mother and everyone a few minutes and we'll come and get you.'

Gently she settled the children with their kindly old housekeeper, giving her a look which said, *Bad news.* Then she rushed out the back to the workshop.

'Philip!' Everyone looked round at her unprecedented shriek along the workshop. The crashing of the drop stamp stopped abruptly. Philip took one look at her and came running.

'It's Georgie,' she said. Her face told him the rest.

'Oh, no,' Philip said. 'Oh, dear God, no.'

She felt her own tears begin. Her gentle, humorous cousin Georgie, father to Jimmy, Ella and little Georgina, husband to Clara. Life began to feel as if it was cracking apart, the way it was in households all across the country.

They went back to number twenty-six to find Aunt Hatt sobbing in Eb's embrace and Clara leaning her head against them. Margaret went and took Clara in her arms and felt her fleshy body break at last into its heart-rending grief.

It was only an hour later, but felt as if they had lived through days; after Eb and Hatt, Clara and the children left for home, to be together and try to take in that their husband, their only son, their father, had reached France only to lose his life almost immediately.

Margaret and Philip tried to go back to work, impossible as that seemed.

'My condolences, Mrs Tallis,' Mr Henshaw said, very formally. 'Mr Watts was your cousin, was he not?'

'Yes,' Margaret said, still feeling stunned, and then thinking, He was my cousin and yet I seem to have seen so little of him. She had grown very fond of Georgie in the past ten years, but he had always been someone who had a quiet, smiling presence, always in the background behind his talkative wife and mother. Did I ever have any proper conversation with him, when you come down to it? she asked herself. Now she never would, and all that seemed to emphasize was the waste of life when you fail to take into account that it all might end. And now it had mown them down like a silent, deathly train.

She accepted Muriel Allen's and Edith Taylor's condolences, still self-controlled. She did not want to give way to her grief in front of them and there were things to do. She was trying to return to her pile of tasks just as Daisy came home from the Jewellery School. When she heard the front door open she expected Daisy to hurry through the house to find Hester, as she usually did. But she came straight into the office.

'Margaret.' There was a pale tightness to her face. 'May I please talk to you for a moment?'

With a feeling of fate, Margaret got up and followed her. Daisy walked a short way along the passage. The doors to all the rooms were shut and she turned with desperate urgency.

'Whatever is it?' Margaret said, keeping her voice low.

'He's dead. He's been killed, in action.'

'Oh, my dear, I know,' Margaret said. 'Aunt Harriet and Clara have been – they only left a short time ago and Uncle's gone as well . . .'

Daisy was staring at her in incomprehension. The tense urgency in her face only increased.

'What do you mean? Who . . . ?'

'Well . . . Georgie,' Margaret said. The distress she had

been keeping at bay began to spill out. 'He'd only just got there . . . They had the telegram today . . .'

'Oh . . .' Daisy gasped. 'Oh, no!' Her eyes filled with tears as well. 'Oh, poor, poor Clara.'

'How did you know?' Margaret said.

Daisy shook her head. She clasped her arms about her suddenly, as if to hold something in. 'I didn't. I meant . . . *He's* dead. They told us at the school today.'

'*He?*' Margaret stared stupidly at her.

'James Carson.' Daisy's face twisted. 'Hester's father.'

Twenty-Seven

Daisy pushed Hester, in her pram, along towards the iron gates of the park. Walking along quiet and solemn at each side were Lily and Clara's youngest girl, Georgina, both of them eight years old.

'That's it, girls, just hold on to the pram until we get inside the gates.'

There was no need for her to say anything as they were holding on anyway. But she felt she needed to speak to break into the leaden sadness of their silence, to find a way of sounding even a little bit cheerful for them.

Lily turned to her in her usual, earnest way, and said, 'Is Hester asleep? Can she get out and play with us?'

The two girls were besotted with Hester.

Daisy forced a smile to her lips. 'She is asleep – but you know our Hester. The moment anything's going on, she'll be up and doing.'

'I want to hold her hand,' Gina said.

Daisy felt as if a hand had squeezed her own heart, looking at the child. She was thin faced like her father, with dark hair and shining brown eyes. And so sad. She could not really understand where her pa had gone. None of them – adults or children – could take in that Georgie was never coming back.

The rest of the family were at the Wattses' house. The warm brickwork of the front was adorned with black crêpe, as was the entrance to twenty-six Chain Street. Aunt Hatt had gone into deep mourning, without even a

224

touch of the jewellery which usually gave off gold flashes of light somewhere about her ears and neck. Margaret was also in black from head to foot to mark the death of her cousin. She had said it was not necessary for Daisy to wear full mourning, but all the same she was wearing the drabbest clothes she possessed for summer – a pale grey cotton frock and black cardigan. She wanted to be in mourning, with all of them – and for him, even for James, though she kept this thought private.

The park was crowded with people from Handsworth and around the area. They sprawled, Sunday relaxed, about the wide expanses of grass. It was the first fine day after much grey, mizzling August weather and everyone was lolling, picnicking and chatting, letting the children run free and making the most of the sun on their faces after days spent holed up in factories and offices.

It was a lovely park, sloping down to a stream and a small lake, with the blackened red stone of St Mary's church in the distance. It was still moist underfoot and as Daisy pushed the pram off the path and on to the grass, she could feel the humid heat coming off it as if the land was sweating. In the far distance she could see people working the new allotments at the edge of the park. The wartime shortages meant making the most of every inch of land to grow food.

'Just leave Hester for the moment,' she said to Lily and Gina as she parked the pram. 'We'll spread out the rug. Now don't go sitting on the grass – it's still wet.'

But a sit-down was not what the girls had in mind at all. They ran and danced about together as Daisy sank down on the rug. She felt more relaxed being in Handsworth. No one knew her, or anything about her. But within a few moments Daisy heard Hester squeaking in the pram. Sure enough, two lively eyes were peering up at her when she looked under the hood.

'You're the end, you are,' she scolded affectionately. Hester would sleep soundly so long as nothing else was going on, but if there was the prospect of any entertainment – especially from another child – she seemed to be able to sense it even in her sleep and wanted to know if she was missing anything.

Daisy picked Hester up and sat her on the rug beside her. But in seconds, Hester was on her hands and knees, wobbling as she desperately tried to crawl to get to her playmates. She made cross noises, not getting anywhere, and put her head on the ground in an attitude of melodramatic despair.

'Hessie!' Gina cried, running over. The sight of her lit-up little face twisted Daisy's heart.

'Don't go too far,' Daisy said. But the water, the only real danger, was a good way away. She watched, shading her eyes as the two girls got down and sat with Hester, both giggling, trying to teach her to crawl. She could hear Hester's delighted gurgles. Daisy wasn't going to stop them. So what if they got grass stains on their frocks?

She watched them, feeling old. She was now the adult in their lives. It was up to her to be strong for them. But she allowed the heaviness of grief to sink into her again now that, for a few moments, she did not have to find a cheerful word for anyone. The Wattses' house was a terrible place. She had offered to take the girls out partly to give them a break from the dark pall hanging over the adults, but also to give herself time to think. The two boys were happy enough together in the garden. Ella, who was nearly ten, would not leave Clara's side. Daisy knew that Margaret and her father were doing the best they could to comfort Eb and Harriet Watts, but for her the place had become unbearable.

She had been very fond of Georgie. They were related only by marriage – Georgie was Margaret's cousin – but as they grew up, living in Chain Street, and especially after Margaret married Pa, he had become like an elder brother to her. He had always been someone who was just *there*, with a smile, a teasing word. Only now did she realize how much. And the fact that he was Clara's husband, Eb and Hatt's only child . . . It was all almost too heartbreaking to think about.

But that other grief weighed on her. Though he had used her, had really thought only of himself, she knew that James Carson had not been all bad. He was a selfish man but also a talented one, and she knew that he had been truly besotted with her. Now he had paid the ultimate price for his country. The thought ate at her conscience. Had it not been for her, would he ever have joined up? He would have been called up eventually, she thought, but he would not have gone then, would not have been in that place at that time . . .

Was it all a punishment – of both of them for what they had done? Was this the price of sin? She never usually thought about this sort of thing. But all of it felt like punishment. She had been denied her youth, her freedom. And, despite it all, he was Hester's father. One day he might have seen Hester, loved her, even – for who could not? Might he have been, at least in some way, a father to her? Now, that was never going to happen. And no one in the family, except her, was mourning for James Carson.

These deaths, of Georgie and James, brought back the feelings she tried never to visit of the day her mother died. She had been taken out of the house while her mother laboured to deliver a second daughter, losing both the child and her own life. That morning came back to her now, tearing at her. Her father's wrenching sobs, his cries that it was his fault, that they should never have let this happen . . .

Only when Lily came running up to say that Hester was eating grass and was that all right, did she manage to break away from these agonizing thoughts and get to her feet. She took Lily's hand.

'Anyone would think I never fed her,' she said, forcing herself to smile at the little girl.

That week, her conscience pricked by everything that had happened, she had visited Den Poole in hospital another time. He begged her to come more often, but what with Hester and work – and because of her own feelings – it was as many times as she could bear.

He was recovering slowly. The shrapnel buried close to his heart had given them reason for concern for a long time but seemed to be stabilizing and he already looked stronger.

'He's a tough lad,' Annie told her. 'He didn't have much of a start in life as you know, but it's made him tough. And he's been lucky compared to some. He just needs the time to heal and hope that bit of rubbish inside him stays where it is.'

The next time she walked back into the ward it was with a sense of dread. She found it hard to face the smells, the suffering faces of some of the boys, the feeling of them all staring at her. She found Den sitting on his bed in his pyjamas, but with his arms now out of bandages. His face lit up when she appeared.

'You've come!' he said.

'You've got your sisters,' she said teasingly, sitting

down beside him, though as far away as she could manage. 'It's not as if you're short of visitors.'

'I know,' he said. His hair had grown and he looked a bit softer, less like a soldier. 'Our Lizzie and our Ivy come in. But our Lizzie's run ragged with that new job –'er's on the gun cartridges like. Money's better.' His face looked granite hard for a moment. 'Soon as I get out of 'ere I'll try and 'elp 'er.' A second later he brightened again. 'But I like seeing you!'

It seemed very simple. He just liked her company. To her enormous relief, he was not making any more declarations of love. 'The sight of you perks me up, Daisy. You've always been so . . . I dunno.' He looked down at his hands, clasped on his thighs. They were strong hands, the veins standing out on the backs of them, a few cuts, now healing. 'You always look nice and you're, I dunno, better'n us somehow.'

Blood rushed to her face. She had still not told him anything, not about Hester or how her life had changed. Den still thought she was the Daisy Tallis she used to be, Queen Bee, taking the world by storm, succeeding in everything she did. And she shrank inside from telling him the truth. Let him go on believing that – why not?

She changed the subject, asking him how he was, about the hospital. There was a magazine on his bed and, desperate for something to say, she picked it up and asked about it. *Southern Cross*, it was called.

'Oh, ar – gives us summat to read,' Den said. 'Only thing is, I don't read any too well. Too much time bunking off school.'

'Would you like me to read you a few bits?'

'Go on then.' He looked delighted and got back on to the bed, waiting, like a child eager for a story.

Daisy smiled, relieved to find something to do. Other

visitors seemed to be chatting away but she was not sure what they could talk about and she did not want to drown him in the family's grief. He had worked with Georgie at the Watts's works. But she did not feel like telling him the news. Not now. Why make things worse?

She flicked through the magazine. It was obviously designed to be cheery: cartoons, a few skits on the hospital, reports of entertainments they had had. She read a few jokes about the food, hospital soup described as 'an onion skin in water', and Den smiled but he added, 'It ain't bad really.'

A poem caught her eye. 'From His Wife', she read (a woman's appreciation of the woman who nursed her husband). That didn't seem quite the thing to entertain Den, but she could not help starting to read it herself:

> 'Dear Sister in the ward to-day
> I could not speak or take your hand
> Tears choked the words I tried to say
> But think – and then you'll understand.
>
> 'To you he's but a patient there
> One of a lot who come and go . . .'

Her eyes skimmed down . . .

> 'But he is all I have to love . . .'

She stopped, because it was too unbearable to go on. 'What's that, Dais? Read it me?' Den said.

'No,' she managed to say, husky voiced. Fighting her tears, she turned the page and smiled up at him. 'I'm sure there are some more funny things in here – let me find those.'

His hand was on her arm suddenly and, despite the tears in her eyes, she was forced to look up at him.

'What's up?' he said. 'Oh, Dais – don't cry. I hate to see yer upset.'

'Nothing.' She swallowed. 'It's just a sad poem.'

Den gazed at her. 'D'you know, you're so beautiful,' he said wonderingly.

'Don't,' she said, looking down again, so close to bursting into tears that she really wanted to run from the room. 'Don't, Den – please. Look, let me find something else to read.'

Twenty-Eight

3 September 1916

Margaret woke to the sound of a church bell tolling in the distance. As happened every morning, she opened her eyes feeling comfortably content on the thick feather bed, enjoying those moments of freshness, of simply being and remembering nothing. When memory came, it brought down once more the dark weight of grief.

Georgie. And the distress of his family. Clara was so upset, so angry at the war leaving her with no husband and her children with no father. Aunt Hatt wept and wept, almost a ghost herself with shadows under her eyes. But Uncle Eb was the one who Margaret found the most heartbreaking.

'It hurts,' he said to her quietly, in the days after they had heard the news. He pressed his belly. 'Here. As if someone's kicked me in the guts. And it never goes away. I can't believe it – my lad, never coming back. Why did they have to take my one lad?' His kindly eyes were full of pain and bewilderment.

Feeling Philip stirring beside her, Margaret said quietly, 'I still can't believe it.'

He turned on his side and drew her into his arms. His chin rested on her head. 'Georgie?'

'Umm,' she said into his chest, already close to tears. He was so solid and comforting. 'I don't understand why

232

we had to have a war. Why someone couldn't just . . .' She petered out. Just what? What, in the end, was it all for?

Philip had no answer. There was no answer. They lay holding each other. From the attic they heard a high little wailing sound: Hester waking.

'I'm sorry,' Philip said suddenly.

She moved her head to look at him. 'What for?'

'Being so hard on her. You were the one who . . . You've been a mother to her, Margaret. A real, loving mother.'

'Shh,' she said. 'I *do* love her. Even if she can be a little madam sometimes. She made a mistake – but it wasn't all her mistake. And in the end, she's the one carrying the can for it all.'

'A woman's lot,' Philip said.

'Yes,' Margaret flared. 'Precisely – but *why*?'

Her husband, realizing that his attempt at sympathy had backfired somewhere, kept quiet and cuddled close to her. He nuzzled her neck and she laughed as his beard tickled her.

'Philip,' she said warningly. 'I've got to get up for church.'

'No, you haven't,' he said teasingly, as he began to caress her.

'I *have*. You wretched heathen.'

'It's early,' he said, his hands moving over her body, his own eyes closing. 'You don't need to go yet.'

'Umm,' she conceded, turning to him and cuddling closer. 'I suppose I don't.' She gave him a playful poke in the ribs. 'You're terrible – on the Sabbath as well!'

Twenty-Nine

'So – you're ready?'

Smiling, Annie stood by Den Poole's bed, where he sat waiting, dressed in the blue uniform of a convalescing soldier.

'Yeah. Think so.' He looked self-conscious, patted the jacket's wide lapels and then tried to pat his pockets until he looked up ruefully, realizing that there weren't any. 'Dunno where we're supposed to put our smokes.'

'I expect they were economizing on cloth,' Annie said. 'Anyway, you'll be back in full uniform all too soon, I should think, by the look of you. You've done well, Den.'

She could see he was nervous. Though he had healed quickly and was certainly well enough to leave the hospital, there was still some way to go. He was being sent for a few weeks' convalescence at the army training camp in Sutton Coldfield.

'Will you tell 'er where they've sent me?' Den said.

'Who – Lizzie? She already knows, Den.' She knew really that he did not mean Lizzie.

'No – Daisy. Thought I might go and call – when I'm up to it. It'd be nice to see Mrs Tallis again an' all.'

'Well,' Annie said, without committing herself. 'You need to go and make sure you rest first. We don't want you overdoing it – do you hear, Den?'

'Yes, nurse.' He grinned up at her and she saw the little lad she had once known plodding barefoot round the streets, selling his pathetic little bits of firewood. She felt moved. Den had come a long way. In his uniform, smart and groomed army fashion, he looked an impressive, handsome man.

'Best of luck.' She held out her hand, trying not to get emotional. 'Your transport must be here – come on.' She led him to the door of the ward. 'We don't want to see you again, Den – not in here, anyway.'

Annie stood watching him walk away with the orderly who had come to fetch him. He turned back for a moment and waved. Almost as if I'm his mother, she thought. She was just about to go back into the ward when another tall, RAMC uniform-clad figure appeared, striding along the corridor at a pace that could only mean something urgent. She waited, with a sudden feeling of misgiving as Fergus came almost running towards her.

'Nurse Hanson!' He drew closer and she could see the tension in his face. In a much lower voice, he said, 'Annie – have you got a moment?'

She hesitated. 'Not really. Whatever is it?'

'Go and ask Matron if Dr Reid can borrow you for a few minutes – no, wait, I'll go.'

He strode into the ward. Matron, who almost melted into a puddle on the floor every time Fergus appeared, could hardly say no.

'Come on.' He led her at a gallop towards the front entrance and out into the autumn sunshine.

'Fergus!' Annie protested. 'Just *stop* and tell me.'

They paused at the corner of the building, away from the bustle of the front entrance.

He hesitated for a second, then looked directly into her eyes. 'I'm being posted.'

Her heart seemed to stop, as if clutched in a tight hand. She remembered to breathe.

'Where?'

235

'France. Not sure where exactly yet. It'll be one of the big casualty clearing stations near the coast – most likely Dieppe or Étaples.'

She stared at him. It was no good saying, *Don't go*. He was under orders. But oh, heaven, how she loved him and how she did not want him to leave! The idea of him no longer being here, striding about the hospital, went through her, an actual physical pain.

'It'll make all the difference,' she said, looking squarely back at him. 'You'll make all the difference.'

They had had numerous conversations about how many of their patients would have fared better if they had been treated sooner. The army was moving the treatment closer to the Front; more operating theatres were being set up, there was the new technique of transfusing blood, and specialists were on hand to deal with the wounds and injuries before too much blood was lost, before death-dealing infections set in. And Fergus, with all his expert-ise, was needed, she knew. It was so obvious that she felt surprised it had not happened before.

'Come with me,' he said, in a very low voice.

Annie stared at him. *Come with me*. A world of pos-sibility opened for a second. Had she not always wanted to travel further, wider than she ever had? She could vol-unteer to nurse in France, in one of the new nursing con-tingents who would cross the Channel to work nearer the Front. She and Fergus, together, striving to save the lives of all those boys, united in love of the work and love of each other . . . She almost said, *Yes, yes, of course I will* . . . But she knew it was not right. She loved her work here, wanted to give support to Lizzie, to Margaret and her family. It surprised her how much she did not want to go.

'I couldn't guarantee being close to you in any case,

could I?' she said. 'You'll be moved again. We might be at opposite sides of the country.'

'In fact,' Fergus admitted, 'I'd really rather you were here, where I know you're safe. I can picture you, keeping the home fires burning.' He smiled, with a touch of irony. 'And with your very nice family, I think that is just what you should be doing. They've lost enough lately.'

They had still never managed to visit Margaret and Philip together. There had simply not been time. She had kept Fergus rather a secret up until then, but she had told him a lot about them and the business and all that was going on. But meeting them was obviously going to have to wait even longer. Their snatched time off had been spent in town.

'When are you going?' she said, struggling to be brave.

'Next couple of days.' He looked aside for a moment, across at the grand facade of the university buildings. 'I imagine it will all be a lot more rudimentary than this.' He reached for her hand. 'My love – I know I have things to do there. I'm bound to go. But leaving you . . .'

Annie's eyes filled with tears. Annoyed at herself, she wiped them away. Heavens, she was becoming a soppy thing.

'It'll be a poor place here after you've gone,' she said. Another tear rolled down her cheek. 'At least I've got that photograph.' Once, on one of their rare visits into Birmingham, it had been early enough for them to go into a photographer's and have their portrait taken together. The idea had been Fergus's and he had, in his usual way, persuaded her.

Fergus smiled. 'You're a sweet little poppet after all,' he teased. But he looked moved and tenderly put his arms round her for a moment.

237

Annie frowned, wiping her face. 'Go on with you,' she said. 'You dreadful man.'

'Have you any time – can we be together?'

She thought helplessly of her rostered hours over the next days. 'Only at about five o'clock in the morning.'

Fergus grinned. 'Well – so be it. Tomorrow at five?' He leaned over and tenderly kissed her cheek.

They met in the mild darkness before dawn, out in the hospital grounds. Annie had been a bag of nerves creeping out of the nurses' quarters again, terrified that someone would catch her. But once she was outside, she could breathe again. She saw Fergus coming towards her, the silhouette of his cap against the sky's uncertain light.

'Come, my darling,' he whispered, his arm round her shoulders while they walked.

After some moments so full of feeling that they could not begin speaking, Fergus said quietly, 'I'm looking forward to seeing what kind of letters Nurse Hanson will write.'

'I'll write,' she said, not in the mood for teasing. 'Of course I will. I'll write and write, and I want to hear everything from you – *every detail.*'

'Well,' he said. 'I'll do my best.' He glanced at her. 'I understand why you don't want to come – and of course, we could have been sent miles apart. So I'll have to describe it all for you. And then, when I come back . . .'

'You'll get some leave at some time, won't you?' she said, seeing months stretching before her, desolate, never knowing when she might see him. Like so many others who were waiting and longing, she realized, feeling it now, truly for the first time. MIZPAH, she thought.

Fergus let the breath hiss out through his teeth. 'Truth to tell you, I don't know. There must be leave, but

238

whether it would be only in France . . . We'll just have to see. But Annie . . .'

He stopped on the wet grass and turned to hold her. As she embraced him, feeling his back, his long body, *him, here now*, she tried to inhabit every second of it as it slipped away.

'When I do come home – when all this terrible mess is over . . .' He stopped. They had talked about the future many times, in tentative, half-joking terms. How many children was it wise to have? Was it better to have boys or girls? A point they could never agree on but, as Fergus said, fortunately it was something nature decided for you. Where was the ideal place to live? But now he was serious.

'Annie, my dearest love – once we are living in a time of peace again, when life can go on without such fear as now – will you promise to be my wife?'

Thirty

'Oh – hello, Auntie Annie!'

Daisy opened the door that Monday afternoon, Hester balanced on her hip.

'Just popping in, Daisy,' Annie said, stepping into the hall. 'Hello, little lovely.' She kissed Hester's cheek and Hester chuckled and beamed at her. 'Ooh, you're a happy little soul, aren't you?'

'She is *now*,' Daisy said ruefully. 'You should have heard her at dinner time – she can blart for England when she puts her mind to it!'

'Are you all right, Daisy?' Annie said, hanging her hat and coat in quick, neat movements. The girl was changed, of course. Thinner, more subdued and mature.

'Yes, I'm all right,' Daisy said. What else was there to say? When so much sadness was all about them, and especially now such a terrible grief had come to the Wattses next door, what were her frustrations about hardly being able to do any of her own creative work set against that?

'You just look a bit pale,' Annie said, peering at her.

Daisy was not about to tell her that she had been staying up very late. She would go into her workroom once Hester seemed settled and everyone was off to bed and work away for as long as she could on her smithing. It made her feel sane, handling her tools, doing the work that she loved, even if only for an hour or two. But it was very tiring and even hammering anything was tricky for fear of waking Hester in the next-door room.

'Annie!' Margaret came out of the office. It was only four o'clock – an odd time for Annie to appear. 'Just in time for a cup of tea.'

They usually took tea in the office with the staff, but as Annie was there, Philip, Margaret and Daisy went into the back room with her.

'Well,' Annie said, as Margaret poured for them all. Daisy saw how excited she was looking, and so pretty. It was as if the old, austere Annie had turned into a swan as the fable went. 'I've not got a lot of time because I must go and see Lizzie after this. Her wages are better at Kynoch's, but she's worried to death about who's looking after little Ann. She thinks the lady looking after her's not feeding her properly – and she's getting on a bit to handle a young child. Ann's been poorly . . . But anyway. I've come to tell you some news.'

'Oh.' Margaret handed her a cup of tea and sat down, looking worried. With Annie, 'news' could mean anything.

Daisy felt herself tighten inside as well. Was Annie about to announce that she was being sent to a hospital at the Front? That would be just like Annie, to go and do something extreme and heroic. And Daisy knew that Margaret would never have another good night's sleep if she did.

'It's all right,' Annie laughed. 'It's not that bad.'

'Glad to hear it,' Philip remarked drily.

'No – it's . . .' She looked suddenly very bashful. 'The thing is – I'm engaged to be married.'

There was a stunned silence.

'*Married?*' Margaret said, looking truly discombobulated.

'Yes,' Annie said, laughing. It was obvious how happy she was.

Daisy felt a pang of grief. This was something that was never going to happen to her now – love and marriage.

'Married. You know – *married*. But not just yet – not while the war's on, anyway.'

'But who on earth to?' Margaret's bewilderment was obvious. She sounded a bit cheated, Daisy thought, that this had all somehow crept up on them.

Annie told them then about Dr Fergus Reid, the nerve specialist who she was to marry but who was already, by now, at one of the casualty clearing stations in France.

Margaret was still asking questions about getting their father's permission and was she sure – as if Annie ever did anything she was not sure about – when Philip stood up. He went to Annie, pulled her to her feet and embraced her.

'Good for you, Annie,' he said. 'That's one nice bit of news at least.'

'Thank you, Philip.' She smiled up at him.

'He must be quite a feller,' Philip added teasingly.

'Congratulations, Auntie Annie.' Daisy went and gave her a kiss.

'We must go and tell Uncle Eb,' Margaret said, embracing her sister. 'It might cheer him up – just a tiny bit anyway.'

When she and Margaret went next door, Watts's had also just finished a tea break and Uncle Eb was in the office with Bridget Sidwell and the others.

When he turned to them Annie was deeply shocked. She had not seen him for some time and he was so much thinner than before. He looked hollowed out, like a man who had not slept in weeks. The demands of the business were always relentless, but Georgie's death on top of that seemed to have aged him by ten years. His once iron-grey hair was almost white and his face looked papery and fragile. Margaret had told her that while Aunt Hatt grieved endlessly for her boy, she thought that in his quiet way, Uncle Eb had taken it even harder.

'Hello, wenches!' He greeted them warmly as usual, then his face fell into a wary look. 'What brings you – no bad news, I hope?'

'No, Uncle,' Margaret said, smiling at him. 'Something good for a change. Go on – tell him, Annie.'

Annie felt bashful delivering her news.

'Ah, well, that *is* good! Now –' he began teasing her and they saw a flicker of his old self – 'if I'm not mistaken, is this not the young suffragist who was never going to get married?'

'I'm still a suffragist – by inclination anyway, Uncle,' Annie said. 'But Fergus . . .' She felt self-conscious even saying his name, but she loved it. *Fergus.* It sounded crisp and interesting, and as if brushed against the Scottish heather of his birthplace. 'He seems to have swept me off my feet! Anyway, this is him.'

She drew out the picture they had had taken, of herself and Fergus arm in arm, he in his RAMC uniform, she in a summer frock and simple straw hat, both smiling with a look of almost outrageous happiness at the camera.

Everyone admired it and Uncle Eb repeated the same sort of sentiments Philip had mentioned, about how this Fergus Reid must be quite a man, it taking some doing to get Annie to agree to marry him, and so on. He was trying his best to be jolly and happy for her, Annie could see. But under this, you could not fail to notice the heartbreaking change in him, the amount it was costing him to keep going day after day, to try and find purpose in his life with his boy gone – his boy who was to inherit the business.

When they were back in number twenty-four, she said tearfully to Margaret, 'Oh, poor Eb. It's terrible seeing him like that.' Their uncle had always seemed to them one of the happiest men in the world – happy in his marriage and family, content and prosperous in his work.

She gathered herself together. 'Look, I'd better get over to Lizzie. See you as soon as I can.'

'Bye, dear,' Margaret said, kissing her. 'And – well, I hope we get to meet this astonishing Fergus Reid soon. I'm very happy for you, Annie.'

A few nights later, Margaret woke, startled by something out of a deep sleep. The noise, which had seemed far away at first, sharpened. It was knocking, heavy and insistent.

'Philip?' she whispered.

There was no reply. Listening, she heard it again. It sounded as if it was coming from their own front door.

On the landing, wearing shoes and a gown thrown hurriedly over her nightdress, she saw that Daisy, similarly attired, was already on her way down the stairs. Daisy turned, hearing her footsteps, and waited.

'I'd just put Hester down again when it started,' she whispered.

As they reached the door a voice behind it shouted, 'Police – open up!'

'Oh, Lord,' Margaret said. She was glad Daisy was up as well. 'Whatever now? Here – let me open.'

In the poorly lit street she saw the unmistakable outline of a policeman, a middle-aged, reassuring-looking man. Only the older men were left these days.

'Sorry to trouble you, madam,' he said, standing as if to attention. 'Nothing for you to be concerned about regarding this property. But I'm trying to gain access to the house next door and I'm wondering if you have a key? Otherwise I shall be forced to kick the door in.'

'Gracious,' Margaret said. 'What's happened? Has there been a burglary?'

'Do you have a key, madam?' the policeman said patiently.

'Oh – yes. Daisy, you know the drawer in the office? But please – what's the problem?'

'We had a telephone call from a Mrs Watts,' he said stiffly, 'to report that her husband has not come home. And,' he added with an air of disapproval, 'even the public houses are shut at this hour.'

'Oh, he's not a drinker,' Margaret assured him as Daisy rushed back with the key. 'At least not to excess.'

The policeman made a sound which could have been scepticism or mere acknowledgement of what had been said.

'Right.' He looked at the two of them in their hastily covered-up nightwear. 'Perhaps the man of the house would be better to accompany me?'

'He's asleep,' Margaret said, irritated by this. 'And Mr Watts is my uncle. My daughter and I will be happy to come with you.'

Daisy unlocked the door of number twenty-six. Nothing seemed out of the ordinary. The lights were off and they lit the gas in the hall.

'If the door was locked he's not likely to be here,' Margaret said. 'They tend not to lock it until going-home time. Unless he was going to leave by the entry. I don't know . . .'

'Oh,' Daisy exclaimed from along the hall. 'The light's still on at the back.'

'Oh, dear,' Margaret said. 'Poor Eb – he's so tired these days.'

But surely, she thought, Uncle Eb was not still working at this time of night? It was one o'clock in the morning! Worry gripped at her and she wished now that Philip had woken up and was here with them. Annie had said what a change she had seen in their uncle. Had he been trying to push his terrible grief for Georgie aside by overworking, burning the candle at both ends? But would Aunt Hatt not have said something about this?

'He's probably sat down at one of the pegs for a moment and fallen asleep,' she said. 'Bless his heart.'

The three of them trooped across into the workshop. Some of the lights were still burning at the front, as if Eb had been working his way back through, putting them out as he normally did at shutting-up time.

Margaret, leading the way, was tempted to call out, but she didn't want to startle him. She looked round at the benches for his burly figure hunched over one of them, but Daisy gasped behind her.

'Oh, Margaret – look!'

Ahead of them, right in the middle of the workshop, between the tightly packed pegs, Margaret caught sight of what Daisy had seen: first the sole of a boot, then an ankle, a trouser leg.

They dashed over, past the lathe and one set of pegs, and in the hissing gaslight saw their uncle prone on the floor, in the passage between two sets of benches.

'Uncle!' Margaret flung herself to her knees at his feet and leaned over him in the narrow space. Eb was on his back, sprawled, his eyes closed. She shook him, crying out. 'Oh, no . . . No! Uncle – wake up. Wake up, please!'

As Daisy and the policeman stood nearby in appalled silence, Margaret felt Eb's hands, his neck, her fingertips feeling their way in the desperate hope of a flickering pulse which would belie the heavy lifelessness of his body.

'No,' she kept saying, hardly knowing she was speaking at all. 'No, this can't be, he can't be dead, Uncle, please, please . . .'

There was nothing. She tried the wrist. But already she could feel that he was stiff and chill.

She bent forward and rested her forehead on his ribcage, feeling how shrunken was the once barrel-like body of this lovely, kindly man. And she knew that he was gone.

Thirty-One

As the news spread, people came to Watts's to pay their respects from businesses all round the quarter. Eb Watts had learned his trade from his father and they were a well-known family, sociable and much liked in the district. Anyone who had ever worked with Eb Watts, like expert enameller Sam Lieberman, and all his pub cronies, called at the door. Bridget Sidwell, who worked in the office, had to deal with this, trying to master her own tears, since there was no Georgie to take over his father's role. Aunt Hatt remained at home, in shock, waiting for her husband's body to be brought to her.

Margaret, who had in any case been up all night, left that morning to go to Aunt Hatt in Handsworth and to get a message to Annie at the hospital, telling her about their uncle's death. It seemed his heart had given out as he went round the works locking up, and that he must have died almost instantly.

Daisy, who was supposed to be teaching that day at Vittoria Street, had to leave Hester in the care of the office staff, who seemed glad to have distraction from all the surrounding grief and pain, in the shape of a lively nine-month-old.

The shock of seeing Eb Watts lying stone cold on his workshop floor stayed with Daisy. She had to keep dragging her mind back to teaching the remaining students in the school. Most of the people she taught these days were young – too young to fight – and the school was battling on, trying to keep everything running.

'Mr Thomas has gone into the army,' the new silversmithing tutor, Mr Grant, told her when she arrived. He was an older man, short and stocky, with tufty white hair. He was very experienced in smithing, though less in teaching. Mr Thomas had taught die sinking.

'Oh, dear,' Daisy said. 'Whoever are they going to get now?' She thought for a moment of Caleb Turner, who now worked at Watts's. But he seemed to be very busy and it was hard to imagine the lugubrious Mr Turner teaching a class of young students.

Mr Grant chatted on, saying had she heard that the school were thinking of installing a gas annealing muffle because the council were complaining that there was a shortage of them for annealing small articles made of sheet metal for the war effort and the school needed to do its bit . . . He broke off, seeing that Daisy did not look too interested in this information.

'Sorry, my dear – not of great moment, I'm sure. Are you all right, Miss Tallis?'

Daisy, though annoyed with herself, felt her eyes fill. But it was good to tell someone and she poured out to him what had happened.

'Oh, you poor dear,' he said. 'What a shock. And poor Mr Watts. I must say I never knew the gentleman, but . . . how very sudden.'

'He was so kind,' Daisy sobbed. Only now, as she told a stranger what had happened, the full agony of it released itself in her. 'And his poor wife – their son had just been killed as well.'

Mr Grant stood in front of her, sympathetic but helpless.

'These are dark days.' He sounded angry. 'In other

times I would tell you to go home and not attempt to teach today. But sadly I really don't think we can do without you.'

She staggered through the class somehow. None of the students seemed to notice and once they were all cleared up and she was left alone, for a moment she even had a pang of missing James Carson's appearance in the room. It would be so nice to see a familiar face. He had let her down, betrayed her and used her – she knew all that. But for a time, he had been the one man she had ever thought she was in love with and she missed that feeling of excitement, of someone paying her attention. And then she remembered Den, his telling her he loved her, and this brought on such a confusion of feelings that she pushed the memory away.

As she stepped out of the school in Vittoria Street, she tried to shut any thoughts of the future, let alone love, out of her mind, because thinking about it filled her with despair. You made your bed – now lie on it. That was what people said. And what choice was there, in any case?

When she reached Chain Street she saw that Bridget had draped even more black crêpe across the window and above the front door of number twenty-six. She was about to walk into twenty-four, filled with dread, when a sudden, light, guilty feeling of joy came over her. Hester. She was coming home to her little girl. How joyful that felt in the face of all this death – her little one who had no notion of how terrible the world could be.

And there was her own work, snatched moments in the attic. She had been up working last night when the policeman arrived, though she had not told Margaret this. Slowly, so slowly, she was completing her tea set. The teapot was proving the most challenging – the oval shape she had chosen.

As she stepped into number twenty-four, the office door was ajar and she heard voices. She looked inside, a smile ready.

But it froze on her face.

Mr Henshaw, seated in his usual place, looked up at her over her spectacles. Muriel Allen was also sitting, but Edith stood to one side of the room with Hester in her arms. Seeing Daisy, Hester let out a squeak of happiness and held out her arms. But Daisy was looking at the visitor, perched uneasily on Edith's chair. Den.

He was in his blue convalescent's uniform, and looking much better than when she had last seen him. He had filled out and his hair had grown a little, softening his face. In that moment, he didn't say anything. He looked at Hester, then at her and back again.

Daisy could see, instantly, that he knew. Even if no one had said anything, Den knew. Her cheeks burned with mortification that he had come here and seen what had become of her. She had told him nothing, had hidden her secret and led him to believe that she was still the same successful Daisy Tallis that she had always been.

Their eyes met and she saw a strange look in his. He gazed steadily at her, as if looking right into her, and in his eyes she read a mixture of pity and of something else which made her cheeks burn even more. A realization. Triumph even. Was it? Or was she misreading him? But it felt like triumph, as if his gaze was saying, *So now I know – you're no better than me. We are equals.*

And then she was glad. This is how it is. So his talk about loving her and all that nonsense, his imagining he knew who she was – at least I'll be free of that, she

251

thought. What does it matter what he thinks? She managed to stare, almost brazenly, back at him.

Without a word, she went to Edith and held out her arms. Hester almost flung herself into them, puttering, 'Ma Ma Ma!'

'Hello, Hessy,' Daisy said, and she held her tight, kissed her cheek, did everything to show she was this child's mother, that she loved her no matter what anyone thought and that was how it was. Almost incidentally, she added, 'Hello, Den. How are you getting along?'

'I'm going along all right,' he said calmly. 'Much better. Thought I'd come down and see you all – and Mr Watts. And then I come and 'eard the news.' He shook his head, looking very upset. Of course, Daisy thought. This was a bigger shock still, for Den. Eb Watts had been his first and only employer.

'I gather you was one of the ones found 'im?'

'Yes.' Daisy cuddled Hester. 'I expect they've told you. Mrs Watts went to the police when he didn't come home. It was Margaret – Mrs Tallis – and I, who went round there. It was terrible to see him.'

Her voice broke and she softened towards Den. What did anything matter when faced with all this? She was free of him, now that he knew what she was really like. And they were taking up time in the office.

'D'you want a cup of tea now you're here, Den?'

They went into the back and Mrs Flett, who was already brewing tea for the office, brought them each a cup.

'Dear, oh, dear,' she kept saying. She didn't need to say anything else.

When Daisy, still holding Hester, was left alone with Den, she busied herself with the little girl, so as not to have to face him. She put Hester down to sit on the floor and gave her a few little toys.

''Er's a lovely baby,' he said. 'Why dain't yer tell me, Daisy?' Rather than triumphant, he sounded hurt.

'Why d'you think?' She looked up sharply. 'Not exactly something you go broadcasting round about, is it? Being a fallen woman?'

Den stared at her. Whatever she had seen in his eyes before was gone and he shrugged, as if this was of no consequence to him. Daisy suddenly heard Annie's voice: Mary Poole, Den's mother, the babies that appeared when there was no visible sign of a husband . . . She saw that this was less shocking to Den than it would be to many people.

'You're not fallen,' he said sweetly. 'Not you. Why d'yer say you are?'

'Well, that's how people see it, isn't it?' she snapped, sitting up straight, wondering why she was directing her anger at him.

'Who was it?' The question was so direct that it seemed to bypass any indignation at being asked such a thing.

'Someone at the Jewellery School.' She met his eyes. 'He's dead. He joined the army, died on the Somme. Before he could marry me,' she added, for her dignity.

'Oh, Dais.' He looked down, leaning forward, rubbing the palm of one hand against the other. His hands were wide and strong looking. Suddenly, tears filled her eyes. This was not what she had expected – that he would be sympathetic.

There was a silence during which she wrestled for control of herself. Was he wondering how to leave now? she thought. She had no idea what to say. Hester tugged at her skirt and she lifted her on to her lap.

'She's a lovely baby,' he said again.

Hester looked at Den and gave a chortle.

'D'you want a hold?' Daisy asked.

'All right.' He smiled faintly and held his arms out for Daisy to put Hester on his lap. He was long used to holding small children. ''Ello, baby,' he said, rather awkwardly. 'Our Ann's a bit older than 'er,' he said. 'Looks poorly compared with this'un, though.'

He joggled her on his knees for a few moments, then handed her over again.

'They're getting ready to send me back,' he said, as Daisy sat down again. 'It won't be long, I don't think. Well, not more than a couple of months, I mean.'

'No – not already?' she said. 'But are you well enough?'

He shrugged. 'Have to be, dun' I?'

There was another silence, and he stood up. 'Best get off then. Ta for the tea.'

When he reached the door he turned to her.

'I've gotta say this. It don't matter to me – none of this.' He nodded at Hester. 'I love you, Dais. I've told yer before – at least I've tried. I'd be your man if yer'd let me. That's all I can say.'

Daisy stood holding Hester. She was disarmed and moved by his words, by the way he seemed to be devoted to her whatever she did in anyone else's eyes. The idea of loving him back was strange to her, would take getting used to. But she liked him, felt for him.

'Thank you, Den,' she said humbly.

'I don't s'pose you ... ?' He stopped himself. 'No, I won't ask. But Daisy – before I go, promise this time you'll write. And I'll write – I'll get someone to do it if I can't. Where I'm going, I need to know you're 'ere – you're the thing that keeps me going.'

Tears slid into her eyes. She longed to be able to say the thing that he could take in his heart back into the war.

To pour out loving words, to tell him how grateful she was that he accepted her no matter what, but they would not come.

'I will, Den,' she said softly. 'Course I will.'

This seemed to give him hope and he walked up to her quickly and kissed her cheek.

'I don't know when they'll send me. I'll try and get over before I go.'

'Will you come to the funeral?' she said. 'Mr Watts?'

'Course I will, if I'm still here.'

And he was gone.

Thirty-Two

December 1916

'Annie? Where on earth are you off to?'

Susannah stood gaping as Annie tore along the passage and into the lavatory in the short morning break.

Inside, the door bolted, she stood for a second, her blood singing. Her hand caressed the pocket in which rested the wonderful, precious envelope she had been waiting to open all morning as she hurried about the ward. The waiting was all part of the pleasure. A letter from Fergus – the fluttering, excited, bubbling feeling of being loved, of knowing he had sat, somewhere in his posting in France, thinking of her, writing his droll, affectionate letters, perhaps smiling a little, those lips turning up under the moustache . . .

But she had waited long enough. Praying that no one else would need to come in for the next few minutes, she took the envelope out, looked at Fergus's small, exquisite, handwriting and kissed the envelope before she tore it open.

Her eyes raced over the words. Was he all right? Was there anything to worry about? She reached the end at a gallop and, reassured, began again.

Since I last wrote, my darling, I have been posted on again. The price of my particular expertise, I suppose, is to be endlessly on the move to somewhere new. I am not allowed to divulge my exact whereabouts. However, that hardly matters since I shall soon be gone – though I am hoping to be here at least until after the Christmas season.

All I can say is, we are of course near the sea and the hospital is as rum a place as I have yet encountered. Spotless and well organized – but in the building of an old seafront casino, would you believe? I'm sure you would disapprove mightily – I can see that Puritan frown appearing on your stern brow at the very thought. But be reassured. No gambling goes on here now – it is a place of great rectitude and endeavour. Though I do find myself visiting patients in wards with the usual black iron bedsteads, but all lined up beneath the most louche-looking crystal chandeliers! The hospital was set up by a titled Lady – in fact, she herself certainly knuckles down, I'll give her that. She goes to work with sleeves rolled like anyone else. Evidently she was an Olympic sailing contender a few years back, and she has an enormous wolf of a dog a bit like my old pal Seamus, and he's a great favourite among the officers – it's an officer-only hospital, by the way. She has also been known, along with several cronies (I suspect I should have my knuckles rapped for endowing such fine ladies with the title 'cronies') to greet the incoming casualties in the most elegant evening garments – tiaras and all!

He wrote a little more about his work, one of the patients who had affected him most – 'a crude, distressing disman-tling of an entire personality'. And she read with interest, moved. But still her gaze hurried to the end, to his loving words.

257

I miss you so much that it fills me with an ache. Of course, the days are busy – and nights too I am forever rushing hither and thither. But you are always with me. I keep expecting to see your busy little figure appearing along a corridor, your face looking into mine, ready to rag me for some misdemeanour. When this war is over, Miss Annie Hanson, what a powerhouse we shall be! You and I – Dr and Mrs Reid – together we can take on the world! I always thought I wanted to settle for ever in London. Now I wonder if foreign climes and unknown customs are not more to my taste. What think you? Are you ready for the adventure? The two of us, always together, my sweet darling?

I suppose I must do duty to my patients by snatching some sleep now. So, across the waves I send you my love once more – holding you in the depths of my heart, my dearest love.

Yours ever,
Fergus

Annie read his tender words of parting, her eyes awash with tears. For a moment she stood with her back to the door, the letter held sweetly to her heart. *I am so blessed*, she whispered. With a twist of pain, she thought of Aunt Hatt, weighed down by so much grief she could hardly bear to think of it. Her cousin Georgie's dark-eyed, smiling face came to her mind, young and kindly, so beloved. No more. She found herself thanking God that her beloved was a doctor, not a soldier on the front line. Safer, the Lord be praised. Eyes closed, she blessed Georgie, then brought to mind the smiling face of her beloved Fergus.

'Yes,' she whispered. 'Oh, yes, my love – I'm ready to go with you anywhere.'

Thirty-Three

25 December 1916

Harriet Watts lay on the deep feather bed of that dark December morning, warm and happy in the deceit of a dawn dream. Her thick winceyette nightdress wrapped round her, hair in a thick plait, she pulled the bedclothes closer.

After a moment she reached out an arm. Eb? She wriggled over to snuggle up behind her husband's broad, comforting shape, to tuck her thighs in behind his as she always did, wrap an arm about his bulky waist and hear him give a little putter of sleepy pleasure, *That's my girl*, or some such. Everything was as it should be. A normal day, Eb beside her, the works humming away, Georgie in charge, Clara and the children – her happy, busy life.

The sheet beside her was cold. Her eyes opened and cold horror – the reality of each day – seized her all over again.

'Oh, heaven, no . . .' she moaned, trying to sink back into the dream of all that should be, all that was good.

No Eb. No Georgie. Both taken from her for ever. All was cold and dead. It was like falling endlessly into a black, freezing well. The day of Eb's funeral came back to her, the gusting wind rocking the trees, the ranks of people dressed in black hats and coats, everyone from the firm, even Den Poole, who was about to be sent back to the

Front, Jack Sidwell with his wife Bridget sobbing beside him. And she, his wife of forty years, trying to stand upright, to drain some comfort out of the Church's words which neither of them ever really believed in. *I am the resurrection and the life.* The words had fallen on her like ash. There might be resurrection, but all she needed was her Eb, plump and warm, smiling and whiskery, beside her.

'Why couldn't you take me with you?' she whispered, the ache of it filling her as it did hour after hour, day after day. The forgetting had been the cruellest. That delusion of things being as they had been before.

Another realization came to her. Christmas Day. The family were coming to her house. Poor dear Clara. Those fatherless children. Somehow, under the load of her own grief, she had to go on, to make Christmas in some way cheerful for them all.

With a groan, she sat up, pushing back the heavy bed-clothes. She swung her legs over the edge and sat, toes brushing the little rug beside the bed.

'Come on, Hatt old thing,' she said, as Eb would have said. 'There's work to be done. Get to it, wench.'

'These are the last of Georgie's potatoes,' Clara said when she arrived later, handing her mother-in-law a heavily filled brown paper bag. 'I've kept them in the dark – they've not sprouted.'

Clara's naturally pale face was still white, the coppery freckles standing out even more, and the blueish half-moons under her eyes of nights with broken sleep. But she was upright, defiant and strong as she had been most of the time since Georgie's death.

'Thanks, love,' Hatt said faintly. She felt as if the breath would not come into her body properly, as if she needed propping up like an old building whose foundations have suddenly given way. Looking into the bag, seeing the soil-dusted vegetables, her chest tightened all over again. Her boy had planted and planted in the back garden before he left in the spring. Though he had never said as much, he had been providing for his family in his absence in one way he could think of. The harvest which had outlasted his own short life was to give them their Christmas dinner. A mercy as the commercial crops had not done well this year and prices were sky high.

'Let's get the dinner together,' Clara said, rolling up her sleeves. They had given Aunt Hatt's cook the day off to join her family. And they both knew the busyness was good for them. 'Come on, Ella,' she called. 'You can come and help now – let's get these potatoes peeled.'

'I've got a bit of beef,' Hatt said. 'It's not much good, but . . .' She looked down, feeling the wave of tears about to engulf her again. In past years they had been in a land of plenty, the prosperous firm, the days when there were no shortages. Everywhere she looked there was loss.

'It'll do us,' Clara said. She was dry eyed, tight in herself and staunch. Hatt had never had anything against Clara. She had always striven to get on with her daughter-in-law for Georgie's sake, even though she had found her rather bossy and officious at times. But now she was seeing the girl grow in stature. She was strong, brave. The two women's eyes met and Hatt felt Clara's strength go into her. 'Give the kids a day, eh?'

Hatt drew in a breath, filling her lungs against death and despair – and any trouble.

'Clara, you won't be unkind to Daisy?'

Clara looked back at her, seeing the imploring look in her mother-in-law's eyes.

'No. I'll keep my thoughts to myself – I promise.' She sighed then. 'What does it all matter, in the end?'

Hatt smiled faintly. 'Let's get to work then.'

Clara reached out and touched her arm. 'Mother, I have something to say to you.'

Harriet Watts pulled her shoulders back. 'I've got something else to say for my part as well. But I'll say it later – when all the others are here.'

They all sat round in the Wattses' cosy dining room, the children up at the table as well. Daisy kept Hester next to her, propped on cushions in a chair. She helped Hester eat and tried to stop her from messing too much with Georgina, who was on the other side of her. Hester was almost a year old now. She had a generous cap of dark hair and her brown-eyed face was full of life and mischief.

The meat course had passed with everyone trying to be cheerful and talk about everyday things, not dwelling on the past. They toasted Annie, who was working on the wards today but might be able to join them on New Year's Eve.

Daisy was full of admiration for the way Margaret kept the conversation going, about people in the office, the weather and asking the children about themselves and getting them to talk. She knew her stepmother was painfully aware of being the only woman in the room who had not lost her man. And Philip had done the honours carving the joint. Now though, glancing at her pa at the end of the table as they finished off the meat and gravy, she saw how exhausted he looked, as if he might just fall asleep there and then.

Everyone looked different, Daisy thought. The most obvious thing was that they were all in black. Hatt's house was draped in mourning, reminders of the loss in every room, in the shape of drapes over pictures and mirrors. All along the mantelpiece were photographs which

Georgie had taken: of the family, of himself, happy and smiling, with Clara and the children. There was so much pain, so many things that had changed in the last year. No Eb or Georgie, no James Carson for that matter. The place was full of ghosts of their lost lives.

She thought of Den Poole with a twist of mixed feelings. Now he was back in France, which in a way was a relief. She did not know what to feel towards him except gratitude for his quiet bravery, for the way he had loved her, stuck by her through everything, even if she could not fully love him back.

She leaned over to take Hester's plate. 'That's enough now – stop playing with it.'

Hester looked up at her, startled. She saw dots of light reflected in the child's dark eyes. I should give her a father, a respectable life, she thought. No one else is going to want me, soiled goods as I am. I should be grateful. He's a good man and I should try to love him as he loves me.

'Now,' Aunt Hatt said, standing at the other end of the table from Philip Tallis. A basin-shaped Christmas pudding sat gleaming on a plate. 'Jimmy – a little job for you.'

Her eldest grandson, now thirteen, got to his feet and poured a tot of brandy over the pudding as instructed, then struck a match. A halo of blueish flame hovered and died and everyone clapped.

Portions were handed out and soon Lily removed something from her mouth, eyes shining, and announced, 'I've got the sixpence!'

John, who had rather hoped *he* was going to get it since Jimmy had done the flame-lighting part, made to snatch it, only half joking.

'Stop – at once!' Margaret said sharply.

Aunt Hatt sat back, tapping a knife against her glass.

Every time Daisy looked at Harriet Watts she felt a shock. The plump, contented matron of the summer was a thinner version of herself. She still had her old, sultry beauty, but she had aged and her face was haggard. However, the new, determined light in Hatt's eyes drew everyone's attention.

'Right. I've got a few things to say.' Daisy could feel the nervousness coming from her in the way she fiddled with her wedding ring, as if to draw strength from it.

'Do you want to wait until the children get down?' Margaret asked.

'No, I don't think so,' Aunt Hatt said. She sat up straighter. 'It's nothing they shouldn't hear.' She cleared her throat and drew in a big breath. Daisy saw Clara's eyes fixed on her, with intense attention.

'These past weeks I've been here, in the house, most of the time.' Aunt Hatt spoke in a rush, as if she was afraid she would not be able to get the words out if she went any more slowly. 'I've been mourning my Eb and our Georgie, trying to come to terms with things . . .'

She stopped, looking down. Daisy felt so much for her, so sad, that her own chest constricted and she was close to tears. How they had all loved Eb and how much worse it all was for Aunt Hatt. She saw Harriet Watts's throat move as she swallowed and composed herself. She spoke, her eyes fixed on the sprig of holly at the centre of the cooling pudding.

'I don't suppose I ever shall.' She spoke gruffly. 'You can't come to terms with losing the two people dearest to you. The war's taken both of them, one way or another. And left our Clara a widow. Both of us are just two of the many widows in this country now, so it's no good keeping on. But I've decided something in the last few days.'

She looked round at them all. Daisy saw that her pa's sleepiness had passed and that his and Margaret's attention, as well as Clara and the children's – even Hester, who sensed the seriousness in the room – were fixed on Aunt Hatt.

'I can't stay here, mourning in this house. I don't want to be like the old Queen, making a project of grief. Oh, I'll mourn all right – to the end of my days. But I've got to *do* something, or I'll lose my mind. And I know what I've got to do. If Eb was still here he'd say, *Come on, wench – there's a job of work to do.* I know the staff are keeping the works going. And Bridget's been a rock in all this. But Ebenezer Watts & Son is like a ship without a captain. And if there's one person who knows that business like the back of her hand, it's me.'

Daisy saw Margaret and her father exchange looks.

'We've the war to win and a business to run,' Hatt said. 'And I'm going to be the one running it. I'm going to be there every day like I used to be and I'm going to do my damnedest to keep the place going at its very best in honour of my husband and my son. That'll be my life from now on.' She looked round fiercely, as if expecting someone to try and stop her.

'Well, I think that's truly *wonderful*, Auntie,' Lily said, so earnestly that suddenly everyone started laughing. Lily looked round, startled, seemingly unsure what she had set off until Margaret touched her head reassuringly and gave her a smile.

'I'm sure the business could do with having you there, Aunt,' Margaret said. She squeezed her aunt's shoulder. 'I've been going in trying to help out but I know Bridget and the others are feeling it terribly, not having one of you there. So if that's what you feel's right . . .'

'It is,' Aunt Hatt said.

'I can give you help if you need it,' Margaret said, looking at her husband. 'We're never far away, are we, Philip?'

He nodded kindly. 'Course not. It'll be good to have you back, Harriet.'

'Well, while we're on the subject,' Clara said, also sitting up tall, 'I've got summat to say myself.'

'Oh, dear,' Jimmy murmured. Again, there was laughter.

'What d'you mean, oh, dear?' his mother said indignantly. 'It's not going to affect you much, young man – you're at school for another year at least. No –' she looked round the table – 'I feel much the same as Mother. If all you do is sit round grieving you sink into yourself. So I've decided what I'm going to do. There's so many women at work now and all needing somewhere for their children. I'm good with children and with my three at school I rather miss it. What I'm thinking is, to start up one of those nurseries for working mothers – for a few children at least. For a small sum. And I can teach them all a little bit if they're old enough. With a clutch of little ones about the place, I won't have time to think – and that will suit me down to the ground.'

Thirty-Four

31 December 1916

'You did *what*?'

Margaret stared in shock at her younger sister. Annie's eyes, looking back at her, were gleaming with mischief. Up until then Daisy had seen nothing but affection in Margaret's eyes, a joy that her little sister, in love, was sitting with them so clearly bubbling over with happiness. Annie had been telling them about Fergus's work in France, laced with details about the eccentric lady who had set up the latest hospital in which he was working.

'I sent him a bottle of malt whisky. It's his favourite – from Scotland.'

'Heavens,' Philip said wryly from his chair as the family sat cosily round the fire. 'Whatever is the world coming to? Are we to toast the New Year in with a tot of the same then, Annie?'

'But . . .' Margaret was so flabbergasted that Daisy and the others all started to laugh. 'We *don't drink*, Annie. We've never touched a drop of that sort of liquor in our lives!'

'She never said *she* was going to drink it,' Daisy pointed out, from the floor where she was sitting with Lily and Hester. They were playing with some of the toys she had made them as Christmas presents.

'I still think . . .' They could all see that Margaret was

shocked to the core. Their strict temperance upbringing had put alcohol – and spirits in particular – well beyond the pale. For a moment their father, William Hanson, stood sternly in the room between them.

'Really . . .' Annie said seriously. She stopped herself. She had longed to say, *All week I have been on duty with a VAD who scarcely knows one end of the human body from another and spends her existence shocked to the core by the male form, and there is one man who howls half the night whatever we try to do for him and a gangrene case which is not improving and that smell – oh, the relief of being here and out of that stench and able to spend the night here with my family – and yet I can still half smell it!* But at the same time she did not want to bring these things into the warmth of the Tallis house and their New Year celebrations. For once she kept her mouth shut.

'Fergus is not very far from the Front,' was all she said. 'Things are . . . I mean, in the grand scheme of all that is happening – really, what does it matter?'

Margaret looked coolly at her, but all she said was, 'Let's make another pot of tea. And John,' she admonished her son, 'if you really have to set up a battlefield in here, take it over there and keep it out of my sight. It's the last thing I want to see in front of me on the Sabbath! Philip, you give him a hand moving it, will you?'

'What's your New Year Resolution?' Lily asked Daisy solemnly. They had moved on to wooden bricks and were building yet another tower for Hester to bash down with her gurgling giggle. She never seemed to tire of this game.

Irritated, Daisy looked at her little half-sister. 'None of your business,' she whispered, giving a smile but not really meaning it. She wanted to be left with her own thoughts, but there were Hester's endless demands as well as Lily. If she only had time to herself, she could sneak off up to the attic and carry on with the new design of bowl she was making. It had meant some very late nights. And when she was experimenting with making the little silver wire toys like the ones she had given as presents – a cat, a flower, some little people, even an engine – she had had an idea for something more ambitious ... Once again, she was angry with herself for feeling so frustrated, so angry with her life when all about her, people were suffering such overwhelming loss and grief.

'Oh, go on – tell me,' Lily said, in her intense way. She was like her mother; she took things very seriously.

'All right,' Daisy teased. 'My New Year resolution is never to let anyone in my room – *ever*.'

Lily looked down, hurt. 'You never let me in there anyway,' she said sadly.

Daisy felt guilty then. Why was she being so mean? It wasn't Lily's fault that she had got into trouble and had Hester and was now tied down and barely had a moment to herself (after all, who did, these days? Pa was working all the hours there were) or that now she had got tangled up with Den Poole and he felt he had a claim on her that she was not sure she had ever given him, and yet she did like him just a little – and who was she to be choosy now? Feelings swelled in her but she tried to be fair to Lily.

'All right,' she said. 'Maybe no one can come in except my very special sister.'

Lily leapt to her feet all lit up and flung her arms round Daisy's neck. 'Oh, *can* I? Can I be the only one allowed in? I want to come and see you working and all your lovely things you make!'

'No, I don't,' Daisy pointed out. 'Not any more. Hardly ever.'

269

'But you *will*,' Lily said, drawing back to look at her with great feeling. 'Because you're very *very* clever and good at it – everyone says so. And you're a *Tallis*!'

This hit home. Daisy looked into Lily's earnest little face and gave a genuine, warm smile. I must be nicer, she thought. 'Thanks, Lils.' She reached over and ruffled her sister's hair and Lily beamed at her.

Over cold ham and pickles, Annie regaled them with the more cheerful hospital news that she could think of, like the Christmas pantomime that had been put on by some kind people from Sutton Coldfield and all the carols and present giving. And soon they moved on to telling Annie the family news.

'So, Aunt Hatt wants to come back and run the business?' Annie looked amazed. 'Well, that's something I never thought to see.'

'Makes sense.' Philip stood up to carve more slices of the precious Christmas ham, sprigged with cloves and baked with mustard and sugar. 'If anyone knows that business back to front it's Harriet Watts. On the quiet she knew more of what was going on than her husband.'

'It'll be nice having her back here more,' Margaret said. 'I hope it doesn't wear her out, though. I'll go and lend a hand in the office if she needs it.'

'And Clara wants to open a nursery,' Daisy said.

Annie turned to her. She was such a fast eater that she had already polished off her meal. '*Is* she? Are you going to take Hester?'

Daisy was stopped in her tracks. Hester? Until that moment no such thought had occurred to her. To have more help than making do with the ladies in the office, with Margaret taking Hester when really she needed to be doing a host of other things ... Why had she not thought? She could work at Vittoria Street without constantly feeling she needed to rush home and relieve someone else, could maybe even – oh, please! – be able to do a little more of her own work again. She saw Annie register the look of excitement on her face.

'I hadn't thought,' she said, bewildered. She realized that she saw her struggles, her lack, as fit punishment. She was soiled, did not deserve better.

'But, how could I?' Her heart was pounding with hope. 'It's rather a long way away.'

Annie shrugged. 'Get up earlier.'

They all laughed at this and Daisy looked round, realizing that she was not seeing opposition in any of the faces around the table.

'But . . .' She didn't want to bring trouble to the occasion. 'I don't think Clara would have Hester.'

They all looked at each other, not needing to have this explained.

'I think she would,' Margaret said gently. 'Clara's very forthright, but she's come to terms with things. She's got too many worries of her own to be . . .' She did not finish the sentence.

'Is she serious – actually taking other children and not just her own?' Annie said, leaning forward in her intense way. 'Because if she were to be running something and needing help – well, I can think of someone who'd be a godsend.'

'Who?' Margaret asked.

'Lizzie Poole. She's at her wits' end with Ann. She could bring her there and work with Clara.'

'Her wages wouldn't be as good,' Philip said through a mouthful, shaking his head. 'They pay well at Kynoch's – best she'll've ever earned, I'd think.'

'Well, Clara would have to charge people – a bit at

271

least. And she'd have to pay Lizzie, of course. But then perhaps Clara wouldn't charge for Ann and she would know she was all right . . .'

'There'd be the tram fare,' Margaret pointed out. 'And she might not want to. You can't just organize everyone's life, Annie. Also, it's a long traipse for her as well.'

'Well, she's already traipsing over to Witton,' Annie pointed out. 'That's further if anything.'

'She could get up earlier?' Daisy suggested, and they all laughed.

Thirty-Five

January 1917

Aunt Hatt and Clara flung themselves into action as soon as Christmas was over and within a short time had formed a plan.

Margaret called into the office of Watts & Son next door as soon as work began again, to find Aunt Hatt bustling about and reclaiming her seat at the helm, prising open a tin of polish to give her desk a rub-over. Margaret took the tin from her hand and completed the job herself.

'That's it, Bridget, bring that chair round here, by my old desk – yes, and that table needs to be pulled further along. My goodness, what's happened to the gas mantles in here – it's like the Black Hole of Calcutta . . .'

The newer two women who worked at Watts's now were scuttling about looking intimidated by the arrival of Harriet Watts, but Bridget Sidwell, who had worked there for years, in the time when Aunt Hatt ran the office, jumped to it, beaming with happiness.

'It's going to be lovely to have you back, Mrs Watts,' she said as Margaret stepped aside to let them move the office's biggest chair into its rightful place behind Aunt Hatt's desk. 'The works has been such a sad place lately.'

She looked stricken for a moment then, as if she might have said the wrong thing in reminding Harriet Watts of her grief, but Aunt Hatt looked back into Bridget's eyes. She reached out to touch her arm.

'It's the only place I want to be now, Bridget. If there's one thing I can do for Eb and for our Georgie, it's keep this place going. And this place is full of *them*,' she added, looking round sadly. 'What's the good of me sitting at home knitting socks for sailors? In any case, the house is going to be overrun with children. I've told Clara, it's no good her trying to run any sort of nursery in her little house and why rent premises when they can have the run of mine, and the garden?'

'Oh, Auntie!' Margaret said, astonished. Was Aunt Hatt's beautiful house really to have a crowd of children let loose on it? 'Are you sure that's a good idea?'

Aunt Hatt gave her a level look. Margaret was surprised to see how her aunt suddenly appeared more like the woman Margaret had known when she first came to Birmingham. Her hair was more faded, it was true, but in her grief she had lost her matronly girth, her face was thinner and somehow more lively, as if her suffering had chiselled her down into a younger, sharper woman again.

'Yes,' she said. 'It's where the life is – young things. Life and vigour. There's been enough death and . . .' She shivered, pulling her cardigan closer about her. 'Terrible things. That's what I want round me more than anything now. What does the house matter?'

Daisy stood in front of Clara, in the big parlour of Aunt Hatt's house. She had carried Hester over on the tram, Hester bouncing excitedly on her lap.

Throughout the journey, although she was nervous, Daisy's mind was full of calculations. Would Clara be snooty with her? Would she accept Hester and if so how much would Clara charge her? Might she be able to work it all out, do her teaching, help Pa in the business and then perhaps reserve a day for making her own things?

She had let Hester loose in the lovely big room, with its glass doors over the garden. Hester immediately half-crawled, half-toddled across to them and gazed out at the lawn. And now the two women stood facing one another. Clara was wearing a workaday brown skirt, her hair wrapped in a scarf. There were a couple of half-filled tea chests on the floor. Like Aunt Hatt, she was thinner than before and the strain told in her face. She looked forbidding and Daisy felt her heart sink. But, finding her courage, she set out to explain why she had come and what she was hoping for.

'So – I was wondering . . .' she finished her nervous explanation, 'whether you might be prepared to let Hester be one of your first children?'

Clara was silent for a moment. Then, as if drawing herself together, she said stiffly, 'I've not behaved the best to you, Daisy. When I heard about – well, you know – I was . . . I don't hold with that sort of thing. It's shameful. But then . . .' Her eyes wandered and a look of acute sadness passed across her face for a moment.

'I was sure about a lot of things back then. I suppose I've had that knocked out of me a bit, me thinking I knew what was what about everything. I don't even really know what happened to you, to tell you the truth, and I don't need to. But you've been brave, Daisy, keeping her and bringing her up the way you have, I'll say that for you. I don't know as I could've done it the way you have, people talking and thinking the worse of you. And she's a lovely child.'

Daisy faced her, feeling emotional at these words.

'Of course you can bring her,' Clara told her, and Daisy saw her soften. 'She's family and she's lovely.'

She indicated the tea chests, into which she had been packing some of the family china away out of reach.

'Let me give you a hand?' Daisy said, eager to please. 'Pa can do without me in the works this morning. He knows I'm over here with you.'

'All right – that'd be a help. Here you go,' Clara said, handing her a blue-and-white vase from the mantel. 'I know it should be out of reach up there, but you never know. Better safe than sorry.'

'I think it's marvellous you doing this,' Daisy said shyly. She had always been in awe of Clara and still felt she had to be careful.

Clara turned, sheets of newspaper held in one hand. Her face was gaunt, and her arms were stick thin.

'Don't ever love anyone,' she said, with bitter humour. 'I've got to do something, Dais, or I'll go off my head. Georgie and me . . .' The tears came then, grief forcing through her brisk manner. 'I loved him, Daisy – God, I did.' She dropped the paper she was holding and sank on to a chair, covering her face with her hands. 'I wake up in the night and I think . . . I can't bear it. And then I know I have to because there's no choice. But my Georgie – he was gentle. He should never've been there. There's hardly any of them should. What's it all for?'

She raised her head then, with a wild look on her face. 'What are we doing it for? All of us? Us and them? The thousands and thousands . . .' She stopped, staring blankly ahead of her.

Daisy dared to come closer and knelt at Clara's feet, her own eyes full of tears. Hester, taking note of the emotion in the room, came toddling over and put her hand on Clara's thigh, which made both of them cry even more. Daisy sat back on her heels on Aunt Hatt's thick carpet and sat Hester on her lap. Poor Clara – and Jimmy, Ella and Gina! It felt unbearable to her that they would never see their lovely father again.

'I know it's not my business, but you lost someone, didn't you, Dais?' Clara wiped her eyes and looked at them both. 'Her father? I don't think ... I mean, I'm sorry if none of us really realized ...'

Daisy cuddled Hester close to her, rocking gently back and forth. Hester put her thumb in her mouth and snuggled up.

'It wasn't like you – not like Georgie, who was a proper man and a husband and father. James Carson was ...' She shook her head. As she spoke his name for the first time in an age, he felt so far away and long ago.

'He was a brilliant man, in his way – an artist, I mean. And I supposed he loved me, or thought he did. But he was selfish and full of himself. And I thought I loved him, but I think I really just liked him being so keen on me. I suppose I was rather full of myself in those days too.' She gave Clara a wry smile. 'A lesson hard learned.'

'It certainly is.' Clara leaned forward suddenly and pressed her damp cheek against Daisy's. 'You're all right, Daisy. You're a great kid. Don't let anyone tell you otherwise. And you can be a help to me. Let's be friends, eh? I'm sorry for the way I've behaved to you.'

Daisy smiled tearfully, warmed by Clara's honest nature.

'Yes, please,' she said. She seemed to have lost so many friends since having Hester, having to be with her all the time.

'So,' she said. 'This nursery. Do you have to tell anyone – ask anyone's permission, I mean?'

'I don't know.' Clara looked as if she had never thought of it. 'All I know is, there are mothers with kids round here who are going out to work and they need somewhere to go. I suppose I might need to register with someone – the corporation? I'll have to find out. But it's something I can do for the war. And I'm good with children. I miss mine being small.'

'Do you know how much you'll be charging?' Daisy said anxiously. 'I'm working for Pa for my keep, and I've taken on another class, but I'm only teaching three afternoons at the moment – although I'd be able to do more if she comes here.'

'Oh, we'll work it out,' Clara said. 'There's her food, of course. But I want to be able to help people. Some of them are getting an allowance.' She frowned slightly. 'Maybe you could as well?'

'I don't know, what with me not being married and everything.' Daisy blushed, looking down. 'I doubt they'd give me anything . . .'

'Well, I tell you what,' Clara said. 'I'm feeling my way here and you've the tram fares to pay as well. What if we start with two shillings to begin with, each time she comes? And I'll see how it goes.'

'Is that enough?' Daisy said doubtfully.

'Well, it'll cover her food. And you're family.' Clara smiled. 'I've already got a neighbour's daughter coming – starting tomorrow! She was desperate. And she's not much older than Hessie.'

The maid came in with a tray of tea and Clara patted the seat next to her. 'Come on – sit down properly and we can talk about it all.'

Daisy, who was used to rolling out of bed and being able to go to work downstairs, did indeed have to get up earlier, but she rose from her bed on wings, knowing Hester would be safe and happy with Clara and she could go back to work feeling freer, younger.

And at last, one precious afternoon of the week, she climbed up to her little workshop at the top of the house. She had tried to work at night sometimes, though the light was bad and there had been a strange, dreamlike atmosphere being there alone in the small hours.

Now, for the first time, she was able to sit at her workbench in the slanting light of afternoon. She stared at her tools – her hammers and saws, snips and files – picking each up, renewing her acquaintance with it in daylight as if it were an old friend. She drew in a deep breath, hearing only the muffled sounds from downstairs, feeling the quiet around her, letting herself expand into it. Her younger self before Hester and who she was now – how far apart they seemed! – could begin to reach out to each other.

She looked at her mother's little jewel box over on the shelf; the stones caught in the light and an ache filled her chest. It was so hard to remember her mother. She had no picture of her and she knew her as a presence, as lovely autumn-leaf hair, an arm about her back as they sat side by side, the smell of lavender.

'I'm sorry, Mom. I let you down so badly. But I'm going to try – really try . . . I'm a mother now,' she whispered. 'And you'll never see my little Hester . . .' A tear fell like a gemstone on to her old grey skirt. 'I wanted to make you proud of me and I don't think you're going to be now. But maybe Hester will make us both proud.'

Almost as if daring herself, she reached down to the lower cupboard and took out the silver tea set she had been making, the jug and sugar bowl, the troublesome teapot and the toast rack. She set them on the table in a thin patch of sunlight. They were solid silver and for now were tarnished and dull, but as the sun shone on them she took in their unusual shape that she had worked so hard to achieve, the angular spout of the jug, the simple lines and minute beading along the edges. She breathed in and out, almost a gasp of recognition. They were good. They were! More tears fell into her lap.

'Oh, Mom,' she sobbed. 'I want to do well. I want to be better – to be the best.'

She froze, hearing feet on the stairs, and quickly, angrily wiped her eyes. Who could be coming up here, just when she at last had a few moments to herself, to commune with her own work?

'Daisy?' Margaret tapped apologetically at the door and walked in. As she stood by the bed, the slanting light brightened a panel of her emerald-green skirt. She took in Daisy's sullen, tear-stained face.

'I'm glad you've been able to come in here,' she said carefully. 'I don't want to interrupt but – well, obviously now I have.' She smiled. 'Oh!' She took in the sight of the silverware. 'Those look ... Oh, they're delightful! And so unusual.'

Gratified, Daisy smiled. 'Thanks. I've still got a lot to do.'

Margaret tilted her head. 'You've been a brave girl, Daisy.'

Daisy felt her eyes fill again. She felt like a fountain of emotion this afternoon, as if suddenly there was space and time for it.

'I know it's been hard for you. But little Hester is – well, she's such a love. Oh, don't cry, dear. I didn't come up to upset you. In fact, what I came for was to give you this. It came in the second post.'

Daisy took the little brown envelope from her. Glancing up at Margaret for a moment, she opened it. She found a note in badly formed writing, with poor spelling, the lines lurching down the page.

Dear Dais,

I hope this gets to you. I'll try and write though I'm not much good at it. Make sure you write to me. You've got my number. Your letters are what I need.

It's snowing here and we're moving forward tomorrow so I don't know what might be next exackly. Everyone's in good heart.

I never said Daisy what you really are to me. Can't really now sept I know Im your man and I hope that's the way you see it now. I can be a father to your baby I know I can. So all I wont now is fer us to be toggether when this lot is all over.

Your mine Daisy I've always looked up to you since we was together all those years ago. Now I can look you in the eye and tell you I love you I would if you was here I've got my courage up now. I was going to ask one of the other lads what to say but 'ive done it myself.

Write soon won't you Dais, my girl.

Your Den.

Her eyes moved as fast over the words as the poor handwriting would allow. One hand went to her throat. *My girl.* In confusion she looked up at Margaret, who was watching her face. She did not want to show her the letter. She was overwhelmed and appalled by it. Had she really given him reason to think he could claim her like this?

'It's from Den,' she said, folding it quickly back into the envelope.

Margaret's eyebrows arched in surprise. 'Oh. He got round to writing! Anything to say? Is he all right?'

'He seems to be,' Daisy said. 'He says they're "moving forward".'

She saw her stepmother wondering, then restraining herself from asking any questions, and was grateful for her disciplined nature. She didn't want questions – she did not know how to answer them to herself, let alone to Margaret.

After a moment, Margaret said, 'You must write back, obviously. Write to him every week.'

'Every week?' Daisy stared back, horrified. She knew Margaret had always had a soft spot for Den Poole, but really, this was a lot to expect. She started to protest, but Margaret cut her off with a movement of her hand.

'You don't need to say much, Daisy. Just write a brief note – tell him things you're doing, day to day.' Seeing Daisy's deepening frown, she said firmly, 'He's not got much – I don't suppose Lizzie writes often with all she's got going on. Be kind to him, Daisy, that's all I ask. We don't know what's going to happen from one day to the next, do we?'

Daisy watched her graceful figure move to the door and heard her feet descending the stairs. She picked up a handful of silver wires and started to twist them restlessly, artfully, concentrating until she saw the beginning of a shape.

Thirty-Six

Daisy hurried along Vittoria Street. The dinner hour was coming to an end, the crowds thinning out, everyone glad to get back inside out of the freezing weather. A trickle of snow was falling. She had her scarf wrapped round her nose and her hands pushed into her coat pockets.

'Oh, why's it still so cold?' she muttered to herself. She was immediately filled with guilty feelings that she was to spend the afternoon in a classroom which, even if the heat from the stove was rather feeble, was indoors and safe and not exposed to the elements. So many grumbles these days were measured against the thought of soldiers in freezing, mud-filled trenches or sailors on the black, heaving sea. And now the sea was not just icy and terrifying in itself; it was patrolled thickly by German U-boats, trying to stop American ships bringing food across the Atlantic.

'They're trying to starve us out,' people kept saying. And now the Tsar had abdicated in Russia and no one knew what the Russians were going to do . . . Every day, the war seemed darker and more frightening.

She did her best to write to Den, struggling to find things to say. 'My life's just always much the same,' she told him. Her letters were short. His even shorter. He just seemed to need contact, seemed utterly delighted that she was in touch with him.

'Your letters are everything to me, Dais. Its like having a lite in the dark.' She was touched by this. The war had brought out a sweetness in Den – at least towards her – that she had never seen before. And now sometimes he mentioned a lad called Wilf, who came from Cannock. It seemed he had made a friend and she realized she had never known Den to have a friend before. In fact, she knew that lately she had been rather friendless herself. It was a very long time since she had seen May, who she had trained with, and now that she had Hester, May felt like someone from another life. Clara's friendship, even though Clara was a good deal older, meant a great deal to her.

'Ah, Miss Tallis! Just the person I was hoping to see.'

She had come in to help Mr Harper run the afternoon class in raising, chasing and *repousée*, but as she unwound her scarf in the corridor, she saw the head of the school hurrying towards her.

'Good afternoon, Mr Gaskin,' she said. She was always pleased to see him and had great admiration for him and for his own work. Since she had had Hester she felt awkward in his presence, uncomfortable with the fact that she had hidden her predicament from him. But now that Hester was older, and being cared for, she felt more relaxed again.

'Spare me just a second, will you, Miss Tallis?' he said, drawing her close to the wall to let the incoming students get past. He smiled sweetly at her. 'I'm sure you can imagine what I am going to ask.'

Daisy smiled. 'I think I might be able to guess,' she said.

'It may not be quite what you think. Of course, as you know, recruiting teachers is nigh on impossible at the moment. So, yes, it is about your perhaps taking on a little more. Might that be a possibility?'

'Yes, of course I'll help if I can,' Daisy said, her heart lifting. How good it felt to be able to say yes so easily, without the explosive sense of panic she would have felt at the thought of who was going to look after Hester.

'I realize you are already working with Mr Harper. But in fact, Mr Cuzner will soon be back to join him and I wonder whether I might poach you for something else?'

'Which class would it be?' Daisy asked.

'At present, I think we can offer you a choice,' Mr Gaskin said with a wry expression. 'It's either model drawing with Mr Bradley or clay modelling with myself.'

'Oh –' she didn't hesitate – 'clay modelling, please!'

Mr Gaskin smiled. 'You never were very keen on the drawing side, despite your excellence at it.'

Daisy blushed. 'I've always preferred shaping things. Like my mother, I suppose.'

'I gather she was an excellent smith in her own right,' Mr Gaskin said gently. 'Anyway – yes, clay modelling. We may be getting some convalescent soldiers from Highbury Hall hospital into the school. But there is something else. Arrangements have been made for someone to go into hospitals in the area to work with some of the men who are able, teaching clay modelling there. Now, we did have someone lined up, but sadly she is rather unwell at present. I wondered if I might persuade you? We could rearrange it so that you teach your other classes during the evening session?'

'Oh.' Daisy was taken aback. Her heart began to thud harder. Arrangements for Hester spun round in her head. She would have to get to Handsworth and back – yes, that was possible – and did this still mean she could keep her precious afternoon for work? And to go and teach men with all sorts of injuries – that sounded frightening. But then she thought of Annie. And she could fit it all in – just.

'Well, perhaps I could. Would it be the First Southern general hospital?'

'That might be one of them – I'm not sure at present. If you are interested in principle, it would be a godsend, Miss Tallis. I can give you the details before long, of course.'

The thought was beginning to brighten inside her.

'I'd like to do something for the war effort. I've never felt I could be of much use before.'

Mr Gaskin gave a wry smile. 'Indeed. We do have a role in retraining men where that is appropriate for them. But I was going to mention another proposal for something more that the school might do for the war effort. We are preparing to install machines, lathes and so on, in various of the rooms, including the elementary silversmith's room – for making Vernier and micrometer gauges.'

'When?' Daisy said.

'Soon – next month, I believe. But the room should be free for the evening classes, if you could manage the three?' He stopped, looking harassed. 'It has yet to be worked out fully, but don't worry – we all have to work round each other.' He began to walk away as if another thought had occurred to him. 'So you are prepared to do the convalescent work?'

He was gone before she could give an answer.

'Come on, Hessie, stop messing about,' Daisy urged her daughter early the next morning, trying to hurry her along Hamstead Road in Handsworth.

It was Friday and this morning she would be working for Pa. After that, there was no class to teach at Vittoria Street and she could have her one blessed afternoon in her workroom. She was already playing in her mind with the design she had begun of a wide, hand-beaten dish. And there was that twist of wire which was forming sinuously into the trunk of a tree . . .

Snowflakes tickled against their faces, although last night's fall had been light and there were only a couple of inches of virgin snow, creaking under their feet as they walked. Hester was entranced by it and not to be hurried. She kept bending down, trying to pick up as much snow in her arms as she could and exclaiming crossly when it slipped back to the ground again. Daisy smiled, in a moment's adoration of her little girl. But, adorable as she looked in a little crimson coat and cream woolly hat, Daisy had to get to work.

'For goodness' sake, we can't fiddle about at this time in the morning! Your grandpa'll be after me – he's got a lot for me to do today.' She scooped Hester into her arms and she squirmed and squealed, but Daisy hurried on to Aunt Hatt's house.

She knew Aunt Hatt would have left by now. She was amazed by Harriet Watts, the way she had inserted herself back into Watts & Son. She no longer had the driver that Eb had provided for her. To everyone's amazement she had said she would travel in on the tram.

'It's not far and I like being out and about,' she said. 'That's how you meet people – not sitting on your own in some private conveyance.'

And now she had opened up her house to other people's children.

Daisy let Hester down on the step of the big villa and was about to knock when the door opened.

'Oh – hello,' she said, smiling at Lizzie Poole. Lizzie, now in charge of all her family, still looked barely more than a child herself. In the bright, snowy light, her face was sallow and unhealthy.

'All right?' Lizzie hurried past, flustered as ever about getting to work. She was still on munitions at Kynoch's.

Clara appeared, brisk and businesslike, an apron over her dress. There was a smell of warm milk and bread.

'She's had her breakfast,' Daisy said, unbuttoning Hester's coat.

'I'll do that,' Clara said. 'And Hessie, you can go and see little Ann.' Clara smiled up at her. 'I've got another new one coming later as well.'

'I'll stop for a cuppa when I pick her up. See you later, Clara!'

As she hurried back along Chain Street, its soot-stained bricks and mucky pavements cheered by the icy whiteness, she felt excitement rise in her. This was her favourite day of the week. She might have to do some boring chores in the office, but Pa was letting her design a collection of silver bracelets in the workshop and then there was the afternoon ... Although they were still steadily selling MIZPAH items, there was a regular demand for other gifts and other jewellery.

She looked along Chain Street, past the carts pulled up at the side of the road, the horses' hot breath puffing into the air, the hurrying people; and as she approached their front door she felt happy, lucky, for the first time in a long while.

As she went to the door, she found someone else moving towards it at the same time. Glancing, she saw a dumpy little lady bundled up in a brown coat and shabby brown velveteen hat with a narrow brim. She thought for a moment the woman must have the wrong address, but Daisy saw her look up at twenty-four and twenty-six Chain Street as if to check, and then move towards the door of number twenty-four.

'May I help you?' Daisy said, from just behind her.

The woman whipped round, shocked. She was small, with a plain, jowly face and startled brown eyes. For a second she seemed so stunned that she could not think what to say.

'I . . . yes . . . I . . .' she began.

'I'm Miss Tallis,' Daisy told her, wondering if the woman was quite in her right mind. 'This is my father's business – Philip Tallis. Is there someone you want?'

'Yes.' She seemed pleased to grasp on to this. 'That's it. I want to see Edith.'

'Edith Taylor? In the office?'

The woman nodded in a heartfelt way. Daisy was about to ask her name but thought this might be a bit much for her, she seemed so overcome, and it was very cold out there.

'Why don't you step inside a moment?' she invited. 'I'm sure Edith will be here by now.'

She looked round the office door. 'Edith – there's someone here to see you.'

She cursed herself for ever afterwards for her terrible clumsiness. Only as she began to climb the stairs did it dawn on her what this might mean. The way Edith's usually gentle expression turned stony as she got up from her desk, the way she got up from the chair as if her legs were like rocks weighing her down.

Daisy was already on the first landing when she heard the terrible, stifled cry from downstairs, the moan of pain which brought Margaret running through from the back room into which, Daisy thought afterwards, she should have taken Mrs Paige in the first place. Mrs Paige who was to have been Edith's mother-in-law when her Arthur came home from the merchant navy.

Arthur, whose ship had just been one of the latest of many to be sunk by a German U-boat.

The sounds of Edith's grief echoing up the stairs tore into her. They were the sounds of someone who loved – really loved – and had lost the most precious thing in her life.

Thirty-Seven

February 1917

'My Darling Fergus . . .'

Annie, propped on the bed, alone in her nurse's room, leaned back trying to position her thin pillow, to cushion her back against the iron bed frame. She thought for a moment, smiling. *My Darling Fergus . . .* When had she ever imagined she would write such words? It made her laugh at herself. She, Annie Hanson, going all soft over a man – who would have thought?

Taking out the photograph she gazed on it for the umpteenth time. She remembered that afternoon – it seemed a short while ago – when she had stood arm in arm with him in the photographer's shop, looking adoringly into each other's faces and laughing at themselves for doing it. Fergus's smile reached out to her from under his military cap, his laughing eyes, almost as if he had just made one of his teasing jokes.

'I wish you were here, you cheeky devil,' she whispered. Her smile faded and her spirits sank. It was rare for Annie ever to sit still for long enough to allow her thoughts to intrude. She was forever busy on the wards or, on brief times off, rushing to see the family, or, even more rarely, Lizzie Poole. But now she let the dark reality of the war filter into her.

Of course, she saw the wreckage of war every day – the

wounds and amputations, the blinding and the wrecked lungs, the nightmares and terrors. Each life that came into the hospital brought with it a calamity of fear and loss, and for almost every man the trauma of having been too young, having been pushed and harried beyond anything that was reasonable for body and soul to withstand.

One of her patients saw Germans everywhere: hiding under beds, striding along the ward towards him or transposed on to the faces of the lads around him. There were the gangrene cases, the lads with trench foot, the boy who shook and shook . . . So often the work came down to one task after another – beds and dressings, observations and hygiene. It helped to stop you thinking too deeply.

Now, the dark pall of it all, the newspaper pages of lists of the dead, the trenches, dug in and trapped in a stalemate, each side taking more lives from the other. All the women dressed in black, the crêpe-draped houses; desperate seances for those clawing at the door of death to hear a beloved voice from beyond. The war was well into its third year now, and for what? Separating loved ones, breaking families and neighbourhoods. She thought of Aunt Hatt, how much loss there was now compared with a year ago. Tears filled her eyes. And how much longer must it all go on?

'Thank heaven you are all right,' she whispered, gently touching the face in the picture with her fingertip. She ached for him to be here, for him to take her in his arms, loving, teasing. But they were blessed compared with so many of the soldiers. Safer than most, anyway. 'Come home to me soon, my love,' Annie whispered.

He had written to say that he was in another place now and though he did not name it, she guessed, from his description – there being a large number of hospitals – that he was in Étaples, on the coast of Picardy.

'There is something exceedingly strange about this place,' Fergus had written.

It's a fishing port and the town is one of poky, scruffy little streets, the places surrounded by villages and farms, but now, well there's the ambulance depot (called Thumbs Up corner, apparently) and then, looking out from the edge of the village, an encampment, spreading for miles – like a town in itself, a sea, almost, of dull huts and pale tents, which make up the collective hospital and staff quarters. I am told there are upwards of six thousand patients here. I cannot say it is an easy place. There is a constant movement of lads going out 'up the line' or back, in, of course, much reduced states. Out of all the places I have visited so far, here there feels a sense of exhaustion, of bewilderment and dread. Or perhaps it is that I am simply tired and a little worn down. I don't have to tell you the nature of the work – the staff are on duty for almost inhuman hours. And because the camp is neither quite France nor England, there is a numbing atmosphere of displacement.

However, I am of course kept busy. Only now – at a very late hour – I have a few moments put aside from sleep to write to you, my dearest love. How sweet, what a salve of blessing is the thought of you – more than I can ever describe. Otherwise this place can feel like nothing but the effort of picking up the pieces of a gargantuan exercise in futility. Words we are not allowed to say, to think. Perhaps some of our patients will, in time, end up in your hands. It is a consolation, dearest, to think of this link between us.

There is so much I could say. Voices and images from the day present themselves before my mind but I am

293

too weary to write all and must – have a duty to – try
and snatch some sleep.

I love you, my dear girl. How feeble those words
seem, compared to what my heart would like to say. But
I send you all the affection and devotion that tired heart
can muster. Apologies for this scrappy note. How I
wish we could talk freely and face to face. I shall write
again as soon as possible.

With my love, sweet one, and goodnight. Fergus.

Annie took her pen again, trying to rouse herself from
the feeling of dark, sinful despair that was washing
through her. She must rally something in her of her
cheerful buoyancy. Fergus certainly did not need to be
sent an envelope full of gloom and despondency.

All is going along as smoothly as ever here. Though I
must say, I am writing this in this crabbed hand to make
the paper last. That is another thing – like so many
others – becoming harder to find.

The family are going along, despite everything. My
Aunt Hatt is like a blazing flame of energy these days,
working all hours in the business. They are of course
still making fuses (I think that's right) as well as the
usual things. She seems to be on a mission. Margaret
worries that she might burn herself out in the process,
but to me it seems the thing which is keeping her going.
Grief has whittled her to a thinner, nervier Aunt Hatt
and it is painful to see. But it must be better than sitting
home alone, dwelling on it all.

And Clara is now running a nursery and gradually
accumulating children. She is a fierce disciplinarian and
something in her has changed and become considerable.
Aunt Hatt's house now has six or seven children there

in the day and Clara has drawn up a programme for
them all. How she manages I don't know, but it is
extraordinary to see the depths in people which the war
has exposed. I am impressed by her – moved in fact. She
is a brave and clever soul.

A few highlights for you, heard this week on the
ward: 'Nurse, nurse? Why are those telephones ringing?
They never stop ringing – why doesn't someone answer
them?' (Said while there is a complete absence of any
telephones ringing at all.)

The padre's visit: 'Sister, what religion is this man?'

Sister, absent-mindedly, 'Oh, methylated, sir.'

There was a lantern lecture this week from a
clergyman called Mr Rees. 'Egypt and What I Saw
There.' Which didn't strike me as the most imaginative
of titles, but the talk itself was a wonder. Shall you and I
travel to Egypt and see the pyramids and tombs, once
all this is over, my love? It seems that dreams are a
flame of life which can hold us all together.

'Dear Den,' Daisy wrote.

She stopped, stumped as ever by quite what to say.
Den's very rare letters were brevity itself. He was not
used to writing, but she found something sweet in the fact
that he tried to write at all.

'Dear Dais, I hope this finds you well. I am getting
on all right. I hope you are all right and the family . . .
I'm thinking of you Dais and wish I could say things
better.'

Other than that, he ended, always, 'Love from Den.'

They did not read like love letters. Except that she
knew they were.

Daisy thought sometimes of James Carson's flowery
outbursts which she had found so exciting at the time and

295

now she wondered which was the more real. James Carson: all mouth and trousers, she thought. It was a phrase she had overheard one of the lads in her smithing class use and she had struggled to keep a straight face. Whereas Den said very little but something came through – the effort of putting pen to paper, his regard for her. Even though they never said anything much it felt warming to receive them. She had no real idea where he was and he never said anything about the war. All she could do was to try and think of cheerful things to tell him.

'I have a nice piece of news to tell you,' she wrote, relieved to relate something other than the daily round.

Yesterday your Lizzie changed her mind about working with Clara and has said she would! Clara is getting new children all the time and although Lizzie says she won't earn what she would at Kynoch's (or not yet, Clara said), she won't have to pay for Ann and she said she would rather play with children than churn out .303 bullets all day. After all, if there's one person who knows about little ones, it's Lizzie! You should see the garden at Harriet Watts's house, Den – the snowdrops are out and the children can go outside and run about. My little Hester is happy as a lamb there and I think Lizzie will be too.

I've been getting along all right and have been teaching some classes with the head of the school, Mr Gaskin. I was nervous at first, but he's a very nice man. And it's all so much better now that Hester is older and I know she is in good hands with Clara instead of having to bother Margaret, which I always felt rather worried about. She has done so much for me, but even so, with Pa being so busy . . .

Daisy stopped, taken aback to realize that it was a relief to have someone to pour out her feelings to. But she had written more than she intended and she crossed out the last part of the sentence.

'I'm going on too long,' she finished. 'When really not much has happened.'

She signed off, 'Kind regards, Daisy.'

She did not want to give Den any false encouragement.

Thirty-Eight

March 1917

'Daisy.' Margaret gave her a meaningful look across the table where they had just eaten tea. Auntie Annie had come to visit and Margaret clearly wanted to speak to her alone. 'Could you please take John and Lily up with you to help get Hester ready for bed?'

Daisy, seeing the pale, strained look on Annie's face despite her attempts to chat cheerfully, got to her feet. Her father did the same.

'I just need to go and finish off out the back . . .' Philip said vaguely, and headed towards the workshop again.

'Come on, you two,' Daisy ordered. To her surprise there was no protest from John. 'You can play with your soldiers while Lily helps me,' she whispered to him.

She could see that they too had felt an atmosphere in the room.

Margaret waited, the tension rising in her, until the door closed behind Daisy and the children. She turned and poked the fire, adding a shovelful of coal. When she looked back at Annie, she saw that the mask of cheerfulness had already slipped and she looked pale and desperate. She worried for her sister. Even nursing in peacetime took its toll, both physical and emotional, but now she sometimes wondered how they all kept going.

'What is it, dear?' she asked, leaning to lay her hand over Annie's as it rested on the table. It was cold as a fish. 'Oh, Annie – are you ill?'

To her dismay, Annie covered her eyes with her other hand and began to sob quietly. Annie, her tough, wiry little sister who almost never cried.

'Oh, my dear – whatever is wrong?' She leaned down, eyes full of worried sympathy, and waited.

'I haven't heard from him.' Annie uncovered her face and her eyes bored desperately into Margaret's. 'Not a word all week. Usually he writes every day – almost, anyway. If he can. And if he can't I know there's always a reason, some sort of rush on so that he's working all hours. But now it's . . .' She calculated. 'Six days since I've heard from him.'

'But . . .' Margaret could see all the misery and worry in her. Her mind raced. Was it that this Fergus fellow had somehow deserted Annie – was now somehow growing cool or disloyal?

Annie could read her thoughts. 'He's not like that. His letters up until last week were . . .' She stopped, keeping all Fergus's loving words privately in her heart.

Annie looked as if she had not slept for several nights, her face gaunt, eyes unnaturally big and haunted.

'Six days is not so very long, in the circumstances,' Margaret tried to reason with her. 'It might just be the post, surely . . .'

'No.' Annie was adamant. 'The post is reliable.'

'But he's not at the Front, is he?' Margaret said.

'No. But they could be shelling the hospitals, couldn't they?' She looked lost. 'Oh, I don't *know*.' More desperate tears came then. 'But there's something wrong – something's happened, I just know it has. We write all the time, like a conversation. It's vital!' She looked wildly at Margaret. 'He would never not write to me!'

'Oh, my dear.' Margaret got up and wrapped her arms round her little sister's shoulders, feeling her shake with sobs. Margaret held her, as she had now held Aunt Hatt and Clara and Edith, feeling the force of loss, of anger or grief or fear in all of them.

Dear Lord, she prayed inwardly, this war, this evil, godless slaughter. Where are you, Lord? What is your divine will? Show us your light and hope – hide not your face from us ... And please, please, don't let anything have happened to this man Fergus, who holds my dear sister's heart in his hands.

'The worst thing is that there's nothing, absolutely nothing, I can do,' Annie raged. She got up and paced the room, fiercely wiping her eyes. Standing near the mantelpiece with a glow of firelight behind her, clenching a fist, she said, 'It's only now that I know what love is – this force, this power, growing in you, inhabiting you, tearing at you. I think of our crucified Lord – and it's only now that I'm even beginning to understand what love means. And in some ways, by heaven, I wish I didn't.'

She prayed as she had never prayed before. Throughout most of her life, Annie's prayers had consisted of intercessions – some very heartfelt, others more dutiful – on behalf of others and their welfare. There were all the villagers she had helped or nursed as a young woman, before she and Margaret made their new home in Birmingham. Since the war began there had been innumerable young men who she had felt bound to remember in her prayers.

Now her reaching out to God was like a howl that she felt from the very core of her. In her agony, she knelt in her room, when Susannah was not there, her head, still often swathed in her nurse's veil, pressed to the floor, hands clenched into claws, begging the Almighty.

Just let him write. Please, please, just let me get a letter from him so that I know he's all right. Why hasn't he written? Oh, Fergus, please . . .

Never in her life had she been in such a state. She remembered what Margaret had told her about Edith, about the heart-rending sounds she had made when she heard the news about her Arthur. Thinking of it made her freeze with dread. Arthur's ship was sunk by a German U-boat. And the lads who went to the Front – Den and all the others – anyone close to them lived with fear day after day. But Fergus, she had thought reasonably safe. Had he just deserted her for some reason? But she knew that this was not the reason, knew him, his love and integrity well enough to be sure he would not behave in such a way.

So where was he? What was happening? On the wards she tried to hide her worry and act the role that was needed. In her room afterwards, she was close to falling apart.

Susannah was kind and sympathetic. She came in one day to find Annie pressed to the floor in supplication.

'Oh, my goodness,' she exclaimed, gently helping Annie to her feet, whereupon Annie burst into further tears. She took her in her arms as Annie sobbed. 'Still no letter from him? Oh, Annie, you poor girl!'

They sat side by side on the bed, while Annie cried out some of the tension which sat like a stone in her all day.

'I'm sure you'll hear soon,' Susannah said, stroking her back. 'They've probably got a rush on of some sort.' But they both knew that there was no big battle going on, or not that they had heard about.

301

'I knew I should never get involved with a man,' Annie said, in a feeble attempt at joking as she wiped her eyes. 'Nothing but blasted trouble.'

Another few days passed and then the letter arrived. Her whole body jolted with hope as she saw an envelope addressed to her, but even as she took it she could see that the handwriting was not Fergus's. It was a larger script, ornate and cursive in blue-black ink. Hope sank, like a stone slowly disappearing into mud. She had just come off an early shift that afternoon and she took the letter and climbed with leaden legs to her room.

Lochiebank House
Auchtermuchty
Fife
March 19th, 1917

Dear Miss Hanson,
    Never have I had to write a more terrible letter than this. My husband has deputed the task to me, since I might address you woman to woman.
    I can hardly bear to write the words, whose meaning, as yet, has still scarcely reached me. This week we heard from his Commanding Officer that our son, Fergus, has died in France. We had clung to the belief that as a member of the Medical Corps, away from the Front, he would be more protected and his life spared in this wicked, terrible war. However, we are told that he died of a form of influenza, endemic in the hospital, which came upon him quickly and, just as expeditiously, ended our dear boy's life.
    Our darling Fergus had written to us of you with great warmth and told us that the two of you were

engaged to be married. Indeed, he sent us a marvellous photograph. I know it has only been the unsparing demands of the war that prevented him from bringing you up here to meet us. We hardly know what to say to you, my dear. We are, and so sadly imagine you soon to be, prostrate with grief at losing the boy who we all held so dear. We send our condolences from hearts that are broken. The future seems now without meaning.

Should your own work ever grant you leave to visit us, Miss Hanson, as one close to our beloved son, the light and pride of our lives, you can be assured of a heartfelt welcome.

With regards and deep regret at having to convey such news,

Isobel Reid

III

Thirty-Nine

April 1917

'But isn't that an asylum?' Daisy said, when Mr Gaskin's assistant directed her to go and run a workshop at Holly-moor hospital, in Northfield.

'Not any more.' The woman smiled. 'Didn't you know? Both the hospitals at Hollymoor and Rubery are war hospitals now.'

Even so, as she walked between the budding young trees towards the rather grand-looking hospital building, its tall tower pointing up majestically in the middle, she felt shaky with nerves. Teaching young – mostly young – students at the school was one thing. But what was she to be faced with here? Men her age or older, with injured bodies and minds.

It was shocking enough what had happened to Auntie Annie. They had all heard the terrible news of the death of her fiancé – not even killed exactly by the war, but by influenza in the hospital at Étaples. The next thing they all knew was Annie turning up at the house in a state in which none of them had ever seen her before – nothing like. She looked shrunken, sick, and she couldn't stop weeping. It was as if she had broken down completely.

'They sent me away,' she sobbed, as Margaret and Philip looked at each other over her head, in utter shock.

'They said I wasn't working properly, that I need to rest. I didn't want to go back to Father . . .'

Of course they had taken her in. Annie had lived in the house, never going out, as if in a shell for the past weeks.

Is that what everyone's going to be like here? Daisy thought. Then she told herself not to be so stupid and selfish. All she was doing was helping out a little – instructing the men for a few afternoons. She stood tall and walked into the main entrance.

Soon she was in the care of a kind orderly, an older, bandy-legged little man with crow-black hair, who chatted away trying to put her at her ease.

'Oh, yes – been taking patients in here since July 1915. Course there's a few beds at Mr George Cadbury's place as well, not far away. The Beeches it's called. But this is on a much bigger scale. Right – come this way, please. You'll be glad to know your package of clay has arrived and is waiting for you, Miss Tallis.'

'Oh, good,' Daisy said, looking about her. She wondered what had happened to all the mental patients who had been in here before but did not like to ask.

'We've got quite a few workshops now – and classes. Got to keep 'em all busy somehow. All sorts, they have. It may surprise you to know that most of the splints and bed frames and that sort of thing which they use in the hospital are made here now. And there's arithmetic, French lessons, Spanish too, I believe, and bookkeeping. That sort of thing. All helps get into a job somewhere after, see. Right, this way . . .' He pushed on the door of one of the outbuildings. 'Your victims are waiting.'

Daisy tried to smile back, feeling even more as if she wanted to run away.

Inside, she saw a basic workshop room with several work tables, around which were seated a number of men.

There were not too many, she saw with relief, counting quickly. Eight. They all wore the blue uniform of convalescing soldiers and their eyes all swivelled towards her. One man had a black patch over his left eye.

'Right, you lucky lot,' the orderly announced. 'This is Miss Tallis from the art school in Birmingham.' With a twinkle he added, ''Er's come to do some modelling for yer today.'

There was laughter and Daisy smiled, feeling herself blush immediately. She knew she was going to have to get the upper hand in this straight away, as in any classroom.

'That'll be clay modelling,' she said. 'In case any of you gentlemen are in the wrong room.'

The lads all laughed again good-naturedly and one called out, 'Shame!'

'I'll leave you all to it then,' the orderly said, retreating.

Daisy licked her lips. The eight men – all young except one who must have been in his forties – were looking expectantly at her.

'We'll get started then,' she said. Her courage returned and she felt the sense of enjoyment she often had standing in front of a class. 'Anyone done any of this before?'

When she finally got back to Handsworth that evening to pick up Hester, some of the other children had already gone. Lizzie had taken little Ann home. Clara was now looking after a varying number of infants of a range of ages on most days. Her own children, still at home for the Easter holiday, were helping out.

Hester was so caught up in a game with Ella and Gina Watts that she hardly noticed her mother's arrival. Daisy smiled wistfully, feeling both relieved and slightly wounded at the same time.

'How did it go?' Clara asked. She had one of the younger children, a stolid-looking little boy, balanced on her hip. 'There's tea in the pot if you need it, by the way.'

'Oh, I really could do with a cup,' Daisy said. She went to the kitchen and brought back cups for herself and Clara. They perched on the sofa.

'It was . . . all right.' She laughed suddenly. 'Yes – it really was. They were very happy just to be doing anything, I think. There're two lads who've lost both legs. The one's quiet, but the other one kept joking all the time, which was almost worse than him being sad . . . Various other injuries but all right with their arms or they wouldn't have been there. Most of them haven't a clue, although one was quite good at it – the quiet one, come to think of it. Anyway, tomorrow I'm off to Rubery as well. And next week I believe they're also adding the First Southern General one of the afternoons – where Auntie Annie works.'

'But I thought you taught at the Jewellery School in the afternoons?'

'They've moved them to the evening now, so I can't hang about long today.'

'Goodness,' Clara said admiringly. 'I could never do that sort of thing.'

'I don't think I could do this.' Daisy looked round the room. However much she loved Hester, the thought of spending every day surrounded by small children was not her idea of heaven at all. But Clara was doing a wonderful job.

She had got hold of several little infant desks which were in a row at the back of the room, and a blackboard and stand were folded away against the wall behind. Most of the toys had been tidied in an orderly fashion.

'No, I wouldn't have thought I could at one time,'

Clara said. 'As it turns out, I quite like it. I just wish . . .' She trailed off, her face full of sadness. 'If I could have done summat like this and still have my Georgie . . .' She looked round at Daisy and in a concerned voice said, 'How is Annie?'

'She's going back to work,' Daisy said. She was about to say more when Hester finally noticed her existence and came running over. 'Mama!' She flung herself on to Daisy's lap and started grizzling, seemingly suddenly exhausted.

'Now now, Hessie,' Clara said. 'You've been a good girl all day. Don't start for your mom.'

Hester raised her head from Daisy's lap with a toddler's tired, tragic expression.

'All right,' Daisy said. 'Come on, you little monkey. We must get home. By the look of you I'll have to carry you all the way.'

Annie stood in the tiny spare room upstairs at the back of twenty-four Chain Street, staring at herself in the glass.

She saw a face so thin and haggard, the eyes almost too big for the shape of it, that she hardly recognized herself. The girl she saw – for she looked skinny and young, almost like a child – wore her old grey wool dress, which sagged limply on her. Her hair hung loose and dull.

For the past few weeks she sensed she had been standing outside herself, with a queer, floating, detached feeling. She could barely eat or sleep and now, staring at herself in her sister's house where she had been staying, she strained to understand that she was the person she could see reflected in the mirror.

I look like a madwoman, she thought. It can't go on like this.

There came a tap on the door. Annie did not turn or answer.

'Annie?' Margaret spoke cautiously, easing her way into the room as if there might be something about to jump on her.

It's not as if I've ever done anything like that, Anne thought tetchily. Since she had broken down at the hospital a month ago, since Sister had ordered her to take time off to rest, she had been here, being a cause of concern. She could see the strain on her sister's face. She was torn between two businesses, between too many cares. What with Aunt Hatt and me, Annie thought, Margaret is caring for the walking wounded herself.

She made herself walk calmly to the bed, sit down with her hands folded in her lap and look up at Margaret.

'I've come to a decision.'

'What, dear?' Margaret came and sat beside her. Her worried tone grated on Annie as well. She was not used to being the one who had to be looked after.

'I am going back to the hospital.'

Without even looking at Margaret, she could sense that her sister was torn between relief and concern at this announcement. She kept having to explain to John and Lily – Lily especially, who adored Annie and thought having her to stay a great treat – that their aunt was not herself, and why. Lily was touchingly loving to her, would come in to her room and say things sympathetic beyond her years.

'I know you have had a terrible shock, Auntie,' she said soon after Annie arrived. 'And when you've had a shock you need lots of sweet tea and rest. I know there's a shortage of sugar so you can have all my sugar in your tea.'

Annie, at that time hardly able to think or say anything without tears dropping from her eyes, was soon wet-cheeked at this and Lily came and sat down, putting her arms around her and leaning on her like a devoted little dog.

Lily was a marvellous child, she thought. But she couldn't just go on like this.

'I don't think you're ready,' Margaret said. 'Your . . . What happened to Fergus has knocked you for six, on top of all the other strains of the hospital.'

For six. She could not put into words the strange darkness that had possessed her mind since she received the letter from Isobel Reid, Fergus's mother. There were dreams, not about Fergus, but which seemed to flood her mind night after night: noxious shadows, images of putrefaction. The butchering and derangement she had seen in so many of the men she had nursed flooded the night, as if it had all been stored up waiting there to overcome her when she was at her weakest. One night all she dreamt of was the torso of a man, with no arms, no legs, no head, which was screaming at her.

She had not confided these images to Margaret or to anyone else.

'I just think,' she said, struggling to remain calm, 'that I spend too much time alone and that it's not good for me. I feel so useless.'

'Not everything has to have a use – not all the time,' Margaret said.

' "Have nothing in your house that you do not know to be useful or believe to be beautiful," ' Annie quoted. 'Wasn't that what William Morris said? I've been sitting uselessly about in your house for nearly a month now. And I'm certainly not adding any ornament to it.'

'Yes – but Morris meant *things*, not people. And whatever else, Annie, you are beautiful.'

'Oh, nonsense. But . . .' She watched the scuffed toe of

her boot, sliding it back and forth along the floor. 'I think that if I were to return to my work, to the care of others, it would help to take me out of myself.'

Margaret leaned round then, giving her a direct, searching look.

'My dear, you have been very unwell. It has been terrible to see you in such a low state.'

'I know.' Annie looked down, fighting the tears which swelled in her. She mustn't weep, not again. 'I have hardly known myself. He . . .' She could not stop her grief any longer and the sobs racked her body.

Margaret, saying, 'Oh, my poor, dear little sister!' wrapped her arm round Annie's shoulders.

'He opened me – in some way I never knew before. I don't feel the same. But . . .' She dragged her hands across her eyes and looked back at Margaret. 'I have to go on somehow. Like Aunt Hatt has to. Like Clara. We all do. I want to carry on our work – his and mine.'

24 Chain Street
Birmingham
April 15th 1917

Dear Dr and Mrs Reid,

My apologies for taking so long in sending a reply to your kind letter. In reply I wish to be truthful and the truth is that since I heard of Fergus's death, I have been unwell. I have not been myself, and have taken a brief time away from the hospital, staying with my sister. However, I am now on the point of returning to my duties at the First Southern General.

Your letter meant a great deal to me. I have read it many times and will treasure both the letter and the

314

deep trust you show in your beloved son in treating
with such kindness a fiancée whom you have never met.

I would like very much one day to come to Scotland
to meet you both, once this is possible. At present I do
not feel able, but I am sure I shall soon feel stronger.

In the meantime, all I can do is to send my
condolences – a word so dreadfully inadequate – for the
loss of a person we all loved so very much.

Yours more sincerely than words convey,
Annie Hanson

Forty

Before long, Daisy found herself travelling about the city on three afternoons each week to different hospitals. At first she was at Hollymoor and Rubery hospitals – both sprawling institutions in large, isolated grounds at the very edge of the city, which had been asylums and were now converted to use as hospitals for the wounded and convalescent, who were brought in by train through Rubery station. Rubery was now known as the First Birmingham War Hospital and Hollymoor as the Second.

Soon, another hospital was added to her list, not, as it turned out, the First Southern General, but Highbury Hall. This was the gracious home of the Chamberlain family, set in beautiful parkland in Kings Heath and which was being used as a specialist hospital for orthopaedics.

'I feel as if I spend half my life on a tram now,' Daisy grumbled to Clara, during her first week of running sessions in all three hospitals. She had just reached Handsworth on yet another tram to pick up Hester.

'You look all right on it to me,' Clara said as the two of them gathered Hester's things together. 'There are roses in your cheeks.'

'Are there?' Daisy smiled, surprised to find that she was, indeed, enjoying life. 'I don't know why – I seem to be rushing from pillar to post all the time. I have just enough time to get home, get Hester to bed and throw a meal down me and off out for the evening classes!'

'Well, it's good to be busy.' Clara slipped Hester's little

coat on to her and bent to kiss her cheek. 'Bye-bye, lovie – see you in the morning.'

'Goodbye, Clara – thank you,' Daisy said. 'It makes all the difference in the world knowing she's here with you. And by the way, you're not looking so bad yourself.'

Clara's freckly face broke into a smile. 'It helps, doing this. I'm loving it, to tell you the truth. If there was anything could bring my Georgie back, that's all I'd want, like a shot.' She glanced over at one of the photographs of Georgie on the mantelpiece. 'But nothing's going to turn the clock back so that things can be as they were. At least I had him for as long as I did – I have my children. Not like poor Annie . . .' She looked at Daisy as if to include her in this, but said nothing. 'I'm just trying to make the best of it.'

At first, Daisy had found facing each new class nerve-racking. As well as having to walk into a room where a group of strange men would be waiting, the thought of their injuries and disfigurements made her feel queasy. But shocking as some of those were – the missing legs in particular – very quickly most of the men she met became individuals whose talents and weaknesses in the work she could address, whose injuries were only a part of them along with their smiles, their voices, their sense of humour.

She soon got to know them: the jokey Canadian called Gilbert, face partly burned, body twisted; Tommy recovering from bullet wounds, who wanted to model nothing but aeroplanes; the tall one with the dark curls and long scar down his left cheek, whose legs ended at the knees, whose long fingers showed skill and sensitivity and who, it took a while to find out, was called Stephen.

Very few were not memorable in some way, though

317

one or two were here today and discharged tomorrow. Most seemed happy to be there though one, a thin, austere man called Francis, was always quiet, seemingly sunk in bitterness. He came to the class as if forced into it. One of the other lads whispered to her, 'His guts are in a terrible state, miss.'

Several of them she knew would stay in her mind because they were gifted. She would set them to work the clay into a particular shape – a bird, an animal. She would show them the tools and explain that the best approach to modelling, to form a strong structure, was to cut away from the central body of the clay. She talked about the underlying anatomy, the bone and muscle informing the shape.

'The best models always honour this knowledge of what lies underneath,' she told them. 'But let's not get too carried away – we'll start with quite simple things.'

But she did bring in anatomical pictures – birds and horses, dogs, even the human skeleton, showing the stretch of muscle over bone. Some of the lads seemed to understand this instinctively; others learned well. Tommy was more interested in wings and propellers. And a few were completely clueless and just seemed to like hacking about with lumps of clay. But it hardly mattered. It took them all out of themselves for a while and passed the time.

There were other boys, among the joking and teasing which went on, who she remembered for other reasons. Amid the talk of the war, and how we were going to thrash the Hun now that the Americans had come on our side, there was the lad who talked excitedly about Russia. The Revolution was taking place now the Tsar had abdicated! That was what would happen everywhere soon! The workers of the world were going to rise up together and claim their rightful share! There would be a new world order, not run by rich toffs! Some of the others grunted in agreement: one or two told him to stick it and find some manners and not keep on about politics.

Joe, the one with the patch at Hollymoor who had lost an eye and suffered bad abdominal injuries, was always sweetly courteous to her in an old-fashioned manner. He said he was from a farm outside Hereford and because his mother died when he was young, he had never actually set eyes on a female of any age until he was seven years old.

'Good gracious!' Daisy said. The lads were all seated round two tables with their clay and she stood moving between them. She saw Stephen, the tall, curly-haired one, raise his head with interest at this. 'Did you never go to school?'

'Nope,' he said. 'I think they just forgot about us all the way out there – me and my brother. Dad put us to work on the farm soon as we could walk more or less, and that was that. We was in bed with the sun, come five or so in the winter – and up with it again. We never knew no different.'

'You poor little sod,' someone else remarked.

'So who was the first woman you ever saw?' another wanted to know.

'Oh, she were quite an old girl from another farm,' Joe said. 'I was out by the road and 'er went past with a cart-load of muck. I never knew 'er was a woman then any' ow –'ad a bit of a moustache on 'er, that one.'

Everyone roared with laughter at this.

'Well, you take a good look at Miss Tallis,' someone suggested, still chortling.

'Oh,' Joe said seriously, 'Miss Tallis looks like an *angel* to me!'

Daisy blushed, touched by his sweet innocence. She saw Stephen smile and look down at his work again.

The scar distorted his cheek when he smiled. 'Now, now,' she admonished kindly. 'Let's get on with our work, shall we?'

There was Albert, another lad who she taught at Rubery hospital, who had lost a leg and an eye and had a badly puckered face. He told her matter-of-factly that the loves of his life were football and a girl called Beatty. Football was something he would now only be able to watch, but Beatty was sticking with him and 'At least I'm still alive,' was his way of looking at it. 'Not like my pal Sam – he bought it on the Somme, left a wife and two kiddies.'

Daisy saw Beatty sometimes, waiting out in the spring sunshine for Albert to finish the class. She was a shy girl, a little older than Daisy, with brown hair swept neatly back and tucked under her hat and a gently pretty face with slender arching brows. She would say hello, but all the time her eyes were searching for Albert and they came alight when she saw him.

For all the tragedy that Albert was so wounded – though he was very determined to get along with a prosthetic leg – there was something about the pair of them that wrung Daisy's heart. Love. Real love. Something she knew she had never had. And I never will now, she thought. Much as she loved her little Hessie, the notion filled her with despair for a moment.

And yet there was a man, Den, who thought she was promised to him. He had started writing, 'To my Daisy,' at the beginning of his little notes. She found herself thinking, If he comes back, if the war spares him, then it's a sign I'm meant to marry him.

One day after seeing Beatty Solomons again, Daisy went home resolved to write to Den as soon as she had time. She had had another letter from him, one of his simple, matter-of-fact, illiterate notes. Each one that arrived gave her a twisted confusion of feelings. On the one hand she was filled her with longing for love, and increasingly with gratitude for his devotion. It was something miraculous to be loved. She thought of the depth of Annie's grief, of Clara and Aunt Hatt. There was so much loss about her – she was the one who was fortunate. Despite all this came a feeling of dread, of being pushed by him in a direction that was nothing to do with her own will.

One Saturday evening, once Hester was settled down, she wrote another letter to him.

'Dear Den.' This was as far as she got for a long time. She sat on her bed in the fading light, hearing John and Lily running up and down the lower staircase, playing some game. Reaching over, she picked up the bundle of silver wire from beside the bed. Running her hands along it, she could feel its twisting shape. She was fashioning it gradually into a tree and it was working rather well. Sighing, she put it down. Working with metal was a lot easier than writing letters.

'I am teaching a lot of classes,' she began again. There did not seem to be any point in going into detail. 'The family are well and so are Lizzie and all the girls. Auntie Annie is better now and has gone back to the hospital.' She knew Den was devoted to both Margaret and Annie, but still could not think of more to say about Margaret. Her stepmother, she realized gratefully, went on, undramatically, from day to day.

She wished him well and signed off. Having written the envelope, she lay it on the bed beside her, trying to confront herself. Den seemed to have gone away to another world. But if he came back, what was she really going to do? Den had overcome a lot, she knew all too well. There was his father's accident, his desertion of the family and later death. And their mother Mary, who had struggled to cope, had died far too young. And yet Den had worked and learned at Watts & Son. He had grown into an impressive man, solid and kindly. And he loved her. What more should she expect? She was hardly in a position to be fussy, she knew that. And it would be good for Hester to have a father – wouldn't it?

Staring up at the darkening window, she wondered whether Pa realized that Den had serious intentions towards her. She had never talked to him about it. The pain of the relationship with her father coursed through her again. Things were much improved on the surface, but her disgrace, her having Hester out of wedlock – with James Carson of all people – had wounded something for ever in their relationship, it seemed to her. She knew that he thought she was never going to do what her young promise had led him to think she would – to live up to him, to her mother, Florence Tallis. To go beyond, to be great.

Perhaps he had washed his hands of her in that regard and would not really care who she married?

Forty-One

June 1917

'How are you finding it, Miss Tallis?'

The conversation with Mr Gaskin came back to Daisy as she sat on the tram, sweeping out of town along the Bristol Road. After their class at Vittoria Street the night before, he had approached her, almost as if worried.

'I hope it's not too much for you? I imagine there must be some . . . some difficult things to witness?'

'It was rather hard at first, but I'm used to it now.' She smiled, realizing how disappointed she would be if she had to stop. 'In fact, I enjoy it – and I think the patients find the classes beneficial.'

'Colonel Marsh has indicated that he thinks very much so – in fact, he has furnished us with a certificate to say so.' Mr Gaskin smiled as if he found this rather quaint.

'It's good to feel I'm doing something for the war effort,' she said. 'How are the gauge-making classes coming along?' she thought to ask.

'Yes, yes, very well . . .' He began drifting away. 'Anyway, that's excellent, Miss Tallis – keep up the good work.'

Looking out at the bright day, as the city thinned and opened into the suburbs, she felt the glow of his praise. It was a long time since anyone had praised her, she thought. Her younger years, full of achievements and compliments, of her own confidence and prizes, seemed another life, many years ago. She thought of the half-finished silver projects in her attic and her spirits sank, wondering for a moment quite why she was making such an effort to keep working on them.

But as soon as she reached Hollymoor she was taken out of her self-absorbed thoughts. Walking through the grounds she heard spring birdsong from the trees, some of which still had frills of blossom on them. Her heart lifted. She wore a silver-grey dress and had plaited her hair up in a coil at the back.

As she approached the workshop, near the door she saw someone in a wheelchair, facing away from her. Drawing closer she began to recognize the dark curls of the man called Stephen. His body seemed to list a little to the right, something she had not noticed when facing him.

As she walked round to greet him, he smiled shyly and looked up at her. 'I thought I'd hold the door open. I think everyone's in now, though.'

'Oh, good – thank you,' Daisy said. Her mind on the class ahead, she was about to step into the workshop.

'Would you mind pushing me in now, please, Miss Tallis?' He spoke apologetically, as if he was bothering her. 'I let the orderly go.'

'Oh, I'm so sorry,' Daisy said, embarrassed that this had not occurred to her.

She manoeuvred the chair, aware suddenly of being very close to the young man, of the delicate shape of his neck, the rich brown, curling hair. In those seconds she was brought up close to the reality of his injuries. His shoulders in the blue uniform tunic were broad, strong looking, though there was that slight tilt to them, as if something within had been shortened in some way. He had a thin blanket draped over the lower half of his body which hung abruptly straight down where his legs ended. It was painful to see. Even though he was facing away from her, she averted her eyes.

'Here we are,' she said brightly, pushing the chair up to one of the tables amid the chat of the other men. They quietened then and called out greetings to her.

'Good afternoon.' She smiled fondly round at them all.

Leaning down, she pushed on the lever to put the brake on. As she did so, she was suddenly acutely aware of her closeness to him. She saw, close up, the weave of his uniform and texture of skin on the back of his left hand, resting on the grey blanket: the pale, sallow skin, the tributaries of veins. She caught a scent of carbolic soap and as she straightened up, her hat brushed against his shoulder.

'Oh, sorry!' She was startled. Even bending so close to him had felt strangely intimate, as if she was doing wrong in some way.

'That's all right, miss – no harm done.' He smiled with a certain irony, as if to say, *What's a little knock from a straw hat compared to all this?* 'Thanks.'

Until now she had paid little attention to him. He was the quietest member of this class and one of the more able, but he would lower his head and fix his attention on the task in front of him, rather than joining in the class chit-chat. Now she found her eyes drawn to him, wondering about him.

'Today,' she said, speaking up to get their attention, 'I've brought a model from the art school for you to work from.'

Before, they had worked mainly from pictures, or even just from memory. She drew it out of her bag with a flourish.

'Ha – a parrot!' someone laughed.

'Yes, well, it's a cockatoo.' The bird was creamy white with a rakish yellow crest, its claws fixed on a stand so that she could set it up on the table. It had been heavy to carry.

'Couldn't you've brought one that was still alive?' asked the lad with the eye patch.

'I think that might have caused me a bit of trouble on the tram, Joe,' she said. 'Specially if it was a bit of a chatter-box.'

'My Uncle Fred had a parrot,' said a new lad, called Windy for reasons she did not care to enquire about. Like many of the others he was not local – came from down south somewhere. Trying to send the wounded lads to a hospital near home had largely gone out of the window months ago. 'Cor, 'e used to make some ripe announce-ments –'e'd been in a pub, Uncle Fred said. One day—'

'Shall we get on with it, gentlemen?' Daisy said sternly.

'Yes, miss. Sorry, miss.'

She saw Stephen look down, apparently amused.

Daisy cut up the block of clay into shares for them all and handed them out.

'I've done a lorra fings in the last few years what I never expected,' said Sid, a man from somewhere in London with a badly scarred face. He held up his lump of clay. 'If you'd asked me a year or two back I don't s'pose I'd've said, well, yeah, mate, I'll be sat in Birming-ham, me chest and fizzog full o' metal junk, making a clay parrot . . .'

The others laughed.

'Well, it doesn't look much like a parrot yet, Sid,' Daisy said and Sid pulled a face like a small boy who has been ticked off.

They settled down, though parrot stories kept emer-ging. By the end of the class a variety of clay cockatoos

326

had appeared from the clay – some of which, truth to tell, looked more closely related to the pigeon, and a few that were really quite good.

All through the class, she felt herself wanting to go and look at what Stephen was doing and for some reason held herself back. The sudden shock of intimacy she had felt at coming so close to him had made her feel shy towards him. But she did not want to look as if she was ignoring him.

Towards the end, as they were packing up and some of the lads who could walk were pushing the wheelchair-bound out of the room – 'Thanks, miss!' – he still seemed absorbed in his work and she walked round to look at what he had done, standing at his shoulder.

'That's very good.' She was truly impressed. He always did a good job, but this was particularly fine. By this time, he was using a thin stylus to mark on the feathers.

'The cockatoo-ness of the cockatoo,' he said, leaning back to look at it. She liked his voice. It was quiet, smooth, unaffected.

'Yes,' she laughed, head on one side. 'That's the thing. You've got the underlying structure – the shape is just right so that it actually *is* a cockatoo.' It was easily the best one in the room. 'You're very good,' she said. 'Have you done any modelling before?'

'No.' He set the bird down carefully and rubbed his hands together. His long fingers were grey with dried clay. 'Not this – but I do work with my hands. Cabinet-making, restoration. I work – or used to – with my father. But . . .' He seemed hesitant to admit this. 'I do a bit of drawing as well. It makes you examine things – really take notice of every aspect of them.' As he spoke he looked ahead of him and she could not see his face. 'I used to paint a little as well – just watercolours, when I had a bit of time. Are you an artist, Miss Tallis?'

He twisted round to look at her then, seeming glad to talk about *something*, not just the joking chatter that went on most of the time. But she also saw a moment's flicker of pain pass over his face. His eyes were greyish blue and like his voice, sincere.

'An artist? No – not really.' She moved to the other side of the table so that he did not have to keep turning in the chair. 'I've had to do a lot of drawing in my training at the art school. We did drawing and a lot of modelling, like this –' she pointed at the cockatoo – 'so I've done plenty, but what I really like is designing things. I'm a silversmith.'

She felt the pride in her voice as she said it and she saw the respect in his eyes.

'Are you? That's an impressive trade.'

'My father and mother were silversmiths. I mean, my father still is – my mother passed away when I was young. She was very good, everyone says,' she said with the usual swell of pride. 'My father taught me a lot, but then they opened the school in Vittoria Street and I was able to go and learn more there.'

'I learned everything from my pa as well,' he said. 'Wood is more our thing – he's marvellous at it. I hope I'll be able to go home soon. They did come over here to visit, once, when I first came back from France, but it's a long trip for them.'

'Where's home?' she said, relaxing back to lean on the other table, facing him.

'Suffolk,' he said. 'Town called Framlingham. Nothing like as big as Birmingham – it's a small town but it has a castle.'

'I've hardly been anywhere except Birmingham in my

life,' she said. 'And we live very near the middle of town – in the Jewellery Quarter as it's called. Hockley. It's a busy place, full of businesses all crowded in, everybody making all sorts of things. The only place I've seen is where my stepmother comes from – a village near Bristol.' She felt a blush come over her, the reason why she had been there the last time coming powerfully into her mind. 'It seemed so small and quiet! I was glad to get back here.'

'Yes,' Stephen said. 'I suppose it must feel very different.'

There was a silence in which both of them looked down, shy suddenly. Daisy, feeling obliged to break the silence, said, 'I wish I was better at painting.'

'Sometimes,' Stephen said, 'I wonder whether after all this –' he gestured towards his absent legs – 'after all that's gone on, painting isn't a completely ridiculous, insane, futile thing. Other times, I think p'rhaps it's the *only* thing to do.'

Daisy met his gaze. 'Creating beautiful things is *the* thing to do.' She sounded so insistent that only afterwards, she thought to add, 'I think.'

Their eyes held each others'. It was as if a long, passionate conversation was opening out, an endless flow of exchanges, and that they could stay there for hours and talk and talk. At least, that was how it felt to her. He would ask a question that mattered and she would say something that mattered and on it would go and how rare and precious that was.

'They'll be sitting down for tea,' Stephen said with a movement of his head and the moment faded. But she could hear his reluctance.

The other lads had gone and she was about to say, *Let me wheel you back inside,* when one of the orderlies popped his head round the door.

329

'Ah, Ratcliffe, there you are!' he said chirpily. 'Thought you must have run off somewhere!'

For a second Daisy was taken aback by the brutal tactlessness of this, before realizing that it was said with a sympathetic irony that brought a grin to Stephen's face and he was lit up with amusement.

'Thank you, Miss Tallis,' he said, still smiling as the orderly swivelled the chair round. 'See you next week.'

She watched him disappear through the door, moved by the sight of his long body in the chair. How must he have looked while standing? she thought, finding sudden tears in her eyes.

Next week seemed a long time away.

Forty-Two

'Aunt Hatt?'

Margaret pushed open the door of number twenty-six Chain Street and went to the front office. They had had a busy day in number twenty-four and she had been intending to pop in earlier. She guessed, though, that her aunt would still be there.

Aunt Hatt looked up from behind her desk. There was no one else in the room and for a second Margaret was shocked by the sight of her all over again. Harriet Watts was so much smaller and thinner than she had ever been – as if grief was sucking her away from the inside.

'Still here then?' Margaret smiled at herself for stating the obvious.

'Hello, love.' Aunt Hatt's face held strain and exhaustion, but she forced a smile. 'Come in – I was just shutting up.' As both of them heard footsteps in the passage, Hatt added, 'Bridget's just on her way out.'

Bridget Sidwell appeared then in her summer coat. Margaret remembered Bridget as a plump, comfortable-looking girl with wire spectacles. Now she had grown into an older, matronly version of herself, married to Jack, who worked upstairs, and bringing up their two lads.

'Ooh, hello, Margaret.' Bridget's own tired face lifted. 'Shall I ask Lucy to make you a cup of tea?'

'No . . .' Margaret was saying but was overridden by Aunt Hatt's, 'Oh, yes, would you please, Bridget? I could do with summat I can tell you.' She pulled out a chair. 'Come and sit with me, Margaret.'

As Bridget was leaving the room her eyes met Margaret's. Bridget looked briefly and meaningfully at Aunt Hatt and back at her. Margaret could see all the sorrow and concern in her eyes.

'Of course, Aunt. Thanks, Bridget.'

Bridget disappeared out to the back. On her way through, she popped in again and said, 'Bye, Mrs Watts. See you tomorrow.' She nodded at Margaret as well.

They heard the front door close. There was a moment's silence, in which the gas mantle hissed, the clock ticked, and two men passed outside, talking. Aunt Hatt sat with her hands folded one over the other on the desk, bolt upright as if she had a wall behind her. From each of her earlobes hung a gold droplet, which Margaret knew that Uncle Eb had made for her. This was a good sign, Margaret thought. Aunt was beginning to wear jewellery again. But after a moment, before Margaret could say anything, Aunt Hatt slumped forward and laid her head on her hands on the desk, her shoulders shaking.

'Oh, Auntie!' Margaret said, distressed. She did not know what else to do but lay a hand on her beloved aunt's back, caressing her as she wept, making soothing noises as she would for Lily or John or Hester when they were tearful. The shock of it went down deep inside her. Aunt Hatt was not someone who cried – not in public. Blarting, she would have said. While she knew the depths of grief her aunt was carrying within her for Eb, for Georgie, usually any tears were in private.

Aunt Hatt sat up after a few moments, looking dazed, almost as if waking from sleep. She pulled a hanky from her sleeve to wipe her eyes. Margaret saw the wet spots of her tears on the blotter.

'Sorry to do that, love,' Aunt Hatt said. She sounded weary and defeated. 'It's just been that sort of day.'

'Oh, Aunt,' Margaret said, removing her hand. She felt the surge of guilt she often experienced that she was the one who still had her husband, that he had been too old to fight, when there were Georgie and Annie's Fergus and Edith's fiancé – all swept so cruelly away. Poor Edith had been very brave but she was like a little ghost.

'Some days I can be strong,' Aunt Hatt said. 'Most days, in fact. I'm going to run this business that my Eb built up and my Georgie. I'm going to keep it going, make sure it's as they would have wanted in so far as I can – even if it finishes me off. It's just that sometimes . . .'

Margaret watched her strained face. *Please*, she wanted to say, *be careful – look after yourself.*

'It's what keeps me going.' Aunt Hatt looked round at her. 'The way Clara's got her little nursery to keep her going.' She was silent for a few seconds before continuing. 'Then there are days like today when all I can see is the two of them, here. I keep expecting Georgie to walk in with that grin of his, and to go out the back and find Eb bent over someone's peg or at his desk or breezing in, smoking that pipe and getting on my nerves.' More tears ran down her cheeks.

The door opened and Aunt Hatt quickly wiped her face as Lucy came in with a tray.

'Thank you,' she managed to say huskily.

'I'll be off now, Mrs Watts,' Lucy said.

Both of them thanked her and she was off and away as well.

'I don't know . . .' Margaret said hesitantly, feeling that anything she said was ridiculous, 'how you bear it.'

'No,' Aunt Hatt said glumly. 'Nor do I, to tell you the honest truth. But then what choice is there?'

333

There was no answer to this.

'Going home at night . . .' She shook her head. 'I keep putting it off. The empty house. No husband. No one . . .' Her face creased again and she put a hand over it, fighting for control. 'The quiet . . . I mean, Eb wasn't the quietest of individuals.'

Margaret smiled gently. 'No, he wasn't, was he?'

Their eyes met and they both laughed then, even though Hatt's cheeks were still wet.

'It's all right when Clara's there – the children. It's busy, full of life. But then . . .' She stopped herself and turned in her chair as if to enter a different mood. 'Look, I must stop wallowing. How's poor Annie now?'

'I . . .' Margaret had been about to say, *I hate to think.*

'I don't exactly know. She's gone back to the hospital.'

The month in which Annie had come to live with them had been one of the most disturbing she could ever remember. Annie, who had always been so full of life and stubborn confidence, had been like a broken, uncertain shadow. She had seldom gone out, even refusing to go to church. She sat for hours, silent and strange, like a wounded animal. Margaret had almost wanted to curse Fergus Reid for ever existing, for doing this to her poor little sister. But when she expressed something of this to Annie once, Annie had flared up.

'He gave me more than you'll ever understand!' she snapped. 'Even if he's gone, if this wicked, cursed, *damnable* war has taken him, I had him, had his love.' She looked wildly at Margaret. 'And I loved *him*. Don't you think that makes me more . . . more human, more of a person than I had ever been before?'

Margaret had to agree. But there was so much pain in the house.

'Edith seems to be getting along all right.' She poured

the tea for them both. 'The funny thing is, Muriel Allen has changed somehow. I'm not sure it's for very noble reasons but she's being much nicer to Edith, as if she sees Edith as being fated to be single all her life now like her – and she doesn't have to feel jealous any more.'

Margaret felt rather shocked by realizing that that was what she thought. But there was a careful kindliness about the office of number twenty-four these days which had not been there before, between Edith and Muriel and even Mr Henshaw, between all of them and Daisy and of course little Hester, the one person oblivious to all the darkness and death around them, who trotted about full of joy and new life.

This thought brought a sudden idea to her mind.

'Aunt,' she said, passing Aunt Hatt the sugar. 'Might it be better if you weren't alone in that big house?'

'How d'you mean?' Aunt Hatt passed the sugar bowl back and Margaret took a lump. One, these days, not two. Everything was in short supply.

'Well, there's you rattling about in there, and Clara. How would it be if Clara and the children moved in with you, instead of just being there in the daytime?'

'She did. She seemed very keen.'

Margaret lay curled in bed in the darkness beside Philip, her arm resting on his body as he lay on his back.

'I s'pose it does seem a bit daft keeping two house-holds going – if Clara's willing,' he said. 'Mind you, it'd mean living with her mother-in-law.'

'They're both busy – Hatt's away from home all week. And it'd save Clara traipsing back and forth. She'd have more room, they'd both have company – and the kids'd love it.'

'Quite a hen house that'd be,' Philip said.

Margaret laughed. 'What with Lizzie as well and the mothers. Mind you, Clara said last week they've a father bringing a child to her now. Poor man – first he was wounded, then his wife died. He's got a little boy to bring up on his own and he's lost an arm.'

'God,' was all Philip said, but she could feel his anger. They all watched, helpless now things had gone on so far, so callously; it was as if nothing could be done to prevent the slaughter, the wiping out of a generation.

Margaret embraced him more tightly and felt his warm hand caress her arm. Thank heaven you're here, she thought. That you and I are here together, now, in the midst of all this. She thought of the desolation of Aunt Hatt and Clara, lying alone in their beds. In the dark it felt as if she and Philip were together on a little island of fortune, of love, amid the churning waters of death and uncertainty.

'My love,' she murmured. 'My dear, dear love.'

Forty-Three

That summer, Daisy came to look forward to Tuesdays – the afternoon she went to Hollymoor, the Second Birmingham War Hospital.

Each of the other classes – in Highbury Hall and at the hospital at Rubery – were also enjoyable and satisfying. Many of the lads really seemed to look forward to seeing her and to working with their hands and learning something new.

But it was on a Tuesday that, as the weeks went by, she would wake up and feel an immediate pulse of excitement.

It was the same throughout the morning when she sat in the office in Chain Street or worked out at the back in the workshop. The MIZPAH jewellery and trinkets were still selling well and Daisy was often designing new lockets and brooches for separated sweethearts, as well as helping with other orders that came in. When working on something with her hands she would be completely absorbed in the work while all around her went on the hammering, the thud of the stamping machine and the turning lathe up at one end. Then she would surface suddenly and remember. This afternoon, Hollymoor. And him.

After their first conversation, she had already begun looking forward to seeing Stephen Ratcliffe again. A couple of members of the class had been discharged, one of them returned to the Front, and they had been replaced by two more.

But Stephen Ratcliffe would not be returning to the Front. Though the loss of his lower legs was obvious to the eye, Daisy could see that he had suffered some other injury, though she did not like to ask. Stephen was out of the war, that was clear, and would need a long period of rehabilitation, artificial legs and who knew what else.

She became more adventurous about the objects she took with her from the Animal Room at Vittoria Street for the men to copy as models. This meant carting rather large, not to say eccentric, items about Birmingham with her on the tram. She would choose one for each week and had begun at first with simpler items. Now that it was high summer and getting about entailed fewer clothes, with less need of a heavy coat or umbrella, she grew bolder. One week it was a thrush, then a pheasant; another time a stoat.

Yesterday she had gone to the school and looked carefully round the collection of stuffed creatures, trying to work out what she could carry without damaging the creature or causing too much alarm to her fellow passengers on the tram. A gleaming little glass eye met hers; a copper-red coat. Yes, that was what she would take! She could wrap it carefully and just about manage to lug it across town.

'You got a whole menagerie at 'ome, 'ave yer, Miss Tallis?' one of the lads asked as they all filed in – some pushed in wheelchairs, some on crutches, others able to walk well.

'Cor – look at that! That's beautiful, that is! You're not gunna make us do that, though, are yer?'

She had placed the fox, on its wooden base, on the table at the front and it did look a very fine specimen, with its reddish fur and fierce eyes, although its brush was a little moth-eaten looking.

'Well, I thought you might like a really big challenge this week,' Daisy said. 'I know it's difficult, but start with cutting away to get the basic shape, just like the other things we've done. You can make him look even finer than he is, if you like.'

There was dubious-sounding laughter at this.

'How d'you know it's a he, miss?'

At the edge of her field of vision she saw Stephen Ratcliffe give a faint smile. He was watching her, waiting for them all to get on with the main business of the class.

'I don't, Reg,' she said. 'And it doesn't matter, I don't think. Are you gentlemen all ready and comfortable?'

She took a lump of clay to each of them.

'Now, I've also got a picture of a fox skeleton here – look carefully.' She propped the pictures up at the front. 'And this one shows you where the groups of muscle are – the flow of them. Look and feel – let's get started.'

There were a few moments of quiet as the men started to cut cautiously into the rectangles of clay. She loved to see their immediate absorption in the task, their seriousness, when usually they were joking around. It brought out another side of them, which moved her.

'It's very warm today,' she said, going to the door. 'I think I'll prop this open for a bit.'

A slight breeze came in. Daisy stood at the threshold, feeling it cooling her face. She had dressed in a frock that she loved but seldom wore because the weather was hardly ever warm enough. It was made of dusky pink muslin, light and fine, with a cotton underskirt sewn into it and little pearly pink beads around the bodice. She had taken her hair back into a loose knot and it was making her rather hot. Surreptitiously she slipped a hand under the heavy twist of hair and wiped her neck.

When she turned back to the room, she saw Stephen

Ratcliffe quickly look away and down at his modelling again. Daisy blushed. He had been watching her. She could tell by the embarrassed look on his face. She wanted to go over and talk to him, but she could never be quite sure about him. Most of the time he seemed so closed in on himself.

She thought guiltily of Den. Another letter had arrived only this week, saying so little, yet always claiming her. Den. Her fate – that was how it felt. She was his fiancée as far as he was concerned, something that seemed to her both inevitable and far distant, since he was never here to make it real.

'That's a good start,' she said, going over to a red-headed lad called George.

He peered at it. 'It just looks too heavy and fat,' he said. He never did get along well but seemed very keen to try.

'You can fine it down as you go. Better than taking away too much at the beginning,' she said encouragingly.

She knew that Stephen would never call out to her as the others often did. He was self-contained, just kept his head down, working away. Gradually she made her way along to him. He was already working the body of the fox with his strong fingers, in the same way that she had seen before, as if he had an instinct for all that lay beneath the skin and could shape it.

'That's a very good start,' she said.

He looked up then, solemnly. 'D'you think so? I'm finding it very difficult.'

'Well, it is difficult. The hardest thing we have done so far. But you have a feel for it.'

He gave a slight nod and muttered, 'Thank you.'

Talk to me, she thought, but he had lowered his head and was once again absorbed in the work. Weeks had passed like this and her frustration grew. After the class the men were taken away for tea and there was never very much time. He had no idea how she longed to linger there talking to him, because he was the one person in a long time who had made her feel excited by his very presence. But he seemed so shy and reluctant to force his company on her.

That day as the class ended, the men in wheelchairs waited to be wheeled back to the main building. Daisy was gathering the models together, some of which looked convincingly like foxes and others like various breeds of rather baffled-looking dog. She stood them in rows across two of the tables. Stephen's, though not perfect, was by far the most fox like. The fox-ness of the fox, she thought.

She felt very shy about talking to Stephen while the others were there. But fortunately, that afternoon, he was left until last. Knowing that any moment an orderly would appear, Daisy steeled herself, her heart picking up speed.

Stephen Ratcliffe was seated in the wheelchair with his hands in his lap. There was, as usual, a grey blanket over his knees. She felt sorry that he always felt the need to hide himself like that when it was so warm a day. The blanket had slipped a little so that one of his legs could be seen projecting forward from the seat of the chair. His trouser leg was folded neatly and pinned over it. The sight of it, knowing that his other leg was in much the same condition, filled her with grief and anger. How must it feel, being cut down like that, knowing you would never walk naturally again? Suddenly what she was going to say seemed impossible, but now she had walked over to him and she had to speak. She was so nervous, it snatched at her breath.

'I wondered,' she said, full of confusion which sent

341

blushes to her cheeks, 'whether . . . I mean, it's . . . We've had some interesting conversations – begun some, anyway . . . But there's never time. Would you like to . . . I mean, I could come and visit at some other time?'

He looked up at her with what seemed a stony expression in his eyes and she felt herself recoil. Her cheeks burned. It felt as if she had got everything wrong, as if this was quite the worst thing to say. He took a while to reply.

'And why would you do that?' There was a cold neutrality to his voice, as if he was trying not to sound angry or rude.

'Well . . .' She felt terrible now, as if she had said some tactless, wrong thing. 'To talk. That's all. I'm sorry. The classes are always rather busy . . . I just thought . . .'

He stared at her. 'Are you pitying me – is that what it is?'

Why would she not pity him? She gazed at him, quite at sea, and could not answer.

And then, to her astonishment, he said, 'Why would a goddess like you, the loveliest girl I have ever seen, want to come and see a man who is a . . . a physical wreck? It's not just my legs, you know.' He spoke with sullen harshness, as if intent on giving her every detail, every reason why she should feel repelled, that she had spoken with no idea what she was talking about. 'I've other . . . wounds. Bit of a mess really.'

Still reeling from the compliment he had given her, she was moved by him, confused but compelled to honesty.

'You needn't think I'm any sort of perfect woman.' She looked down, her blushes deepening. 'You mustn't think that. I'm not. Not at all. And all I meant was – it's nice to have a conversation. I don't get many good conversations.'

This seemed to disarm him. 'No,' he admitted, almost sulkily. Nor me.'

They were both silent for a moment and he sat and looked wretched, despite his proud words.

'Look,' she said, her mind calculating the arrangements of her life, her teaching hours, Hester. 'There's only one afternoon when I'm not teaching – Mondays. I could come then? Perhaps we could sit outside?'

'Right, Mr Ratcliffe – ready to roll, are we?' the black-haired orderly said, appearing in his jovial way.

'All right,' Stephen said to her formally, with no show of enthusiasm. 'That would be nice – thank you.'

Forty-Four

That afternoon, as if by a miracle, in between hurling showers of rain the sun shone for a time, hot and strong.

Daisy walked beside the wheelchair as the orderly wheeled Stephen's chair across the grounds. She had offered to push him herself, but the man had insisted.

'The grass ain't been cut for a while, with all this rain,' he said. 'I think you'd find it a job, miss.'

The swathe of lawn behind the hospital buildings was already scattered with a few convalescents and their visitors, all making the most of the sun's rare appearance during that wet August. There were wheelchairs with chairs set beside them, a few who were seated on the ground on rugs, people turning their faces to the brightness.

As Daisy walked beside Stephen, she could sense the pain in him as the chair laboured across the grass. His hands gripped the arms and once or twice the orderly said, 'Sorry, pal – doing the best I can,' as Stephen's body lurched in the seat, though he made not a sound of complaint.

Already she was aware of a melting sense of tenderness towards him. She felt for him: for his pain; for the passive place to which he had found himself condemned, unable to get to anywhere he wanted on his own; for the useless stumps of his legs sticking out in front of him under the rug; for his quiet suffering. He did not look round and seemed remote from her as she followed, carrying another rug to put on the ground.

344

A goddess like you, the loveliest girl I have ever seen . . . His words had been playing over in her head all that week, exciting, unsettling her. Is that what he felt? And what did she feel? She warned herself – just because someone admires you, you are not obliged to admire them back . . . But admire she did. More than admire. Was touched by, affected by.

'This do?' the orderly said, reaching a spot on the lawn close to a young tree. And they agreed it would.

The orderly bent to put the brake on the chair, though it was hardly necessary since it was difficult to get the thing to move anywhere.

'What I'd really like, Fred,' Stephen said to him, 'is to sit on the grass.' He spoke quietly, in a confidential way as if he was embarrassed that Daisy should hear.

'The grass?' The man straightened up with a slight air of impatience. 'But it's soaking wet, pal.'

'We can put the rug down,' Daisy said. 'And my coat.' She could see at once that both of them on the grass together would make them more equal. All she could think of was trying to please him, to make things better. 'I can help.'

'Oh, no – yer all right, miss.' Fred spread the grey blanket and almost nonchalantly scooped Stephen up from under the arms and deposited him on the grass, covering him with the blanket again. She saw Stephen wince, but then a small smile of satisfaction came to his lips as he settled on the rug, leaning back on his hands.

'Won't be quite so much fun getting you up again, Mr Ratcliffe, but we'll cross that bridge when we come to it.'

'Thanks, Fred,' Stephen said abruptly. 'Appreciate it.'

'All right, pal – see yer later,' Fred said, taking off back to the hospital.

Daisy stood awkwardly for a second, feeling the sun

pressing on her back. It was so warm that the grass was lightly steaming. Stephen sat upright, legs out in front and he reminded her pitifully for a second of Hester when she first learned to sit up, rooted to one place by her inability to move.

He patted the place beside him on the rug. 'Coming down?' He didn't turn his head.

She laid her coat down on top of the rug and sat beside him. There was almost a guilty feeling as she stretched out her legs, whole legs, in front of her. But then they were side by side, for the first time at the same height and looking out at the grass and trees. A bee flew past. She heard a scattering of laughter on the breeze.

Stephen breathed in deep. 'It's so good to get out of that blasted chair.' He reached out and stroked the grass.

'It's a lovely day,' she said. This seemed so obvious a thing to say, but she hesitated in the silence which followed, not knowing what they might and might not talk about. 'I suppose,' she said haltingly, 'you'll be able to . . . I mean, there are artificial legs you can have?'

'Peg legs? Oh, yes. We're working on it. The stumps are healed pretty well now, though I've had to have a number of ops. It's hard when you've lost both – I suppose I'll always need sticks or something in the long run, if I can get used to the new legs. But first of all they've been dealing with – well, the other bit of trouble.'

He glanced round at her and seeing her attentive face, said, 'I expect you're wondering. People find it so hard to ask for some reason. I was in the First Norfolks – joined up in 1915. I sort of thought I should. Over there in East Anglia you can hear it, you know – the sound of it comes right across. I bet it's loud and clear, now they've started off again in Belgium. Ypres again.' He shook his head and was silent for a moment.

'It was last September, Morval – on the Somme. They say I'm a bit of a living miracle. Should have been dead long ago.'

'Oh?' Daisy said, intrigued. 'Why? I mean why apart from . . . sorry – that was a silly question.'

'Well, obviously I was in a war and I got hit.' He spoke with a bitter kind of humour. 'But it wasn't just my legs. A bit of stuff went into my belly – well, I say belly. About here . . .' He gestured towards the lower right side of his body.

'A bullet?'

'No – some other bit of rubbish. They got me to a CCS pretty soon – but the thing is, apparently I owe my life to something called the *"omentum majus"*.'

Stephen looked into her puzzled eyes. Suddenly he laughed, a boyish, delighted laugh which lit up his face. It was a beautiful face. Something in her already soft towards him deepened, the way everything had been changing little by little since she met him.

'One of life's miracles,' he said. 'There's a thing in the body, apparently, like a kind of skirt – or raincoat . . .'

Daisy laughed now at the absurd sound of this.

'One of the medics explained it to me. It sort of hangs from your stomach and floats round your innards – sort of folds itself round them. Anyway, one of the things it can do, apparently, is wrap itself about something it doesn't like the look of – like a spider wrapping up a fly – something like a spot of trauma or an infection. I had both, I think – a lump of stuff getting infected . . . I mean, I can't remember much about any of this, I was out of it. But the "O.M.", as he called it, isolated the thing inside me by wrapping it up and they were able to get it out while I was still in France. It's made a mess of me down there – I seem to be a bit off kilter. But it's healing.

347

I've been lucky beyond anything you could ask, really. Most lads I saw who got hit in the belly – well, that was that.'

'I've never heard of anything like that before,' she said. 'It's a kind of miracle.'

'It is,' he agreed. 'And even though I'm alive and kicking . . . Well, maybe not kicking . . .'

Their eyes met and when she saw the rueful laughter in his, she allowed herself to laugh as well.

'At least they won't send me back. I know they're desperate but I don't think a soldier with neither leg to stand on is even a glint in any of the generals' eyes yet.'

He turned to her then. 'It feels nicer than I can tell you just to have a conversation outside of there, with . . . well, with someone who's not another patient, or a nurse for that matter, although they're very good.'

'It's a pity you're so far from home,' she said.

'In some ways.' He looked ahead of him. 'But if they'd sent me somewhere else I wouldn't have met Miss Tallis, would I? Will you tell me about yourself, Miss . . . ?'

'Daisy,' she said. Panic filled her suddenly. How could she tell him – about Hester? Or . . . She thought with a rush of guilt about Den. What was Den, exactly? How could she tell him the truth about anything when all she could think of now was him, Stephen Ratcliffe, this sensitive, wounded man beside her who she found occupying her thoughts more and more? It was as if he had become one of the only things that mattered.

'Well,' she tried. 'I think I mentioned – my family have a silversmith's business in Chain Street, in Hockley, very near the middle of Birmingham.'

'Your mother was a silversmith as well?'

'Yes.' Daisy flushed with pleasure. 'She died when I was four – having my baby sister. The baby died as well.

My mother was called Florence Tallis. She was a . . . They say she was very, very good. I've got a few of her pieces. And I was going to . . .'

She stopped abruptly. Going to be good. Going to win every prize, going to prove to my father that I was as good as her, better, I was going to make him proud. But then . . .

It didn't come spilling out – couldn't. How could she tell Stephen about James Carson or Hester or any of it? He most likely saw her as an innocent, virtuous girl, when the truth was so much more shameful. And why was she even here with this man? Why did he disturb her feelings so and why did she let him when it was all so hopeless?

He looked at her, waiting for her to finish. But Daisy couldn't. She lowered her head, full of confusion, caught between the truth which could not be told and lies which could not be told either.

She could feel him waiting for her to finish.

'Going to what?' he said gently.

'Oh – nothing.' She looked up again, forcing a smile. 'Just going to follow in her footsteps. I am – trying to. But that's all about me really. I'm just – well, I'm just from here. Why don't you tell me some more about you?'

She was a little late getting to Handsworth that evening. The few hours of sunshine had vanished and clouds were beginning to gather ominously to the west. Clara opened the door looking harassed and weary and Daisy immediately felt contrite.

'I'm sorry I'm late, Clara – hello, Hessie!' Her daughter, grizzling with tiredness, came and wrapped her arm round Daisy's legs. 'I got a bit held up.'

'I thought this was the day you didn't teach?' Clara said rather sharply.

349

'It is. I just went to see someone – one of the patients,' Daisy said. 'Come on, Hessie – stop that now.' She picked her daughter up, guilty for her lateness. 'We'll go home and see Nana, shall we?'

Hester nodded tearfully and stuck her thumb in her mouth.

Clara peered at her. 'She's been a good girl, haven't you, Hess? She was perfectly all right until she saw you. Hey, Daisy – you're looking like the cat that's got the cream. What's happened?'

Daisy's cheeks flamed. She longed to pour out her feelings to Clara, that she had met a man who made her feel like no man ever had before – and yet was so injured that how would his life be possible? Getting him back into the wheelchair alone had taken two of them and anyway what about Den, who thought she was going to marry him . . . And this was what she felt – yet it was all impossible to put into words.

Forty-Five

In the classes she treated him no differently from anyone else. Stephen worked away quietly, but every so often he would look up and if their eyes met, it affected her like a jolt, sending her pulse to a gallop. She would give him a faint smile and look away, afraid that the other lads would notice.

She was aware of his presence every second of the time, like a glow, a fire, forever attracting her attention so that her senses were alert to any movement from him. She remembered the time when Mr Carson had paid her attention, how she had also been aware that he was watching, waiting. But this was different. It felt right and full of tenderness.

The next Monday she visited him, and the next. It rained and rained and they were not able to sit out on the grass again. Instead they sat at a table in a room in the hospital, facing each other, which at first made it harder to talk. But Stephen told her more about his life in Framlingham, about his parents and younger sister Catherine.

'She's a good girl,' he said, with a hint of wistfulness. 'She's nearly twenty now, but her health is not good. She fell ill when she was – I don't know – fourteen, I think. She's never fully recovered.'

'What's the matter with her?' Daisy asked. Her own health had always been so robust that she could hardly imagine being ill for so long. But she did remember

Margaret telling her that she had had a similar period of illness in her younger years.

'I don't know,' Stephen said, frowning, almost as if he had hardly thought about it before. 'I suppose the truth is we all just got used to it a long time ago. Cath runs out of energy – gets ill easily.' He shrugged. 'Nothing you can quite put your finger on – she's just delicate. She used not to be.'

He smiled and Daisy felt herself fall deeper. When his face lit up like that, he was such a good-looking man.

'When Cath and I were young we were great play-mates. We used to go and play round the castle – lovely grassy slopes you could run and tumble up and down. She'd roll right from the top to the bottom, laughing all the way down.' He looked at the window beyond Daisy, his eyes sad for a moment. 'And Ma and Pa took us up to the coast at Holkham a time or two. Sand dunes and – oh, it's lovely up there. You should see it!'

'I'd love to,' Daisy said. 'I've never seen the sea.'

But, her heart sinking a little, she realized how different his life had been from hers. She could scarcely imagine this quiet place, the rolling dunes he described facing the North Sea, the cold east wind in the winter, his father's work as a local baker.

'It sounds lovely,' she said, not quite sure whether it did.

'It is, in its way – but very quiet.' He smiled. 'Too quiet, some might say. Although I'd settle for somewhere peaceful now.'

There was a silence. The rain drummed down outside and the lower portions of the long panes were blurred by cuticles of condensation.

'It's like Noah's flood,' Stephen said. After a moment he added, 'Over there as well.'

News of the fighting – Ypres again – reached them every day. The heavens had opened across northern Europe. They seldom talked about the war, the Front, but now she said, 'Are your ... are the Norfolks there?'

'I'm not sure – but very likely,' he said. He stared ahead of him again, his expression sombre. 'I don't know how many of 'em I'd know now.'

This statement said so much in so little that Daisy was silenced. *Tell me*, she wanted to say. And at the same time, wondered if she did want to know. The lads did not talk about how it was – their maimed bodies spoke of terrible things – but mostly, in a crowd, they joked and kept things light and on the surface.

Each time she saw Stephen and sat talking with him, the atmosphere between them grew more intense with feelings that neither seemed able to express. All week, all she could think of was being back with him again, of seeing his lovely face, topped by the dark, curling hair. Sometimes, seeing his long, sensitive fingers restlessly tapping the table as they so often did, as if he was longing to move, to be off and away, it was all she could do not to reach out and take his hand in hers, to still it, cradle it. Each night now, she thought of him, imagining lying in his arms. She was troubled by the thought of what had happened to him. It was impossible not to wonder about his injuries and the loss of his legs, as if she needed to *see* and come to terms with it. To know the worst. But above all what she felt was love. Tender, longing love – the need to hold him, care for him and be held in return.

She saw longing in his eyes too, and fear and doubt. The more time they spent together talking, week after week, the more intense it became. But she could not break through it. She knew he was afraid of what he was. And she had the same fear. She had not told him about

353

Hester, about her own past. He was such a straightforward man, from a quiet, country background. And didn't he see her as some kind of goddess – an ideal, virginal and pure? If he found out what she really was it would break the spell. How could they even begin?

That third week in August she had visited Stephen on the Monday afternoon and passed the time talking about drawing and smithing and working with wood. Daisy told him about her mother and stepmother, about John and Lily. Their talk was about everything except all the feeling that was gathering between them, even though with every week it seemed to grow more powerful. She got up to leave, feeling as if here, with him, was the only place she was meant to be, and that to leave was tearing herself apart.

'I'd better go and brave the weather,' she said, managing her patient-visiting, cheerful voice as she buttoned her coat. She had dressed carefully in her dusky-pink frock, a cream wool cardigan to keep warm and her blue coat.

'Daisy.' Stephen's voice was low, cautious, but behind it she could hear the emotion he was keeping at bay. She looked into his eyes.

'Your coming here – it's . . . it's the best thing that happens all week. And the classes. But this . . . I . . .' He looked down, with a sad expression. 'I wish I could just declare myself like a man – a whole man who could be any good to you. That's what I feel.'

Daisy was so moved that her eyes filled with tears. She reached for words, honest words, but found herself overcome by emotion.

'Stephen . . .' To her embarrassment, tears began to run down her cheeks and he looked horrified.

'I'm sorry. I didn't mean . . . I've said the wrong thing.

Stupid, stupid ...' He banged a fist on the table so that some of the other visitors looked round.

'No!' She sat down again, leaning across to try and gain some privacy in the crowded room. Fiercely she wiped her eyes. 'No, it's not stupid. I'm sorry, Stephen. Only ...' She still couldn't say it, not with all honesty. *There are so many things you don't know about me, that will disgust you. If I tell you, you might never feel the same again.* She groped for words which were kind, which would tell him what she felt.

'It's not your legs. It's ...' she began in a rush, then stopped abruptly. For the first time she reached out for his hand. She saw the effect it had on him, a dawning, a hope, and he grasped hers back as if it was the most vital thing he had ever found. His hand was cool, slightly clammy as if from fear.

'What then?' he said desperately. 'But it *is* my legs, isn't it? Be truthful, Daisy. I'm a wreck. Why would any woman ...' He trailed off, looking down miserably.

'*No*. It's not that. It's just a bit fast – a bit soon,' she said, feeling like a liar. 'I love talking to you, Stephen. I ...' She cut herself off, hating her lack of courage. Drawing in a breath, she sat up straight, still holding his hands. 'Stephen – I'm not what you think. There are things about me that – if you knew, you wouldn't think the same of me at all.'

He looked at her, a look of irony, of scorn, almost, crossing his face. 'Oh, really – you think so? And what could they possibly be, Miss Tallis? Are you some kind of criminal?' He leaned towards her then, face softening into vulnerability. 'Come closer.'

Hesitant, she bent and he put his lips close to her ear.

'I love you, Daisy,' she heard him whisper. *He* could say it, could risk himself. 'You're the most beautiful, amazing girl I've ever met.' He held her hand in one of his and stroked it wonderingly with the other. 'If you can feel anything for a mess like me – well, that means the world to me. It's the only thing that matters . . .'

For a second, she wanted to pour everything out: the reality of her life, Hester, everything, to lay herself at his mercy. But Pa's words, back when he had been at his most bitter – *You're no earthly use to anyone now* – blocked her mind like a wall. Stephen's disability was a result of his doing his brave duty, inflicted by someone else – hers, her own stupidity and wantonness. And because of that, she had thought that Den Poole was the only man who would ever want her now; Den, who had persuaded himself that she was promised to be married to him . . . She drew in a breath to speak, then let it go again. All she could do was to squeeze his hand in return.

His face fell and he released her hand, looking away. 'I see. Well, now I know.'

'No!' she protested again. 'Please – don't think . . . It's just that I can't . . .' In frustration and fear she petered into silence. She was afraid she was going to burst into tears and started hurriedly gathering her things together. 'I think I'd better go. We can . . . we can talk again . . .'

She nodded goodbye to him, not trusting herself, and swiftly left the room.

Forty-Six

'Guess who's here?'

Clara opened the door when Daisy went to pick up Hester that afternoon. She looked cheerful and Daisy forced a smile on to her own face.

'Hello, Daisy!' Auntie Annie appeared from the big room where the children spent most of their time, Hester trotting along beside her. Hester saw Daisy and ran over to her. 'I finally had a day off, so I came to help Clara and Aunt Hatt with the move today.'

'Lovely to see you.' Holding Hester by the hand, Daisy went and kissed Annie, smiling. But she was appalled at how Annie looked. She was so thin that her eyes seemed even bigger in her face. Though Annie had lived in their house for a month after the death of her fiancé, growing more gaunt by the day no matter how much Margaret chided her to eat, Daisy still found her appearance a shock. It was heartbreaking to see. She could hardly imagine how Annie managed her work on the wards. But there was nothing she could think of to say that would help.

'Well, now Clara's moving in here they needed some help rearranging things,' Annie said. 'And it meant I could see Lizzie too. I've been very bad at visiting.' She smiled sadly and Daisy saw the bones of her jaw moving under the skin.

A moment later, Lizzie Poole emerged from the room as well. Lizzie, as a contrast to Annie, looked stronger, even a little taller. Her hair was tied back and she wore a

357

flowery overall over her frock. Though Daisy saw Lizzie most days now, it was only seeing her beside Annie that she realized how much more grown up and substantial Lizzie looked. Her face was a good colour and she moved about vigorously. In fact, Lizzie seemed to be blooming. Though she was a pale girl, with mousey hair, Daisy took in, for the first time, that Lizzie was really pretty.

'All right, are you, Daisy?' Lizzie said. 'She's been a good girl today – but then she usually is, aren't you, Hessie?' Little Ann Poole came along in Lizzie's wake.

'Hello, Daisy!' Aunt Hatt came down the stairs then as well. 'It's all go here, I can tell you.'

She had obviously already seen Annie, but even so, Daisy saw her eyes rest on her niece for a moment in a troubled way. Aunt Hatt seemed perkier, Daisy thought. Having Clara and the children living in the house would be good for her.

'Have all the children gone now?' Aunt Hatt asked. 'We can have some tea.'

'There's just little Joseph left – his dad'll be here any minute.'

'Well, we'll get the kettle on,' Aunt Hatt said.

'Perhaps Mr Higgins would like a cup as well, poor man?' Clara said. 'I don't suppose he gets much company. And you don't need to rush off, do you, Lizzie?'

'Well . . .' Lizzie hesitated and Daisy thought she saw a blush rise in her cheeks. 'I don't suppose a few minutes will hurt. Ivy can get the tea on.'

Daisy took Hester back into Aunt Hatt's big room and found a little boy of about two years old quietly and solemnly playing with some wooden pegs, which were to be fitted in various shaped holes in a board. He had a round, babyish face and big blue eyes.

'Hello, Joseph,' she said. He stared at her warily, before going back to his game.

She gathered Hester's things and within minutes the tea was ready and another knock at the door brought Tom Higgins. Daisy had never seen the man before and she was taken aback by how young he looked. She could see where Joseph had inherited his big blue eyes from.

'All right?' he said shyly, coming into the room. She saw that the left arm of his jacket was pinned up, above the elbow. 'Hello, Joseph.'

The little lad went to him in his solemn way and buried his head in his father's knees.

'He's ever so good,' Daisy said.

'Sometimes too good, I think,' Tom Higgins said, sounding worried. 'A bit on the quiet side, you know. Course, he misses his mother, but he don't know how to say so. It was only . . .' To her surprise, she saw the young man's eyes fill with tears. 'Just six months ago – today. I was still in hospital with this.' He looked down at his arm.

'Oh.' Daisy felt her own eyes fill. 'Oh, how awful.'

'Yeah – well.' Tom Higgins sniffed manfully. 'You just have to keep going. Come on, Joey.'

'Mr Higgins,' Lizzie Poole said. 'Mrs Watts says would you like a cup of tea before you go?'

'Oh!' He straightened up from bending over Joseph, seeming shy and at a loss for a moment. 'Well – yes, all right. Ta very much.' To Daisy he added, 'Not as if there's any rush to get home really.'

As they all sat and drank tea together, with a bit of dry cake, Mr Higgins told them that he and Joseph now lived back with his widowed father and got by the best they could. He had a clerical job at Fort Dunlop.

'I was there before the war,' he said. 'Could do the job

with both hands tied behind my back if I had to! That's summat good anyway.'

Little Ann Poole kept toddling up to Tom Higgins, apparently fascinated by him, and they all laughed.

'She doesn't see many men, you see,' Lizzie explained shyly.

'Oh, why's that?' Tom Higgins said. 'It's the opposite problem in our house – all men for Joey. That's why it's good him coming here.'

'I look after my sisters,' Lizzie said. 'My brother's away – he's in the artillery.'

'How many sisters've you got then?' Mr Higgins seemed most comfortable talking to Lizzie of all of them.

'There's three apart from me,' Lizzie said. 'Our Ivy's nineteen now, so 'er's out working. Ethel's nine so she can get herself to school, and there's Ann here – she's two.'

Ann stood staring mesmerized at Tom, with her mouth open, and he looked at Lizzie. They both laughed.

'I'd better be off,' he said after a time. 'Pa's trying to find someone who could cook for us but no luck so far. The women all want factory work these days. So he's trying his best for now.' He rolled his eyes. 'Not sure what's on tonight!'

'Poor man,' Lizzie said as Clara let Tom Higgins out at the front.

'Something about a house with only men in seems even sadder than one with only women,' Aunt Hatt said, sitting back with her cup and saucer. She appeared to wilt. 'Oh, I feel quite exhausted.'

'He's nice, isn't he?' Lizzie said to Daisy. 'Don't you think he's a nice man?'

'Auntie Annie says she'll come and see us a bit later,' Daisy told Margaret, when she had reached home through the cloudy gloom of the afternoon. She stood at the door of the front office, where her stepmother was still busy.

'Oh!' Margaret looked up quickly at the clock. 'I'm almost finished.' She looked concerned. 'How did she seem?'

Daisy could sense both Edith and Muriel listening intensely. The sight of poor Edith also wrung Daisy's heart. She was so pale and drawn, though, they all agreed, very brave.

'Well, still rather thin and tired looking,' Daisy said carefully.

'Did she say she was coming for tea?'

'No,' Daisy said, smiling. 'But she most likely will. She never thinks of things like that, does she?'

Margaret rolled her eyes and smiled. 'No. Hello, Hessie – have you had a nice day?'

Hester nodded sullenly.

'She's tired out,' Daisy said. 'I'll go and get her ready for bed.'

'Can I help?' Lily said, appearing from the back room.

'All right,' Daisy said. 'She likes you singing to her.'

Lily happily led Hester to the stairs.

'Oh, there's a letter for you.' Margaret passed her in the doorway and went into the back room.

Den, Daisy thought, with a sinking heart. All sorts of mixed feelings woke in her – guilt and dread and confusion.

'It's not from Den this time.' Margaret voiced her thoughts, holding out a pale blue envelope.

Relieved but puzzled, she looked at the rounded, careful handwriting on the envelope, almost like that of a child. She put it in her pocket, frowning.

Upstairs, she waited while Lily sang to Hester in her sweet voice, 'Rock-a-bye Baby' and 'Jack and Jill' until

Hester's tired tears faded to hiccoughs and her eyelids grew heavy.

'Thanks, Lil,' she whispered. Lily was nine now and the two of them were getting along better. Lily was a serious, grown-up girl for her age and Hester adored her. Daisy watched fondly as Lily tiptoed out of the room with exaggerated care.

She sat looking down at Hester, full of love for her. She was such a beautiful-looking child, her dark lashes flickering lightly as she settled into sleep, her chubby face and thick, dark hair. It seemed impossible now that Hester had not always been in her life. With a terrible pang she thought of the agony of the time when she had given her up. She might have left her in the village and never seen her again . . . The idea of it was so painful that she forced herself to stop thinking of it.

Leaning over, she lightly stroked Hester's head and the child gave a little murmur and smacked her lips.

'My little love,' Daisy whispered. It was all impossible and her heart ached. Hester was her love – and Stephen. His face appeared in her mind with that lovely smile. The face of the man she loved. But he had such a wrong idea of her, as if she was some kind of saint. How could she possibly tell him about Hester? But how could she ever have any kind of real friendship with him if she did not?

Getting up, she left the room very quietly and hurried up to her own. The tree she had begun fashioning from silver wires was on the chest of drawers. She had splayed the ends at the bottom and neatly soldered them to make tapering roots and she was working on a complex mesh of branches.

One day Margaret had come in and seemed drawn to it.

'Oh, that's beautiful, Daisy – it's the tree of life!'

'Is it?' Daisy said.

'From Matthew's gospel – the tiny mustard seed grows into a great tree and all the birds of the air come and shelter in its branches. It's one of my favourite stories. The tree is like love – embracing everyone.'

'Oh,' Daisy said. She had smiled. 'Yes, that is lovely. It's not finished yet.'

For a second, she was sorely tempted to pick it up and start working on it. It was absorbing her, adding little twists and curlicues, leaves and tiny birds.

But there was no time. She had to get changed and ready to teach at Vittoria Street that evening. Moving briskly, she took her shoes off and felt the rustling of the envelope in her pocket. She sat on the bed and pulled it out. The handwriting meant nothing to her.

The Kemptown Hospital
Eastern Terrace
Brighton
25th August 1917

Dear Miss Tallis,

I am writing to you on behalf of your fiancé, Denis Poole, to let you know that he has been wounded and is here at the Kemptown, in Brighton. I am one of the VADs caring for him on the ward and he has asked me to write this for him as he is not able at present, due to his injuries.

He assured you that he is on the mend and in good spirits, but requests that you visit as soon as is possible for you.

Yours most sincerely,
Lucinda Barkham

Forty-Seven

'I'll come with you,' Margaret said. 'You've no idea how to get all the way down there – across London as well!'

When Pa pointed out that neither did she, Margaret retorted, 'Two heads are better than one.'

Pa looked up from his plate of cheese and pickles with that stony look in his eyes when he didn't like something.

'It'll cost a bit. You won't do it there and back in a day, will you?'

Margaret just gave him one of her forthright looks which said, *In this case, Philip Tallis, I know what's right better than you do and this is what's right and you can say what you like.* She would never have actually *said* those things, but that was what the look meant. Daisy, thinking about it later, on the train as they rumbled south towards the coast, turned away from the window where she had been watching the wet green fields sliding past outside. Margaret, in her best hat and coat, sat calmly at her side, scanning a copy of *The Times* which someone had left on the seat.

'Thank you, Ma,' she said softly. She knew these were words she did not use often enough.

Margaret looked up and lowered the paper into her lap. 'I'm fond of Den too.' She gave Daisy a very direct look. '*Fiancé*, Daisy?'

Daisy could only hold her stepmother's gaze for a

moment before she looked away again. She could not think of anything to say.

It was blustery and grey in Brighton and the temporary hospital was a good walk from the railway station. They had been told that the local train which they might have taken was exceedingly slow, so they decided to see something of the town on foot. They had to keep asking the way, but apart from those exchanges, they walked in silence. Daisy carried the small overnight bag in which they had each put the few things they needed with them.

It began to drizzle, the wind buffeting their faces with moisture, and they had to hold their hats on. Margaret gave up on using her umbrella, unable to manage it in the wind. But it was only when they were finally close to their destination that they caught their first sight of the sea, a grey, ruffled expanse at the end of a wide road sloping downwards towards it.

'Oh!' Margaret said. Both of them were lifted out of their thoughts. 'Shall we go and have a look – first of all?'

Neither of them had seen the sea before. The street, like so many others, was lined with tall, imposing houses. They tried to hurry, but were battling in the face of the wind which snatched their breath.

Stepping out on to the parade at the end, they were suddenly in the open. Beyond the road, and the stalls selling winkles, the railings and the downward drop to pebbles below, Daisy saw a belt of greyish gold sand. Fussing at its edge came the froth of the endless, pushing waves. And far beyond, the white-flecked blackness of the sea met a watery grey sky. The wind boxed them, exhaustingly.

'Oh!' Daisy shouted over it, exhilarated. 'It's so . . . wide!'

'Yes!' Margaret smiled valiantly, hand pressed to the top of her hat. 'What a wide, wide world! It's wonderful – but goodness, it's exhausting!'

They were relieved to return to some shelter between the hotels and boarding houses.

'It must be almost visiting time,' Margaret said. 'Shall we have a quick cup of tea first?

Daisy realized she wasn't the only one who wanted to put off the moment when they had to walk into the hospital.

Eastern Terrace was a curve of pale, gracious houses tucked in behind Marine Parade.

'Goodness,' Daisy said, forgetting herself for a moment and giggling with nerves. 'Fancy Den being in there!'

Then the reality of their visit came to her again in a plunge of dread. The two of them stopped at the entrance to number five. Margaret looked up at the long-windowed frontage, clutching her umbrella. Margaret was different in many ways from Annie, and Daisy realized that she found hospitals and the sick and suffering rather difficult.

'Right.' Margaret braced her shoulders. 'Come on then.'

In the wide hallway, a young woman in an overall, showing a glimpse of copper-coloured hair from under a white headscarf, was mopping the tiles. She looked up, her freckled face smiling at them. Another woman seated at a small table nearby said irritably, 'Do let the visitors past, Josie. I've told you not to get in everyone's way.'

'Sorry, Miss Perkins, sorry, ma'am,' the girl said to Margaret.

She sounded Irish. Feeling sorry for her, Daisy rolled her eyes at her sympathetically as she passed and the pretty girl's eyes lit up with mischief. She looked down to hide her smile.

The irritable middle-aged woman at the table directed them to the staircase.

'Up on the left – someone will point you in the right direction. Oh, and you may leave your belongings with me if you like? Here – put that behind me. It will be quite safe.' Obediently, Daisy put the bag down and they left the umbrella.

The someone, at the top of the stairs, was a very young-looking VAD, petite and wiry looking, pale hair taken back under the white kerchief, a large red cross on the front of her apron.

'Ah,' she smiled and searched out Daisy. Her deep, well-spoken voice contradicted the childlike frame. 'Well, this is lucky – I am Lucinda Bailey. It was I that wrote to you, I believe. You are Mr Poole's fiancé?'

Daisy opened her mouth to reply no, then closed it again without saying anything. How had it become so established a fact when no one had ever asked her? This must be what Den had told her, what he was clinging to in his mind.

'This is Daisy Tallis, yes,' Margaret said calmly. 'How is Mr Poole?'

The VAD's expression sobered. They were standing on a landing from where, through a doorway, they could see a number of beds. Lucinda Bailey drew them aside, speaking quietly.

'You may find it a shock when you see him. It's the bandages – I know it's not easy. He can't remember much about how he was wounded. He has had two operations to remove –' she paused, as if realizing she was about to embark on too much detail – 'shell damage. One piece went in rather deep.'

'He already has something in him from the last time,' Margaret said.

'So I gather,' the VAD said. She cleared her throat. 'The thing is, it appears that he was lying outside for some time, wounded. In the meantime, he received a dose of gas – mustard gas, it seems. I don't know if you know anything of the effects?'

They both shook their heads. Daisy felt everything inside her tighten with dread and all the more so because the young woman seemed reluctant to enlighten them.

'Unfortunately, if you are exposed for long and it gets into the clothing, it has a blistering effect. Of course, overall it makes them very ill. You can perhaps imagine.' She paused. 'Any part of the body to be in contact with it . . . And the eyes . . .'

Margaret touched the young woman's arm. 'I can see this is difficult,' she said.

The nurse looked startled for a moment, then grateful.

'Is he blind?' Daisy whispered.

'Well . . .' Lucinda Bailey seemed to have to force herself to look into Daisy's eyes. 'For the moment at least, yes.'

The shock deepened in her body. After a second, she reminded herself to start breathing again.

'And will he . . . will he always be . . . ?'

'It's impossible to say yet, I'm afraid. I don't want to give you false hope, Miss Tallis. Some men do regain their sight. It depends on the extent of the damage.'

Daisy leaned against the wall. It was as if a great heat was sweeping through her and she struggled to unbutton her coat. The white walls seemed strange and too bright, and lights began to flash at the side of her vision until suddenly blackness blotted out everything.

Forty-Eight

She was seated on a chair, leaning forward, and someone was pressing firmly on her shoulders. She felt sick and hazy and wanted nothing but to lie down and go to sleep. She gave a low whimper.

'Daisy dear?' Margaret squatted down, trying to see into her face. 'Can you hear me? Look – here's a glass of water.'

'Try and sit up now if you can, Miss Tallis,' the nurse said. 'That's it, there's a good girl.'

Daisy sipped the water and felt the heat gradually ebb from her to be replaced by a chill. 'Sorry, Ma,' she whispered.

'Not to worry,' Margaret said. 'But we should get on and see him now. Can you manage?'

No, she wanted to say. The sweat was cooling on her and she felt shivery. *I don't ever want to see him.* But she was full of pity and sorrow as well. Poor, poor Den.

'I gather he has some family,' the VAD said.

'Sisters,' Margaret said. 'But dear Lizzie, the eldest, is working hard trying to manage everything for the little ones. It was easier for us to come.'

Daisy handed the glass back to Nurse Bailey and stood up. 'Let's go in now,' she said, feeling she must do it or she might run away.

'Second on the left,' Nurse Bailey told them unnecessarily, since she was leading the way.

The room contained seven beds, arranged three along

369

each side and one in the middle, jutting into the passage-way.

A couple of the men turned to look at them as they came in and Daisy blushed, wishing to goodness that there was no one else there. How was she to manage this, let alone in front of an audience? Others were lying prone. On the bed second on the left, under a neat, floral bedspread, the figure lying flat with bandages covering every part of him except for his nose and the lower part of his face, was Den.

'Mr Poole?' Nurse Bailey said, leaning over him. 'You have some visitors. Miss Tallis and . . .' She turned, enquiringly.

'Mrs Tallis,' Margaret said.

Den made a small sound and turned his head as if to look, although unable to see anything.

'I'll fetch a chair,' their nurse said. 'You might have to take it in turns – difficult with space in here.'

Daisy could not move her feet. Flirting with Den had been one thing, responding to his attention, a boy and girl playing with each other, none of it serious . . . But this . . .

'Den?' Margaret stepped over and went to take his hand, but realizing they were each swathed in bandages, made an uncertain gesture with her own and withdrew it.

'Mrs Tallis?' His voice was hoarse and as soon as he spoke he started coughing, before managing to say, 'Is Daisy here? Did you bring 'er?'

'Yes.' Daisy forced herself forward and Margaret stepped out of the way. 'Hello, Den. I . . . How are you?'

'Can't see,' he rasped, then coughed again. 'Can't see yer. But they say I might be able to . . . soon.'

'Yes,' she said. 'That's what the nurse said.'

'Yeah.' He paused, then added with bitter feeling, 'Bastard Hun.'

370

There was a silence as Den moved his head, as if trying to see out from behind a wall, then stilled again, defeated.

'Dais?'

She prickled with discomfort – this conversation in front of strangers in the ward, in front of Margaret. It did not seem to matter to Den – he could not see who was there in any case.

'Yes?' She leaned closer as if to ask him to speak more quietly, but of course he could not see that either.

'Give us yer hand?'

'Won't it hurt you?'

'No – s'all right. The bandages pad them. They're blistered, like, but not too bad.'

Gently, glad he could not see her reluctance now that all this had become so serious, she placed her right hand over his.

'You have the chair,' Margaret said, as Nurse Bailey came and placed an upright wooden thing in the space between the beds. 'I'll step out of here a moment.'

Still holding Den's hand, Daisy took a seat. Pity filled her, and sorrow and panic. How had she got herself into this? What could she say to him?

'Does it hurt, Den?' she tried.

'Dais?' He ignored her question. 'You've come. My Daisy. You're what keeps me going. Your letters – knowing you're there . . .' His voice cracked and she thought he was going to cry, but he must have stopped himself. Possibly it would hurt even more.

'Oh, Den.' Her chest ached yet no tears came, just a feeling of utter desperation.

'They say I might get my eyes back. I'll be all right, 'part from that. I'm getting better already. Promise me summat.'

'What?' she asked faintly.

'I wouldn't expect you to marry a blind b—' He bit back a swear word.

Marriage – how had they got on to marriage? She wanted to backtrack, to contradict, but how could she, to this poor, broken figure in the bed, the man who said that she was everything to him? This man to whom she had somehow promised far more than she realized.

'What good'd I be to yer like that? I wouldn't do that to you, Daisy. But promise me – if it does come back, if I can see again and I can get through this war in one piece . . .'

'Oh, Den,' she said desperately. 'Of course you will! Aren't you out of it now, for good?'

She thought of Stephen Ratcliffe then, who at this moment seemed part of another life, and, sitting here now, she could not decide which of these lives was the real one or to which her feelings should direct themselves.

'If it's got two arms and legs it goes to the Front. If I get my sight back . . . Oh, they'll send me back for a third dose all right.' He coughed, then tried to turn over, before wincing, falling on to his back again. 'Promise me you'll be my wife, Daisy? If I'm a whole man again. You're beautiful, you are, Dais – you're my life. Promise me, will yer? It'd be everything to me to know you're waiting for me.'

Margaret said not a word about the visit until they were in the room they were to share in a modest lodging house a few streets away. The window looked on to the houses opposite and inside, apart from the brown linoleum, everything from the eiderdowns to the lampshades was some shade of green.

Daisy put the bag down on the floor and Margaret had just sunk wearily on to the bed and was taking the pin out of her hat, when the cheerful landlady's voice floated upstairs and across the landing.

'I expect you'd like a cup of tea, wouldn't you, Mrs Tallis?'

Margaret raised her eyebrows as if to say, *Oh, yes, wouldn't we?* Daisy hurried to the door.

'Yes, please – that would be very nice,' she called in the direction of the staircase.

'Come down to the back here in a few minutes – I'll have it ready. And a bit of cake.' Daisy heard receding footsteps.

'Oh, how lovely – just what I need!' Margaret groaned. 'I feel all in. It must be all the new sights and sounds.'

Daisy was bending to reach down for the little case on the floor, when Margaret straightened up.

'Daisy?' Her voice was suddenly sharp as if the import of all that had happened that afternoon had just sunk in.

'Umm?'

'What's going on?'

'How do you mean?' She looked down, feeling the heat rise in her face.

'You know what I mean? What did Den say? When I went in to see him he seemed to think . . . Did you lead him to believe that . . . I mean, is it true?'

'Is what true?' Daisy asked carefully. She looked up.

'That you have agreed to marry him?'

Daisy could not read Margaret's face. She seemed to be struggling with mixed feelings which only aggravated Daisy amid her own confusion.

'Would that be so terrible?' She hardened her tone. 'After all – who else is going to want me?'

Margaret paused, looking away towards the window. Daisy could see her struggling to find an honest answer, as was her way.

'No-o,' she said carefully. 'I mean, if . . .' She stopped, trying to be tactful.

Daisy looked at her, feeling wounded. Did Margaret not think Den was beneath her – would she not have felt that at one time? But now, of course, everything was different.

'Well,' Daisy said, sarcastic now. 'I suppose you'd say he's a nice man – all things considered.'

'Yes. He's a remarkable man, Daisy, when you think of the start he had. What happened to his father, the state they were living in, then with Mary scraping by. Den's a good man, and a skilled man now as well. I'm very fond of him – you know I am. I also don't want to see him hurt – or you.'

There was a pause. Margaret looked up at her. 'Did you promise him?'

'He said, if he gets better, gets his sight back – then would I promise?'

'And did you?'

She hesitated, then whispered, 'Yes.'

'Tea's ready, Mrs Tallis!' came trilling up the stairs.

'Coming!' Margaret called back.

She hauled herself up from the bed and came over to Daisy, putting an arm round her shoulders, her eyes solemn.

'Well, if you have promised that, then you have promised. All we can do is to wait and see. But Daisy, remember, you have given him something to hope for. You may have been rash – perhaps you were just trying to be kind. But I'd hate to see you break a promise.'

Forty-Nine

'You all right, Miss Tallis?'

Daisy's mind was startled back into the workroom, the men all sitting round. She had been standing by the window as the lads got on with their work, looking out at the patch of faded grass beyond. Joe, the red-headed lad with the eye patch, who was close to her, swivelled round in his chair.

'Yes.' Her heart was pounding. 'Of course. How are you getting on, Joe?'

It had been so hard coming back here today. She felt very out of sorts and had not had time to go and find them any sort of model to copy. Instead she gave them free choice of what they wanted to make. Tommy, delighted to be given free rein, was finally making his aeroplane.

'Bottom wing's're all right,' he said, sounding disillusioned. 'Can't seem to get the top ones right with the supporting bit being so thin.'

'I did warn you.'

'No, you dain't, miss.' He sounded genuinely affronted.

'No, perhaps I didn't. Well, I should have done.' It was true, she had not had the energy to argue that making a biplane out of clay was going to be a tricky job. She cranked her face into an appeasing smile. 'That's the way to find out, though, isn't it?'

She went to look at the other lads' work, leaving Stephen until last, putting it off. She had not once looked fully in his direction throughout the class. And of course she had not come in to see him yesterday either.

They had reached Birmingham in the middle of the afternoon on Sunday, she and Margaret both exhausted from all the new experiences and the journey and the emotion of it all.

When they got back, Pa and the others had been all eager to hear about it and Daisy had seen Margaret give Pa one of her looks that said, *I'll tell you about it later, properly.*

Over Mrs Flett's tea of stew, much padded out with barley, they had told the family about the trip. John wanted to know about the trains, Lily about the nurses and about London, and both of them were agog to hear about the underground trains which whisked you along beneath the city.

'Oh,' Lily said, wide-eyed. 'I'd be scared! I'd rather sit on the omnibus and *see* everything!'

'And how's the lad?' Philip asked, once the first flurry of excitement was over.

Daisy looked at Margaret, imploring with her eyes, *Don't tell them!*

'He's . . . comfortable,' Margaret said carefully.

'And what does that mean?' Philip said, a little more sharply. 'The lad's had all this before. What's happened to him this time?'

'He's had two operations,' Daisy said. 'He was . . . well, he said he couldn't remember but he was in an explosion. And . . .' She couldn't go on. The factor on which her promise – *promise!* How had she promised like that? – rested was too much for her and she had such a lump of distress and panic in her throat that she could not speak.

'Gas,' Margaret said, quietly. She seemed reluctant to

talk about it in front of Lily and John. 'He's been gassed. He's all bandages – it blisters the skin. And . . .'

Daisy looked up and their eyes met. She saw Margaret register the look of desperation in her eyes.

'He's . . . he can't see,' Margaret half-whispered it. 'For the moment. They say it might get better, but they're not sure.'

'Blind? Oh, good Lord.' Pa sounded horrified. 'That's terrible! How's he ever going to work again if he can't see? Course, the lad's alive, but what sort of life will he have to look forward to?'

'Not much,' Margaret agreed.

The words twisted down inside Daisy, deepening the wound she felt at all times. Was she the one thing Den had left to look forward to?

Now, in the workshop at Hollymoor, she made her way very slowly round the room, spinning it out, advising, encouraging. She bent low over the table next to each of the lads, trying to pay close attention to them, though conscious of the closeness, of her femaleness among the male smells: Woodbine-scented breath, sweat mingled with rough hospital soap. But she could not put off talking to Stephen any longer.

He was modelling a hare. As soon as she caught sight of it, she gasped, taken out of herself.

'Oh – that's marvellous!'

Of course, everyone else looked.

'Ha – teacher's pet!' one of the others teased. Stephen sat back, looking bashful. But there was an air of pain, of sulkiness about him now and he did not meet her eyes.

'That is damn good, though,' someone else conceded. 'Look at them ears – and the shape . . .'

The hare was sitting upright, alert, one ear cocked slightly back, as if about to take flight. You could almost sense its fear, its breathing. Stephen was marking its coat, hair by hair.

'I wondered if the shoulders are really in proportion,' he said modestly. 'Not having a picture, it's hard.'

'But you seem to know exactly,' Daisy said, unable to contain her admiration for the artistry of it.

'There are a lot of them around the lanes where I come from,' Stephen said. 'You often see them tearing along up the road in front of you. Rarer to see one sitting still like this.'

'It looks as if it's about to run,' she said. 'Poised ready.'

Realizing she was getting drawn in, just as she had vowed she would not do this week, she moved away, saying briskly, 'All right, everyone – five more minutes and then we'll have to clear up.'

She made a great show of being very busy helping everyone place their work on the side table, clear up the tools and clean the tables. To her relief, the orderly who came to collect Stephen was on time today and she made bright conversation with him, seeing the dull, hopeless look Stephen wore as he was wheeled away. There had been no time to talk.

Sidelong, she watched as he left the room, more unsteady in the chair than the men who still had their lower legs to balance the weight of their bodies. The set of his shoulders, his curling hair and the helpless wobble of his torso as the chair hit any bump, all moved her to such tenderness that she wanted to run after him and beg him to stay, for them to talk. But in seconds he was gone from the room.

When she reached Handsworth that afternoon, to pick up Hester, she hardly knew how she had got there. As she walked to the tram stop, then in Birmingham to catch the second tram, her thoughts were in turmoil.

It was as if she had two lives, two realities and she could not reconcile them. She felt paralysed. There was the life she lived and knew so well, that contained Ma and Pa and Hester, her beautiful little girl who she had fought for, would give her life for. And there was Den, who knew her, really knew her, for the fallen woman she was. He was prepared to accept her, to take all of it on – she, Daisy, Hester, the shame of it – everything.

But that look Den had given her when he found out about Hester would not leave her. The gleam of something in his eyes – triumph, almost glee – still disturbed and repelled her, despite his devotion and his claim that he adored her. On the other hand, Den had proved loyal. He was clever and strong. And now somehow, without even having willed it, she seemed promised to be his wife, a promise that honourable Margaret, her stepmother, would try to see to it that she kept.

And Stephen . . . But she wrestled with herself, trying not to think about lovely, artistic Stephen. He had a quite unrealistic view of her, saw her as some sort of perfect angel and would feel very differently when he found out about her, about Hester.

All the same, as she walked through the quiet suburb to Aunt Hatt's house, she found herself whispering a terrible, wicked prayer . . . *Please don't let him get his sight back. He only said I had to marry him if he can see again. Please God – save me.*

Hester dawdled so slowly from the tram stop that Daisy had impatiently scooped her up into her arms and was carrying her when she walked into twenty-four Chain Street. She heard low voices from the back room and went to put her head round the door, saying that she would give Hester a bath.

'Oh!' she stopped, startled. 'Hello, again, Auntie Annie!'

They saw so little of Annie now that she was back at the hospital that her appearing twice in two days was a real rarity. She and Margaret were sitting with a tray of tea between them.

'Hello, Daisy.' Annie forced her lips up into a smile, which did nothing to dispel the wan look of her face. Daisy stood, not sure what to say.

'Annie has been given some more time off from the hospital,' Margaret said carefully.

'*Enforced* time off,' Annie said. But even her fury was muted. 'Hello, Hessie.' She smiled at the little girl.

'They're worried about you,' Margaret said. 'And quite rightly so. We all are.'

'I'm all right,' Annie said irritably. 'And we're so busy – the casualties coming from Belgium are . . . Well, we're overrun.'

'She only said take a week off,' Margaret said. 'And she would never have said it with things so busy if she hadn't thought you were more use off the ward than on it.'

Annie had the grace to look chastened by this brutal truth.

'You can stay here, of course,' Margaret said. 'Any time you need.'

'No,' Annie said, sitting up straight. 'I'm not going to do that – although thank you, of course. As I've a whole week, I'm going to go to Scotland. Tomorrow. To meet Fergus's family. His mother wrote me such a nice letter and invited me.'

'Oh!' Margaret said. 'But – are you sure that won't—' Her voice was full of doubt and worry for her little sister.

'Won't what?' Annie interrupted. 'Make it worse?

How could it possibly *be* any worse? I want to meet them.'

Daisy decided she would keep out of it and slid off round the door again. As she went to the stairs she heard Margaret say, 'Do you have enough money to go all the way up there?'

'Of course I do,' Annie said wearily. 'When do you think I ever get time to spend money?'

Fifty

For the first part of the long journey north, Annie was cold to the marrow. She had stowed her modest Gladstone bag on the rack above and sat huddled in her coat with its black band about the arm and a black woollen shawl over the top. Her body was so thin that she felt the cold terribly. Even though it was only September, her feet were so icy she could scarcely feel them.

She was positioned between the window and a whiskery man who immediately fell asleep and snored rhythmically. And it felt to her like the first time she had sat still since going back to work at the hospital. She had not wanted to be still, did not want, ever, to have time to think.

But now, as they rumbled between the dingy, soot-blackened factories and warehouses, broken by momentary glimpses of working boats on the cut's inky water, her spirits reached rock bottom in a way she never normally allowed. All these years since she and Margaret had come to live in Birmingham, she had been happy here, had loved the place. Now, the very sight of it dragged her even further down, her own despairing spirits making an entire city appear draped in a pall of death.

I must stop this, she thought. She closed her eyes, feeling the train gradually picking up speed. Rocking gently with the motion, light snores coming from the gentleman on her right, her thoughts whirled round, flaying her like a storm of biting, sharp-edged leaves.

He is gone, gone for ever. Oh, Fergus, my love, my love ... And the ache which had taken hold of her since she had heard of his death spread through her chill body, turning it into one complete united pain.

You have had love and it is gone, gone for ever. You are thirty years old, too old – your chance is gone. Now you will never stand in anyone's arms ever again, never feel how it would be to lie with him, to lose your virginity. You will never bear his children, never bear any – not now ... Never live the life of love and adventure which you might have done with him ...

And Fergus was so far away. His body, the body of her beloved, was buried in French soil somewhere near Étaples ... And that Fergus who she had loved so much, those strong shoulders, the long body which she had never seen naked but had so many times imagined, came so clear in her mind, his smiling face, moustache, those eyes, so alive and full of love and mischief ... But then she saw them covered with shovelfuls of soil. Would it be black, brown, red? She did not even know how the soil looked where they had buried him, covering his lovely face ...

A physical sensation swelled in her, so powerful that her eyes snapped open and she sat up, gasping. The howl that was rising in her, trapped in her, seemed to close her lungs so that she was fighting to breathe.

'Are you all right?' the woman opposite her asked fearfully. She was elderly, bespectacled and swathed in black with a fur cape. 'You're not going to be sick, are you?'

'No,' Annie managed to say. She fought for a breath. 'It's nothing – I'm all right. Thank you.'

Closing her eyes to shut out the woman's wary expression, she thought, I must look like a madwoman. Perhaps I am. Perhaps this is what it feels like.

Everything was dark and distorted, overwhelming, as if layers of flesh had been removed and replaced with a thin tissue that could scarcely protect her. And what on earth was she thinking, going all the way to Scotland to his parents for five days? She had to go via Carlisle, then to Edinburgh, where she would change for Kinross Junction and, finally, to Auchtermuchty. What a journey! Fear and dread added themselves to the bitter sorrow. What on earth was it going to be like after all those miles – how would they talk to one another?

Yet, go she must. And Mrs Reid's letter had been kind and welcoming. She knew she could do no other.

She got to her feet suddenly and struggled along the train in search of a cup of tea. Back in the compartment, warmed by the hot drink, she slept and slept for a long time, finding comfort in the rocking of the train.

Many hours and two trains later, after putting up for the night in Edinburgh, and having rumbled across the Forth Bridge, after which she had changed at Kinross Junction, they were chugging east across the lowlands of Fife. It was a bright, blustery morning and Annie looked out, fascinated and moved. This was Fergus's place. She had already seen the grey majesty of Edinburgh and now, as they pulled into the little station at Auchtermuchty, fields stretching flat away towards the pale sky, she felt she was entering a different world. It was both a new adventure and one that brought her even closer to the man she had loved. Strange as it was, it filled her with a sense of purpose.

Stiff after the long journey, she stepped down on to the platform of the little station. Glancing about her, all she could see was the humble station building, a green flatness and the grey beginnings of the town. The wind was fresh and tinged with salt, chasing clouds across the sun and drawing the smoke from the train off to one side. It was ten-fifteen in the morning, and the few passengers apart from herself getting down here, soon moved away.

Along the now almost deserted platform she saw a woman waiting. Annie's heart picked up speed. She was a short, almost dumpy figure in a tweed coat, a mourning band around the arm. She wore black, workmanlike boots and a wide-brimmed black hat with a diaphanous black scarf tied over it and under her chin so that the brim had a slightly eccentric look to it. This figure seemed to fit Fergus's description of his mother, Elspeth Reid, as a person with 'a mind of her own – rather like you, my dear'. So that, before she had even reached her, Annie already felt a sense of recognition and of liking for her.

'Annie?' She stepped forward with a start of uncertainty which warmed Annie's heart even more. 'Ah, yes – I can see it's you, my dear. I have the lovely photograph Fergus sent of the two of you.'

Elspeth Reid came close. She was not much taller than Annie, and under the hat a mop of rather wild-looking grey hair seemed desperate to escape. Her cheeks were wind-chaffed pink, the eyes pale grey and kindly sincere.

'I'm Elspeth – Fergus's mother.' She gazed at Annie, who saw a look of concerned pity enter her eyes. 'You do look very peaky, dear – or peely-wally as we say up here.'

To Annie's surprise, she found herself being taken into Elspeth Reid's arms and pressed against her comfortable, tweedy form.

'Oh, my dear,' Annie heard her say, distressed. 'My poor child.'

The ache spread and ruptured and Annie found herself sobbing and sobbing, soon aware that the woman who was to have been her mother-in-law was also weeping as they held each other. At last, at last, the one person she needed to be with, who had loved Fergus since the day he was born.

'I loved him . . . I loved him *so much*,' Annie sobbed. Never in her life before had she expressed her emotions like this, not to anyone. Her grief and loss and love all came pouring out.

'I know, I know – we all did,' Mrs Reid said and Annie could feel the woman's body shaken by the grief that they both shared, her voice cracked with heartbreak . . . 'Oh, my poor wee girl . . .'

Gradually they both surfaced. Annie stood back, wiping her eyes, feeling the wind cool her cheeks. Dazed, she looked up at Mrs Reid, who was mopping her face with a handkerchief. There seemed no need to apologize. Their eyes met in fond understanding.

'Let's go home,' Mrs Reid said. 'Are you all right with your wee bag? You're obviously a light traveller.'

'Yes,' Annie said. 'Thank you, Mrs Reid.'

'Oh, call me Elspeth, for goodness' sake,' she said. 'We've never been ones for formality. Now – Fergus's sister, Isobel, is coming tomorrow. She's longing to meet you. We'll go home and have a bite to eat. Dugald, my husband, will just be finishing off his surgery . . .'

She linked her arm through Annie's. 'Come on, dear. It's not far.'

They walked through the austere little town to a large house close to what Annie learned was called 'the Cross'. Its grey stone walls were picked out in paler stone at the corners and round the windows. The front door was draped in black, the ends of the crêpe shifting in the wind. And to the right was a plaque advertising the presence of 'Dr. D. J. Reid' with his letters in a string after his name.

Annie looked up at the house, impressed. She could already see many of the kindly, solid aspects of Fergus's life and upbringing that had made him into the confident, clever, humane man he had been.

'Which was his bedroom?' she asked.

'Well, when he was a wee boy we were living in Edinburgh,' Elspeth Reid said. She seemed touched by the question. 'We moved here when Fergus was ten and Isobel getting on for eight, if I recall rightly. So we've been here a good while. Fergus's room faces over the back, though.' She hesitated by the door and looked back at Annie. 'I wasn't going to put you to sleep in there – but if you'd like to . . . ?'

'Oh, no,' Annie said hastily. She felt almost afraid – of her own emotion, but also of transgressing. Surely his mother would prefer his room left as it was? 'Thank you, but no.'

'I wouldn't mind,' Elspeth said. 'But perhaps wisest not. Isobel might not be pleased.'

They stepped into the stone-flagged hall, where there was a homely scattering of gum boots, walking sticks, a boot scraper, coats and dog leads. Immediately an enormously long-legged dog of indeterminate brown-grey colour, with a shaggy face, mooched along the hall to greet them.

'This is Seamus,' Mrs Reid said, untying the scarf under her chin as the dog sniffed gently at Annie's shoes. 'He's an Irish wolfhound – don't mind him. He wouldn't hurt a fly. Of course, he was Fergus's originally, but he's long been left to us.'

'Oh, I've heard about this old chap,' Annie said, delighted. This dog had been such a part of Fergus's life! She was just about to squat down and pet him when another door opened nearby and Annie saw a tall man, lean and moustachioed, but with such a look of Fergus that she started for a second.

'Ah,' Dr Reid said. 'Excellent timing. The last of my victims has just left.' For a moment she thought she saw, on the man's long face, the ravages left by Fergus's death. Like his wife, he wore a black armband. But he came to her, took her hand with a little bow and twinkled at her, his lined, saggy face suddenly lit up. Annie realized immediately that with Fergus's parents she was in the presence of two remarkable people.

'Miss Hanson.' His hand was large and warm. 'We are more than delighted to meet you. Leave her alone, Seamus.' He pulled the dog away. Seamus sat, looking mildly resigned. 'I hope your journey was a good one? And you are a nurse, I gather?'

'Yes.' She smiled. 'As some of my own victims would testify.' Dr Reid chuckled and she saw his eyes crease at the corners just the way Fergus's used to, which was a joyful agony.

'Come along.' Elspeth Reid bustled along the passage. 'Let's go and stow your bag and make a nice hot drink. You must be starving, you poor wee girlie.'

Fifty-One

Annie was amazed by Fergus's parents.

She had been both longing to meet them and dreading the crushing weight of emotion that she knew must be contained in that large, stone house in Scotland. And as she walked about the place, in any part of it, she knew that Fergus must once have done the same. Washing her face in the bathroom and seeing her own thin, strained features in the mirror, she knew he must have stood in this very spot where she stood now. The bedroom that had been shelter for his lovely young body since his infant years was only next door. Every step along the landing and down the staircase would have been as familiar to him as his own body and he had often talked to her about the house. His presence was all around her. It was terribly painful, but it was also lovely and reassuring to feel him exist here as he existed nowhere in her Birmingham setting except in her own mind.

She rested for a while, and afterwards, for much of that day, she and Dr and Mrs Reid spent the time talking.

When she went down for what Dr Reid called luncheon, there was a shepherd's pie with cabbage and extra swede. ('We're overrun with swede in the garden.') And as soon as they were seated at the table in the big, echoing dining room with its dark wooden furniture and long curtained windows looking out to the green of the garden, they both began talking and Annie hardly had to say a word.

'When we got the news,' Mrs Reid said, spooning cabbage on to her plate, 'we just couldn't believe it. I still can't, fully. After all, he was in a hospital . . .'

'Well, there do tend to be a lot of sick people in hospitals,' Dr Reid said.

'You know what I mean, Dugald,' his wife said. 'All those poor lads dying . . . And our poor lamb being taken not *by* the war exactly, but *in* it.'

'It's all part of war,' Dr Reid said. 'Think of the epidemics at Scutari – more died from infection than bullets.'

'I know, I know.' Mrs Reid put the half-empty bowl of cabbage down on the table. 'But knowing the facts doesn't necessarily prepare you. The mind doesn't work like that.'

'Well, yours doesn't, my dear, of that I'm sure.' Dr Reid spoke drily, but there was no malice in what he said. He smiled at his wife and their eyes met, full of sad understanding.

'I felt the same though,' Annie said. 'I just thought he would be safe. Even though I know it's not just those in the front line who get killed. Enough boys on the wards have told me things . . .'

They asked her then about her work and Dr Reid was very interested in the First Southern General and Annie telling him about the teaching rooms all converted to wards and therapy rooms, the Great Hall full of beds.

But soon they started on Fergus again. Through the meal, followed by weak tea, then a walk along the farm tracks in a brisk wind, then more tea, and later the evening meal, with some lulls in between, Fergus's parents reminisced unaffectedly, and without reserve, about their son.

'He was such a good student,' Mrs Reid said as they walked. They took Seamus, who, old as he was, set off on his long legs as if he was on springs. The damp wind buffeted their faces and snatched at words so that everything had to be said loudly and facing the person you were talking to. 'Always very good at school, keen and clever . . .'

'Even if the wee laddie could hardly get his clothes on the right way round,' his father said. They were walking alongside a stone wall and as Dr Reid spoke, his voice cracked and he stopped abruptly.

His wife, in her firmly tied hat once again, took Annie's arm, glancing back as her husband fought for control of his emotions behind a handkerchief.

'Oh, dear,' she said. 'It takes us like that – every day, on and off.'

'I know,' Annie said, her own eyes filling. The two women looked at each other with silent understanding and Elspeth Reid squeezed her arm.

'I hope this isn't all too much for you, dear. I suppose Dugald and I . . . Well, we're here all day just with each other and somehow you don't know how to help each other because you're suffering yourself. So, we end up not saying anything. Your being here allows us to remember our boy with someone who loved him. But we don't want to overwhelm you.'

'Oh, no,' Annie said. 'It's . . .' And she was in tears herself. 'It means so much,' she sobbed, as Mrs Reid put an arm round her shoulders. 'No one at home really knew him. And when so many other people are dying, it just seems . . . You just have to go on.'

'You do,' Mrs Reid agreed tearfully. They could hear Dr Reid coughing behind them. 'And that's the hardest thing of all. Going on with the empty chair that you know will never be filled.'

She drew herself up and turned Annie towards the view.

'Over there, those are the Lomond Hills – that's our

391

highest point, here in Fife. It's not like the highlands! Mind you, they look very fetching with a dusting of snow, do our hills. Fergus loved this view. He used to come up here a lot with old Seamus here, whenever he came home.'

Dr Reid came and stood beside them, seemingly recovered. Annie was still arm in arm with Mrs Reid, and standing on her other side, he suddenly reached for Annie's hand and held it tenderly in his own.

After dinner they sat in the cosy sitting room at the back, a fire cracking and roaring in the grate. It was a comfortable house, with big leather armchairs and oil paintings of cold-looking mountain landscapes which Annie assumed to be in Scotland. In one, a group of men with guns were filing through the heather. There was a profusion of brass fire tools inside the fender and the side tables were piled with books and periodicals.

Mrs Reid handed Annie a cup of tea.

'Come nice and close to the fire, dear, next to me. Come along now, Seamus,' she said to the dog, who was stretched right along the hearthrug, giving off smells of hot, damp fur. 'Do move over and let our young friend Annie have some room as well!' The dog got up with a grunt, gave Annie a look of gentle reproach and curled up again on the rug. 'Now – shall we show you some photographs?'

Out came the albums. Dr Reid sat back, listening, chipping in, holding his cup and saucer as his wife regaled Annie about each of the sepia prints.

'Dugald was always keen on taking photographs,' she said. 'He had a camera even when I met him! I'm so glad now.'

Annie thought of her cousin Georgie taking his pictures and her heart twisted. Thanks heavens for these cameras! Otherwise, what would she and Clara and everyone else have had to hold on to?

And there was Fergus, a round-faced child in a floppy hat and white Victorian petticoats, gazing round-eyed at the camera. Annie gazed back at him. There were already the eyebrows, a child's, but still arched at the same angle she remembered.

'He'd have been almost two there,' Mrs Reid said.

'Wasn't he beautiful!' Annie said.

The boy grew and thinned out, the shoulders widened, his poses almost all sporting – with a cricket bat, rowing a boat, running along plastered in mud, an occasional posed studio portrait, his graduation from medical school. And in each Annie drank in the sight of the man she had loved so much, seeing his happy, healthy boyhood and the fruits of all his hard work as he grew into a caring, well-qualified man with the urge to help and heal – he had been living that out as he died.

She looked up at Dr and Mrs Reid, her face wet with tears. They, now, seemed calmer. Mrs Reid leaned forward and laid another chunk of wood on the fire, which crackled and spat.

'You have so much to be proud of,' Annie said. 'You gave him a wonderful upbringing and he was so kind, so keen to be of service to others. He was the finest, nicest man I ever met.'

She could see that Fergus's father was moved by this and Elspeth Reid touched her hand.

'Thank you, dear,' she said.

The next day they were expecting Fergus's sister Isobel with her two children. Though she was full of a sense of comfort and gratitude towards Fergus's parents, Annie felt much more nervous about meeting his sister. She had seen photographs of her in the album along with Fergus's, a pretty, confident-looking girl pictured running or on horseback and later, standing in a ball gown on the arm of a tall, dark-haired and classically good-looking man with a moustache, on the steps of an impressive-looking building.

'Oh, that was the ball Angus took her to when he proposed – right outside the university!' Mrs Reid said. 'Angus is a teacher of science at the university. Chemistry. Though he's out east somewhere at the moment.' She gazed sadly at the picture. 'None of us knew what was coming, of course. Now they've the two little boys – I hope they recognize their father when he ...' Annie heard her stop herself saying *if he gets home* . . .

'What are the boys' names?' she had asked. 'And how old are they?'

'Oh, they're twins,' Mrs Reid said. 'They're coming up to their sixth birthday.' She rolled her eyes fondly. 'They certainly keep our Isobel on her toes.'

Annie wanted to ask more. *Was she close to Fergus? Will she like me?* And other foolish, unanswerable things. Fergus always spoke affectionately of her.

'Would you like to walk down to the station with me, to greet them?' Mrs Reid asked.

Annie looked doubtfully at her. 'Perhaps you'd prefer me to stay here and give you some time to yourselves?' she said. The arrival of Isobel made her feel suddenly awkward, an outsider who would be in the way.

'No,' Elspeth said. 'Don't be silly. She's looking forward to meeting you.' She looked intently at Annie and smiled gently. 'She wants to meet the woman who her brother loved so much.'

*

It was another beautiful clear day, though still breezy. Waiting on the quiet platform, the only ones there, they saw the plume of smoke in the distance long before the rhythmic sound of the train came to them. Standing in her hat and coat, Annie felt her innards tighten. No matter what kindly Mrs Reid said, she still felt fraught with nerves at meeting Isobel.

Even as the train slowed, a hand was waving out of the window.

'There she is!' Mrs Reid said as it moved ahead of them so that they walked along the carriages to meet it.

Annie saw a lovely face with big, grey eyes smiling at them and soon Isobel descended from the carriage, an elegant camel coat tied over a darker brown skirt, a deep brown hat with a long feather curving from the brim and a little bag held by a strap over her left arm. But though she was elegant she hurried to them like an excited child.

'Hello!' She held her arms out. 'Hello, Mother!' She kissed and embraced Elspeth, with a certain skill in not entangling their hats, and then, arms held out, 'And this is Annie – I'm so happy to meet you!'

'Well, where are the boys?' Elspeth asked indignantly as the two young women embraced. 'Have you not brought my wee grandsons to see me?'

'No,' Isobel said, 'I left them with Angus's mother 'til tomorrow. I can't stop long and I promise to bring them up very soon. But oh, it is nice to have a little rest from the wee darlings – and I wanted to see you and Annie without having to answer a hundred questions every five minutes and have them careering round the house with Seamus like a couple of hoodlums!'

Annie had to confess to a certain relief at this as well and was warmed by Isobel's enthusiasm for meeting her.

'Anyway,' she said, as they left the station, 'it'll do Mrs

M good to see what it's like having to deal with two at once!' She grinned wickedly.

'Oh, dear,' her mother said, from which Annie concluded that Angus's mother was evidently a bit difficult. 'I do hope they'll be all right.'

During a lunch of lamb chops, Isobel chatted with her parents, updating them on news of Angus and the children, but she took care to include Annie in the conversation, explaining things that she would not understand and often smiling at her.

Afterwards, when the two of them were in the sitting room and Mrs Reid still somewhere about the house, Isobel said, 'Oh, I see the fire has been lit in your honour!'

'Has it?' Annie said, surprised.

'Oh, yes. Mother doesn't hold with fires until at least October. It's our cold Scots blood, you see. She must think you're a soft southerner.' Again, the teasing was good-humoured.

'Well, I suppose I am,' Annie said, as she had been feeling cold most of the time since she had been there.

'You're very thin,' Isobel said. She sat down across from Annie, looking closely at her. 'I . . .' A spasm of grief crossed her face. 'I loved my brother a great deal. He was always very good to me – well, almost always.' She struggled to find a smile. 'I don't know if that's unusual – some siblings fight like cats and dogs but he was always so easygoing and such fun. I miss him terribly. But for you . . . I know you've lost someone who you loved and hoped to make a life with.'

Her eyes filled and Annie felt her chest tighten so that she could hardly breathe, her own eyes already spilling tears. She nodded, looking down.

'I always thought . . .' She wiped her eyes, trying not

396

to start sobbing out all her sorrow in the face of Isobel's kind sympathy. 'When I was young, I always said I would never marry. I wanted to do other things, great things, I thought – you know, make great changes in society, in the world.'

'That sounds ambitious.' Isobel smiled tearfully.

'Until I met him,' Annie said. 'Fergus – our Fergus.' She looked up at Isobel. 'I know we were only engaged, not married. But I hope you don't mind me saying that?'

'No. Of course not. He was crazy about you. He wrote and told me he'd met the most astonishing woman and how you'd made a proper man of him.'

'Me?' Annie said, startled. 'He said that?'

'He did. You probably thought we Scots are all dry, puritanical types, but Fergus was very emotional, when he was with people who knew him. If he said that, he must have loved you like *anything*.'

'He did,' Annie said. 'And he was the love of my life – of that I'm sure. He changed me.' More tears came. 'He made me know what love is. And it's made me suffer more and sometimes I curse that. But I know really I would never be without it.'

Mrs Reid soon came in and once again, they all talked and talked. They took another walk and very quickly, Annie realized that Isobel was to become a genuine friend.

'If you had married Fergus,' Isobel said as they walked the track again, the thin sunlight on their faces, 'you would have been my sister-in-law.' She squeezed Annie's arm. 'And I would have loved that. I've always wanted a sister. You have one, don't you?'

'Yes,' Annie said. 'Margaret – she's my elder sister.'

'But no brothers?'

'Our brother John died in infancy.'

'Oh, how dreadful! And are you close to your sister, Margaret?'

'Yes. I'd say so.'

Isobel was silent for a moment. 'Well, I don't suppose you'd be needing another one? My husband is from a whole string of boys and now I've got sons ... Sometimes I feel as if I live in a male clubhouse! It can be rather lonely at times.'

Annie was deeply touched by this.

'I'd like that. Will you write to me?'

'Of course – as long as you write back. Real writing, not the weather.'

Annie laughed. As if she would write about the weather! 'Real writing. Yes – I will.'

Fifty-Two

'Daisy?'

She looked up from her bench in Pa's workshop that Friday morning to see Margaret hurrying towards her, a strange expression on her face.

Daisy was helping with an order they had received for a set of plated silver sports trophies to be sent to somewhere in Scotland. She stood up, wiping her hands on a rag. The lathe kept turning at the other end of the workshop. All Daisy knew about these small parts they were turning out day after day, was that they were for Mark 4 tanks. A few of the women workers had glanced up as Margaret came in, then respectfully went back to their work.

She held out an envelope and then Daisy understood the look on her face. It was from Brighton.

'Take it out of here and read it if you like,' Margaret said very quietly.

Daisy nodded. She took it up to the attic, and only then looked closely at the handwriting. Once again, it was not Den's and she did not recognize it. Unlike the rather stylish hand of Lucinda Bailey, the VAD, it was looped, rather childish writing, and the top line of the address was smudged. Her heart was thudding but she felt a sense of fate come over her. This would decide things. Something outside her control would decide her future and what she deserved in this life.

She had given Stephen no reason to hope. Despite his

hurt glances, she had not been to Hollymoor to visit for the last few Mondays and when she was teaching on Tuesdays she had been distant, treating him like any other of the men there, polite, encouraging, but nothing more. She had avoided his eyes and, she realized, soon he had stopped seeking out hers. It was better that way, she knew. Stephen had her on a pedestal. She could not bear to think of the look that would come over his face when she was forced to tell him the truth. The shame of it washed through her even at the thought of it.

Calmly, her hands not even trembling, she slit the envelope open and drew out a single sheet of paper. There was neither an address nor a date at the top, as if the writer was not well versed in the art of letter writing. The lines of the letter sloped downwards and the spelling was shocking. 'Dazy' was crossed out and replaced with the correct letters of her name:

Dear Daisy Tallis,
    I am writing for Denis Pool and he says to tell you that he has the bandages off of him now and is going along allright he can see and he says what he wants to see is you when you can come doun.
    Signed Josie O'Toole.

She set off the next morning.

'I know what to do,' she had said to Margaret. 'Now we've been once. I'll do just what we did last time – I'll be back tomorrow.'

Margaret did not ask anything, did not start handing out advice or instruction. She just gave one of her calm, penetrating looks and said, 'Think carefully, Daisy. You have made a promise, remember. Promises are easily made.'

'I know.' She did not, could not, say any more, except, 'Thank you for looking after Hessie for me.'

She kissed her little girl goodbye and set off for the station.

Sitting on the train, as rain streaked the windows, she tried out words she might have said to Hester. *I'm going to see your daddy – the man who will be a daddy to you.* Den Poole. Den, the man who had always loved her, who had been there waiting for her all the time. That was what she should have said.

All the way down, she thought soberly about her life. She made herself replay the weeks when she was in the thrall of James Carson, the horrible months of her pregnancy, of sickness and shame and hiding, having to go off to that village with Margaret's stiff, disapproving father, the thought that she might have just handed Hester over to a stranger who would be raising her now, out of sight.

And all the time, Den had moved in and out of her life. Den who had lost his father, his little sister, then his mother, all so tragically. Den, who she had treated with a sort of amused condescension. She saw his handsome, smiling face, heard all the things he had said, *Write to me, Dais . . .* But she also recalled the look on his face when he saw Hester for the first time. The look of . . . triumph? Was that what it had been? As if something had shifted, had brought her down. As if he had known then that he was in with a chance.

He knew her all right. Den knew her both good and bad, the truth of her and what she had done. And he was prepared to stand by her. He was a skilled man – he could have a great future after the war. He and she would make a good team, could run a business as she had always wanted . . .

She stopped herself. *Sufficient unto the day is the evil*

thereof ... One of Margaret's sayings. First, she had to deal with today. And, it seemed, Den had regained his sight, and she must keep her promise.

But why, she wondered, did he get this person Josie, who could barely shape her letters, to write for him? Could he really see again, or was it just an excuse to get her to come ... ?

Den was still in the hospital at Eastern Terrace. She hurried there through the blowy drizzle, again having to keep a tight hold on her hat. She was glad to get inside. The same woman was sitting at the table downstairs, and as before invited her to leave her bag. But it was a different nurse who guided her upstairs, this time to a different room. *Down at the end,* she said, *on the left.*

Daisy hesitated in the gloomy light of the passage outside the ward and drew in a deep breath. She could hear a murmur of talk and when she found the courage to step into the room, with a feeling of fate, she saw someone standing beside the bed at the far end to which the nurse had directed her.

She stopped, narrowing her eyes. She recognized the girl in her overall, leaning on the handle of a broom or mop, talking to Den. She had been cleaning the ward last time. In that second, she took in that Den was looking back at the young woman – there were no bandages about his head this time – and it was certainly the look of a person whose eyes were taking in what was in front of him. He was smiling, his face lit up. He could see.

Den could see, and she was here as she had promised.

It was the girl who spotted her. She said something and Den looked round. As Daisy walked towards him, his face lit up.

'Daisy!' He was beaming at her as she reached the bed.

'I'll leave you then, so,' the girl said, moving away with the broom.

'Ta, Josie,' he said as she went off along the ward. 'That's the girl who wrote the letter for me,' Den said, his eyes alight with life. And it was only in that second, finally, as his eyes followed the young Irish woman along the ward, the smile still playing about his lips, that she knew she had done the right thing coming here, that she knew what she must do.

'Hello, Den,' she said. 'Look –' she could say 'look!' – 'I brought you a bun from a shop along the road.'

'Ooh, ta – Chelsea, is it?' He was boyishly enthusiastic. 'My favourite.'

She put it on the table beside the bed and looked round for a chair. There was one at the far end of the ward and she fetched it.

'How're you feeling, Den?' she said quickly as she sat beside him, perching on the edge. She felt strong, she realized. Much stronger than she could ever remember.

'I'm all right,' he said, sounding surprised. 'You'd never've thought, would yer? I mean, I've got all sorts of bits and pieces of scrap in me somewhere, they say. Right mess to begin with. But the burns are better – and as it turns out it didn't finish off my eyes though it might've done. When I was lying out there, after I was hit, I managed to get my mask on in the end but it burns through your uniform, see? But when they took them bandages off – oh, I can't tell yer what it were like.' He beamed at her. 'Like being a little babby again and seeing everything for the first time. It were bostin, it were. That girl – she were one of the first things I saw!'

'But does that mean . . . ?' She frowned at him, still finding it hard to believe. 'If you're all right, will they send you back? Not again, surely?'

403

'Most likely,' he said, with surprising cheer. 'Wouldn't put it past 'em. Eh, Dais – pass me that bun, will yer? I've got a hunger on me now – eating like a horse.'

Laughing, she passed him the bun. It was nice talking easily like this and seeing him better, looking like the old Den, and she thought, Maybe we can just go on like this, chatting like friends without having to go into anything else just yet.

But almost immediately, Den, after some enthusiastic chewing and swallowing, said, 'I don't mind what happens, Dais – all I need to know is that you're there. That you're going to be my missus. That's enough to keep me going through anything.'

She felt everything in her tighten and she pulled in a deep breath, having to gather herself swiftly. Now. She had to say it now. Reaching out she laid her hand on his, on the arm of his chair.

'Den.' She looked very directly at him, feeling herself tremble, but she had to go on. 'I need to talk to you – to be truthful with you . . .'

And, from eyes which looked out from a scarred face, he gazed steadily back at her.

To her surprise, she slept soundly that night in the guesthouse where she and Margaret had stayed before, with the kindly landlady. When she lay down, it was like a light being switched off and the next thing she knew, it was morning.

And all the way back to Birmingham, she felt her mood grow lighter.

'Hello, Dais,' her father greeted her as she walked into the house that afternoon. His face altered from being glad and relieved to see her, to concerned. 'Everything all right? Good journey?'

Hester heard her voice then and came running out, with Margaret and Lily in pursuit.

'Mama!'

Daisy scooped her into her arms and kissed her soft, warm cheek. 'Careful, Hessie, you're nearly throttling me!'

'There's tea in the pot,' Margaret said. 'Come on in and tell us all about it.'

Even though the children were in there playing, Margaret and Philip sat down with her and it all felt like a special occasion.

'So,' her father said, stiff with shyness on these matters. 'What's been going on, love?'

'Are there to be wedding bells?' Margaret asked, carefully.

Daisy's heart skittered in her chest. She felt suddenly girlishly nervous.

'I *think* so,' she said. Blushes rose up her cheeks as she allowed all her feelings of love and hope to flow. 'I hope so – if he'll have me. But Pa, Ma, you must come and meet him first because I don't think he'll be able to come here and see you just yet. His name is Stephen Ratcliffe.'

1918

Fifty-Three

24 Chain Street
Hockley
Birmingham
15th December 1918

My dearest Annie,

Well, my darling sister, the first thing for me to say is that we are missing you! The weather has been foul and each time I set foot outside the door I wonder how much worse might it be in Scotland? But I fear (selfishly and to my dismay) from the tone of your last letter that yourself and Edinburgh are already on fond terms, you and the Royal Infirmary even more so, and that you are settling alarmingly well. And that you now have a new sister in Isobel Munro and have quite discarded your old one . . .

There – all my grumbles and pettiness from missing you are out of the way. What I really want to say is I am so happy that these terrible years of war which brought you so much darkness and pain might be brought to a close. I am pleased for you that you have found a place where you can start afresh, may remember your beloved Fergus with the friendship of his loving family and cast off the shadows of death and grief, of which being here in Birmingham could only constantly remind you. So you see, my dear, I do understand.

But still. John and Lily keep asking, when is Auntie Annie coming for Christmas? And Philip and Aunt Hatt are nearly as bad. (I think Philip misses your terrible stories.) So – we shall be patient as it is not too many days now. And even if we were not inducement enough I know you would never miss Lizzie's wedding. She is like a lily in bloom these days, that poor little waif who you befriended. And she is impressive, this young woman she has become. She is, as ever, full of organization and is to have Ivy, Ethel and little Ann as bridesmaids and Tom Higgins's boy Joe as their little page. There is such a shortage of men that she has asked old Mr B to give her away! This all sounds rather lavish, but she is being very sensible as Lizzie always is – but just wanting to let everyone possible play a part. It is sad to think how many members of her family are missing when she is still so young. And Tom has not much family either, but I believe his father and brother will be there to support him.

Aunt Hatt is well, though I do worry about her and keep telling her to slow down and employ more help in running the business. She assures me that Watts & Son is now her life and she wouldn't know what to do without it. Clara is also well, although now she is no longer needed to do anything for the war effort and is on the loose in Aunt Hatt's house. At first she was relishing a more tranquil life, but lately I notice her becoming rather restless. Jimmy, Ella and Gina are of course all at school and Clara says she finds the days hang heavy. Is there something wrong with that? I asked her – but in fact I am very occupied myself and would not take to having too many idle hours. She has begun talking about becoming a teacher of young children.

Aunt Hatt is rather horrified, but I can see Clara being very good at it.

I have saved a good piece of news until last. Daisy has just heard that the silver tea set she has been labouring over for so long in between all else, which she sent down to South Kensington, has just won a Gold Medal in the silversmithing category. It is very beautiful and was much lauded by the judges as an exemplary piece of Arts and Crafts smithing. I've hardly ever seen her – or Philip for that matter – look so happy!

We are well under way looking for new premises for her, but for now I rejoice in our very full, but happy household. And our workshop which no longer contains any trace of the manufacture of war, but only of utility and beauty.

And, my dear Annie, I am waiting with great excitement for your arrival and overjoyed that you are meeting new friends and gathering a new life about you. We shall see you very soon to hear all about it.

My fondest love for today and may the Lord bless you abundantly,

Margaret

Fifty-Four

That Monday, last year, after her visit to Brighton, Daisy had been to see Stephen Ratcliffe at Hollymoor.

The orderly wheeled him into the visitors' room. As he was brought across the room to the table, he did not meet her eye. His face had a hard, tight look as if he was clenching his jaw.

Even when the orderly had settled him, sideways on to her, and left them together, he sat, staring ahead of him. Daisy had been full of words, of explanations and heartfelt apologies for her cold behaviour to him, but at this moment none of them would seem to come out of her mouth. For long moments they sat in uncomfortable silence. Daisy, hands in her lap, lowered her head and rubbed one thumb again and again across the other so hard that it hurt.

'Why have you come to see me?' Stephen said at last. He sounded hard, almost aggressive. She dared to look up, but he still could not meet her eye. 'After all, you don't seem to be able to stand the sight of me in the classes any more. And you haven't been . . .' He shrugged. This was her first visit on a Monday for some weeks now.

'I'm sorry,' she said. How weak it sounded to her.

It would have been so easy to make something up, to keep him in the dark about Den as she had so far about Hester. But it would not do. Complete honesty and have done with it, she told herself. That was the only way and if he rejected her when he saw who she really was, well,

412

that must be what she deserved. She would have to accept it. It still did not mean that her life was meant to be with Den.

'Stephen?' She forced herself to speak into the uncomfortable silence. 'May I just talk to you for a few moments? Just tell you some . . . things, that you need to know. I think you'd better just let me talk, or I'll never do it.'

She could see he was listening. He still did not look at her, but he gave a nod.

Where to begin? She took a breath.

'On Saturday, I had to go to Brighton. Back to Brighton, I should say. Someone I know, who I grew up with, sort of anyway, is in hospital there. He was wounded – for the second time. He's in the artillery and he's come back from Ypres. While he was lying wounded, he was also gassed – and blinded.'

Stephen was sitting very still and she could feel that she had his complete attention. The murmur of other voices in the room seemed to fade and they were intent on each other.

'It was the second time I had been to see him. I went in the summer, and he was . . . he looked terrible. You could hardly see him for bandages and no one knew whether his eyes would recover. And while I was there I promised him that if his sight returned, I would marry him.'

Stephen did not move but she sensed something from him, like a kind of inner flinching.

'At least – I didn't exactly promise. But somehow he believed that I had.' As she spoke she realized how peculiar this sounded. If his sight returned? Did she love the man or not? Surely it was not dependent on his sight?

Stephen cleared his throat. 'And did it return? His sight?'

'Last week I got a letter from him, telling me that it

413

had. That he could see again. But even though I had . . .'
She hesitated, looking down for a second. 'Promised – or
he thought I had . . . He didn't exactly force me, but he
put me in a position where he just kept believing I had
said . . . Anyway, I went to see him to tell him that I could
not marry him – even though he had his sight. That it just
wasn't right, or where I . . . I wanted to be . . .'

She saw Stephen's chin lift slightly, as if at the impact
of this. He turned and looked at her then and she saw the
hurt and bewilderment.

'But why did you promise?'

'Because . . .' She looked away for a moment, trying to
find the courage. 'I've known Den for years and he's been
fond of me for a long time – or so he said. The truth is, I
never thought about him seriously, not like that. I wasn't
the most humble of people back then, Stephen. And then
later . . . Well, I thought he was the only man who would
ever want me and so when he kept on about marrying
him I didn't say yes, but I didn't really say no, either. Because I thought, things being the way they are, that perhaps I should marry him. But by then I had met you . . .'

Their eyes met for a second and she looked away, her
face lit with blushes. She felt washed in shame.

'Daisy,' he said slowly. 'What on the earth are you talking about? Here you are, the most beautiful, the most—'

'Stop!' She spoke urgently, and too loudly. She looked
round for a moment then lowered her voice almost to a
whisper so that Stephen leaned in closer. 'Please, Stephen.
This is the trouble. You think I'm so good or pure or
something . . . That's so false – you've got completely the
wrong idea.'

They were close together now and she made herself
look into his eyes, her gaze intense and fearful.

'I know you think you want me, but you don't know

414

anything about me.' She couldn't stop now. 'I am not what you think, Stephen. What if I told you that I already have a child – a little girl who is two years old?'

She saw it register in his eyes, the look of hurt, of disillusionment.

'You're already married?'

She shook her head. 'No.'

'A widow then?'

She just looked at him.

'I see.' He looked away. 'No, in fact I don't really understand. You'll have to tell me.'

'He was a teacher, at the school in Vittoria Street. He's dead now, Stephen. He was killed on the Somme. I was young – in fact I'd known him since I was a child. I thought I was in love with him and he thought he was in love with me. But he was already married even though they were living separately. He was rather absorbed in himself, but I really think he did love me – or thought he did. And I . . .' She stumbled into silence, cheeks burning with shame and embarrassment. 'I allowed . . . it to happen. A kind of affair, I suppose. Not for long. But for long enough. And he went away and then he was dead.'

She did not feel like going into all the ins and outs. Her father's rage, James Carson's callousness about the child. What did it all matter now? She could not look up, not until she heard his voice.

'What's her name?' he asked, sounding stunned.

'Hester. Well, she's Hester Florence Margaret – the second names are after my mother and my stepmother.'

She waited, staring down at her long, pale fingers lying in her lap. There was a silence, in which she waited, as if for an axe to fall. Other people talked in the room. Chairs scraped on the floor; the door banged. The moment seemed to go on and on.

415

At last she heard his voice over the other voices around them.

'Should I care?'

Daisy looked up, startled. She could see that he was shocked, moved, and his face was full of emotion.

'What d'you mean?' she said, confused.

'I mean – am I supposed to condemn you? Is that it? I love you, Daisy. You're the most wonderful woman I've ever met. And in fact – this might sound an awful thing to say – but you seemed almost too perfect. And here am I . . .' He looked down at himself. 'A wreck of a thing.' He looked at her very seriously. 'But I do want you to know that apart from the bit of junk inside and the legs, all else is in working order.' His cheeks flamed as he spoke. 'And I shall learn to walk again – I know I shan't always be just stuck like this. I'm determined. If you were prepared to take this – all this – on, I'm yours. You're the woman for me. I know that. If you can accept all this.'

She smiled through the tears that were already running down her cheeks.

'Yes . . .' She reached out a hand and Stephen grasped hold of it with such gladness, drinking in her words. 'I am – of course I am, dear, dear Stephen! I'm so sorry, but I just couldn't let myself talk to you. Not while Den still thought . . . But seeing you every week has been the best thing that has happened to me in . . . well, ever. I love coming here to teach the class but the best thing has been seeing you, talking to you. You just . . .' She gave a small shrug. 'I just love you – I can't help it. Like no one else, ever.'

Stephen let out a laugh that was almost a shout and nearly everyone in the room looked round.

'It's all right,' he said, looking round. 'It's just that this beautiful girl has just told me that she loves me, that's all!'

416

There was laughter and a scattering of applause and Daisy, cheeks burning even more, stood up to reach over and fling her arms round his shoulders and hold him tight.

'I don't want to marry you until I can stand beside you – one way or another,' Stephen told her. 'I'm not going to the altar with my girl in this blasted chair.'

Over the following months, as they grew to know each other more, love each other more, there were so many things to think about, in terms of how they could live, how they would manage with all Stephen's difficulties.

Daisy brought Hester to visit and the two of them, though each shy at first, finally charmed one other.

And Stephen spent months going back and forth to the Uffculme Hospital in Kings Heath, where he was fitted eventually with two prosthetic legs. The torment of soreness and struggle and frustration that this entailed for him weighed on Daisy. But Stephen was utterly determined.

On one of the last days of 1917, Daisy had received a letter. The handwriting was instantly recognizable and she felt a pulse of dread. It was Den's. Surely he was not going to go on pursuing her? He had steam-rollered her into a promise before, but now, surely, she had made herself clear?

She read the letter, written in his usual style, in private, up in her attic bedroom.

Dear Daisy,

So there sending me back again soon as Christmas is over I'll be on my way to France. I don't want to leave without saying a thing or two to you. You've all of you your family and Mr Watts and all of them have always been decent to me and I want to keep things right. I didnt like you coming saying what you did but you was right. You and me aren't meant to be together even though I'd like to see you I'd always like that.

Just in case like I want to tell you I got wed last week. A girl called Josie O'Toole you saw her I think. Lovely Irish wench her is and we'll make a right Mr and Mrs together, if I'm spared and Ile bring her back to Birmingham.

Say a prayer for us Daisy and I hope well meet again later one day.

With fond wishes,
Den Poole.

1919

Fifty-Five

'Do you realize,' Stephen said, 'that it's twenty-one months and three days since you first told me that you loved me?'

He rolled over and seized Daisy by the waist, nuzzling into her back.

'Hey – stop – you're tickling me!' She giggled and twisted round to look at him, his lovely face, the *right* face, and his curly hair dark against the pillow. 'You're not *still* counting, are you!'

Stephen picked up the end of her thick, pale plait and tickled her nose with it. 'Oh, I am. I'll go on counting for the rest of our lives.'

'And driving me mad!' she laughed.

She looked round the bare room, as yet unfamiliar and with almost nothing in it except the bed. This had been the first night in their new home, and it was in Caroline Street, only a few minutes' walk away from Chain Street and Pa and Ma and everyone else.

Stephen pulled himself up on one elbow and looked down into her eyes, as if to say, *Remember?*

'Ma said she'd come and help today,' Daisy said. 'Or at least keep an eye on Hessie anyway.'

'Good of her.' Stephen fixed his gaze on her, caressing the curved belly through her white nightdress. 'And how is *my* flesh and blood getting along?'

He spoke teasingly, but not once, since they had been courting and married, had he ever shown an ounce of difficulty with having Hester in their lives. Life was life, was his view. He was lucky enough still to have that and everything added on was a bonus – including Hester, who already adored him. She loved to be close to Stephen while he was working and Stephen teased Daisy about it.

'This one is born to work with wood. We'll have her by my side as a cabinetmaker once she can see over the table.'

'Oh, no – she's going to be a silversmith!' Daisy protested. 'It runs in the family.'

'Hmm. Well, we'll see, won't we?' he said.

And now, miraculous as it seemed, they had their own place and were starting to get settled in.

'So – let's be sure about what we're doing,' she said as his warm hand moved over her tight flesh.

'We've been over and over it.'

'But are you sure you don't want us to sleep downstairs? There's room and we could . . .'

'No. Look, I can do the stairs – and it's only really at night I'll need to go up. Your business upstairs, mine down. Our room upstairs, and the children – just normal. We don't need to do anything special.'

Once they were up they looked round the house again like excited children, Hessie running through the empty rooms, excited by the clatter of her feet on the bare boards. Her hair was long and wavy down her back now.

'So, did you like your new bedroom, Hess?' Daisy said. The children's room was at the back of the house. 'Soon you can share it with the new baby.'

'When's it *coming*?' Hessie asked impatiently. 'It's taking too *long*.'

'Oh, soon. But it's not taking any longer than you did!'

Her own workroom looked out over Caroline Street and Stephen's was to be downstairs at the front – the two rooms letting in the most light. They had already had two woodworking benches carried into the room and he had brought his tools from home. Their living room and kitchen would be at the back.

Finally they went outside and stood in the street, looking up at the house, in a row of high terraces with long windows. Before ever moving in they had had two brass signs made, and fixed one above the other beside the front door:

'Stephen Ratcliffe – Cabinetmaker and Furniture Restorer,' read the first, and above it:

'Daisy Tallis – Silversmith.'

'Looks very fine,' a voice said behind them. Startled, Daisy turned to see her father, a portly figure now, in his big coat and hat, looking up at the premises which would be their home. He was holding something: her silver-wire tree.

'Gran-pa!' Hester cried, running to him.

'Pa! What're you doing here?' Daisy said. 'I thought Ma was coming?'

'She will be a bit later,' he said. 'I just wanted to have a look. You're both doing a good job. Brought you this as well.' He handed her the tree. 'It's a lovely thing.'

'Come inside,' she said, taking his hand. 'You can help me decide on my workshop.'

Both of them knew that she did not really need help, but it was a lovely thing, a shared thing. They stood back a respectful distance as Stephen struggled into the house with his sticks, Hester urging him from behind. Their eyes met, Daisy's saying to Philip, *I know it's hard – and I love him for all of it, for all of his love and determination.*

They went upstairs and she carried the almost finished tree and set it down on her workbench. She and her father talked benches and light and tools and then stood by the

423

window looking out. To her surprise, her father shyly laid an arm around her shoulders.

'I'm proud of you, young wench. And your mother would've been too. Proud as punch, the pair of us.'

Her tree gleamed in the light, its shape flowing this way and that, over the branches and leaves and creatures, all the birds of the air which were welcomed and settled in its branches.

And she rested her head on his shoulder, satisfied and content.

Acknowledgements

Once again my thanks to the staff of the Hockley museums, Birmingham, Museum of the Jewellery Quarter, especially Steve Whyte; to Evans Silversmiths, especially Sheila Askew; and to the volunteers at the Pen Factory.

My thanks also go to Sian Hindle at the School of Jewellery and Silversmithing in Vittoria Street for taking me on a tour and answering all sorts of questions; and to Fiona Waterhouse for her assistance at the archives at Birmingham City University. Also to Laura Cox, archivist at the Museum of the Jewellery Quarter, and to the Cadbury Research Library at Birmingham University, where are housed copies of *Southern Cross*, the magazine of the First Southern General Hospital, which was at Birmingham University during the First World War.

A great many books were helpful, but especially: Shena Mason's *Jewellery Making in Birmingham, 1750–1995*; Bernard Cuzner's *A Silversmith's Manual*; David S. Shure's *Hester Bateman, Queen of English Silversmiths*; Birmingham Museums and Art Gallery's *Arthur and Georgie Gaskin*; Kathleen Dayus's *The Girl from Hockley*; Sian Roberts's *Birmingham, Remembering 1914–1918*; Terry Carter's *Birmingham in the Great War, Mobilisation and Recruitment, The First Eighteen Months of the War*.

And to Debbie Carter for all her help.